FATAL PRESUMPTIONS

Merville Thomas

Merville Thomas Books

*To Emma, Matthew, Madison, Carson and Ava - five
very special human beings who bring happiness
into my life every time I think of them, and who
just happen to be my grandchildren.*

CONTENTS

Title Page

Copyright

Dedication

Prologue

Fatal Presumptions

Chapter 1: Behind Every Good Man — 1

Chapter 2: Portent — 8

Chapter 3: Seeking a Path to a Reckoning — 10

Chapter 4: Caller Unknown — 16

Chapter 5: Sisters, But Not Twins — 22

Chapter 6: The Center — 28

Chapter 7: Set-back — 32

Chapter 8: Faceless — 36

Chapter 9: Threats — 40

Chapter 10: The Next Step — 43

Chapter 11: Monday Retribution — 48

Chapter 12: Aftermath — 54

Chapter 13: The Appointment — 61

Chapter 14: You've Come Back! — 69

Chapter 15: Gargoyle — 72

Chapter 16: Priming an Enquiry — 78

Chapter 17: Now a Widow — 85

Chapter 18: Let Me Spell It Out for You — 94

Chapter 19: Assembling the Best — 99

Chapter 20: Bric-a-Brac 107

Chapter 21: BTO and Ibuprofen 113

Chapter 22: Call Me Rod 118

Chapter 23: Keeper of the Records 127

Chapter 24: Just Wanted to Help 131

Chapter 25: The Brain Trust 137

Chapter 26: A Good Neighbour 148

Chapter 27: A Killer at Lillian Metcalfe? 159

Chapter 28: Ida Said 166

Chapters 29: Sinners, Repent 171

Chapter 30: Banished 173

Chapter 31: Another Casserole 175

Chapter 32: And Then There Were Three 179

Chapter 33: The Lady Doth Protest 187

Chapter 34: The Truth Will Set You Free or Not 190

Chapter 35: Exorcising Demons 199

Chapter 36: How Do You Like Me Now? 209

Chapter 37: Setting the Record Straight 220

Chapter 38: Faubert's 224

Chapter 39: Mother Warrior 229

Chapter 40: Advocate 238

Chapter 41: Warrant 243

Chapter 42: A Foul-Smelling Creek 251

Chapter 43: Push Comes to Shove 257

Chapter 44: Farewell, Peter 268

Chapter 45: Prosecution Scorned 273

Chapter 46: If I Could Turn Back Time 279

Chapter 47: Pursuit 284

Chapter 48: Doldrums   295

Chapter 49: Up Close and ...   299

Chapter 50: ... Very Personal   303

Chapter 51: Crossing T's and Dotting I's   317

Chapter 52: Reverberation   322

Chapter 53: One Saturday in April   324

Epilogue   333

Acknowledgement   339

About The Author   341

Books By This Author   343

Fatal Presumptions   345

PROLOGUE

The naked girl continued to stare at her. Those penetrating, grey-green eyes set above a button nose and a full-lipped heart-shaped mouth held her gaze. The expression on the girl's face was appraising, suggesting an assessment of … what? … assets? … flaws? What is she looking for? What does she see? She must see the pretty face with eyes as engaging as those of her own; the momentary shy smile, flashing a hint of straight white teeth beaming an inviting warmth; the blooming breasts heralding the promise of a statuesque figure; the narrow waist serving to accentuate the curve of the hips; and, a pear-shaped butt atop long legs with muscular thighs and calves and slim ankles. Is she seeing all this packaged in a fit, model-worthy five-foot, seven-inch frame? Or is she seeing something else entirely? Do others see what she sees?

She intensified her scrutiny of the girl's face searching … searching for a clue as to her thoughts, her judgements. In response, the girl's serious expression morphed into that smile, the one that communicated the secret they shared, the one that made the girl's appraisal and any conclusions she might draw irrelevant because they both knew that the one person who mattered had already proclaimed her beautiful, sexy and intelligent. He'd not only told her so repeatedly but treated her as she thought she should be treated given her status as his girlfriend, his special girl, his partner. And indeed, he did make her feel special and relevant, feel loved. He'd awakened in her feelings she had no idea she could have. Despite her uncertainty and reservations early in their relationship, with time she had become much more comfortable in his company. She imagined what she felt for him now was love, because she thought about him all the time when they weren't together, always looking forward to their next rendezvous.

Why do I love him? Not simply because he is drop-dead gorgeous. Not just because he has a ripped body. And not purely because he has proven to be patient and caring. I love him because he makes me feel good about myself. He makes me feel pretty, sexy and smart. I feel safe with him, that he knows how to protect us from anyone who might want to come between us and what we have. I know I love him because I want to be his, no matter what.

She thought back to the first time they made love. She'd told him that she was performing with her school's cheerleading team at a local shopping mall and he'd showed up to watch. She'd purposely shunned company to walk home alone after she left the mall and, like a fantasy made real, he'd approached her with the offer of a drive. It wasn't as though they hadn't spent time together before this happened because there had been ample opportunities for them to be in contact with one another, not all of them by chance. Those encounters had started with polite social conversation and then gradually included more and more personal exchanges, his positive comments about her appearance, her wardrobe, her personality, and her "delightful" manner. Following his lead, she'd reciprocated in kind. She hadn't been completely naïve to the possibilities that accepting his offer of a ride brought with it, but she hadn't been prepared for the physical and emotional fallout of such a dramatic shift in their relationship. Thoughts of that experience cluttered her mind as she looked at the naked girl who had started to slowly and rhythmically sway and move to music playing in her head.

He'd been very patient, very gentle with her, but she'd been anxious, hesitant. He'd talked her through it, asking her permission at each step. She allowed him to guide her, agreeing to go further each time he asked her if she was OK with it. It had hurt and she'd wanted to tell him to stop. But she didn't.

x

After it was over, he'd held her and comforted her when she'd started to cry. She'd wept, not because she had been hurt, but due to the immense relief she felt at having been able to get through her first experience with sex. It had all been rather overwhelming for her. However, it wasn't long before that relief was replaced with feelings of guilt. She couldn't believe that she had actively participated in an act that had taken their relationship into forbidden territory and past the point of no return.

She shook her head almost imperceptibly as she thought about the mess she had been back then, her face flushed, her eyes red, raw, eyelashes matted with tears. She recalled feeling doubt, fear, and, more powerful than all, that sense of guilt. How had she let this happen? But he'd come to her rescue, physically cradling her, stroking her hair, wiping the tears from her face and professing his love for her, calling her his special one and proclaiming that someday when the time was right everyone would know of their love. That he wanted her and only her forever. He had promised that it would not hurt her next time.

Maggie turned abruptly away from the full-length mirror in her bedroom, her face feeling the burn of the shame and embarrassment her remembrances of that early encounter with him generated. She hastily began donning her after-school clothes which had remained neatly folded on her bed awaiting the completion of her extended contemplation of her image in the mirror. She then picked up her school clothes and her underwear from the floor where she had discarded them before losing herself like Alice through the looking glass. While hanging up her clothing in her closet and placing her underwear in the laundry hamper, she considered once again the conflicting emotions this was causing her. On the one hand, the secret status she enjoyed as his special girl, his lover, brought with it a kind of excitement and happiness which she had never felt before. She could not discount the pride she felt in the power she enjoyed in the relationship, like that of an adult on an equal footing with another adult. Yet, no matter the things she might think of to justify it, she knew their relationship was wrong and she could not shake the feeling that the longer it continued, the closer it brought her to disaster.

FATAL PRESUMPTIONS

XIII

CHAPTER 1: BEHIND EVERY GOOD MAN

Thursday, January 18

Dr. Peter Simpson flipped the switch and plunged his small, but comfortable inner office into darkness, effectively stamping *closed* on his psychotherapy practice for another day. It was only 5:30 in the afternoon but any sunlight this late January day had enjoyed was long gone by now. Passing through the compact reception/waiting area of his office suite, vacated just moments before by his girl-Friday, Sue, he paused, letting his eyes move over the room before him. It contained the now so familiar black quartz reception counter with a glassed-in booth on top, a modification Sue had insisted upon for security purposes, though he could think of no client he had ever seen who might pose such a risk. He smiled when contemplating Sue, single and in her mid-forties, who looked ten years older, and who was anal about the neatness and precision of her work area. She regarded it as the vital nerve center of the practice of which she was its ever-alert sentinel. In this, she was a living paradox because he recalled his astonishment when he first saw her apartment with its mementos, decorations, greeting cards, pictures in frames, and frilly things, the detritus of a lifetime, placed on virtually every flat surface available. Accepting her invitation for coffee when dropping her off after work, he'd felt the proverbial bull in the china shop, fearful of knocking something from its roost simply by walking past it. He still had difficulty reconciling the fastidious Sue of the vital nerve center with the one whose home was a scene of obscene clutter.

Back in the here and now, his eyes took in her solid mahogany desk and posh, high-backed leather chair and the wall-to-ceiling file cabinets and shelves behind them, along with the tasteful wall hangings that completed the professional appearance of this, her nexus. Peter had long held the suspicion that Sue had come to work for him, not because of the salary he offered or because she was agog over his winning smile, but because of the promise he had made to give her carte blanche in the furnishing of the office suite. To his dismay, this promise had led to the purchase and installation of elegant leather chairs for the relaxation of waiting clients. Sue had argued that people with the weight of the world on their shoulders deserved some comfort before starting or continuing on the often difficult road to unburdening themselves. At the time, Peter had quipped that as their therapist that was his role not that of the chairs, no matter the comfort. He smiled to himself as the array of fine cowhide before him gave testimony to whose argument had carried the day.

As he stood there in the quiet of day's end, his mind went back to the first time he had viewed the office space which had been previously used by a failed travel agency. That was almost six years ago. It had been a dark mid-winter evening, not unlike the present one. The real estate agent had apologized for the unappealing state of the rental unit explaining that it had been summarily abandoned by the lessees some six weeks before, leaving all their furniture and office materials in place and their former employees unpaid. Yet, Peter, a brand new Doctorate in Psychology in hand, and his beautiful new bride, Karen, had not seen the worn and stained carpeting, the flaking wall paint or the thick patina of dust. Rather than the odour of neglect, their optimism, Karen's in large part, allowed them to sense the lure of opportunity. Offer and counter-offers had led to the signing of an advantageous agreement with the building's owners - one which required that he and Karen roll up their sleeves to renovate the space in return for bargain basement monthly payments for the first two years of the lease. He couldn't have done it without Karen, of course. She had been a tigress, vigorously encouraging him to set up the practice and backing up her confidence in him by contributing a portion of her substantial inheritance from her maternal grandmother to the financing. With her support and advice, he had generated such a burgeoning caseload that he was referring prospective clients to other practitioners and giving consideration to hiring another therapist. Without question, he had had doubts but remembered how skillfully Karen had erased his fears and boosted his shaky resolve when needed. She had always been his sometimes tough but caring cheerleader, particularly in those first few months.

Man, I've come a long way in a short time! From grad student to highly sought-after psychotherapist with a practice that this past year has netted me a comfortable six-figure salary after expenses.

He lived in a large house in Halifax's south end that was presently assessed at 1.8 million dollars. *Grammy's bequest coming in handy once again.* He had moved quickly to join the Rotary Club and had been accepted as a member of a most prestigious golf and country club, something that was unheard of given the fact that he was considered a newcomer, perhaps even an outsider, by the *old money* sitting on the Board of Directors. Karen and he were being invited to social events judged to be exclusive, for the social elite only. Social media had carried pictures of Karen and him either entering or leaving social functions for the city's wealthiest and most powerful. His celebrity had been further enhanced by the fact that he had become a *media darling,* frequently sought after for interviews and expert commentary. Feature articles which focused on both his professional success and their meteoric rise within the City's social hierarchy had appeared in both an online news service and a regional magazine. No doubt, he was well on his way. Even his mother, if she had lived, would have had to admit that he was doing well. The sudden memory of his mother cast a shadow over his feeling of well-being. It brought back memories of his childhood, a childhood where he could never do anything right, and of a severe, unrelenting parent he tried so hard to please but who, despite his best efforts, made him feel flawed, inadequate, only capable of making decisions with guidance ... *hers, of course.* As an adult, he had been able to gain perspective, to come to understand how his mother's cold and demanding nature was her problem, not his, and was an aberration in her personality, not one in his. It was evidence, however, of the powerful influence of one's early upbringing, and how even a reasoned adult perception sometimes could not dispel feelings of inadequacy, of not being quite good enough.

As he switched off the last of the lights and locked the outer door of the office, Peter shook off the depressing recollections of the past and allowed thoughts and images of the present, of Karen, to flood his consciousness. She was a striking woman with long-lashed, deep-set shimmering blue eyes set in a perfect heart-shaped face framed by a thick mane of shoulder-length brown hair. And that body ... still the hourglass figure of her youth despite the birth of their first child, Solynn. Now, as in the past, when out in public with Karen, Peter invariably suffered from a conflicting mix of emotions as his wife turned the heads of men and women alike - pride with a sense of violation, of resentment even. More than once, intense feelings of jealousy had been aroused by the attention his wife attracted from men. In these circumstances, his emotions often got the better of him, leading to bitter arguments with Karen as though it was her fault that men found her attractive and flirted with her. On rare occasions in the past, his feelings of worthlessness mixed with rage had taken him to the edge of the marital abyss, its precipice demarking a point of no return in a relationship. During one heated interaction following a social gathering where a man simply complimented Karen on her dress, he had chosen to berate her all the way home in the car, accusing her of encouraging the man, of secretly wishing to have an affair with him. Karen's protestations to the contrary held no sway with him given the bout of irrational emotional turmoil he was in. When he regained his composure and a degree of rationality, he understood that his jealousy, his possessiveness, was a fear that he was not good enough for Karen and that she sooner or later would reject him. He realized that he could thank his mother for the emotional dysfunction that threatened his relationship with his wife. Despite the insight, he continued to allow the anomalous mothering he'd experienced as a child to shape both his feelings and behaviour well beyond the time considered healthy for an adult. Fortunately, Karen seemed to understand the demons with which he was dealing and had accepted his apologies for his boorish, sometimes abusive behaviour, while reassuring him of her love and fidelity. *If only words were enough* he thought. Hers never were. Total peace and security were only available to him during the times she was submissive during sex. It was unhealthy he knew but, thus far, he had been unable to make the necessary changes he understood needed to be made if his marriage was to survive.

Although it may have been Karen's exceptional good looks and accompanying sex appeal that first drew him to her, it was her buoyant, optimistic personality and enjoyment of life that had perfected his utter and complete seduction. Much to his surprise and good fortune, she had communicated a similar interest in him. *And why shouldn't she?* He'd been in great physical shape when he met her, and still was, within five pounds of his weight as a senior in high school. And good-looking and charming he'd been told repeatedly, a fortuitous combination from the family gene pool - deep brown eyes, high cheekbones, a lights-out smile with an ability to charm the frostiest of humanity. As for turning heads, his observations suggested that he was equally as good at it, if not better, than his wife. *Smart too!* The highest aggregate in his high school graduating class, an honours undergrad degree in Psychology, and a published Doctorate dissertation with a thriving practice were evidence of that. Smiling to himself, he thought that if Karen had not agreed to marry him, he might have married himself. Then why was he so full of nagging self-doubts that seemed to present themselves almost anytime he faced a challenge?

Now he remembered that three months after their introduction to one another by a friend in common, he and Karen were having hot chocolate at that little café in Montrose Place following an afternoon of tobogganing. There, chocolate moustache to chocolate moustache, he had asked her to marry him. Despite the almost six years which had passed since that time, Peter was still able to recall, and feel, the growing intense apprehension, almost a panic, which pervaded the few seconds between his proposal and her acceptance. During that short interval, he'd felt the crushing emotional pain of her rejection, although it never came. It was as if he had never fully considered what her refusal to marry him might mean to him, might have done to him. It seemed to him that it wasn't until the very moment his proposal escaped his mouth that he understood that life without Karen was not a life worth living. That realization had frightened him profoundly.

As he neared the full glass front doors of the office building, his reverie continued and a precious little bundle of humanity came into focus. Solynn, born just eighteen months after the start-up of his practice, marked the beginning of a wonderful new chapter in his life. Both Peter and Karen had agreed that their daughter was their top priority. Karen, who had been working part-time in his practice and as a volunteer in a local seniors' complex, would stay home - for a while, at least - to care for the baby. Adjusting to the role of mother as well as being that of wife and homemaker seemed effortless for her. The joy and peace of mind she exuded conflicted with Peter's conception of motherhood. In this, he realized he had been conditioned by his mother's frequent complaints about the excessive physical and emotional demands caring for him placed on her. As an only child, whose father's sales position had him on the road much of the time, it was his mother who was the dominant influence in his formative years, holding him close physically but spurning him emotionally. Even when at home, his father seemed little more than a meek, powerless figure who succumbed to the all-consuming force that was his mother. More and more, he had felt certain that, in Karen, he had selected a life partner who was the complete opposite of his mother, and wondered if that choice was motivated by a subconscious desire to prove he was not the man his father was. While one would have predicted that such thoughts would have brought with them relief, they generated a discomfort in Peter which sometimes took on physical manifestations - persistent headaches, and bouts of rapid heart rate with occasional palpitations, and frequent, shallow breaths. His professional training told him that his strong emotional reactions to having a woman so different from his mother in his life may well be related to the independence Karen forced upon him. There was no one there to tell him what to do.

CHAPTER 2: PORTENT

S tepping outside, he recognized that the day had turned colder and the slight breeze from the northeast had picked up since he entered the office this morning. Fluffy snow swirled in the wind and flakes danced in the glow of the streetlights as he exited the building and filled his lungs with cold air. Trudging through the newly fallen, yet to be cleared, snow of the dimly-lit parking lot, he could see stars littering the blackness through the swirling clouds of vapour his exhalations created. The overcast skies which prevailed during the day were clearing. His thoughts turned to the imminent prospect of seeing his family shortly and to the anticipation of having some alone time with Karen. His momentary depressive thoughts were immediately replaced by excitement which elevated his mood once again. He had some definite ideas about how they might spend some of that alone time later this evening. This thought reminded him to stop and pick up a bottle of their favourite wine on the way home. As he continued to re-surface from his internal thoughts, Peter mused contentedly about his good luck in life, but consistent with his effort to be more assertive in his approach to that life, he immediately adjusted his internalized self-talk and made a spontaneous audible proclamation.

"No, I am not lucky! I am an intelligent, hard-working man who has made good choices and those good choices have been rewarded!"

A little embarrassed about his impulsive vocalization, he quickly looked around to determine if anyone might have heard. In his line of work, it wouldn't do to have rumours circulating that he talked to himself.

His reminiscing had distracted Peter as he approached his car, the only one left in a more remote area of the small parking lot. Coming up to the late model black BMW sedan, while reaching in his pocket to make sure he had his key fob, he noted for the first time that the otherwise unmolested snow in this area of the parking lot was full of fresh footprints in and around the immediate vicinity of the BMW. Upon closer scrutiny, he saw that the footprints circled his car. The trail led from the nearby street, went around the BMW and then returned to the street.

Uh, uh, some kid looking to see if keys were left in the car! Peter concluded, as he looked up and visually scanned the area for a possible suspect. There was nobody to be seen.

He had lost track of his keys more times than he liked to think, and some of these times he had, indeed, left them in the car. He was thankful that today had not been one of those occasions. Making his way to the driver's side of the car, he was somewhat taken back to see that someone had printed *U piece of shit* in the snow and frost adhering to the car's windshield. Following the initial shock, he once more did a quick 360-degree search for a culprit but came up empty again. A fleeting anger shaped by his sense of violation and the disrespect the message represented replaced his surprise. This emotion quickly gave way to a feeling of greater comfort in the explanation of a random act of a kid thumbing his nose at the adult world in the safety of anonymity. Yet, he recognized the incident as one of a number of unexplained happenings over the past couple of weeks. An anonymous note berating his ethics stuffed under the door to his office, and an article on sex crimes in the mail from an unknown sender, were just two of the most recent instances. Entering his car, however, he made a mental note to pay more attention to where he put his keys and to park closer to the office building in the future.

CHAPTER 3: SEEKING A PATH
TO A RECKONING

Sheila was very pleased with herself. She had initiated a couple of small steps of the plan she had formulated to exact the justice she felt was necessary for her little sister. Almost as soon as this feeling of accomplishment had set in, that part of her mind where doubts reside overflowed and overwhelmed her usual sense of optimism.

You hardly have a plan for Christ's sake! No plan really, Einstein. The things you've done don't accomplish anything.

Fighting back, she reminded herself she had taken action, albeit limited, when the opportunity had arisen.

I do have a plan, one that requires patience, seized opportunity and determination, but getting there depends on my having the guts to take advantage of openings when they present themselves. Like today.

She considered the incursion she had just made into his life - a small step, for sure, but one which showed that she could take a risk, could take action. Perhaps it hadn't advanced her plan that much, but she imagined that it had made him feel uncomfortable, while it made her feel better - like she was doing something.

Sheila knew she was smart and attractive. The School Psychologist had done tests and said she was scholastically gifted, could qualify for Mensa. Teacher feedback further attested to her competence and a level of academic performance which could be even higher "if she applied herself a little more". As for her looks, the interest and often all too predictable approaches of boys and men suggested her ability to attract males. Her thick long brunette hair cascading over her shoulders bordered a stunning face featuring unblemished olive skin, sparkling grey-green eyes, highlighted by her astute use of make-up, and full-lipped mouth which turned up slightly at the corners. At five foot, eight, and 140 pounds proportioned to advantage, she was blessed with an outstanding athletic ability and superior eye-hand coordination. She was a star on both her basketball and volleyball varsity teams. Beyond that, she was into drama and had auditioned for, and won the leading roles in her school's past major productions of *Alice in Wonderland* and *The Lion King.* She'd even won scholarships to prestigious, limited-enrolment drama workshops the past two summers. It was through her avid interest in performing and acting that she identified in herself something about which many had commented, something that gave license to behaviour she otherwise held tightly in check. In short, performing was a rush. She enjoyed losing herself in the roles she had taken on. Acting allowed her to become another person, another personality, someone with a life she could infiltrate, someone who could make decisions that she, herself, might not make in her own life. Although she was not by nature impulsive, she was, indeed, a risk-taker when it came to acting, willing to put herself out there, to become the character she was playing. Yes, she recognized her assets and she knew she would need them to pull off what she intended to do.

Once she had decided to act on her sister's behalf, she started her - *What did the police call it? ... Oh, yes. ... Surveillance.* In the beginning, she hadn't known what she would do other than keep an eye on the *asshole* whenever she could. This often meant travelling to the small park opposite his office building right after she finished school in the afternoon, sometimes at noon hour when she had the first period after lunch free, and occasionally, on the days she skipped school altogether. The park, which wasn't a park at all, was an ideal vantage point for observation. It was positioned at a location where three city streets intersected and formed a kind of roundabout. The park was the green area hub - although it was hardly green this time of the year - with grass, shrubs, benches and resident pigeons. Sitting there on a bench, Sheila was allowed a clear view of the building in which he had his office and of its parking lot. On the other three sides were an assortment of shops and businesses including a place to buy burgers and fries. During periods of surveillance, she read, fed the pigeons and took short walks, all the while maintaining a sight line on the building. Despite the cold and the occasional park visitor, one or two of whom had viewed her warily, she had persevered. Over four weeks of diligent watchfulness, she had learned what days he worked, the times he and his secretary arrived in the morning and the times they left for the day, what kind of car he drove, and had even identified some of the people she felt sure were visiting his place of business. Not surprisingly, she'd thought, the majority were female. During week two, she had used a ruse to borrow her parents' car to follow at a discreet distance behind him and his fancy vehicle and had learned where he lived. The house was a huge Spanish-style construction with a two-car garage located on a short, secluded horseshoe-shaped street lined with houses of similar size and grandiosity. Sheila couldn't imagine what houses like the ones on his street would cost, but she knew it would be astronomical. Despite the lack of both foot and vehicle traffic and a suitable observation position, which combined to make cover almost impossible, she had begun watching his residence on the weekends. During her staggered bypasses of the large and expensive home, she had, from time to time, observed in the yard or by a glimpse through a window, the beautiful lady who was his wife. Sheila recognized the woman from pictures she had come across online through the comprehensive internet searches she had done on her target. On a couple of occasions, once with a small child bundled up against the cold, the woman had looked across the street from her front yard in Sheila's direction. Although a bit unnerved,

Sheila was sure the woman had not paid her much attention, and even if she had, she would have no reason to be suspicious. Other than the occasional absent-minded looks the woman had given her, she hadn't noticed anyone paying any particular attention to her presence.   She was just another passer-by in the minds of anyone who saw her, she hoped.   Sheila was quickly filling the pages of a Hilroy notebook with the observations she had made, and it was from these observations and her sense of poetic justice that the flesh of her plan had begun to coalesce around its skeletal outline.

***

Trudging home in the snow with the frigid wind penetrating the long maroon Hudson's Bay coat her parents had bought her for her last birthday, Sheila thought back to that awful day that had changed everything. She had heard Maggie return from an outing "with a school friend", quietly climbing the stairs, entering her bedroom and closing the door. Looking for a reason to take a break from an English Literature homework assignment, Sheila put aside the laptop she had been using on the bed, swung her legs over the side, stretched out her tight muscles and then crossed the hallway to her sister's room. As was their practice, she had opened Maggie's bedroom door while simultaneously knocking and uttering a greeting which she had aborted abruptly. One look at her sister's face had told her something was seriously wrong. Not only had Maggie looked very distressed, but it had been apparent that she'd been crying. From the point in time that Sheila, alarmed by what she saw, had asked Maggie what was wrong to the ending of their conversation almost an hour later, Maggie, albeit reluctantly, confided some information that rocked Sheila's world. First was Maggie's admission that she had had sex for the first time. Despite obviously being troubled by the experience, she had remained extremely tight-lipped about providing further detail, including who her partner had been. Sheila hadn't even known Maggie had a boyfriend. Slipping into her sibling protector role, she had asked her little sister about whether or not protection had been used. Maggie's response, designed to put her sister's concerns at rest, established that her partner had used a condom, and appeared to be very knowledgeable when it came to safe sex. Sheila had tried to reassure her sister that she understood that having sex for the first time is a big deal and can cause girls to feel all kinds of unsettling emotions which are quite normal. She then cautioned Maggie to be prepared for the potential fallout from an immature boy claiming bragging rights for his sexual conquest. Maggie had dismissed this concern with a mirthless laugh and told Sheila not to worry because "he definitely doesn't want anyone to know". Just before being called for dinner by their mother and in reaction to Maggie's intransigence regarding who her partner had been, Sheila had started asking questions which might narrow down the possibilities. She even started suggesting the names of students she knew who might be prospects. This had seemed to lighten Maggie's mood and she even giggled at some of the preposterous suggestions her sister put forward. One particular suggestion had led to an outright guffaw followed by Maggie blurting out "Stop guessing, he's not a student!" When Sheila had asked, "Who's not a student?" Maggie's face had fallen, communicating a recognition that she had said too much. She had pleaded with her sister to forget what she had just said and not to tell anyone about any of the things she had confided, particularly their parents. Sheila knew that their parents' marriage was fragile. She had heard the vitriol-laced exchanges, noticed her father coming home from work late more frequently, and the increasingly distracted, anxious demeanour of her mother. Though neither parent had said anything to them about their problems, intuitively, Sheila recognized, as she was sure her sister did, that revealing what Maggie had shared could only make things worse for their parents. Therefore, she vowed to keep Maggie's confidence provided that Maggie told her who her partner was. Initially refusing, in the end, Maggie had begrudgingly complied. Looking back now, Sheila imagined that it was at this point that her need to protect had mutated into a drive to exact revenge.

CHAPTER 4: CALLER UNKNOWN

As he drove out of the office parking lot after clearing the snow and ice from his car, Peter, as was his habit most days, began reviewing the sessions he'd just had with clients. Mrs. MacNutt, a retired teacher who had recently lost her husband to cancer, had made significant strides in dealing with the aftermath of serious depression and anxiety triggered by grief. That improvement continued to be evident during therapy today, and Peter considered the gains made in this case a testament to the positive impact that psychotherapy, competently provided, can have. Miss Larson was the next client he remembered. Miss Larson's presenting problems had proven to be a moving target - they seemed to change over time or became obscured by a non-stop commentary about anything but the purpose of her presence in his office. He remembered he had asked questions in aid of improving clarity with consequent responses about her house, her two Pekinese and the faults of the younger generation. Becoming mildly frustrated, he had spoken gently but firmly.

"Miss Larson, forgive me, but I have not been able to get a clear idea of why you have come to see me. What has made you feel that you need the services I offer? Each time I ask you about it, you seem to avoid the question and talk about other things. I need to know what brings you here so I can start therapy."

He recalled the uncomfortable, extended silence that filled the space between them before the tiny 70-year-old sat bolt-upright, looked Peter defiantly in the eye and, in a quavering voice, chided him.

"God almighty, man, I'm lonely. Can't you see that? I am paying good money to visit and talk with you. There, is that good enough for you?"

Thinking about Miss Larson brought a smile to his face although he also felt saddened by the experience. He had arranged with Miss Larsen to engage the services of a Social Worker colleague to find her more suitable opportunities to deal with her loneliness and to engage with others.

He was snapped out of his world of inner thought by something on the edge of his consciousness which came rushing into full awareness. Abruptly pushing down hard on the brake pedal, Peter, aware of the screech of the tires and the long, loud blast of the horn of the motorist behind, turned sharply to the right into the entrance to *The Abbey Winery.* While doing so, he waved apologetically to the irate motorist while getting a profane gesture in return. He never ceased to be amazed at how getting behind the steering wheel of a car turned some people into potential raging maniacs capable of showing others great disrespect, and, in a thankfully small number of cases, of causing others harm.

Once back on the road, a bottle of top-quality Australian Shiraz on board, his thoughts shifted from the ugly display of road rage he'd just experienced and from today's sessions to those scheduled for the last day of this week. As he did so, his mind settled on Friday's agenda, and the therapy sessions he had been contracted to conduct with students who had sought assistance through Lillian Metcalfe High School's Teen Health Center. Checking his reflection in the rear-view mirror, he was met by the image of a face smiling back at him.

***

"Daddy, Daddy!" filled the air as soon as Peter closed the door between the two-car garage and the mud room of his comfortable home on Sanford Avenue just a 10-minute drive from his office. Solynn darted from the kitchen where she was "helping" her mother prepare supper and began her trek down the short hallway, past the laundry room and into the mud room. There, she latched onto her father's leg, momentarily forestalling any further removal of his boots and coat. Gathering the squealing little girl into his arms, he hugged and kissed her, then carried her, along with the bottle of wine he had bought, down the hallway to the kitchen. Once there, another exchange of hugs and an elongated kiss took place under Solynn's approving gaze.

The kitchen air was ripe with the tantalizing smells of one of Karen's culinary adventures, a Philipino recipe with chicken he remembered her mentioning when he had phoned between appointments earlier in the afternoon,

"Amazing! May I have a little taste?"

"Why thank you, kind sir. But you'll just have to wait, it's not quite ready."

Giving Karen a meaningful look, Peter responded.

"I wasn't referring to the food."

His wife gave a little laugh while making priorities clear.

"Like I said, it's not quite ready. And I am referring to the dinner as well as the dessert you may have been thinking about. Solynn, you want to help Daddy set the table?"

Passing by Karen on his way to the cutlery drawer he placed a hand on her back.

"By the way, I picked up a bottle of wine for us - Australian Shiraz this time. It's right there in the bag on the counter."

"Oh my God. I picked one up too. I didn't think you'd remember. Not Australian though."

"Great minds think alike. Why didn't you come in and say 'hello' while you were out?"

"Solynn and I just went over to the Nova Scotia Liquor Commission store in the Mall for the wine. I didn't have time to drive anywhere else today, but if I had, we would have dropped by."

Peter almost blurted out "Just as well you didn't as it turns out" on his way to telling Karen what he had seen printed on the window of his car. However, he caught himself in time. For some reason which he had yet to identify, he didn't want Karen to know about the series of unusual messages he had been receiving lately. He'd convinced himself that he didn't want to worry her. Initially, he actually didn't think there was anything to be concerned about, but, with each new incident, his discomfort grew, leading him to consider what he would do if they continued to occur. Trying to bolster his resolve, he castigated himself for allowing such thoughts to preoccupy him. *Alright, alright, I'm building mountains out of molehills, taking it too personally.*

***

Three hours, one bath in a tub populated with floating toys and one happy but sleepy little girl, and a few "just one more" bedtime stories later, Peter and Karen were relaxing with their second glass of wine of the evening in the spacious entertainment room. Solynn tucked in her crib and fast asleep, they took a few minutes to just be with one another. As was often their practice after Solynn was in bed for the night, they lounged in this room containing a 60-inch LED television with an elaborate surround-sound system and reclining theatre seating.

"That dinner was incredible, delicious like the chef," said Peter initiating conversation.

In return and using her favourite tactic of feigning insult and demanding retribution, Karen, with furrowed brow, pouted.

"Do I detect a hint of surprise in your voice? Do you think I just got lucky tonight and my cooking is usually not up to snuff? Peter, I'm hurt, really hurt!"

As was his pattern in such situations, Peter jumped into the breach, spinning a little mischief of his own.

"No. No, I wasn't suggesting any such thing. You're a great cook. Your meals are always...well, usually...excellent... fine restaurant quality."

"What do you mean 'usually'?"

"I see you have conveniently forgotten the culinary disaster of last Christmas and, let us not forget, the infamous dinner for your parents in 2021. I think there must be a term for that type of memory loss, maybe epicurean amnesia. All kidding aside, you know I love you for many, many reasons, and one of those reasons is your superior abilities as a chef."

Playing her role to the hilt, Karen, looking as though devastated by Peter's playful insults, used a sad, small voice through the beginnings of a smile.

"I accept your apology. But if you want to make it up to me, you can tackle those pots and pans in the kitchen."

Twenty minutes later, pots and pans washed, dried and returned to their appropriate places in assorted holders and cabinets, Peter rejoined his wife in the entertainment room and, realizing he neglected to do so, asked how her day had gone.

"Every day is an adventure with Solynn, you know that. Today, we attended our Kindergym class where she performed for all in attendance, and quite the performer she is, our daughter. Then, we baked the cookies that you had for dessert tonight, and following that, spent an hour playing at camping out. We used a blanket over the chairs of her play set to make the tent, and she insisted I get inside with her. I'm reliving my childhood again. Oh, I did receive an odd phone call a few minutes before you got home from work. I forgot to tell you. Someone was definitely on the other end of the line but didn't say anything. I said "hello" a couple of times, and then just hung up. That, with camping, made for an exciting day."

"Yeah?" said Peter, "That's a bit weird. You sure someone was on the other end?"

"As sure as I can be without the other person saying anything. I'm pretty certain I could hear breathing, not heavy breathing, and there was no dial tone."

Peter thought for a moment, then said, "What about caller display?"

"'Caller unknown' came up on caller display. It was probably just a prank."

"You're probably right, but let me know if it happens again, will you?"

Peter absentmindedly reached for the remote control and turned on the TV. While gazing at the screen not seeing a reality show contestant auditioning to be the next great singing star of the modern era, he experienced a distinct feeling of unease as he considered what Karen had told him about the call she had received.

CHAPTER 5: SISTERS, BUT NOT TWINS

As the hammering noise that her rapidly beating heart was creating in her ears gradually lessened, Sheila became aware of the voice penetrating the closed door of her bedroom. She listened again and heard her mother yell up the stairs, "Dinner's ready, Sheila. I'm not going to tell you again. Come and get it, now!"

With a deep sigh, creating a consequent huge expulsion of air, she stared at the hand which held the mobile phone she had just used. Her reaction to making a 15-second phone call, during which she said nothing, alarmed her. She had not anticipated that she would have such a dramatic physical reaction. If something as mild as making a short anonymous phone call caused her heart to beat the way it had, she couldn't imagine the state she would be in when putting the next step of her plan into play. She had to get it together and quickly.

On the way to the dinner table, she met Maggie at the head of the stairs. Before descending, and using a hushed voice, her sister asked her where she had been today. Conspiratorially, Maggie continued whispering, saying that she had been approached by Mr. Foreman, the principal, who asked about Shelia, inquiring if an illness was the cause of her absences from school. A little alarmed, Sheila asked what her sister had told the Principal. That feeling of apprehension found no salve in learning of her sister's response that she did not know why Sheila was absent. With that, she dismissed Maggie's inquiry with a curt, "I'll tell you later. OK?", and headed down the stairs.

Eating one of her favourite meals, whole wheat spaghetti smothered in her mother's special thick meaty pasta sauce, Sheila raised her eyes from her meal catching sight of her mother, seated at the end of the solid maple dining table, in one of her disengaged trances, lost in her thoughts, in her own world. She noticed, not for the first time, how tired and haggard her mother's face had become lately. She knew that despite the problems her parents were having her mother would be the strong one, the rock, the one who would recognize what needed to be done and do it. Her father, like most men, was weak, a runner. A little adversity and he was nowhere to be seen - AWOL again tonight. He was a waste of time. Sheila suspected her father was drinking again. Good old Arthur, up to his old tricks, pursuing his own needs and destroying his family in the process. Her father's on-again, off-again affair with alcohol had resulted in so much heartache and humiliation for all of them. Sheila was sure her negative attitude toward men and her distrust of human beings had their roots in Arthur's intoxicated, addle-brained behaviour. She didn't see him as a parent, more like a boarder in their home, and refused to call him by any appellation which suggested he had parent status in her eyes. To her, he was Arthur, and no more. Looking at her beautiful, but unhappy mother at the end of the table, Sheila found it hard to understand why such a smart and capable woman did not see this coming before she married that poor excuse for a human being.

Following dinner, Sheila, having returned to her bedroom with the stated intention of doing her homework, reflected on two key things which had grave potential to interfere with her plan. First, there was the information which Maggie had just passed on to her before dinner. Obviously, "Dick Foreskin" was becoming concerned about her absences from school and if Richard Foreman could stick it to her, she knew full well he would. It was only a matter of time before he contacted her mother to seek an explanation for her absences. This would mean that she would either have to reduce her surveillance time or move up her plan's timetable. Second, her anxious, almost panicky, physical reaction to making the anonymous phone call, gave rise to the question as to whether or not she had the *cajones* it took to pull it off. This seemed the more critical of the two issues because just the thought of moving up the timetable for execution was already causing her distress. In fact, despite her best efforts to remain optimistic, she found that she was suddenly consumed by fears and doubts. As she began to consider whether or not she could cope with the stress, there was a light knock at her bedroom door.

The door opened part-way and Maggie stuck her head through the opening. "Is this a good time to talk, Sheila? I know something's going on. What is it?"

"If you're talking about me missing school today, I was just taking a mental health day. I couldn't take another day of the boring shit that they call teaching. I caught the downtown bus and went shopping. I don't need to tell you that I'd rather Mom didn't know anything about this."

Giving her a questioning stare, Maggie pressed the issue.

"I don't think you're telling me everything. I was speaking with Noah from your class, you know Noah Baldwin, the good-looking guy you're always going on about, and he said you've been skipping school a lot recently. He said that mutant, Larry Quintel, saw you in that little park near the burger place we went to a couple of weeks ago. He said you were just sitting there in the cold. When he waved, Larry told Noah you pretended not to see him. And it was last Tuesday, the day you told me you were going to hang with Noah after school. Don't you think it's time to tell me what's going on?"

"You little shit! What business do you have checking up on me? Who do you think you are? I don't answer to you! Keep your damn nose out of my business!"

Sheila had turned on her sister and spoken with such ferocity that Maggie's face registered shock and she took a quick step backwards through the doorway. Observing this, Sheila quickly recovered her composure. She couldn't believe it. She had attacked the very person she loved most in her life like she might have her worst enemy. Maggie didn't deserve this. Her pretty, trusting, sometimes too trusting, vulnerable baby sister had looked at her with such trepidation that Sheila had stopped ranting immediately. Simultaneously, her pent-up anger and frustration melted away.

"Oh God, I'm sorry, Maggie, I'm so, so sorry. I didn't mean it. I don't know what's wrong with me. I seem to be losing my temper so easily these days. Please forgive me."

Before Maggie could respond, they heard their mother's voice filtering through the hallway and stairwell from the kitchen.

"What's going on up there? Do I need to come up there?"

Sheila adroitly steered Maggie by the arm back into her bedroom and just before closing the door, said, "No, everything's okay, Mom. We just got a little carried away. Sorry."

"Are you sure?"

"Yep. We're good."

With the bedroom door securely closed and after listening for her mother's footsteps on the stairs for a minute, Sheila turned her attention to her younger sister. A tear or two had made their way to her dimpled chin. Guilt applied its iron vice felt in Sheila's chest. The last thing she wanted to do was hurt Maggie as she had just done.

Maggie looked up at her big sister with what seemed to Sheila like an expression that registered hurt and something else - maybe an appeal for understanding, recognition of some sort. Haltingly, she whispered in a hoarse voice, "I'm sorry. I didn't mean to upset you. I just wanted to tell you that people are noticing that you're not in school."

"I should be the one to apologize, not you, Maggie. I was the one that was out of line. I'm having trouble controlling my temper. You've got enough on your shoulders because of that son-of-a-bitch, and I shouldn't be adding more to that simply because I can't control my own problems."

The sisters hugged and promised each other that they would not let this happen again. Sheila emphasized that she always wanted Maggie to come to her with anything that was bothering her or if she just wanted to talk.

After Maggie left the bedroom, Sheila thought about how close she felt to her sister right now. They'd always been close really. In fact, despite a little more than two years between their ages, they looked so alike that they were unmistakable as sisters. Some people had even thought they were twins. Maggie was the prettier in Sheila's mind, with the same deep brown hair and similar eye colouring. Yet, somehow her sister's combination of delicate facial features made her look absolutely gorgeous. She was also very smart and her school performance was at such a high level she'd not had to endure teacher caveats about doing more to perform at her potential as Sheila had. The differences between them were probably most apparent in personality. Unlike Sheila, who was cautious around others, if not downright suspicious, Maggie was very open, trusting to the point of making herself vulnerable. *Vulnerable* - if there was a word that described the main difference between them that was it. In true Maggie form, she always seemed to be taken off-guard when others played cruel jokes, verbally attacked her or excluded her. And, as with any girl with the looks and brains Maggie had, this type of targeting from those envious of her had been a common occurrence. Over the years, Sheila had found herself becoming Maggie's self-appointed protector, a role to which she seemed suited and at which she had become proficient. In contrast to her sister, Sheila felt herself much more pessimistic about the true intentions of others, on her guard at all times. She had learned a lot about life, men, and herself during the two relationships she had had with older boyfriends, one of whom had been twenty-four when she was sixteen. With those doomed relationships had come too many parties, too much to drink, and occasionally finding herself in places with only the foggiest of memories of how she got there. Fortunately, she had been able to step back from the void, but she sometimes worried that her experiences during her "bad boys" phase had warped her thinking and caused her to be needlessly suspicious and distrustful of all males. But then, she need only contemplate the behaviour of those supposedly highly respected males around her, her father among them, to know that her suspicions were usually well-founded.

Returning from internal reverie, Sheila, with renewed resolve, promised herself that this was the last time she would lose control, and the last time she would doubt the necessity of pursuing her plan. This confirmation sparked a mental image of the next and most challenging step in her strategy to date.

CHAPTER 6: THE CENTER

Friday, January 19

It was Friday, boasting a cloudless, sunshine-flooded sky permeated by a frigid cold only the most warmly dressed of those venturing outside could tolerate. Peter awoke that morning with a sense of exhilaration. As he completed dressing after showering and shaving, he looked at himself in the bedroom mirror and tried to identify the source of the euphoria he was experiencing. He didn't have to give long consideration to the matter. It quickly became obvious to him that working with teenage clients at the Lillian Metcalfe High School Teen Health Center was an appealing change in his usual routine. He found the minds of adolescents to be pristine in the sense that they remained largely uncluttered with the mental detritus that served to impede progress during therapy with older clients. Thus, his efforts with adolescents were rewarded more regularly with positive gains and outcomes. It wasn't that he was unhappy working with his older clientele, it was just that he felt more productive as a therapist when working at the Teen Health Center.

Parking his car in the part of the snow-lined lot adjacent to the wing of the school in which the Center was located, Peter, an extra spring in his step, walked briskly toward a door in the building which gave direct access to the facility. Physically, the Teen Health Center was made up of two large classrooms which had been reconfigured to create one large integrated space containing two small offices, a small meeting room, and a lounge with a reception desk. As usual, the desk was unmanned and he found he was the only one present this morning. This was as it always had been since he started working there. The Center, a joint enterprise of several government agencies, operated on a shoestring budget and was dependent on community agencies to pay the salaries of any professionals who provided services there. No permanent staff members were attached to the project. Consequently, it was common for outside professionals to find themselves the only service provider in the Center on their scheduled days. Early on, Peter had explained to the school administration and the Board of Directors of the Center, that for the protection of both client and therapist, there was a need for, at least, one other responsible adult to be present when he was conducting therapy sessions. In response, the Board of the Center had declared there was no money to pay for the additional staffing, and the school administration cited the Teen Health Center agreement which limited their responsibility to the provision of the space in which the Center was housed. However, the Principal did agree to have a rotation of teachers, who had scheduled instructional prep time outside the classroom, undertake that preparation in the Center; thereby, providing the presence of a second adult. Unfortunately, Peter's experience, thus far, had been that, in practice, this arrangement had fallen prey to unanticipated problems - teachers being late in arriving for their shift or forgetting the responsibility completely, periods when no teachers were scheduled for prep and therefore no one was available to the Center, teachers being called away from the Center during their shift - the list went on. Peter complained further, extracting a promise to try to do better. This morning, looking around the empty Center, save the young student who had just arrived and was waiting to see him, he suspected it would be more of the same.

"Good morning, Frances, I am waiting for Mrs. Ralston to show up", Peter said greeting the seated student. "As soon as she gets here, we'll start our session. OK?"

"Mrs. Ralston's not here today, Dr. Simpson. I think she might be sick or something. Anyway, she's not in school."

No sooner had Frances finished speaking than the two-way PA system filled the Center with the voice of Richard Foreman.

"Dr. Simpson, are you there?"

"Yes, indeed, Mr. Foreman, Frances and I both", replied Peter mentioning the student's name to emphasize their readiness to start therapy.

"I apologize, Dr. Simpson, circumstances beyond my control. As you know, Mrs. Ralston was scheduled to start the day in the Center this morning, but called in sick late. The substitute is en route but won't be here in time to cover the Center. Sorry."

"There's nobody else?" asked Peter, hopefully.

"Fresh out of bodies, I'm afraid, Dr. Simpson. And we may have trouble covering other times today as well. We have had a rash of teachers call in sick today. You can send Frances back to class, if you wish."

"No!" whispered Frances, "I really need to see you today! Please!"

"But, Mr. Foreman, I am booked into the Center for the entire day. If I wait on teachers who may or may not be available, I could lose the day or most of it from what you're telling me. Since Frances is already here and she wants to talk to me, I will start the day with the hope that you can provide a teacher as soon as possible."

"Do as you think best, Dr. Simpson. I will do what I can but don't hold your breath."

With a smile, while motioning Frances toward the office he used for his sessions, Peter said, "OK, Frances. Shall we get started?"

Apart from a 30-minute break for lunch, Peter's day at the Center was a busy one with all six students scheduled for sessions that day showing up on time while only one of the five teachers scheduled to do prep in the Center appeared, and that teacher was fifteen minutes late. After the final student had left, he remained at the desk in the small office dictating the case notes that were part of the product of the sessions he had just conducted. He took his time, more time than he would've taken if doing the dictations in his own office. As the minutes passed, he experienced an ever-building feeling of anticipation and excitement. He had just completed putting the last of the documents in his briefcase when there was a light knock at the door.

As he walked toward the young girl standing in the open doorway, Peter smiled while looking intently at her face, searching for a sign, a hint of what was to come.

"Hello, Maggie. I'm so glad you came. Come on in."

As Maggie Munroe moved into the office, Peter closed the door on the emptiness that was the Teen Health Center at 4:00 pm on a Friday.

CHAPTER 7: SET-BACK

"**S**hit! Shit! Shit! What the hell was I thinking?"

Sheila chastised herself about lost time as she stomped off to catch a bus home.

An hour earlier, she had caught a bus immediately following school dismissal that had taken her to the little park and reviewed again the big step she would take today. The pigeons had come to know her and the bounty associated with her, and they had gathered quickly. Glancing at the office building across the street, she had absent-mindedly begun to cast bread crumbs on the frozen ground around her feet. *Something is wrong! What is it? Something seen or perhaps unseen?* She had looked over the scene once again. *That's it ... his car ... missing ... not in its usual place in the parking lot. Maybe he's there, but didn't bring the car ... maybe using his wife's car ... no, that's not there either. Someone dropped him off, that's it! Call and make sure.*

"Good afternoon, Dr. Simpson's office", the pleasant voice sounded in her ear.

"Er ... is Dr. Simpson in?"

"Dr. Simpson will not be back in the office today. May I help you?"

Not coming back? ... Christ! He always comes to his office after finishing at the Teen Health Center. Goddamnit!

"Hello?"

"Uh ... no, thank you, I'll call again."

***

Sheila, as if wakened from a dream, found herself standing in front of the back door of her home. Having been so psyched up, ready to take that next step, only to have providence snatch the opportunity away at the eleventh hour was deflating. She had experienced a psychological nose-dive that had left her in a kind of daze. She could only remember snippets of how she got from the park to her house.

No sooner had Sheila entered her home through the back door than she heard her mother's voice. And she sounded pissed.

"Sheila, where have you been? And where's that sister of yours? I specifically asked you and Maggie to come home right after school to help me carry out that stuff we're getting rid of. Now the man with the truck has come and gone and that junk is still in the garage. What have you got to say for yourself? "

"Oh, Mom, I'm sorry. I forgot all about it. I can take that stuff out of the garage to the curb right now if you want. And I don't know where Maggie is. I didn't see her at school today."

Looking at her mother's face and seeing annoyance, but worse, hurt, she felt shame. She was letting everyone down lately. She really did need to get it together.

"It's too late to take those things to the curb now. But the next time I ask you to help with something, I expect you to show up. As for your sister, I'll deal with her when she gets home."

Thinking that this day was competing for one of the worst of her life, Sheila headed for the stairs and the refuge of her bedroom. She had not even mounted the first step when her mother's voice sent a sensation not unlike an electric shock through her.

"By the way, Mr. Foreman called this afternoon."

Sheila froze with her right foot and leg suspended in mid-air before the first step of the stairway. Staring straight ahead of her, mind racing to find plausible answers to anticipated questions, her Mother continued.

"He asked if Dad or I had arranged for Maggie to see a Dr. Simpson at the Teen Health Center at the school. He told me that he was working late at the school this afternoon and he happened to see Maggie leaving the Teen Health Center with Dr. Simpson. This was about 4:30, well after school had been dismissed. Did Maggie say anything to you about staying after school to go to the Center?"

Sheila was reeling. What the hell was Maggie thinking? Her mother's next questions indicated that she had noted Sheila's hesitation in responding.

"You know something about this, don't you? What's going on, Sheila?"

Recovering, Sheila lied, convincingly she felt.

"Actually, I don't know anything about it. I was just surprised by what Dick Foreskin told you. I can't see Maggie needing any kind of counselling, can you? Maybe she just happened to be there and helped to carry something to the car for the guy and Foreskin couldn't wait to make something of it."

Used successfully in the past, she waited to see if the tactic of using crude language deflected her Mother's pursuit of the topic. Her mother had proven to be predictable in this way previously.

"Shelia, I've told you time and again not to use that kind of language. It's not only vile, but disrespectful. As long as you are living under this roof, you are not to speak like that!"

Mission accomplished.

Her mother, voice more conversational in tone now, continued.

"Besides, Mr. Foresk… er …."

Looking at one another and failing in their efforts not to smile at her mother's faux pas, they finally broke out in gales of laughter that brought tears to the eyes of both. In due course, regaining their respective composures, Sheila's mother reverted to her prior serious demeanour.

"Mr. Foreman said Maggie got in Dr. Simpson's car and they drove off."

Sheila was having trouble reconciling the emotionally distraught, tearful girl of just days ago with the behaviour described by her Principal. It just didn't make sense. If 'Dick' was correct, and Sheila couldn't think of any reason he would lie, then there was something Maggie wasn't telling her. She needed to talk to her little sister, the sooner, the better. For now, at least, Sheila felt confident that the worst had passed regarding her mother's queries.

"Well, I don't know what to tell you, Mom. You'll have to ask Maggie."

CHAPTER 8: FACELESS

Two huge uniformed cops stood at the front door, holding their peaked caps in their hands, knocking. The door opens just as the older of the two cops raises his fist to knock a second time. He lowers his arm and addresses the woman who appears before him.

"Are you Elizabeth Munroe?"

"Yes, I am. What can I do for you?" replies the faceless voice, sounding puzzled.

"I'm Sergeant Fox and this is Constable Fitzgerald, Halifax Regional Police. May we come in for a moment, Mrs. Munroe? We'd like to speak with you."

"Of course, come in. Let's have a seat in the living room. What's this about?"

Seated, the older cop speaks again.

"You have a daughter, Maggie, Mrs. Munroe?"

"Yes, she's my youngest. Why?"

"I'm very sorry to have to tell you this, Mrs. Munroe, but we have found the body of a young girl we have reason to believe is your daughter, Maggie. We suspect she has been murdered."

"NO! NOOOO!" Screams filling her head, Sheila became aware that she was sitting up in bed, gasping for air, heart racing, perspiration forming on her brow. Moments passed as her mind fought to reset and sort things out. A dream?

A small voice now entered her consciousness: "Sheila, Sheila, are you OK? You were screaming! It woke me up!"

Sheila looked toward the voice coming to her from the darkness. Maggie? Yes, Maggie. Like a small stream made a torrent by a sudden downpour, tears ran freely while she reached out for her sister.

***

Wide awake in bed after Maggie had left and returned to her bedroom, 3:00 am on the digital alarm clock, memories of yesterday late afternoon and evening came flooding back. She had phoned Maggie's mobile to give her a heads-up about the call from Mr. Foreman and what he said he had witnessed. She had paused waiting for her sister to explain why she was meeting Simpson, hoping against hope that Maggie would deny seeing the man and call into question "Foreskin's" report. The silence created by that extended pause had been excruciatingly long and uncomfortable. Finally, Maggie put off answering by saying she would explain everything when she got home.

Back home at 6:30 pm and within 30 minutes of Sheila's call to warn her, Maggie had bustled into the house through the back door, spewing apologies to her mother for being home late and for forgetting that she was supposed to help carry junk to the curb. Her explanation included hanging around the school grounds talking with friends, then hitching a ride downtown with Dr. Simpson who had happened to be leaving just as the group of friends was dispersing. Anticipated follow-up questions from their mother were answered with ease.

"Why did you go downtown without letting anybody know?"

"To buy a birthday present for your birthday next week."

"That's very thoughtful of you but why did that take till 6:30?"

"Because the cost of the gift was more than I thought and I didn't have enough money for the bus ride so I had to walk home."

"I didn't see you carrying any bags or parcels when you came in just now. Where is this gift?"

"I dropped it off at Bonnie's for safekeeping, so it would be a surprise."

Forgiveness was then extended on the condition that it didn't happen again.

Later that evening in Maggie's bedroom, the sisters had squared off facing each other while sitting on the bed. Sheila, watching her sister's reactions carefully, made a demand for a truthful explanation of the afternoon encounter with Simpson.

"OK, let's have it. What the hell is going on? You admit you were with that slimy bastard when he is the last person on earth I would think you could stand to be near. I'm confused, Mags, really confused. Enlighten me."

"Look, I know this looks weird, but I got to thinking that maybe I was partly at fault in this whole thing and it wasn't fair to hold him entirely to blame. I went to see him to say I was sorry for anything I did to contribute to what happened, and that I was not going to see him anymore. He said he understood my decision and offered to give me a lift downtown because I had mentioned I was headed there."

With fire in her eyes, and in a tone that betrayed her astonishment and anger, Shelia, in a voice too loud for the clandestine nature of the conversation they were having, had vented her outrage.

"That's it? He just said 'OK, nice knowing ya'? You've got to be kidding me! The slippery bastard! Listen, Mags, he's a freaking mature man and you're fifteen. No way you're to blame for any of this. Do you hear me?"

"Shhhh…for God's sake, the last thing we need is for Mom to hear any of this. Look, we both agreed it was over… done. OK? I'm OK, alright? I just want to forget it ever happened. Please don't make it worse!"

Later, still fuming as she'd gotten ready for bed, Sheila had come to a fateful decision. Just because her little sister did not understand how she had been victimized and had had her thinking distorted by misguided feelings of guilt, didn't mean that Simpson was any the less evil and should be allowed to escape any consequences. All the more reason her plan should be pursued, and with renewed urgency.

CHAPTER 9: THREATS

Saturday, January 20

"**T**hank God you're home, Peter! I just got another call but this time there was a voice! It was terrible!"

It was Saturday morning. Peter had barely opened the door after returning from a grocery run with Solynn when Karen had greeted him with this. He put the little girl down to play, gave her a number of her favourite toys, then hugged his distraught wife whose face wore the acute distress she was feeling. She had been close to the back door when he arrived home, waiting for him. After a few seconds, he disengaged from his wife, stepping back to look at her face while lightly holding her at arm's length, a hand on each of her shoulders.

"Do you mean that phone call you told me about, the one where the caller didn't say anything? You got another one?"

Her eyes wide, fixed on his, she answered with a virtual avalanche of words.

"Yes! Yes! There was no speaking from the other end at first and *caller unknown* came up on call display. So, I thought it was the same asshole. I was angry and I made the mistake of saying, 'Whoever you are, you must be sick to do this. Do you know who my husband is? If you did, you would think twice about doing this again!' That set her off and this angry tirade came from the other end. She said she damn well knew who you were and if anyone was sick, it was you. That you were evil, but most people didn't know it yet, but they would soon enough. She said you kept it secret, you fooled people, even me; that you didn't deserve to walk around free; that you would be stopped. She said she felt sorry for me. Oh, God, she said Solynn deserved a better father and that if she were me, she'd pack up, take Solynn and run as far from you as she could. She even told me to ask you why you were so late getting home Friday afternoon, to ask you what you were doing. Peter, I was speechless, so upset I just slammed the phone down. That was about ten minutes ago. Who would say such things? She must be mad, crazy. I don't care if it doesn't sound politically correct, it's true. Peter, I'm frightened. She knows Solynn's name! She knows us!"

Listening to Karen's bombshell, he saw the fear and questions registered in her intense expression, and he felt slightly unnerved. He had never seen her quite so upset before. He knew it was largely due to shock. This kind of unexpected phone call, one ripe with innuendo and threat directed toward someone you loved, was a form of personal attack, an assault. He sought to reassure his wife while trying to get as much helpful detail from her as he could. That detail might well help him to decide on what to do next.

"Karen, this is awful. I'm sorry you had to be on the receiving end of such a bizarre call. We are changing our phone number immediately. I am now convinced we need an unpublished number. I will report the call to the phone company first thing on Monday morning and request a new number. You said 'she', a female then. Did she sound young or old?"

"Young, I think, quite young actually. Peter, you should let the police know about this as well as the phone company."

Peter made a point of checking his watch.

"OK. And the call came in just before Solynn and I got back? That would make the time around 11:40."

"Uh-huh."

"Did you notice anything about the call that you haven't mentioned yet? Anything more about the voice or the language used? Any other things she might have said?"

With calm reasserting itself, Karen considered Peter's questions.

"No, I've told you everything she said. The voice was clear, not distorted or disguised, and angry. The language, the little I heard, sounded like that of someone with some education - no double negatives or stuff like that."

Nodding his head, Peter continued:

"Any sounds other than the voi -?

Peter's question remained unfinished as he saw Karen suddenly start to run to the front of the house where she looked out the window of the vestibule while practically shouting, "I heard the chainsaws! You know, the arborists cutting down that dead tree across the street! I heard the chainsaws in the background! Jesus, Peter, she was phoning from right outside our house!"

CHAPTER 10: THE NEXT STEP

Sheila was beside herself. She had always prided herself in her ability to quickly adapt to challenging situations, to maintain her composure and focus in the most trying of circumstances. She was often the recipient of compliments from others as to her calm and steadiness under fire and her ability to control her emotions no matter the pressure. And what had she done? Flown off the handle, abandoned any semblance of self-control and railed at the woman like an elementary school kid during a tiff on the playground. *Oh my God! I even used the little kid's name during the rant. His wife isn't my enemy, for God's sake, certainly not the child. If only the woman hadn't said what she did, suggesting he was this formidable person who could use his almighty power to swat a bug like me. No, he's the bug and I'm the swatter!*

Sheila was dejected, sitting in a bus shelter two streets over from the street on which the Simpsons lived, trying to think, trying to assess the damage she'd done. *What have I revealed? The woman heard my voice, and could likely tell I was young rather than older. I used the kid's name so they are now aware that I know something about their family. Shit! My remark about asking him why he was so late coming home indicates I knew what he was doing, about where he was. Putting myself in the wife's position, I would be scared and feel threatened. I would want something done about it. Oh no, the cops, she'll want the cops involved. OK, so what? They won't be able to trace my pay-as-you-go mobile. Everybody knows that. Anyway, he's not going to want the cops involved ... no way! That could put him in the line of fire and he doesn't want that. OK, what else? The Simpsons don't know me. I'm not connected to them in any...Oh, shit! He's going to think it was Maggie!*

Alright then, what will he do? He'll want to talk to Maggie, ask her what's going on and try to defuse the situation. How can he do that without drawing unwanted attention? Her mobile? Surely she wouldn't have given him her number? Even if she did, would he take a chance on calling her? Wouldn't it be safer for him to wait to talk to her face-to-face? No, he won't wait, he needs to talk to her sooner rather than later. Wait a minute, wait a minute. It's a good bet that he'll get his phone number changed immediately, especially if his wife is freaked. He will feel that a new number, unknown to Maggie, will prevent her from getting through to his wife if she should try to call again, thus giving him more time to arrange a discreet meeting. But can I count on that?

Having mounted the steps of the bus, paid the fare and seated herself alone at the back, Sheila gave further consideration to the new and emergent situation her intemperate phone call had created.

Does this change my plan? Should it? What problems, if any, does it cause me? It might make him more cautious, more suspicious. He could start damage control in some way. Not sure he can though … the horse is already out of the barn. If he suspects Maggie made the call, he will want to talk to her to find out what's going on. But when she denies it, and if he believes her, his antennae will really go up then. Might he come to suspect me as a result? Unlikely, unless Maggie tells him about me and that I know everything. I need to know if they communicate about the call before I take the next step. I will simply ask Maggie before I initiate…what shall I call it? Operation Samantha? Yeah, Operation Samantha. If she says they haven't, I'm laughin' and can move ahead.

***

Arriving home at just after 1:30 pm, Sheila removed her coat and boots quickly, her focus on a conversation with Maggie. On her way to the stairs, she noticed her father and mother in what appeared to be a serious discussion in the TV room. She couldn't hear what they were saying but her mother was very animated, a very determined look on her face. Her father, on the other hand, seemed to be trying to placate her. She had seen it all before, the inevitable banging of heads after another of Arthur's Friday nights pissed to the eyeballs. Better leave them to it and avoid any questions about where I've been.

Music, coming from behind Maggie's bedroom door, announced her presence. Sheila knocked lightly and entered. Quickly taking a seat on the bed next to her sister, Sheila started what she'd planned as a subtle probing.

"You know that stuff we talked about earlier today, 'bout you seeing Simpson again yesterday afternoon? I got to thinking. Have you guys communicated in any other way than when meeting at the Center?"

OK, maybe not so subtle.

Maggie, looking up from her Teen Vogue magazine, turned to Sheila.

"What do mean? Did we meet elsewhere? We always met at the Center after school."

"Yeah, that too, but also did you ever talk on the phone, for example?"

"Nope."

Oh, the hell with being subtle, it's not me.

"Does he have your mobile number?"

"What's this all about, Sheila? Why are you asking these questions? What's up?"

"Just curious that's all. Well?"

Maggie's audible sigh suggested she was resigned to her sister's questioning.

"No. He doesn't know my mobile number."

An inner relief spawned an unexpected excitement touching every nerve in her body because Sheila knew Samantha was still a go.

***

Saturday evening and the usual routine and accompanying rituals saw Solynn sleeping soundly in her bed which was adorned with Little Mermaid decals. Her parents were now in conversation, having retired to the kitchen.

Following her return to relative calm from the shock and subsequent fear she had felt that morning, Karen had had time to reflect and was struggling with a question she wanted to ask her husband. It was a question that she needed to put to him but knew the very asking of it would make it look as if she might be putting some credence in what the caller had said. Coming to her decision, she turned to Peter.

"There's something still bothering me about that awful call this morning. It was like someone reaching right inside your home to attack you. I feel violated. What is particularly frightening is that the caller knew things about us. She almost came out and said she knew of your whereabouts. What do you make of her saying that I should ask you why you were late getting home Friday afternoon?"

There I asked it.

Peter, contemplative in an extended moment of silence before answering, replied calmly and definitively.

"If she knew where I was and what I was doing later that afternoon, she would know that I was adding to my case notes after finishing sessions at the Teen Health Center, spoke to a student who unexpectedly dropped into the Center to see me, and then drove home, taking a short detour to drop the student off downtown to meet her friends."

"Her? A female student? Could she be the caller? It sounded like a young female."

Again, Peter gave the impression of careful reflection before answering.

"I can't think this student would do such a thing. I don't really know her very well. I've only met with her a couple of times. But she seems like a typical adolescent, and I can't imagine the motivation for such a call if she was the one."

"'Typical'? She must have been referred to you for some problem or problems. You don't see 'typical' clients, surely?"

Peter responded, immediately this time.

"Karen, for the most part, the majority of my clients are well-adjusted but have an issue or issues they need help to address. I only see a handful of truly abnormal clients. Anyway, she wasn't a referral. She just dropped in one day when I was there to ask me about the study and practice of Psychology. She is thinking of studying to become a Psychologist."

"I see." Karen said, nodding her head, "Are you in the habit of driving teenage girls around in your car?"

"For God's sake, Karen, she said she was going to catch the bus downtown, practically on my way, so I said I'd drop her off. That hardly constitutes a habit."

Backing off, Karen smoothed the waters, although her words belied the knot she felt in her stomach.

"Sorry, Peter. I'm a bit on edge still. Of course, I might have done the same thing myself. Only I think you need to be careful about being alone with young girls. You have to be as vigilant outside therapy as you are during therapy."

CHAPTER 11: MONDAY RETRIBUTION

Monday, January 22

Opening her eyes Monday morning, Sheila immediately identified an acute sense of purpose and anticipation. She felt a controlled excitement, a feeling that was, at the same time, both motivating and threatening. Lying in bed for a few minutes, sheets and body entwined as silent testimony to troubled sleep, her mind flashed back to images of the many hours devoted to preparation and rehearsal over the past few days. It seemed the fatigue she felt from this driven behaviour had not been the kind conducive to uninterrupted sleep. She had found sleep elusive, getting perhaps three, maybe four hours a night since Friday.

Although she was almost certain there had been no contact between Maggie and Simpson during the weekend, she would arrange to meet with Maggie briefly right after school today to ask one last time. Sheila's repeated query about whether Simpson had made contact or not, was clearly perplexing to her sister. She was wary, Sheila could tell, but Maggie remained ignorant of the drama that would take place.

Choosing to walk alone to school and, while there, spend her lunch hour and off-period in isolation, Sheila yet again mentally rehearsed a role designed to fundamentally change an imbalance of power, the role of a lifetime. Outside this final mental preparation, concentration was not afforded to revelations about Calculus, the power of the words of Robert Frost, or the intricacies of the binding of electrons to the surfaces of various types of matter. *Real life is going on here, people!*

The final minutes of the school day ticked away and the long-anticipated dismissal buzzer sounded. Just as she'd done for Friday's aborted mission, Sheila quickly packed up her school bag and made her way to her locker, opened it and removed a small overnight case. She placed her school bag in the locker, closing and then locking its door. Laser-focused now, following a script embedded in her mind by countless mental rehearsals, she located Maggie at their pre-arranged rendezvous near the stands of the school's soccer field. No contact had been made by Simpson, Maggie confirmed. Maggie noticed but did not ask about the overnight case. Time 3:34 pm.

***

Case in hand, Shelia disembarked from a bus not far from the little park at about 4:15 pm. She walked directly to the park and confirmed the presence of the two cars she'd identified from observations made on her frequent visits here over the past number of weeks - seemed like months now. She hardly noticed the welcoming committee of pigeons gathering around her feet. *Sorry, no crumbs today, guys.* She then turned and walked to the public bathroom in the cobblestoned shopping area a block to the west of the park. Emerging from the bathroom twenty minutes later, she walked directly back to the park, and confirmed that both cars were still present, then took a seat on a bench. Time 4:45 pm.

***

The outside office door opened and closed quietly. *Sue, leaving for the day*? It must be 5 o`clock, Peter realized, looking at his watch for confirmation.

Feet up on his desk, a small tumbler of scotch whiskey from the bottle he kept in his desk in hand, he celebrated finishing the dictation of case notes from his final session that ended at 4:30. *Thank the Lord for speech-to-text software programs.*

Leaving the house this morning, Peter once again assured Karen he would call the phone company to change their present home number to a new unlisted one. He had made good on that promise first thing after arriving at his office. As for contacting the police as Karen had suggested, he thought it wise to put that on the back burner. He had been giving some thought to the call Karen had received and to her warning about his being alone with young high school girls. He wondered if the call might have come from someone who had seen him and Maggie Munroe together and was making assumptions. Someone who knows something about me and my family. No way I'm inviting the police into this quagmire.

Drink finished, referring to his watch once again, 5:10 pm, he began packing his briefcase with the case files he needed to review prior to tomorrow's sessions. The knock at his office door was unexpected. Sue's forgotten to tell me something before she left.

"Come on in, Sue".

His back to the door, pulling files from the cabinet behind his desk, he heard it being opened.

"You could have called me at home rather than coming back to tell me, you know."

"Dr. Simpson?" A female voice - not Sue's. Peter turned toward the door.

Standing in the doorway was a stunning young woman, tall and lean, long slim neck highlighted by thick long dark brown hair swept up on her head adding to the sense of height. Face made-up, yes, but would be breath-taking without any make-up he thought.

Struggling with the temporary paralysis his first glimpse of her created, while succeeding in keeping his facial expression neutral, he failed to prevent his voice from cracking.

"Sor … excuse me….. Sorry. Thought you were my secretary coming back to pass on a message she'd forgotten to give me before she left. Yes, I'm Dr. Simpson. The practice is closed for today. You can call Sue - that's my secretary - tomorrow to book an appointment, if you want. You did want an appointment, didn't you? Maybe, you're just looking for directions to the nearest MacDonald's?"

He barked a brief nervous laugh while flashing a broad smile.

The woman did not smile in return, but wore a rather intense facial expression, as though she was gripped by a grave concern, perhaps by fear. Peter had seen that look many, many times, but perhaps never on a face where its presence did not detract from its essential beauty. However, he knew it signalled vulnerability.

"Oh, I do want to see you, talk to you. I've heard such wonderful things about you, that you are an excellent Psychologist, very understanding, very good with your clients. I know this is a great imposition, Dr. Simpson, but I'm desperate!"

Tears beginning to form in the corners of entrancing grey-green eyes, and fumbling for a Kleenex from her coat pocket, the woman continued her plea.

"Please, a few minutes of your time. Just to see if you think it is something you can help me with. I don't know where else to turn."

Peter, without hesitation, slipped into his caring, empathetic persona, one with which he made his well-paid living, one which would connect him emotionally with her.

"I can see you are very upset and seem a bit overwhelmed. Of course, I can spend a few minutes talking with you. Please, take off your coat and have a seat. Can I get you a drink of water?"

"Oh thank you, thank you for this. No water, thanks."

The full-length, maroon coat, still swinging slightly on the coat rack by Peter's jacket, the woman had effectively unveiled a tantalizingly perfect figure, *statuesque* came to mind. Long tapering legs were accentuated by a snug skirt ending a full six inches above the knee. Her knit V-neck sweater kept no secrets.

Taking a seat in front and to the left of his desk, one which provided her no cover and Peter an unobstructed view, she introduced herself as Samantha. *Friends call me Sam.* With some effort and encouragement from Peter, she then filled the next twenty minutes with a chilling description of the scene of a head-on collision between a car carrying a family of four and a fully loaded tractor-trailer. She, as the first driver on the scene, had stopped her car to try and help but was rendered helpless by flames which by then had enveloped the car and its occupants. Although she said she couldn't be sure, she thought she saw a child's face appear momentarily at a window of the car before the car's fuel tank exploded. She explained that since witnessing this tragedy, she had been plagued by intrusive flashbacks and horrific dreams that made her fear falling asleep. She frequently broke down and subsequently recovered while relating her grisly story. Peter made the obligatory statements of sympathy and asked a few questions. At the appropriate time, Peter brought the session to a conclusion.

"You have been struggling with an immense emotional burden. I think you need some help dealing with it and I think I can provide that help. Let's fit you in this week."

Handing Samantha one of his business cards, he suggested the setting of an early appointment.

"Give Sue a call tomorrow for an appointment time that's convenient for you. I will tell her it's a priority."

Rising from her chair and walking slowly toward the door, Peter following closely behind to see her out of the office, Samantha added to her disclosures.

"Thank you, Dr. Simpson. I feel like I am going crazy because I can't seem to get it out of my head. It's like pictures and memories are hiding in my brain and I can't control when they pop into my mind – like I'm being controlled by someone else who lives in my head. Isn't that weird?"

Stopping abruptly while turning to face him, Peter stumbled into her causing him to reach out to grab her shoulder to steady her from the impact. The maneuver left her face just inches away from his. He could smell her scent, feel her body heat.

Moments passed during which time seemed to be suspended before she spoke.

"You have been very kind, so understanding - so very different from the men I've known."

She suddenly placed her arms around his neck, pulling him in and kissing him on the cheek far too near his mouth. She then moved her head slightly and the kiss became mouth to mouth. She knew she'd achieved her goal when the kiss became prolonged and the tip of her tongue brushed his closed lips causing them to part. Time 5:52.

CHAPTER 12: AFTERMATH

*A*bsolutely unbelievable! I did it! Sheila, on an emotional high, was sitting on a bus headed for home; in her hand the ultra-slim mini-digital audio recorder she had strapped to her abdomen with its highly sensitive wire microphone running up under her push-up bra. She'd thought she was done when their bodies had come together during the kiss and trapped the mini-recorder between them. He hadn't seemed to notice.

She hadn't listened to the recording yet but knew it would be crystal clear because she had experimented with it in the most compromising of circumstances and it had always provided high-quality audio, capturing voices clearly. Upon leaving she'd put the recorder back in her overnight case she'd left just inside his outer office door.

As the bus rumbled toward her home, stopping in its regular pattern to disgorge and pick up passengers, something at the back of her of mind tried to intrude on her mental celebration. She pushed it away, attempting to bury it. But it persisted. Finally, she gave in to it, giving it her attention. It bloomed. She remembered him pulling away, apparently embarrassed, and apologizing.

"Samantha, I'm sorry. This is highly unprofessional of me. I'm very embarrassed. Look, under the circumstances, I can't be your therapist, it would be unethical. I will give you the names of other Psychologists who I can recommend. I apologize for agreeing to be your therapist one minute and then doing something so stupid and having to renege on that agreement the next. But it is for the best, honestly."

Taking on a look of confusion, transitioning to one of desperation, two of the many facial expressions to accompany anticipated emotions she had practised over and over again in the mirror in her bedroom, Sheila had continued to play Samantha.

"But I don't want anybody else! I want you to be my therapist. We can forget about what just happened, no one needs to know. I feel so close to you. I don't want to lose that."

She remembered how Simpson had become more and more confident in his position, more resolute in his responses.

"No, I'm sorry, Samantha, that can't happen. I've been a fool. You are a very attractive woman and I was immensely flattered by your apparent interest in me. I acted on an impulse that I should have been able to control. This is entirely my fault. I hope you can forgive me. The worst thing about this whole thing is that I have betrayed my wife."

Without another word, Sheila had turned her back on him and walked swiftly out of the office suite, not once looking back. She hurried from the building into the cold night which was spitting flakes, elation mounting as she passed the little park with its nesting pigeons and their little snow-capped heads, and on to the public washroom to change once again before moving on to the bus stop.

* * *

At the window of his office, thrown into darkness now, as he had been quick to extinguish his office lighting as soon as she left, he watched her hurry across the street and past the park. He noticed the overnight case she hadn't had with her when she was in his office. The sensation of something foreign attached to her body, something unusual, something that should not have been there, had brought him to his senses mid-kiss. At the time, he had truly been experiencing a raging see-saw battle between conflicting emotions, his surprisingly intense need to have a beautiful young woman want him while trying to submerge his need to protect what he had with

Karen. So balanced were the scales, he could easily have found himself making love to the woman right here in the office. As a consequence, he considered it fortunate that he had felt whatever it was. It had tipped the scales. From that moment on he had moved into strategic retreat, his mind frantically searching for a way out. What he had done, what had come out of his mouth in those few minutes that followed had astonished him. He had seemed to be on automatic, almost as if he had given over his will, his future to someone else. But the result was, perhaps, the best that could have been expected under the circumstances.

Now, who is that pretty thing? What is she after? The best scenario would be that she isn't after anything other than therapy as she said. If so, it is likely there is no damage done and this will all go away. Could she actually want me? Think about it. The whole thing seems too contrived, every man's dream served up on a platter. How likely is that? Could it be money? The purpose of the little drama designed to compromise me so I can be blackmailed? Possible. But it would be her word against mine. There's no proof. While it is true that just the accusation could be damaging, it would not be catastrophic. Practitioners frequently have false accusations made and survive professionally.

While he had been giving his energy to speculating about possible motives, a stirring in the recess of his mind had been coming into sharper focus and now grew into a clear idea which, in turn, generated a distinctly heightened anxiety. The thing he'd felt during the kiss - *oh, God, maybe she does have evidence!*

***

The highly charged energy that had exploded from every cell in her body was starting to dissipate now in the aftermath of her triumph. Sheila, now among the disgorged at the nearest bus stop two blocks from her house, was walking slowly, starting to weep. She felt fatigued in the extreme, so much so that she was seriously wondering if she could make it home without first sitting down to rest. She was becoming aware of an inner emptiness, like all the joy she had felt just minutes ago hadn't happened. *What is this? This feels like it did when I first moved here and left all my friends behind. I didn't know anybody and I felt so alone.* Approaching a small street-side public rest area, she sat down on a bench and tried to make some sense of the melancholy feeling which had usurped the heady, almost giddy, state she had achieved in the minutes after leaving Simpson's office. As she did so, a tangle of conflicting thoughts began to intrude.

The bastard sexually assaulted an 18-year-old! ...... Did he? He thought you were older, an adult woman. You dressed and presented yourself that way. You planned to set him up and you did, so what did you expect? He didn't coerce or threaten you. Everything you did and said was intended to convey the message that you were up for it. You were consenting.

But he's a professional Psychologist engaging in sexual contact with a client. He's unethical. He knows very well that kind of thing is forbidden.

True. But it might be argued that technically you were not his client yet. That it wasn't official. You had not had a formal session yet. Either way, he recognized, albeit a bit late, his misjudgment and pulled back apologizing, asking forgiveness and acknowledging the ethical problem and the need to refer you to another Psychologist. He did the right thing under the circumstances, really looked sorry and sounded genuine.

But he said it himself, he betrayed his wife. What kind of husband does that? A low-life, that's who!

And he will have to live with that. But he confessed to you that he is married. He expressed guilt and self-loathing for his actions. That's got to count for something.

And so it went, back and forth, give and take in a mental

struggle that had consumed her remaining concentration and energy. Slowly, a reality outside her head made its presence known. It gently imposed itself in her awareness, coalescing in the recognition that the driver of the car that had parked curbside, lights out, less than half a block away from where she sat, had not gotten out since parking there five minutes ago. Without moving her head, using her peripheral vision as best she could and with the aid of backlighting provided by the headlights of a passing car, a silhouette of the driver's head and shoulders was clear, still sitting in the driver's seat. She couldn't make out anything about the car except that it was dark in colour. *Probably nothing. Anyway, time to get home.* She stood abruptly and continued walking but at a much more rapid pace. As soon as she resumed walking, she heard the car's engine start and noted the illumination of its headlights from behind her on the street in front. She began to jog, and then, house in sight, she sprinted the final fifty yards, hiding quickly behind a large bush to one side of the front entrance to her house. Peering out, she registered a black sedan driving slowly with the driver, unrecognizable, staring at the house as the car passed.

***

Pulling his car to the curb, Peter fumbled with his briefcase, keying the code into its cylindrical lock. He snapped the spring-loaded fasteners causing the lid to fly open and pulled out his small laptop computer. Powering it up, he looked for a non-secure network he could use to search for the address where he felt sure the woman had gone. She had taken him by surprise when she started running, but he'd seen her head into the shrubbery in front of a house, and then, had seen her again in the passenger-side mirror just as she ran up the walkway of the same house. He had not been able to get a good look at her in the dark, but he was certain she was Samantha and he had managed to get the address. As luck would have it, he found a network with a fairly good signal he could use. Employing reverse address lookup, he typed in the address and the city and moments later the names 'Robert and Elizabeth Munroe' were matched with the address. *Robert and Elizabeth Munroe? Munroe? Jesus!*

***

He followed me! The bastard followed me! Why would he follow me if he was as distraught and self-blaming as he seemed to be? Something's wrong. Did something tip him off? Now he knows where I live. He will soon know who lives in this house. It is only a matter of time before he puts it together and figures out that Samantha is me.

Sheila felt it slipping away, her carefully orchestrated plan unravelling. Any hope of anonymity while controlling Simpson with threats to reveal what he had done to her, was out the window now. She had had the intention of giving him a copy of the audio recording to heighten his tension and soften him up for her demands. Her demands were well-considered and came out of her research on child abuse, sexually deviant personalities and treatment for those afflicted. They were to be simple and non-negotiable. First, he would never see Maggie ever again. Second, he would no longer counsel children and adolescents, and any who were his clients at present would be referred to other Psychologists immediately. Third, he would donate $15,000 annually to charities which specialized in the support and treatment of child and adolescent victims of sexual abuse. And finally, he would seek treatment as an abuser himself.

Shit! It would have been so great to have… Hold on! Wait a minute! So what if he knows it's me? That makes it even better. I'm a student. He is in a position of power and authority and he used that to engage in sexual contact. The only thing that changes is that he will now know who is applying the vice to his nuts. I love it!

***

Peter spent a night of fractured sleep and endless mental rumination trying to make sense of what he had learned about the woman, the so-called Samantha. During the evening he had been distracted, removed from the life of his family going on around him. More than once, Karen had asked him if anything was wrong. A couple of times, he surfaced from his self-imposed mental isolation to hear her voice.

"Earth calling Peter, Earth calling Peter, come in" and "Peter. Peter. Solynn is trying to get your attention."

He eagerly sought alone time so he could think, see if he could see where all this was going. Although he did not know a lot, he reviewed again the facts of which he was reasonably sure.

The woman went into a house that is the residence of Arthur and Elizabeth Munroe. They are the parents of Maggie Munroe. Coincidence? Not a chance. The woman can't be Maggie's mother, she's too young. Maybe she's a friend or a relative? No, she's appeared to be too old to be a friend of Maggie's. But you never know. Maybe a relative then? Maggie mentioned a sister, but I can't remember if she said the sister was older or younger, but I remember her saying they went to the same school. If she's an older sister, it's possible. Surely to God, though, a schoolgirl could not have pulled that off? Leave the 'who' for now, and consider the 'why'. Why do this? Money? Most likely. If so, I will hear from Samantha again. Adventure? The adrenaline rush of dipping your toe in the forbidden pool? That seems a stretch.

Suddenly, the penny dropped.

The anonymous phone call that Karen received. The innuendo and implied threats. *Oh, Lord! This whole charade was intended to expose me to Karen, perhaps, to the community … my colleagues, my friends, the police, even. Everything I've worked so hard to achieve could be ruined … I might lose Karen and Solynn, my reputation, my licence to practise, everything! Calm down. Calm down. It's 'he says, she says'. No witnesses. No proof that I know about…..yet. Too soon to panic.*

CHAPTER 13: THE APPOINTMENT

Tuesday, January 23

As was her practice, Sue, a neurotic winter driver, had left her apartment allowing a twenty-minute cushion to slowly pilot her compact sedan to the office. One never knew when winter conditions might cause delays and Sue seemed to feel it almost a sign of virtue to arrive before necessary for work. No chances were to be taken in this regard.

It was 8:05 am when she walked through the office door, some twenty-five minutes prior to the scheduled start of her work day. She was pleased to have once again avoided any chance of being late and set about doing some filing she had been meaning to get to for some time now. Not having become part of the age of paperless filing, she hummed Christmas carols as she pulled files from steel cabinets, added documents to them and then replaced them. As she worked and hummed, she reflected on how the tunes and songs of Christmas stuck in your head for a while after the holiday, then were gone and didn't find their way back until the next year.

Sue liked her job and, in particular, her boss. She liked being useful to him, having him depend on her. She enjoyed his company. She knew she was being silly. She was more than a decade older than Peter and knew she was not particularly attractive. Besides, he was married and she liked Karen. Yet, he continued to be a frequent participant in her fantasies and dreams, sometimes in a sexual context which disturbed her immensely. When this happened, she became upset, reproving herself and punishing herself for having such thoughts by denying herself her little pleasures, her favourite chocolates, her preferred television show or going out to eat. As a practising Baptist, she had even sought spiritual assistance to banish these unbidden and unwanted thoughts and fantasies once and for all. Nothing had worked to date, so she had been left with castigating herself when she caught herself having "disgusting" thoughts and forcing herself to think about something else.

At 8:30 Sue had almost finished the filing when the first telephone call of the day announced itself with a loud warbling that startled her. Recovering, she picked up the receiver.

"Good morning, Dr. Simpson's Office, may I help you?"

"Yes, I would like to make an appointment to see Dr. Simpson. What might be available this week, the early part of the week is best for me."

Well, don't we feel entitled, thought Sue.

"I'm sorry, but there is nothing available this week. Dr. Simpson is booking new appointments three weeks from -"

The caller, apparently oblivious to the fact that Sue was still talking, interrupted.

"I spoke to Dr. Simpson about my reasons for wanting to see him yesterday and he asked that I call you today to make an appointment for this week. He said he would talk to you about prioritizing it."

Special treatment, eh? You must be a special person, my dear. I wonder who you are.

"I see. Well, Dr. Simpson hasn't come in yet. I will have to check with him, of course. Could I have your name and the telephone number where I can reach you after I have had a chance to check with him?"

"My name is Samantha Henning. Unfortunately, I will be on the move today and I don't have my mobile with me. How about I call you back at about 10:15 to confirm the appointment date and time?"

"I should think that would be fine. Thank you for calling."

Sue returned the telephone receiver to its base feeling this was an unusual method of securing an appointment; however, it wasn't the first time Peter had forgotten to tell her something. Nevertheless, something about the bold and aggressive attitude of the caller had put Sue off.

She had just returned to complete what little was left of the filing when Peter entered the office. Sue was struck by his drawn and pale face and his far-away look. He gave the appearance of being ill.

"Good morning, Dr. Simpson. You look tired. Are you feeling alright?"

Looking at her in a way that suggested that he was taken aback by her presence, Peter struggled to find the words to respond.

"Oh ….. well … I'm OK, Sue, just had a difficult time getting to sleep last night."

"I know what that's like. You pay the price the next day, don't you? May I get you something, a coffee, juice maybe, something to eat?"

Responding with a half-hearted smile, Peter declined.

"No, no thanks, I'm good, Sue."

As he proceeded toward the open doorway of his own office, Peter heard Sue's voice once again.

"Oh, Dr. Simpson, I had a call from a Samantha Henning this morning asking for a priority appointment. She said that you knew about it, said she had talked to you about it yesterday."

Peter stopped in his tracks, a momentary pause giving the impression he was trying to recall.

"Oh, yes. My goodness, she didn't waste any time, did she? Yes, she spoke to me late in the afternoon, and it is a priority. Please fit her in today, Sue. I know the schedule's tight. Perhaps it would be best if she came in after the last appointment of the day, say 5:00 pm."

"Of course, Dr. Simpson, I will arrange to stay beyond my usual time to accommodate the appointment."

"That's not necessary, Sue. You can leave as usual. Not to worry."

"No imposition at all, Dr. Simpson. I don't mind."

"It's nice of you to offer, Sue, but please leave at the usual time."

Sue, feeling the affront, began to ponder.

My, my. What's afoot here?

***

So it's money!

Peter, now sitting behind the desk in his office, awaiting his first client of the day, drew this conclusion from the fact that Samantha wanted to meet again. It was the only reasonable inference that could be drawn. She's coming to make her pitch, her demand.

Despite the continuing threat, he felt relieved, almost elated. Blackmail as a motive is so much better than some crazed crusader hell-bent on ruining him. He was sure he could deal with a blackmailer, seeing a scenario which gave him more time to consider his options. The first step though was to find out exactly what this shake-down artist wants. Without remembering when he started, he found himself humming the tune of the same carol he heard Sue singing when he first entered the office a few minutes ago.

***

Punching the End button on her mobile phone, Sheila disconnected the call that had just told her that the next act featuring Samantha Henning would take place at 5:00 pm today. *But it won't be Samantha, will it?* She had made the call during the mid-morning break at her high school as she had planned when setting the call-back time with Simpson's secretary.

OK. OK. Let's review. Simpson may know, or at the very least, suspect Samantha is me. But that doesn't matter at this point. If he has connected our house address with who lives there, he will be alarmed about Samantha's apparent connection to Maggie. He may suspect this is about Maggie, but if that is the case, he might wonder why all this drama. Why not simply report Maggie's allegations to the police? Therefore, he will suspect that it's about blackmail, and, of course, to some degree, it is. Although he could not have known, he may think Samantha has something incriminating to back up any threats, any demands. He will want to know what it is.

Thinking of the two extra copies of the audio recording she made in the school's computer lab early this morning, Sheila was content with the thought that she will be more than happy to accommodate his quest for that evidence. Although the appointment has come much sooner than she expected it would, she is confident that she is ready.

***

Peter, anxious and mentally exhausted, had been waiting for Samantha for thirty minutes now, since the end of his last session at 4:30 pm. He was too keyed up, too distracted to dictate case notes. At last, he heard Sue leave with a cheery "See you tomorrow" through his closed door and, soon after, noted that the reception area had fallen silent. Three to four minutes later he heard the outer office door open and close, and within a minute thereafter, a knock on his door. Gut clenched, his voice was tight and his mouth felt extremely dry.

"Come in!"

Taking a deep breath, Sheila turned the knob and pushed, walking into the now familiar office, into a drama in which she is playing herself, not Samantha. She could feel how nervous she was, not unexpectedly, much more so than she had been as Samantha.

Looking at each other across the small room, Sheila was the first to speak.

"I believe you have been expecting me or some version of me. I'm Sheila Munroe."

A high school girl, unbelievable! Peter struggled to match the attractive adolescent before him with the mature beauty he had met yesterday. Yet, he noted the same colour hair now falling freely around the pretty, makeupfree face, and the dead giveaway, the stunning grey-green eyes. Any further comparison was foiled by blue denim bib overalls over a pink turtleneck sweater effectively hiding Samantha's curves, thighs and cleavage. The surprise was apparent in his face.

"Actually, I was expecting a client. Do you have an appointment?"

Uninvited, Sheila sat, back straight, on the edge of a chair directly in front of Peter's desk, and used a tone which was cold and aggressive.

"Cut the bullshit! I'm not wired today. Let's get down to the reason for this little get-together right away because I'm getting nauseous being in the same room with you."

With this, Sheila extracted the digital recorder from a pocket of her maroon coat which she had unbuttoned but hadn't bothered to remove, pressed the play button and a reedy-sounding audio filled the space between them with the words they had both used 24 hours ago. If Peter had let the recording play on, he would also have heard the muffled sounds hinting at the physical contact they'd had just before Peter had broken away. However, after listening intently for a couple of minutes, his facial expression suggested his mounting anger. Trying to establish a bit of control over the situation, he almost shouted.

"Alright! Alright! Shut the damn thing off! What are you after?"

Pausing the recording, she then extracted a memory stick from her coat pocket and tossed it onto the desk in front of him.

"Thought you'd like a copy. What do I want? What I want is for you to be in jail. But what I will settle for are the following non-negotiable actions on your part."

Proceeding to list her demands as Peter stared at her disdainfully, she itemized them one at a time and went on to further emphasize her commitment to seeing the demands are met.

"You can save your marriage, your career, and your reputation by doing what I have just laid out for you. I will need proof that you have taken action on what I require from you. So, I will be back here at the same time two weeks from now to receive that proof. If you do not produce satisfactory evidence, I will tell both your wife and your professional association what you did and provide a copy of the recording you have before you as evidence. Now you can crawl back into your hole."

With that said Sheila stood and strode to the office door, a commanding exodus planned. Reaching for the knob, intending to dramatically exit the office and the building into the cold darkness without once looking back, Simpson's voice delayed her withdrawal from the stage.

"You don't want money for yourself? I don't get it."

Turning back, she could see that he had come from behind his desk and was walking toward her. She felt a prickle of fear but maintained her position.

"It was never about money. You know exactly what it's about. You're not fooling anyone. You need help and you better get it if you know what's good for you."

Standing very near her now, Peter was still looking confused but sounded annoyed.

"For God's sake, I thought you were an adult woman. I was attracted to you and you were giving me signals that you were receptive. I made a huge mistake in judgment, I know that, but I did pull back. You know I did. Have you never made a mistake you wish you could reverse?"

Feeling the increasing threat inherent in his proximity, Sheila once again turned her back on him and resumed her trek through the building to the freedom of the night beyond. Just before leaving the outer office, she delivered a parting shot.

"You haven't even got the decency to admit to your criminal behaviour, you creep! You will have to answer to God and, of course, to me."

This time she made it to the street, but she hadn't managed it without looking back just as she was about to exit the front door of the building to see the perplexed look on Simpson's face as he stood by his inner office door. Her exit had been so swift with her attention on listening for indications of Simpson pursuing her, she hadn't noticed Sue scrambling to conceal herself behind the reception area counter the same way she had done when Sheila had first entered the office twenty minutes before.

CHAPTER 14: YOU'VE COME BACK!

By the time she had reached the bus stop near the little park, Sheila was exhausted, as if all her psychic energy had been spent, gone like the air from a punctured balloon. Joy, even euphoria, had come and then disappeared in the few minutes it took for her to exit the office building, pass through the park and continue on her way to the bus stop. She was experiencing a sudden overpowering feeling that she had failed. Despite doing everything she had planned and undertaken it without a single serious glitch, a troubling doubt was taking hold, and with it came an accompanying sense of desperation. Initially, a whisper she had ignored, it was now a blatting bullhorn transmitting an accusation that Simpson was getting off far too lightly, an unscrupulous user and abuser was being tut-tutted instead of being called to task for the criminal he is. In her despair, Sheila began to obsess about her failure to exact the appropriate pound of flesh. She sat on the bench in the bus shelter in the dark, bent over with elbows on knees, head in hands brooding and thinking. Her bus came and went when she had made no move to board it. She was consumed by her thoughts. Finally, she stood and started walking in the direction of the little park and the pigeons, her face set in an expression of fierce determination replacing the one of despair that had preceded it.

***

Peter, before him a tumbler of scotch and the half full bottle from which it had come, sat at his office desk lost in thought. He was profoundly disturbed about the exchange with Sheila Munroe, a.k.a., Samantha. Yes, he was annoyed with himself because he had allowed a schoolgirl to manipulate, to play, him. However, what made him seethe with anger was the disrespect to which he had been subjected by another *goddamn female*, thinking she is better than him. Any feeling of admiration for the gutsy manner in which she had pulled off the extortion was lost in the overwhelming sense of violation he felt. He drained the last of his third glass of scotch and then topped up the tumbler again.

As he sat replaying the exchange with Sheila in his mind, he continued to have the same recurring niggling feeling that he was missing something. Her demands, which he was extremely reluctant to meet, might well be doable if push came to shove, and, if handled with care, would have minimal impact on his life and career. But the nature of the demands themselves had surprised and confused him, at least, initially. First, she had not demanded money for herself. The requirements to exclude children and adolescents from his clientele and to refer those who were presently on his caseload to other professionals seemed rather bizarre at first blush; however, it was the stipulations that he make an annual donation to organizations dedicated to helping victims of sexual abuse and that he get treatment himself that made the message conveyed by the demands most clear. *She actually said that she preferred to see me in jail. What did Maggie tell her?*

Again, Peter couldn't shake the feeling that he was missing something important, something that had remained unspoken. He was just raising the glass of amber liquid to his mouth when a knock sounded on his closed office door. Putting the glass down, he looked towards the closed door.

"Heyyy …. Good. Yer back! I need …. Ah've got questions. Yep. Ah've got questions. Come in. Door's not …. locked."

***

Arriving home at 7:45 pm, Sheila made straight for the bathroom to splash her face with water after which she retreated to her bedroom, and there, lay on the bed virtually comatose. She had the sensation that somehow her body seemed like that of someone else, that she was disembodied somehow, disconnected. At some point, she must have fallen into a deep sleep because she did not re-enter the conscious world until 7:40 the following morning. As she opened her eyes, first the right and then the reluctant left which required a little more effort to get unstuck, and oriented herself, first one mental image and then one image after another assaulted her. She sat bolt upright and gave a stifled whimper, her heart beating quickly and her respiration rapid and shallow. Her body started to tremble. *Dear God, what am I going to do?*

Getting out of bed, she crept out of her bedroom and heard voices below on the first floor of the house. Moving in the direction of the voices, she was nearing the bottom of the stairs when she heard Maggie's exclamation.

"Oh my God! That can't be true! Read that again."

Entering the kitchen, she saw a pyjama-clad Maggie sitting at the kitchen table, before her a breakfast of scrambled eggs untouched, and her mother standing, looking down to read from her tablet propped up on the kitchen countertop.

"'Prominent Local Psychologist Found Dead' is the headline. It goes on to say, 'Well-known psychotherapist, Dr. Peter Simpson, was found dead in his office last night where a member of the night-time cleaning staff came upon his body. Halifax Regional Police spokesperson, Constable Frank Temple, stated that the police investigation, although at a very early stage, is treating the death as suspicious'."

Sheila suddenly bent forward at the waist while bringing her hands to her mouth, and forcefully vomiting. Falling to her knees, the taste of bile in her mouth, she was seized with the sudden realization that her life had changed forever.

CHAPTER 15: GARGOYLE

Tuesday evening, Wednesday morning, January 23 and 24

Detective Sergeant Michael 'Mickey' MacKinnon's gaping, jaw-cracking yawn shook his whole body. He sat at his desk in the small office he shared with his partner, Detective Constable Francine Deveaux, at Halifax Regional Police Department headquarters in Halifax, Nova Scotia. The office, barely large enough to accommodate two undersized desks, two desk chairs and a single filing cabinet, was a claustrophobic nightmare. A crumpled wrapping from Burger Supreme, "the burger that dares you to eat it" as its advertising goes, and an empty extra-large waxed coffee cup adorned MacKinnon's desk the way many hundreds of its kind had done in the past.

It was 11:15 pm. His partner had clocked off duty three hours ago, leaving him to finish the final preparation, including the review of a small mountain of reports, for another of their cases about to go to trial. Francine had had little sleep over the last few days because she was spending nights at a friend's, a single mom, helping with the care of a newborn baby girl delivered by C-section. Consequently, she had been getting up at least twice a night to feed and change the infant plus working long hours on the Job. She was much in need of some sleep so he had offered to finish the paperwork and sent her home. He didn't mind because he had no particular reason to go home to the rented 3-room flat, where he lived alone, other than to sleep. Besides, he was good at pulling together and remembering information. Mickey knew that his prodigious memory and impressive ability to synthesize facts were two of the things that made him a good detective. It had never let him down. He had a reputation among his fellow officers as having a photographic memory. He'd once looked that up on

Wikipedia and came across the term *eidetic memory*, another name, it seemed, for photographic memory, which essentially bestowed upon him *an extraordinarily detailed and vivid recall.*

With the onset of another jaw-stretching yawn, he decided, eidetic memory or not, he had to get some sleep. He was in the process of donning his faux fur-lined overcoat preparatory to heading home when his desk phone rang.

"Yeah?"

Listening, he jotted down some information on a scrap of paper on his desk and hung up after saying, "OK. Got it", and made a call.

"Yo, Frannie. We've been called out. Pick you up in twenty. Tell you about it in the car."

Fifteen minutes after pulling out of the parking lot of police headquarters at 11:25 pm, he was nearing the nondescript wood-frame building where Francine rented her apartment. He knew she would be waiting for him outside as she always did when he picked her up. He had never seen the inside of her apartment, or her building for that matter. He had picked her up and dropped her off countless times since they had been assigned as partners, but she had not once invited him in. He was uncertain as to why his partner seemed intent on maintaining this degree of social distance between them. They got along well as partners. She seemed to respect him as he did her. Maybe he was interpreting her behaviour all wrong, maybe it was a generational or a woman thing, maybe she feared that opening up some sort social connection with a colleague would suggest something she did not intend.

As he approached the building, he saw her waiting at the curb for him to arrive. She seemed to be engaged in a kind of modern dance as she clapped her hands and stamped her feet to ward off the cold, her breath producing a fog which swirled around her body. She had the backpack she was wearing off and the passenger door open before he could bring the car to a full stop. After bustling into the vehicle, she quickly buckled up and then set about extracting a huge thermos and two paper cups from her pack, pouring what she called "liquid gold" from the thermos into the first cup which she handed to him, then into the second for herself. As soon as Mickey saw the thermos, he began to pray it contained coffee and not herbal tea again. His nose told him that his prayers had been answered before he took a swig of what tasted like a medium roast, piping hot. He was taking his second long swallow before anything in the way of a greeting was exchanged between them. Francine was the first to blink.

"Merde, it's cold. Seeps right into your bones. OK, what's up?"

Although they had been partners for better than a year now, he recognized that Francine, a twenty-six-year-old French-Canadian from Gatineau, Quebec, was still comparatively new to homicide investigations. Despite that, Mickey trusted her implicitly. He knew she brought exceptional credentials to her work – first in her class at the Atlantic Police Academy at Holland College in Prince Edward Island, an exceptional record during her time with Traffic Division, recruited as a fast-track candidate, and most important of all, she had proven to be an invaluable asset on the investigations they had worked together. Yet, there were those among the ranks of the Department who sought to diminish her meteoric rise by attributing it to her being female and to being able to converse in Canada's two official languages rather than to her competency. Mickey knew it was just sour grapes. He was simply grateful that she had gotten to where she was and that she was his partner. He had quickly come to know that he could depend on her efficiency and diligence to carry out the assignments given her, and more importantly, he benefited greatly from her assessments, opinions and gut feelings.

Despite the late hour and the sudden call-out, Mickey noted

that Francine's appearance and demeanour gave no hint of the fact that she had minimal sleep over the past few days. Rather, she was disgustingly bright and chipper, eyes aglow with the anticipation of a new adventure, a new case. He had seen this before in newbies who had yet to develop the emotional defences necessary to fend off the psychological assault that was the reality of many homicide investigations. He had given it six months tops for that I'm-up-for-anything attitude to turn into the cynical pessimism of the initiated - senior officers like himself. However, Francine's bright-eyed eagerness and optimism, her let-me-at-it fervour was apparent months after he had predicted it would perish.

Once he'd merged back into traffic, he brought his partner up to speed about where they were going and why, while they continued to enjoy what Francine informed him was a Guatemalan dark roast. *Who cares, as long as it's not herbal tea.*

Arriving at their destination just before 11:45 pm, Mickey brought his car alongside a patrol cruiser parked in a small parking lot to the side of a small flat-roofed, single-story, vinyl-sided office building. He observed that the parking lot was otherwise empty except for a van with a MacFadden Cleaners' emblem visible on its sides and a black BMW. As he unbuckled his seatbelt, he gave the benefit of his thoughts to his partner. It was one of Mickey's ways of mentoring, of imparting the wisdom of the veteran.

"At least the cowboys from the patrol had sense enough to turn their turret lights off. Otherwise, gawkers would be descending on this place like it was a rock concert, with the media not far behind. Hey, and good news. The media didn't beat us to the scene this time. Let's go find who belongs to that cruiser."

Extracting his bulk from behind the steering wheel, a task which seemed to take more effort than he would have liked, he and Francine set about finding the officers who were first on the scene. Francine, as had been her practise since starting to work with Mickey, retrieved the black case from the trunk, and then, carrying the case, the so-called crime investigation kit, trotted along after MacKinnon. After catching him as he opened the front door of the building, she muttered to herself, "No, no, don't wait for me. Not to worry, I like carrying this fucking heavy case all the time. Hold that door for me or so help me I'm going to drop this on your goddamn foot."

Mickey was well aware of the sight he and Francine presented to others when they rolled up to scenes like this. He, the senior officer, was the grizzled, slow-moving veteran at fifty-six, carrying two hundred and fifty pounds on a six-foot-two-inch frame and sporting a face that frightened children. That face boasted bright inquisitive blue eyes surrounded by features which effectively negated their appeal - a large bulbous nose pitted with an army of crater-like pores, a network of facial wrinkles that attested to long hours of work and excessive stress, a thick neck with prominent double chin and coffee-stained teeth with a significant gap between the upper incisors that seemed too small for a head his size. *Maybe I'm too hard on myself when it comes to my looks because I seem to be able to attract the odd woman or two. Or, maybe some women are just into gargoyles.*

In contrast, she was a relative neophyte, energy personified with a lean, well-toned body, the poster child for proper diet and exercise. In Mickey's estimation, she was not a beautiful woman, in the sense of being a knock-out, but she was attractive, exuding a definite femininity but not girly. She had a dark complexion with a virtually unlined face which sported dark gray eyes, a petite straight nose, full lips, and perfect, white teeth. Her dark hair was long and fell to shoulder length, but when at work it was always worn in a style that kept it close to her head making it harder to grab and pull if she found herself in a physical confrontation. Mickey doubted she was the five foot, six inches in height she claimed to be, but she carried herself like a tall woman, with long fluid strides and straight back with her head held high. Aware that certain of his prejudices died hard, he still tended to think of her as far too pretty to be sorting through the refuse of homicides. Fellow officers, pals that they are, had dubbed them "Beauty and the Beastly".

CHAPTER 16: PRIMING AN ENQUIRY

Entering the building, they found themselves immediately in the embrace of an expensively decorated and furnished combination reception and waiting area. Its design, furnishings and décor were high-end. He'd never seen such elegant genuine leather chairs in a waiting room before. Dr. Peter Simpson, the name stencilled to the glass of the entrance door, must be doing very well for himself … unless, of course, he is the victim. Standing outside what appeared to be the closed door to an inner office or room was a young uniformed female Constable. Upon seeing Mickey and Francine, she began walking toward them while launching into an unsolicited recitation.

"Detective Sergeant MacKinnon, I'm Constable Chloe Barkhouse. Me and my partner, Corporal John MacLean, were dispatched to the scene at 10:52 pm and arrived to find the deceased, one Dr. Peter Simpson, in his office. A night cleaner, one Maria Gonzales, found the body. She called it in. She's with my partner just inside the door of the deceased's office."

She paused to take a breath, but before she could speak again, Mickey headed her off.

"Thank you, Constable Barkhouse. It's *my partner and I* by the way. That partner of yours, Corporal MacLean, is not mucking about in there is he? I'll have his tiny ones if he is. Listen, Constable, I want you to cordon off and secure the front entry to the building. Your partner will join you as soon as I am finished with him. OK?"

"Yes, sir. I'll take care of that right away, Detective Sergeant."

As Barkhouse hurried off to the entrance of the building, Mickey quickly donned 4-millimetre, precision nitrile gloves and protective booties taken from the homicide kit. He then opened the door to the room the Constable had referred to as Dr. Simpson's office. He immediately took in the scene - a Hispanic woman of about thirty sitting in a leather office chair talking with a uniformed police officer, obviously Corporal MacLean, sitting in another. In full view of anyone in the room was the body of a man sprawled on the office floor to one side of the desk. What appeared to be blood had pooled on the floor under the head. He observed that MacLean had neglected to put on gloves and booties. *Jesus Christ almighty! What the hell is this dunderhead doing sitting with a witness next to a dead body, a potential murder victim?* However, the words he uttered when he addressed the police officer gave no hint of his irritation. He would save his rebuke for a more appropriate time.

"Ah, Corporal, I'm Detective Sergeant MacKinnon. I assume this is Ms. Gonzales. If you would, I'd like you both to leave this room without touching anything and take a seat in the reception room outside. Please remain seated and don't move around the room touching anything there. I will be with you in a few minutes."

After seeing the Corporal and Ms. Gonzales seated in the reception area, Mickey motioned for Francine, now in gloves and booties, to join him in the inner office. Taking in the scene before him a second time, Mickey witnessed a small, neat office with an extensive selection of professional books on bookcases along the interior wall to the right of the door. The single exterior wall, directly opposite the door, featured a small window facing the front of the building. There was a large, highly polished solid wood desk, which looked very posh, positioned to the left of the door with a two-drawer wood file cabinet next to the wall behind it. Three expensive-looking leather chairs surrounded the desk. Two of the chairs sat at the front of the desk, presumably for clients or visitors. The third was positioned on a large Berber area rug which covered the floor under the desk as well.

Observing what he could of the body, dressed casually in black slacks with a white shirt and baby blue V-neck sweater, he saw a nasty four to five-inch gash in the back of the head. Blood from the wound, now tacky and turning darker in colour, had run from the wound, down the side of the head, before finding its way to the floor. He leaned in to take a closer look at the ruptured skin and thought he could see a small particle which reflected the light, although it was hard to be certain with the damp blood also acting as a reflector.

Stepping back from the desk, Mickey reviewed his observations.

"No signs of forced entry ... no signs of a struggle ... no observable signs of trauma other than the wound to the back of the head. Victim is an adult male, likely in his thirties, who appeared to be fit and in good physical shape at the time of death. Weapon not observed at the scene. The ME and crime scene investigators will be able to tell us more."

Turning to Francine, he went on.

"Frannie, contact the Medical Examiner's office and get someone down here. See if you can get Bill Walters. Also, get a team from the Forensic Identification Unit. Oh, and get on to Henry at HQ and tell him to find out the name and details of next of kin. OK, let's talk with Ms. Gonzales, shall we?"

Henry DeLong was one of the Halifax Regional Police Department's technical support specialists, a young officer with a particular set of skills which allowed him to mine the internet for information, both public and not so public.

Before moving back into the reception area, Francine pulled out her mobile to set critical parts of the investigative process in motion by making the calls Mickey had just instructed her to make. Having sent Corporal MacLean to assist Constable Barkhouse with security at the front entrance of the building, Mickey and Francine interviewed the cleaning lady.

Unfortunately, it turned out that Ms. Gonzales had little to offer the investigation other than the fact that she discovered the body about 10:35 pm shortly after arriving to begin cleaning. She said she hadn't observed anyone in and around the office building, but had found the front door of building unlocked which was unusual, but that it had happened before.

While Mickey was seeing Ms. Gonzales out of the building, Francine had taken two incoming calls and a text on her mobile. She subsequently informed her partner that the first of the calls confirmed that Dr. Walters was the Medical Examiner on call. The second call was from the Forensic Identification Unit (FIU) informing her that a Forensics team had been dispatched and was on its way. She then handed him one of her business cards with the name and contact information of Peter Simpson's next of kin, his wife, written on the back. The source of that information was the text she had received from Henry DeLong.

Satisfied that all the gears required to get his investigation started had been engaged, Mickey addressed next steps with Francine.

"Once Bill Walters has finished and Forensics is on scene, you and I will then visit Mrs. Simpson. Make sure she knows we're coming, will you? I'm going to call the boss to let him know what's going on and to ask him to spring Garcia and Stott to help us out with canvassing the immediate area and to check for CCTV cameras which might have caught something."

Detective Sergeant Jorge Garcia and Detective Constable Marlene Stott had been members of an investigative team Mickey had headed several months ago. Both had Mickey's complete confidence and both had made significant contributions to that investigation which led to the solving of a case involving multiple homicides and the death of a serial killer.

Mickey punched in the numbers on his mobile phone which

would wake his recently appointed superior officer, Inspector Mark Harvey. Harvey was a creature of the political machinations that operated in many, if not all, police services. He was a well-educated, socially skilled and well-connected officer who had enjoyed a rapid series of promotions that had catapulted him to the rank of Inspector at the age of thirty-one. Despite the fact that the Inspector had bypassed a number of more senior, more seasoned, though less-educated officers, Mickey, unlike many of his colleagues, did not resent the man. His limited investigative experience notwithstanding, Harvey seemed to have the good sense to listen to his Senior Investigating Officers which had the dual benefit of assisting his career advancement while not impeding the investigations. Although Mickey had only worked with him on a few cases since his boss took the helm, he found Mark Harvey someone he thought he could work with. He didn't kid himself, however; he knew their relationship was built on the understanding that Mickey, as an SIO, was there to make the Inspector look good. If that didn't happen, there was no doubt in his mind that their symbiotic bond would deteriorate rather quickly.

Mickey, cell phone to his ear, was about to make further use of the positive connection he seemed to have with his superior officer. However, after Harvey answered on the third ring, Mickey hadn't finished stating his case for a second team of detectives before Harvey promised the presence of Garcia and Stott by tomorrow morning. He then ordered Mickey to keep him informed of progress on the investigation before abruptly hanging up. Dial tone sounding in his ear, it was clear to Mickey that a sleep-interrupted Harvey was not a happy Harvey.

***

Mickey and Francine met Dr. Walters and the crew of crime scene investigators from Forensics as they entered the building at virtually the same time. Mickey thought this had to be one for the record books for it seemed that detectives were forever waiting on one or the other to arrive at crime scenes. Mickey led them to the body and the choreographed sequence that was crime scene investigation protocol proceeded.

First, the crime scene photographer, protective paper covers over boots, hair covering in place, camera flashing from various locations and at different angles, did her job at capturing a visual record of the body and the immediate environment in which it was found.

Next, Dr. William (Bill) Walters took center stage. Short and rotund in stature with salt and pepper hair and matching moustache, he was an extremely competent ME with an understanding of the demands faced by the police, particularly detectives. Consequently, he made every effort to get whatever forensic information he could into their hands as soon as possible. On the other hand, he was methodical in his approach and would never sacrifice accuracy and precision for haste. He had the type of personality which made him approachable, and likeable. Always willing to chat with investigating officers about the implications of his findings, he had built a reputation which had taken on almost legendary proportions in the Department. The downside was that every SIO in the division wanted Walters as ME on their cases. There just wasn't enough of him to go around.

Having approached the body booted and gloved, in full-body Tyvek that made him look like the Pillsbury dough boy, he initially did a visual inspection without touching the body. Once finished, he then manipulated it just enough so that he could carefully scrutinize more of the body. He took body temperature, checked the eyes, scanned the clothing and visible skin, and last but not least, the wound at the back of the head. He then bagged the hands and feet using plastic bags fastened at the wrists and ankles so that any evidence contained on the hands and feet would not be lost or contaminated during the removal and transport of the body to the morgue.

Seeing Dr. Walters step back from the body and start removing his gloves, Mickey slipped up beside him.

"What can you tell me, Bill?"

"Well, my impatient friend, the blow to the back of the head is the only visible trauma, but it seems to have been delivered in a critical spot with enough force to possibly be the cause of death. I'll know more after the autopsy tomorrow. Given the body temperature, the advancement of rigour and the fact that room temperature was constant, I am confident that death occurred within the last six hours. Can't tell you more at this point. The body can be removed when you and FIU have finished."

"Thanks, Doc. I'll be attending the post-mortem tomorrow. What time?"

"Since it's you, first thing, say 10:30."

Before he and Francine left the further examination of the Simpson offices and the collection of potential evidence, including fingerprints, to the technicians of Forensics under the obsessive eye of Crime Scene Manager Detective Sergeant Terry Tremblett, Mickey mentioned to Tremblett the possible light-reflecting fragment he thought he had seen in the wound.

"Not sure what it is, if anything, Terry, but keep an eye out, will you?"

CHAPTER 17: NOW A WIDOW

During the short drive to Karen Simpson's Sanford Avenue address, Mickey asked Francine what she had made of the crime scene. She usually looked forward to these opportunities to discuss their respective observations and the possible implications, if any. She viewed it as a win-win situation for her because she not only learned from the thinking and analysis of her experienced partner, but she was able to show her stuff, her ability to read a crime scene and her deductive reasoning. However, recently she had noted her lethargy when it came to sharing her thoughts when asked, and if she was being honest, a rather alarming laissez-faire attitude toward her responsibilities as a detective in general. So much so, that she sometimes had to practically will herself to complete tasks that had previously been second nature to her. Despite lacking the motivation to engage in the exercise Mickey's question was designed to initiate, she gave him what she thought would satisfy him.

"As you mentioned earlier, there were no signs of a struggle. That suggests the victim may have known his assailant. Another possibility is that the assailant was a stranger but managed to take Simpson by surprise. Also, I think it is very unlikely that Simpson would agree to see someone he didn't know after hours. Yeah, he knew his assailant.

"As to the murder weapon…."

Mickey interrupted her flow to take a call and by the time it was finished, he was guiding the car into a pressed concrete driveway in front of a large Spanish-style house with attached two-car garage. It was 1:39 am.

"Hold that thought, Frannie. We're here. I liked your thinking about the perp being known to Simpson. We'll pick up the discussion later."

Exiting the vehicle, Mickey felt the same trepidation he always did when having to inform family members of the death of a loved one. He'd handled many such situations during his career, and as he had done many times in the past, he silently reviewed how he'd approached survivors previously as he walked to the front door and rang the bell. Chimes could be heard sounding in the interior of the house, and a few seconds later, a pretty young woman in a bulky white housecoat answered the door.

The woman's face was etched with apprehension and she abruptly cut Mickey off as he began to introduce himself and Francine.

"Yes, yes, I know who you are. Come in. Somebody called and said you'd be coming, but they didn't say what it was about. It's about Peter, isn't it?"

Standing inside the front door in a large vestibule, Mickey sought to clarify the situation.

"Are you Mrs. Karen Simpson, ma'am? And your husband is Dr. Peter Simpson?"

"It is about Peter, then! I knew it! What's going on? I've been going crazy!"

Then, visibly trying to calm herself, she drew a deep breath.

"Yes, I'm Karen Simpson and Peter's my husband."

Following this confirmation, Mickey asked if they might sit down before proceeding.

"Oh, sorry. I'm distracted, worried about Peter. Have you found out anything? Was he at his office? Let's sit in here." She gestured toward an open doorway off the large vestibule.

Remaining silent, he and Francine entered an exceptionally spacious living room which was elegantly and tastefully furnished and decorated. Despite the seriousness of the occasion, it occurred to him that he had just taken a seat on one of the most comfortable fabric sofas on which he had had the pleasure of placing his posterior. He chased the thought away as he began a well-practised sequence.

As he looked up to address the woman seated across from the sofa in a leather, winged-back chair in a moss-green colour, he witnessed her face transform from apprehension to panic. Wrapping her arms around her upper body as though trying to protect herself from the cold, she blurted in agitation.

"Oh my God! Something's happened to Peter!"

Undeterred on the outside, nerves in mutiny on the inside, Mickey zeroed in.

"Ma'am, I'm sorry to have to tell you that we have found the body of a man about your husband's age in offices which we believe are the place of business of your husband. The identification found on the body is that of your husband and a member of the cleaning staff has identified the body as that of your husband."

Mickey paused and watched as the young woman looked at him disbelievingly, and then at Francine as if seeking a second opinion. She, then, lowered her head and began to cry quietly. Less than thirty seconds elapsed before she appeared to bring her weeping under control. Although she protested what she'd just been told, Mickey sensed that the woman may have been simply going through the motions. *She has to have considered the possibility that her husband's unexplained disappearance could have been due to something as serious as his death.*

"This can't be true! Peter was young… and healthy! He can't be dead! What happened to him?"

Much to Mickey's relief, Francine took the reins of the interview seamlessly. Since becoming partners, he'd looked to Francine, who had proven to be genuinely empathetic in these situations, to take the lead.

"We're sorry, Mrs. Simpson. Although we cannot say with certainty what the cause of death is, we are treating the death as suspicious."

Now shock registered on the pretty face that acted as a screen on which was projected the expected range of emotions that are the natural product of hearing such devastating information.

"What … what does that mean, 'suspicious'? Are you saying Peter was murdered?"

"It is too soon to say that with absolute certainty, Mrs. Simpson, but there is some reason to believe that a person, or persons, at present unknown, may have caused the death of your husband."

What the hell! thought Mickey. *That sounds like something I would say, right from the Department guidelines for dealing with death notices to next of kin.* At this point, Mickey interceded to support Francine who seemed to be struggling a bit with something she usually did better than any cop with whom he'd worked.

"What Detective Constable Deveaux is saying, Mrs. Simpson, is that there are indications that your husband was murdered; however, an official cause of death awaits a full examination by the Medical Examiner's office. In the meantime, we are commencing an investigation on the grounds of suspicious death."

Mickey's interjection seemed to bring the caring, compassionate Francine back into the moment.

"Is there someone we can call to stay with you, Mrs. Simpson? Maybe a family member, or a friend or, perhaps, a neighbour?"

Eyes fixed, seeming to look at nothing in particular, as if in a daze, Karen spoke in a low, almost inaudible voice.

"I'll call a friend. She's a neighbour, Ida Williamson from across the street. My parents will come from Toronto but it will take a day or two for them to get here."

Francine continued, voice soft, gentle, apologetic.

"Mrs. Simpson, I know this is a very difficult time for you, but we have a few questions. It can wait if it's too much for you right now. However, it is sometimes very helpful to our investigation if the questions we have are answered sooner rather than later."

A Kleenex tissue materialized out of the pocket of Karen's housecoat and eyes were dabbed and nose blown as she nodded.

"Please go ahead. I understand. I'll be OK."

"Thank you. When was the last time you saw or heard from your husband?"

Taking in another deep breath that seemed to give her strength, she answered.

"I last saw him this morning… well, yesterday now… when he left for the office a little after 8:00 am. And I last talked to him after lunch, maybe 1:30, when he called as he often does between clients."

Noting that Karen seemed a bit calmer now, Francine pressed on.

"What time did Dr. Simpson usually get home from work? Did you expect him to be delayed getting home yesterday?"

"Sometimes he stayed on to complete case notes or to make follow-up calls, but he was usually home by 6:00 or 6:30 at the latest. He said nothing about expecting to be delayed yesterday, but I didn't start getting anxious until about 9:30 when he still wasn't home."

Francine appeared to be considering what Karen had just told them. After a few seconds of apparent deliberation, she asked her next question.

"It was not until 9:30 that you became concerned? At that time he was at least three hours beyond the latest time he usually returned from work, and as many as 4 ½ hours beyond the normal time."

Mickey looked up quickly at his partner, then at Karen Simpson who, as might be expected, appeared to be stung by what she seemed to perceive as the accusatory nature of Francine's comments. Her back straightened, her eyes widened slightly and her jaw stiffened perceptibly while answering in a challenging manner.

"I put Solynn, our daughter, down for the night around 7:00, came downstairs and poured myself a glass of wine, then sat down to watch television while waiting for Peter. I simply fell asleep on the sofa and did not awaken until 9:30. Of course, Peter had not returned and after calling his office number, his cell and his secretary and getting no response at any of those numbers, I thought to look for his car in the garage. It wasn't there. Then, I started to worry."

"What did you do at that point?"

Mickey noticed that Karen's voice had taken on a slightly higher pitch … and he understood why, given that Francine had practically accused her of not giving a *shit* about the welfare of her husband while he was missing. *Again, what the hell!*

"I did nothing for a while because I had convinced myself that there was some perfectly ordinary explanation for his delay in getting home. It hadn't even occurred to me until then to check our voicemail for a message from him. As the time got closer to 11 o'clock, I couldn't stand it any longer and I called the police. They took my information and said they would send a patrol car around to his office to see if he was still there."

At the beginning of the interview, Mickey had taken out his notebook and from time to time had scribbled a note in response to her answers. There was a pause while he completed taking the last piece of information Karen provided. Then, he asked some questions of his own while Francine assumed the note-taking.

"Did your husband have any enemies? Anyone that might bear him ill will? Any clients he may have mentioned who were particularly difficult? Or who made threats?"

Karen paused for a few seconds to give the questions some thought before responding.

"Peter very seldom talked about his clients. I'm sure there must have been those who weren't happy or satisfied with their lives for one reason or another and blamed Peter for not fixing it, but I don't know who they might be."

"OK. Has anything outside his work happened recently, something your husband may have mentioned, or anything you might be aware of which struck you as unusual?"

As if waiting for this question, Karen responded immediately.

"Yes! I received a most unusual call last week - Saturday in the morning. The caller didn't identify herself. She said some horrible things about Peter."

Karen continued to describe in detail the phone call including the impressions that she had of the caller and the conclusions she drew from what the caller said. Mickey asked a few follow-up questions, then, thanked Karen for her patience. Standing up to leave and apologizing for having to make the request, he asked her if she would attend a viewing at the Centre for Forensic Medicine to identify the body presumed to be that of her husband. He told her he would send around a police car to pick her up first thing in the morning, "say 2 pm". She agreed but insisted that she would arrange transportation herself.

After again expressing their condolences, they saw themselves out. Once behind the wheel of his car, Mickey turned to Francine and asked her about her approach to questioning with Karen Simpson.

"Detective Constable, you know I seldom have reason to second-guess you, but what was that with Karen Simpson."

Francine face betrayed the words she spoke in response.

"What do you mean?"

Mickey was sure she knew exactly what he meant, but he went on to articulate his concerns anyway.

"You demonstrated a distinct coolness toward Mrs. Simpson who, by the way, is a grieving widow and not a suspect. Yet, you all but accused her of not being concerned enough about her husband to postpone a nap and unreasonably put off reporting him missing. I've never seen you do anything like that before. What's going on? Are you OK?"

Francine dug in with her response.

"Look, I noticed that she immediately talked of her husband in the past tense. It is more common for loved ones in shock and confusion after first learning about the death of a family member, particularly where death is sudden and unexpected, to talk about them in the present tense until they adjust. Did you note that her voice became more, I don't know, strident maybe, when she perceived that I might be accusing her of delaying action in response to her husband being very late. And who doesn't think to check voicemail as one of the first things to do when worried about someone overdue?"

Mickey listened carefully and waited a beat before he spoke.

"You don't think just having been told your spouse has been murdered and having a cop suggest you demonstrated a suspicious lack of concern could account for that?."

Her response was too quick, too rigid.

"No, I don't."

As they drove out of the yard, Mickey tried to make sense of his partner's actions and responses to his questions over the past forty-five minutes while he absent-mindedly noticed a woman, who had left a house on the opposite side of the street, hurrying up the Simpson entranceway. Ida Williamson, he presumed.

CHAPTER 18: LET ME SPELL
IT OUT FOR YOU

*W*alters' domain, what a horrible, soul-eroding world. Yet, a world in which Bill Walters thrived, where he was a star. Mickey scanned the stainless steel tables, gurneys and refrigerators that pre-dominated the visual landscape of this area of the Centre for Forensic Medicine. He breathed in the noxious odours, formaldehyde, mixed with disinfectant and a hint of the nauseating aroma of rotting flesh. Adding further to the overall charm of the place were the Y-incisions, shoulders to pubis; the removal, examination and weighing of organs; the draining of bodily fluids; and the removal of stomach contents, a special olfactory treat. If all that was not enough of an indignity to inflict upon the dead, the haphazard replacement of the organs in the abdominal cavity; followed by the crude sewing up of the abdomen provided the icing on the cake. He fully understood Francine's aversion to witnessing autopsies. He had to give his partner her due though; she had made it through this one.

It had only been ten hours, four of them spent trying to sleep, since he and Francine had left the Simpson residence. Stifling another yawn, eyes dry and stinging, irritated by the air-borne vapours coming off the chemicals, Mickey waited for Dr. Walters to dictate the last of his autopsy notes and remove his face shield and gloves. Francine, he noticed wasn't looking quite as eager and energetic as she normally did this morning. Rather, she was pale and drawn, human after all. Both of them were anxious to hear their favourite ME's conclusions about the autopsy he had just finished on Peter Simpson.

As Bill Walters approached them now, he smiled and quipped.

"Wake up, MacKinnon. Enjoy the show? Excellent staying

power this time, Francine. Now, I suppose you want me to solve your case for you."

In return, face taciturn, Mickey returned the sarcasm.

"That would be nice, Bill, but we'll settle for the scant facts you usually provide and expect us to do something with. Give us the highlights, will you?"

Walters, eyes sparkling, continued to spar with Mickey.

"If you had been paying attention during the autopsy you would already know the highlights. Oh well, let me spell it out for you. My estimate for the time of death hasn't changed much as a result of the autopsy. I can narrow it down a bit – sometime between 5:00 and 9:00 pm, probably closer to 5:00 than 9:00. Cause of death was a single blow to the head with a blunt object wielded with considerable force causing bone splinters from the skull to penetrate the brain. Death was most likely instantaneous or within a few minutes of receiving the blow. Three very small particles of what look like glass shards were embedded in the head wound. I sent them for further testing as I did the stomach contents and samples of bodily fluids. I have ordered a full toxicology screen. We should get those results over the next few days depending on the lab schedule. Otherwise, the man was a healthy and physically fit thirty-three-year-old male at the time of death."

Mickey paused as though waiting for the ME to go on. When Walters remained mute, he inserted the barb.

"That's it? I told you not to get your hopes up, Francine."

A broad smile erupting on the face of the pudgy ME, he gave a dismissive wave of his hand and countered.

"You're welcome, you ungrateful SOB. How about a drink at the Castle Gate after work today, say 5:30?"

Mickey, an experienced campaigner in this sort of give and take, upped the ante.

"That would be lovely. You're buying, of course. You have to do something to make up for the time we wasted here this morning."

Francine, seeking to put an end to this witty old boys' repartee, interceded.

"For God's sake, give it rest, you two. Count me out for the drink, Dr. Walters. I promised to give a friend a hand after work, but thanks just the same."

Walters, face feigning shock and disappointment, took his last shot.

"Don't do this to me, Francine. I only made the invitation because I thought you would be there, and now you go and sentence me to the hardship of having to cope with MacKinnon's dull company on my own. Oh, well, the sacrifices I make simply to have a beer or two. Sorry you won't be there. See you later, Mickey."

No sooner had Dr. Walters left them to get ready for his next autopsy - "full house today" he had said, than Francine pulled out her cell which she had set to vibrate during the autopsy. After announcing herself, she listened for close to a minute and then ended the call.

"Thanks, Terry."

Turning to Mickey, gauging from the questioning look he gave her that told her he had guessed the call had been from Terry Tremblett, Francine summarized what the Crime Scene Manager had reported.

"Terry says they found several very small pieces of glass, very difficult to see, in and around Simpson's office. Also, the tech collecting the glass pieces, who was on hands and knees at the time, detected the faint smell of alcohol close to the floor, probably coming off the Berber area rug which was still damp in places. With regard to fingerprints, there are pristine prints that belong to Simpson. Many others were found but no hits when they were run through Canadian Criminal Real Time Identification Services. There are an incredible number of smudged and partial prints from the reception/waiting area, little of any use. However, he said they would continue to try to plough through it.”

Setting off for an exit to the parking lot and the much-needed fresh air awaiting them outside the forensic facility, Mickey assessed what Francine had passed on from Terry Tremblett.

“OK. Fingerprint evidence is unlikely to help us unless we identify a suspect whose prints put him or her in the inner office without a good explanation. The glass fragments in the wound and on the floor around the body suggest the blow to the victim’s head was from a glass object. So where is it? If it broke on impact, why aren’t pieces all over the place?”

Francine once again played Watson to Mickey’s Holmes. He posed questions, she generated possible answers, and they moved forward in a synergy she had always felt was special and effective.

“It could be that the killer cleaned the mess up afterward, but missed the tiny fragments that were hard to see. He or she didn’t want to leave any pieces big enough to have fingerprints on them. If this is the case, no gloves were worn. So, maybe the murder wasn't premeditated but happened unexpectedly. Yet, the killer had the foresight to clean up after killing Simpson. He or she obviously took the broken glass and dumped it somewhere.”

The Q and A continued, Mickey posing another question.

“OK. OK. Possible, maybe even probable. So, was the glass object already there in the office or did the killer bring it?”

Francine gave an exaggerated sigh before responding in a tone which suggested her irritation.

"Look, you know the answers to these questions as well as I do. Don't you think these little Q and A sessions you like to put me through are a waste of our time? I'm a big girl now."

Mickey, taken aback by his partner's comment and tone, was unable to follow-up before Francine spoke again.

"But to answer your question, if the attack was not premeditated as I previous suggested, then the bottle was probably already there."

Cognizant of the impending first meeting of the Special Investigations Team being assembled for this case and scheduled for 2:00 pm, Mickey decided not to immediately address Francine's unexpected outburst but rather checked his watch while walking to the car.

"Come on, Frannie. Time to meet the other boys and girls who will help us pin the tail on this donkey. But we need to talk later, yeah, we need to talk."

CHAPTER 19: ASSEMBLING THE BEST

Halifax Regional Police headquarters was a large flat-roofed brick structure located on Gottingen Street near a major Halifax landmark, the City's famous national historic site, Citadel Hill.   Some thought the location highly appropriate, not only because it was situated close to the City center, but also because of its service parallel to that of the Citadel when it was established in the mid-1700s, and designed to protect its citizen settlers from attack.

Travelling the seven or so kilometres from the Centre for Forensic Medicine to HRPD HQ, Mickey and Francine had refrained from conversation and had been engaged in their own thoughts. As the car flashed by the buildings and homes of this Nova Scotia city, his home for over three decades now, Mickey's thoughts returned to his roots. Images of Cape Breton, an island connected to the Nova Scotia mainland by a short causeway, and the small island community of his birth scurried through his mind. Like so many communities in Cape Breton when he was growing up, his hometown had found itself in the economic death throes resulting from the collapse of the coal mining and steel manufacturing industries. He was witness to the devastating social and economic consequences the loss of these industries had on the community, his neighbours, and most importantly, his family. Out of work, as were the majority of the men in the community, his father, until then a proud man and a caring and loving husband and father, went into slow decline. Before Mickey left home and Cape Breton at eighteen years of age, his father had become a stranger, a drunk who spent most of his time and what little money he had in the local tavern. He had remained husband and father in name only. Thank God for his mother, that little woman who never gave in, who worked tirelessly to make sure the family's basic needs were met, who stuck with her husband though many would not have, and who dedicated her life to giving Mickey and his brother every opportunity for a better one. While his father's death from cirrhosis of the liver stirred little in the way of emotion in Mickey, his mother's passing due to a massive stroke had been devastating. It had taken months for him to extract himself from the black hole of despair in which he had found himself. As he came to recognize that life must go on, he pledged in his mother's memory to make the most of his life, the life that she had fought so hard to give him.

Francine's voice, stating that they had arrived at HQ in record time, brought Mickey back from Cape Breton. He used his handkerchief to blow his nose and to surreptitiously wipe a tear from his eye as he exited the car.

Minutes later they entered Special Investigations Room 2 or SIR-2 for short. This was one of three large rooms dedicated to the use of teams formed to pursue major criminal investigations such as homicides. Each SIR had four workstations equipped with telephones and computers adjacent to three of its walls. Even though Special Investigations Room 2 was spacious, a huge centrally-located boardroom table which seated up to twelve people dominated.

Sitting around this table when Mickey and Francine arrived was Detective Constable Henry DeLong, computer wizard extraordinaire, a twenty-eight-year-old officer who had used his special competencies to assist Mickey in bringing a killer to ground eleven months earlier. He did not fit the stereotype of a computer geek. He didn't wear thick black horn-rimmed glasses, neglect his dress or hygiene or talk only in a cyber language few others could understand. Rather, he was an attractive man, six feet tall with longish black hair cut stylishly. Unlike many officers, he was clothes-conscious; a walking advert for what was currently fashionable. Talking to DeLong was Detective Constable Marlene Stott who was about the same age. Stott was new to Homicide, an officer whose career Mickey himself had a hand in advancing after he first met her as a wet-behind-the-ears rookie. She had proven to be a quick study advancing rapidly in a few short years to her present rank. An intelligent and extremely thorough officer with the potential to be an elite investigator, Stott had proven to be a definite asset to the investigations she had been part of to date. She was physically fit and devoted herself to a workout regimen designed to keep her that way. Although a rather plain-looking woman, whose wardrobe suggested she gave little attention to current fashion trends, Mickey knew Marlene Stott would draw notice nonetheless – not because of her looks or the clothes she wore but because of her professionalism and competence. Detective Sergeant Jorge 'George' Garcia, a balding, heavy-set man and a grandfather at fifty-three, was Stott's partner. Like Mickey, Garcia was a senior officer who was often asked to be the lead on Special Investigations (SI) Teams. Unlike Mickey, he preferred to leave the leading to others. A tenacious investigator who thrived on fieldwork, George did not aspire to the administrative ranks. Virtually all SI lead officers wanted Garcia on their team if he was available. Mickey felt fortunate to have landed him.

With a couple of minutes to spare before the scheduled start of the meeting, Detective Sergeant Terry Tremblatt, Crime Scene Manager, entered the room. As with all the others in the room, Mickey knew Terry well. The thirty-eight-year-old father of three daughters was a key player on most SI Teams, the funnel through which much of the forensic evidence for criminal cases flowed. He was a highly intelligent man and an extremely competent forensic scientist, a professional who not only understood his responsibilities but carried them out proficiently.

Walking to his place at the head of the table, Mickey got down to business.

"As you all know, I've been assigned lead and George has agreed to be my deputy. Go to him if I am not available, otherwise I want to be your first port of call. Terry will attend our meetings as required and pending his availability, as will Henry. OK, let's pool what we have to date. Francine, start us off, will you?"

Referring to her handwritten notes, Francine described the crime scene as she and Mickey had found it including the observation of what turned out to be glass slivers in the victim's head wound and on the floor near the body. She emphasized that there were no signs of forced entry and no signs of a struggle. She noted the ME's initial autopsy findings including the 5:00 to 9:00 pm range in which the time of death was estimated to have occurred.

George Garcia's deep bass voice, one in keeping with a man of his large physical stature, sounded from her left.

"Sounds like the killer was someone the victim knew or trusted or, at least, didn't suspect was a threat. And, given the times you mentioned …you know, the cleaning lady entering the Simpson office and finding the body after 10:30 but before 11:00 and the time of death estimated to have occurred after but nearer 5:00 than 9:00, it seems the killer had a reasonably wide window of up to five to six hours during which he or she could have carried out the murder with a high probability of going undetected. Was the perp just lucky or had he or she planned to carry out the attack giving him or herself that generous window? And why was Simpson still in the office that late? Perhaps, he had planned to meet his killer."

Francine knew Garcia liked to think out loud. He also tended to put his deductive thinking on display like this as a way of generating a fuller discussion of the facts and what they might indicate. Yet, she was becoming surprisingly annoyed by his loud articulation of facts she had already presented and his self-evident speculation. Suppressing her exasperation, she responded, relating the reasoning which suggested the killing was not planned, and then used Garcia's question about why Simpson was staying so late at the office as a springboard to summarize the interview with Karen Simpson, including her mention of the anonymous telephone call she had received, and to note the anomalies observed in Karen's behaviour.

Garcia's voice continued to add to the discussion.

"I don't know if I would characterize the wife's behaviour as unusual after just being told her husband has been murdered. One can't always predict how people will react under acute stress and emotional shock."

Mickey had been watching Francine carefully during her exchange with George Garcia and sensed her mounting frustration. When George mentioned alternative interpretations of Karen Simpson's behaviour, a topic that he had learned was a sore spot for Francine, he had seen the fire in her eyes and moved quickly to head off a confrontation.

"Thanks, Francine. Terry?"

Tremblatt, referring to points listed on a sheet of paper on the table in front of him, reviewed the glass and fingerprint evidence and then concluded.

"Given what we have plus the tech's report of smelling alcohol near the floor around the area of the body and on the damp Berber rug, it could be hypothesized that the murder weapon was a glass liquor bottle that shattered on impact, and the pieces swept up and taken away by the perp."

Francine jumped in to support the CSM.

"That's our hypothesis too, Terry. We think the bottle was there in the office and was used opportunistically by the killer. Then, he tried to hide any fingerprints he may have left on some of the larger glass pieces by collecting and taking them away."

Mickey then called on Garcia to report on their canvass of neighbourhood businesses, interviews with employees of those businesses, and the identification of any CCTV sources that might be helpful.

In addition to being rather loud, George Garcia has a rather gruff voice, one which makes him seem angry when he's not. However, those who have been unfortunate enough to incur his wrath have no difficulty distinguishing between gruff normal and gruff angry. Gruff normal is today's voice.

"As you know Mickey, we just started the canvass this morning when most businesses opened. Marlene and I first targeted those businesses that had sight lines which included the office building in which the victim had his office. There are six which met that criterion. Of the four businesses having CCTV security systems, only two had outside cameras and one of those had its outside camera trained on its outside entrance only. As luck would have it, the second of the two businesses has an outside ATM with one of those HDR cameras which gives more defined background imagery. It may have caught a piece of the parking lot near Simpson's building. We have asked for the footage from Tuesday for that camera. Since only two businesses were open after 5:00 pm on Tuesday, we started with them with regard to employee interviews. Of course, we haven't interviewed everybody who could have seen something yet, but of the five we have seen, no one saw or heard anything unusual late Tuesday afternoon or before they booked off work in the evening. However, two of them said they had noticed an older adolescent, perhaps, a young adult, female, frequenting the little park in the center of the roundabout down there. You've seen it, just opposite the Simpson office building. Apparently, she just sits there feeding the pigeons, reading sometimes. Both people reported seeing her there multiple times over the past number of weeks. Neither person said they knew her. Anyway, we'll keep on it and will update you at the next Team meeting or before, if we hit gold."

Mickey found himself getting anxious to distribute assignments so that the meeting could be adjourned and they could get on with what they were tasked to do, suss out Peter Simpson's killer and bring him or her to justice.

"Thanks, George. Keep me abreast of your progress with the canvass.

"Now, before we adjourn, I want to clarify assignments. George, I want you and Marlene to expand the parameters of the canvass. Given your witnesses' information about the female seen multiple times in the park over the past few weeks, get the recordings from the ATM camera going back over the past, say, four weeks. Get those recordings to Henry to see if they have anything that might be helpful, particularly anything that might show the female. In light of Karen Simpson's characterization of the voice of the anonymous caller as female and quite young sounding, we need to pursue this possible connection vigorously. Also, after completing the canvass of the businesses near Simpson's office building, expand your area of coverage to a one-block radius. Focus on businesses around locations where the female might have been more likely to have spent time, bus stops, taxi stands, etc. Terry, as always, speed is of the essence. I want to get the tox analysis ASAP to see if alcohol was on board and to make sure he wasn't drugged and unconscious when struck which might put an entirely different spin on things. And keep slogging on the fingerprints. Even if there are no hits on CCRTIS, they could prove useful when we have a suspect. Henry, as mentioned, George and Marlene will be feeding you CCTV recordings, so do your stuff and let me know right away if you get anything. I also want you to do background checks on Simpson and his wife, histories and financial status. Francine and I will be arranging a thorough search of Simpson's offices, trying to identify clients of Simpson's who might be potential suspects. Karen Simpson told us his secretary's name, Sue Reynolds, I believe. She can help us with that. Henry, you might as well add the Reynolds woman for a background check. Oh, and Henry, check the phone call records for the Simpsons. I'm particularly interested in a phone call received on the landline at the house on Saturday morning. That's it, folks. Our next Team meeting will be tomorrow at 4:30 pm. Terry, you can beg off unless you feel you have something you need to share with the group. See you all tomorrow then."

CHAPTER 20: BRIC-A-BRAC

Once again wolfing down a burger and drinking a diet pop, Mickey sat in the passenger seat of an unmarked police Impala, Francine driving, as they made their way through streets made slushy by a warming temperature following a 5-centimeter snowfall. It was late-afternoon, some 70 minutes after the Team meeting had come to an end. Francine had entered Sue Reynolds' address into the vehicl's GPS and ten minutes later, a monotone, stilted female voice was telling them to turn left, one kilometre to their destination on the right. Five minutes later they pulled up in front of a well-maintained four-story wood-frame apartment building that was probably three or four decades old. Typical of buildings of this vintage, security required residents of the building to use keys issued to them to enter the front door. Visitors, on the other hand, could press a button to activate an intercom assigned to each of the sixteen units to communicate with tenants. If they so desired, tenants could buzz visitors in by remotely unlocking the front door. Upon exiting the Impala, Mickey had expanded his lungs with the deep intake of warming air that reminded him of Spring, and then moved to the intercom and buzzer system and pushed the button for S. Reynolds. After a couple of attempts with no response, he and Francine had turned to walk back to the car when a tentative, guarded voice emanated from the speaker.

"Yes? What do you want?"

Quickly moving back to the intercom, Francine introduced herself to the voice.

"Detective Constable Deveaux, Halifax Regional Police, ma'am. Are you Sue Reynolds?"

The voice, now sounding incredulous, again rose from the

black speaker.

"You're a woman! How do I know you're who you say you are? I want some identification."

While Mickey rolled his eyes and was about to speak, Francine shushed him with a finger placed to her lips and continued.

"It is very wise to be careful, Ms. Reynolds. I can prove my identity in one of two ways. I can give you my badge number and you can call Halifax Regional Police Headquarters for verification that I am who I say I am, or you can come to the front door of the building and I can show you my identification through the glass. The latter would speed things up if you don't mind coming to the door."

A long pause suggested some consideration of what Francine had said was taking place. Then, a decision was made.

"I'll be down in a minute."

Ten minutes later they were seated in the most cluttered living room Mickey had ever seen. Knick-knacks, ornaments, pictures, doilies, throw cushions, and afghans abounded, covering every available surface. He had already sent several objects teetering back and forth when he accidentally bumped into a table as he walked from the apartment door to the sofa indicated by the somber-faced woman. It was clear that she had been crying - the whites of her eyes were red as were her puffy lids. Beyond the evidence of her tearfulness, her face looked strained, deep furrows in an almost ashen complexion.

"You're here about Dr. Simpson. I went to work as usual today and there were police all over the place, the front entrance with that yellow tape around it. I asked a man who was standing behind the police cordon what was going on. When he told me, I didn't believe him, but a woman who overheard us said it was true, that it had been in the news. I just turned around and came home. I don't even remember driving back."

Keeping as still as possible so as not to cause any further tremor among the bric-a-brac near at hand, Mickey addressed the stricken woman.

"I know this must be a shock, Miss Reynolds, but we need to ask a few questions and, perhaps, enlist your assistance with Dr. Simpson's office records."

Without giving her a chance to respond, he moved on.

"How long have you worked for Dr. Simpson? And where did you work before that?"

With a sigh and eyes beginning to become watery again, Sue seemed to pull herself together, answering the question with a hint of pride in her voice.

"I have been with Dr. Simpson since he started his practice over five years ago. I keep the office humming so he can help the poor people who need him. He's a wonderful man. Oh dear, my life will never be the same."

Belatedly, she remembered the second question.

"I worked for the accounting firm of Terrell, Turner and Mahoney for twenty-one years before starting with Dr. Simpson."

"Twenty one years? That's a long time. Why did you decide to leave?"

Anger infused Sue's face pushing the despair away temporarily. She seemed to be furious. The sudden, rapid transition was a little unnerving.

"Well, sir, I didn't choose to leave. It was suggested I seek employment elsewhere because they told me the firm was going to downsize and I was to be redundant ... me, a senior employee, redundant? There was something more behind it, but they didn't tell me what. I knew I wasn't wanted so I started looking around and got the job with Peter ... I mean, Dr. Simpson, within a week. I tried to give notice but they said it was not necessary and my last day of work was the day I told them I had a new position. What a way to run a business. At least they gave me a good reference and generous severance."

Commiserating, Mickey empathized on his way to his next question.

"Sometimes employers march to their own drummers, for sure, Miss Reynolds. How did you find working for Dr. Simpson?"

Anger vanquished, Sue's mood lightened only to plummet again shortly after she started speaking.

"I loved it. I felt so part of what was happening. Dr. Simpson is wonderful … was wonderful, as a boss and a human being. Oh my goodness, what am I to do now?"

Ignoring her lament, Francine quickly jumped in.

"Miss Reynolds, please think carefully if you will. Did Dr. Simpson have any clients who might be dangerous or who might have wanted to harm him?"

Pausing to think, Sue responded.

"Not that I can think of. His clients loved him and spoke highly of him. I can't remember any client expressing dissatisfaction with Dr. Simpson. He is …was a caring therapist and his clients sensed that."

Clearly, the woman is a fan thought Francine before posing her next query.

"What about any problems with people who were not clients? Or any unusual or out-of-the-ordinary events you may have noticed at work?"

A lightning-fast reply with eyes averted, a single-word answer hung in the air while the two detectives waited for more which wasn't forthcoming.

"No."

Thanking Sue, Mickey raised himself into a standing position very carefully, mindful of the booby-trapped environment. He was almost at the apartment's front door when he said, in an off-hand manner, Columbo-style.

"Miss Reynolds, would you mind telling us your whereabouts from late afternoon to 10:00 pm yesterday?"

Stopping dead as she was seeing the officers to the door, her response exhibited an undisguised huffiness, obviously perturbed to be asked for such an accounting.

"I don't see how that's relevant unless I am considered a suspect. How could you possibly think that? I loved him!"

***

After arranging to meet with Sue at the Simpson offices at 9:00 am the next morning to review client files, Francine couldn't restrain her excitement when she and Mickey returned to the parked car in front of the apartment.

"She lied! She bold-faced lied to us when I asked if anything out of the ordinary had happened at the office. Did you see her reaction? Yeah, and she has no alibi, just said she left work as usual at 5:00 pm, drove home and spent the evening watching her favourite TV shows, nobody to vouch for her."

Stroking chin stubble, feeling like he needed a beer, Mickey looked out the windshield of the car.

"I agree, Frannie. But that doesn't make her the killer. Do you really see Sue Reynolds as someone who would use a liquor bottle to smash her beloved Dr. Simpson with such force as to cause a portion of his fractured skull to penetrate his brain?"

Unconvinced, Francine shrugged.

"Stranger things have happened. You know better than to exclude a suspect simply because he or she doesn't look the part."

"Jesus, when did this start? The student has become the teacher. Let's get a drink. I believe the good Doctor awaits us at the Castle Gate."

CHAPTER 21: BTO AND IBUPROFEN

Thursday, January 25

Mickey awoke to the pain of someone applying a drill to the region of his head between the eyes while simultaneously using a hammer on the back of his skull. Lying in his bed trying to make sense of the misery he felt, he remembered the Castle Gate, Bill Walters and a drink or two or three too many. Thank goodness he'd dropped Francine off at her friend's apartment as she requested. She hadn't been there to see the word-slurring, equilibrium-challenged yob that alcohol had created being bundled into a taxi to be taken directly home. On the positive side, this time he remembered what happened.

Hauling himself into a sitting position on the side of the bed, he waited for the easing of the drill and hammer, the intensity of which had suddenly increased with body movement. Head down, eyes closed, he was just beginning to feel some recovery when the Bachman-Turner Overdrive's "Taking Care of Business" ringtone sounding on his mobile gave rise to another frontal lobe eruption. Head in the grips of a spasm, he reached out toward the nightstand intent on silencing Randy and the crew.

"Yeah, what is it?"

"Well … good morning to you, too, Sunshine. Jesus, you sound bitchy! That time of the month, is it?"

Mickey recognized the voice of Henry DeLong which was far too perky for this time in the morning or any time for that matter.

"Look Henry, cut the bullshit and get to it, if you would, my fucking head feels like my goddamned brain is being pushed out through my eyes. And you better hope Francine never hears you making a quip like that or you'll be wearing your balls on the inside."

An uncertain chuckle was heard at Henry's end of the line during the short pause before he responded.

"Say no more, Boss. Want to hear the highlights of the preliminary background checks on Dr. Peter Simpson, his wife, Karen, and his secretary, Sue Reynolds?"

"Jesus, Henry, what do you think … that I asked for those checks for the fun of it? Let's have it."

The tone of Henry's voice in response did not hide the fact that he was starting to take offence at Mickey's abrupt and sarcastic manner. A formal, all-business Henry resumed the conversation providing summary information.

"Peter Eugene Simpson was thirty-three years of age when he died, born in Halifax, the only son of William and Constance Simpson, both deceased, natural causes. Peter was an all-round student in high school, with high academic marks, first in his graduating class, a good, if not superior athlete, and played on a number of high school varsity teams, basketball, soccer and the like. After high school, he attended Dalhousie University where he graduated with an Honors Bachelor's degree in Psychology maintaining a 4.0 grade point average. While attending Dalhousie, he lived at home. His mother became ill during his final year at Dal and died of pancreatic cancer shortly after he graduated. His father died of a heart attack approximately a year ago. Peter met Karen Rose Pendleton when they were both students at Memorial University of Newfoundland in St. John's. Karen was an undergraduate taking a B.Sc. in Psychology and Peter a Doctor in Psychology degree, a Psych. D. I think they call it. He was a graduate student teaching assistant and Karen was a student in one of his classes. Both graduated from MUN.

"Peter established a private practice with the help of an inheritance his wife received from her maternal grandmother. Karen comes from money, but I'll get into that when I chat about her. Peter's practice has done phenomenally well. So well, he was able to pay off student loans amounting to some $95,000 in his first four years of work. He and Karen have a home valued at 1.8 million dollars with a manageable mortgage balance of $425,000 given his income. Overall, their debt load is minimal. Apart from the house, they seem to pay as they go.

"The one possible blemish on Peter's otherwise pristine and enviable record is that he was accused by an 18-year-old, first-year female student in an Introductory Psychology class he was teaching at MUN of trying to extort sex in exchange for improved grades. Both University and police investigations concluded that there was not enough evidence to take any punitive or legal action against Simpson. It was 'he said, she said' and the girl's credibility was damaged by the revelation that she had accused another male, a professor, with something similar earlier in the term."

Mickey yawned audibly and, with a tone which did little to disguise his impatience, posed a question.

"OK, OK, Henry, have you put this together in report form yet?"

Taking a breath, Henry answered defensively.

"I get the sense you don't want to hear this now and would rather wait for the written report. The reason for my calling you is I had assumed you wanted this information ASAP. If you don't give a shit, I won't waste your time or mine."

Another pissed-off colleague heard from. The landscape of Mickey's career seemed to be littered with them. Contrary to the attitude and tactic his pounding head was advocating, Mickey's social intellect took him down a different route.

"Please don't get pissy with me, Henry. I'm sorry if I sounded impatient and irritable, but the fact is that I am impatient and irritable, but that's not your fault. Please go on with the background information, if you don't mind."

Mickey heard a pause and then a sigh on Henry's end.

"Karen Rose Simpson, nee Pendleton, is a rich girl. Her father made millions in the shipping business, mostly imports, and her mother comes from old money. She seems to have been Daddy's little girl and, given there was no male heir, her old man was grooming her to take over from him. Seems he was sorely disappointed when she married Simpson and effectively renounced all interest in Daddy's plans for her.

"She was born in St. John's, was a straight A student throughout public school, entered MUN on a renewable scholarship, as if she needed it, and graduated with an Honors undergrad Psychology degree. She and Simpson were married shortly after she graduated. She has no record of trouble with the law or with anyone for that matter. Since their marriage, Karen appears to have devoted herself to her husband and child, a daughter named Solynn, four years old.

"Susan Elizabeth Reynolds is 47 years old and lives alone. Has never been married. Graduated from Nova Scotia Community College with a certificate in Office Administration and went directly to a position with the accounting firm of Terrell, Turner and Mahoney where she stayed for 21 years before leaving to start work for Simpson in his private practice. She's a bible-thumping Baptist as were her parents before her, regular church attendance.

"Financially, she does OK; however, like most of us, needs employment to get by. No criminal record. She appears to live simply and quietly. No obvious stains in her history.

"That's it concerning the backgrounds, Boss. George and Marlene are bringing in some CCTV recordings later this morning. I will let you know if we find anything. Oh, and before I forget, a call came in from the Centre of Forensic Medicine late yesterday afternoon. As expected, Peter Simpson's wife identified the body as being that of her husband."

During Henry's report, Mickey had managed to swallow two 400 milligram ibuprofen gel caps chased by cold beer from the fridge.

"Henry, anything come up about the reason Reynolds left Terrell, Turner and Mahoney? She told Francine and me that she was essentially let go for a reason that made no sense to her."

"Nothing in that regard, Boss. We will probably have to ask that question directly."

"Yeah, thanks, Henry. See you at the Team meeting this afternoon. And again, please excuse me for being a bit of an asshole just now."

A split second before hanging up, Henry responded.

"No worries, Boss, that's just you being you."

Mickey opened up his mouth to fire a return salvo, but the dial tone in his ear made it clear he would be wasting his ammunition.

CHAPTER 22: CALL ME ROD

Once again Mickey found himself chauffeuring food, a breakfast sandwich and an extra-large double-double, on his way to pick up Francine at her friend's apartment. Approaching the high-rise brick and glass building, he was engrossed in thoughts about parenthood. Mickey had had relationships with women, a couple of them serious ones, but in the end, they recognized what their lives would be like married to a homicide cop, and in particular, an obsessive homicide cop, and backed out before it was too late. He didn't blame them, but it was becoming clear that it was highly likely that he would remain a bachelor. With this realization came a feeling like grief, a mourning of the loss of the opportunity to be a parent, a father.

As he pulled into the driveway of the apartment building, he saw Francine exit the front doors of the building and make her way curbside. She looked quite unlike Francine this morning. As she opened the passenger-side door and got in the Impala, Mickey noted that she looked pale with both bags and dark circles under her eyes, hair somewhat askew as though she had quickly tried to comb it. Also, she was unaware that what he took for baby formula, or rather regurgitated formula, had found its way onto her sweater just above her right breast.

"Looking good this morning, Frannie. Must have been a good night."

Without looking at him, Francine pulled down the visor and looked at herself in a mirror located on its back.

"Va te faire foutre, trouduc. Oh, merde! I've got crap all over my sweater! Got a Kleenex?"

Smiling, Mickey was secretly pleased to see that Francine

could, indeed, have bad days too.

"I am soooo glad I can't understand French right now. I don't know what you just said, but I suspect that if I did, I would have to write you up for insubordination. Sorry, I don't have a Kleenex. We'll stop on our way to see Mr. Rodney Turner of Terrell, Turner and Mahoney so you can use a public bathroom. OK?"

***

"There it is, 1543 Melvin Drive. Looks like they even have a client parking lot to your right. Quick, turn right, Mickey, right there."

Francine, baby vomit removed without any evidence that it had ever been there unless one counted a big wet spot on her sweater, had taken advantage of a pit stop to comb her hair and apply make-up as well. Hence, a closer approximation of the attractive, energetic, go-get-'em Francine, the one that made Mickey feel young. Despite the physical transformation, he had a strong suspicion that something was amiss with his young partner.

Alighting from the Impala, he noted the two-story stone-faced building, constructed circa the 1930's he guessed, with a large brass plaque by the front door that announced to the world that, indeed, the building housed the offices of Terrell, Turner and Mahoney, Chartered Accountants. Mickey had called ahead to arrange the interview with Mr. Turner, one of the three senior partners, without having to say any more about the purpose of the meeting other than it was a police matter. As it happened, Turner was the only partner available since Terrell was off work due to illness and Mahoney had yet to return from a mid-winter vacation.

His eyes scanned the spacious reception area which was decorated, appointed and furnished in a manner that informed all who entered that the services provided by Terrell,

Turner and Mahoney were not for the financially faint of heart. Even the receptionist, dressed in a smart, expensive business suit, and coiffed and made-up just so, visually communicated that you get what you pay for. Mickey knew she had seen them entering the reception area, but she made a show of seeming only to notice them when they had come to a halt in front of her see-through glass desk. She looked up at them holding their badges out for inspection while introducing themselves and informing her of their appointment with Mr. Turner.

After escorting them to the biggest, fanciest office Mickey had ever seen and asking them if they would like a beverage, an offer they declined, the receptionist left saying that Mr. Turner would be with them in a moment. Door closed, Mickey whispered to Francine.

"Have you ever seen anything like this? My math teachers should have been much clearer about why math is important. If they had, maybe that would be my desk and I'd be meeting you for the first time regarding a 'police matter'."

Francine forced a smile but before she could respond the office door opened and in walked a small trim man of about fifty, with black hair sprinkled with grey which was more predominant at the temples. In contrast to the formality emanating from the office décor and furnishings, he was dressed very casually in black wool slacks, open-neck white dress shirt and a grey pull-over crew-neck sweater.

"Good Lord, I'm in the middle of a real-life detective drama. Detective Sergeant MacKinnon, Detective Constable Deveaux, you've added some intrigue to a day that was destined to be 'boooor-ring' as my daughter would say. I'm Rod Turner. What can I do for you?"

Rather than sitting at his desk, he invited Mickey and Francine to sit at a small glass conference table. As they were seating themselves and Francine was readying her notepad, Turner looked at the young DC.

"This is a very politically incorrect thing to say, but Detective Constable, I don't think I have ever seen a homicide detective as pretty as you are. I didn't think pretty women aspired to the kind of work you do."

Mickey caught Francine's eye and gave a look which warned her about going for Turner's jugular. She got the message.

"Thank you for the compliment, Mr. Turner. In the police force, as with virtually all kinds of professional work, women of all sizes, shapes, religions, philosophies, values and, indeed, physical appearances are making a contribution to society. It is that contribution which is important and not one's looks, don't you agree?"

Turner, a smile of genuine admiration on his face, looked directly at Francine.

"Touché. I've been expertly put in my place and feel only a bit of a fool."

Mickey, an almost imperceptible nod to Francine indicating she should lead the interview since Turner found her such a treat, took out his notebook. Message received, Francine began.

"Thank you for seeing us on such short notice, Mr. Turner -."

"My pleasure, my pleasure, Detective Constable. And please call me Rod."

"OK. Rod, you had an employee by the name of Susan Reynolds working for you about five years ago. At about that time, she left your firm after twenty-one years of employment here. She told us it was not her choice to leave, but was essentially forced out. I wonder if you could tell me the circumstances that necessitated Miss Reynolds being canned."

Turner, Rod to his friends and those he hoped to get to know better, took a big breath and then exhaled over an extended number of seconds before answering.

"'Canned' is such a disagreeable word, Detective Constable. 'Redundant' seemed a much more palatable term to us at the time. However, I don't think she bought it. She wasn't a happy camper. Look, the three partners felt it was the best thing to do for everyone involved, and that included Sue. She had no claim on the position. She was a contract employee whose contract was up and we decided not to renew. She found alternate employment and we did not require notice from her, and gave her a generous severance package."

When Turner stopped as though he had answered Francine's question, she raised her eyebrows, inviting him to go on. What happened next made it obvious he found it difficult to turn down that invitation.

"OK, OK. Tension had been mounting in the workplace because of Sue's unusual behaviour, bizarre even. She seemed to have formed a strong emotional attachment to Manning Mahoney. In conversations with other employees during break times, she would describe Manning in terms which put him on a pedestal, made him seem larger than life. That is not to say that he is not a good guy, of course, he is. It would seem Sue, in her mind, had created an image of him which transcended reality. At first, her fellow employees thought it was funny that Sue, in her forties, was infatuated with a man, one of her bosses, ten years younger. However, a number of them started to become uncomfortable because her comments about Manning were becoming more personal, as though there was a relationship beyond that of work between them. She was also looking to do more and more of Manning's support work here at the office and even started volunteering to do personal things for him, like picking up his dry-cleaning, and buying groceries for him when he was pressed for time. She even offered to assist him with the decorating and furnishing of his new condo. Unfortunately, Manning was blind to what was happening, as were Roy ... that's Roy Terrell ... and I, until Victoria, our lead Executive Assistant, asked to meet with the partners to discuss her concerns about Sue. She explained to us that she had been worried for some time, and finally decided to speak to Sue about the appropriateness of her behaviour. Well, it did not turn out well and Vicky said Sue became furious, accused Vicky of trying to come between Manning and herself, and, at one point, stated that Vicky would be very sorry if she tried that. Vicky is an experienced employee and a sensible woman and is used to handling people in job situations, so when she said that she had become a bit fearful of Sue that spoke volumes to me. We did, however, interview other employees confidentially and they supported what Victoria had told us. We did not feel we could talk directly and openly with Sue about this without putting Vicky, and perhaps others, in a vulnerable position. So we took the action we did."

Both Mickey and Francine paused to complete their notes before responding to what Rod Turner had just told them. Seconds later, Francine followed up.

"Are you saying that Victoria felt her safety was compromised because of the threat Sue made?"

Turner stood up and started walking to the office door while speaking.

"Best I get the horse so you can hear it from her mouth. I'll send Vicky in so you can put those questions to her. I'll be working in the boardroom if you need me. If not, it has been a pleasure. Detective Constable, if you ever need an accountant, for taxes or whatever, please contact me. No charge of course."

In the time it took Rod Turner to close the door and for Victoria to open it again, Mickey took the opportunity to wiggle his eyebrows at Francine and smirk. In turn, she told him to "'piss-off". Ms. Belli was a 30-something clone of the receptionist, power suit, make-up perfect, and long blonde hair looking like that of women pictured in posters on the walls of beauty salons. Mickey was beginning to wonder if the fact that Sue did not fit the power suit mould was a factor in her dismissal. Hand extended, Victoria walked directly toward the table at which they sat.

"Hello, I'm Victoria Belli, Administrative Lead with the firm. You must be Detective Sergeant MacKinnon and you, Detective Constable Deveaux. Pleased to meet you. How can I be of assistance?"

Sitting with legs crossed and back straight, nothing less than perfect posture, Victoria Belli exuded confidence. She awaited their questions which Mickey initiated.

"Thank you for speaking with us, Ms. Belli. I understand from Mr. Turner that you brought up some concerns with the partners here about the conduct of Sue Reynolds, a former employee with the firm. Could you please tell us about that?"

Victoria Belli's version of events was very similar to that given by Rod Turner. She added a little more about the nature of her conversations with Sue which she said were cordial until the topic of professional office conduct was interpreted by Sue to mean that Victoria disapproved of her relationship with Manning Mahoney.

"I honestly don't know if Sue was in love with Mr. Mahoney, or thought she was, or if she just wanted to be close to him and that was enough. I wondered about the latter because she never talked about him in sexual terms. It almost seemed that she was lonely but did not know how to appropriately engage men. Instead, she seemed to be creating a reality in which Mr. Mahoney was some kind of saviour or superhero, and she was his faithful partner or follower, doing everything she could to ingratiate herself by seeking out ways to be of help to him, to support him. Know what I mean?

"The last time we talked, Sue got terribly angry with me.

Accused me of wanting to come between Mr. Mahoney and her so I could be with him, and she made a veiled threat if I persisted. When I took my concerns to the partners, I was not looking to get Sue dismissed. Rather, I simply wanted to give them a heads-up, particularly Mr. Mahoney, because I don't think they had any idea what was going on. I was also hoping that help could be arranged for Sue because I felt she needed it."

***

Tramping to the Impala nestled under two to three centimeters of snow which had fallen while they were in the Terrell, Turner and Mahoney offices, Francine asked Mickey how he felt about Sue as a potential suspect now.

"If she is a suspect, what's the theory? That she became addicted to Simpson in the same way she seemed to be doing with Mahoney and he spurned her in some way which unleashed a homicidal rage ending with her crushing his skull with a heavy glass object?"

It was out of her mouth before she could stifle it, an intemperate, emotionally charged, angry response laced with sarcasm.

"Lord God almighty, Mickey! Of course, it's a motive! One I should hope even the most junior and inexperienced detective would think should be given consideration. Yet, here you are virtually giving a suspect a pass because you, the all-knowing Mickey MacKinnon, has decreed the motive and suspect unlikely. Well, I think it's bullshit!"

Noting the vehemence of Francine's retort and the apparent disconnect between her anger and the context in which it was being expressed, Mickey sought to defuse the situation and conceded the point he thought she was trying to make.

"OK, OK, Frannie, take it easy. I agree. I promise you we'll explore all avenues the evidence suggests, all possible motives, all possible suspects. With that in mind, I certainly want to interview Sue again, and since we are meeting at Simpson's offices to review client files with her help at 1:00 pm, I think we can do it then. Second, I want to talk to Karen Simpson again and push her a bit this time. Will you contact her and arrange a time, perhaps this evening or tomorrow morning? I haven't heard from George and Marlene regarding the expanded canvass or from Henry about the CCTV recordings. Maybe they will have some more information to share at the Team meeting later this afternoon."

Remaining silent but nodding her head to acknowledge Mickey's comments and the action he had given her, Francine turned to face the passenger door window. In doing so, she successfully hid the tears threatening to expose her.

CHAPTER 23: KEEPER OF THE RECORDS

Francine was behind the wheel of the Impala as they drove to the Simpson offices for their prearranged meeting with Sue Reynolds to go through Simpson's client files. Mickey was relegated to the passenger seat because of his inability to lunch at the Castle Gate without having a couple of beers. Although she had never commented on his indecorous habit of washing down his meals with lager while on duty, Mickey could feel Francine's disappointment and disapproval. He told himself it didn't matter. This is the way he had always been and he wasn't going to change just because Miss Goodie-Two-Shoes had her knickers in a twist. Besides, he had developed a foolproof plan of masking any hint of beer on his breath with the judicious use of a couple of post-meal cigarettes and copious breath mints.

As they pulled into the parking lot adjacent to the office building, Mickey noted the yellow police tape still in place and a parka-clad Sue Reynolds waiting for them while talking with a man in a full-length black dress coat. Seeing the Impala, Sue nodded in the direction of the car, causing the man to turn and look as well. The presence of the man was unexpected, and in Mickey's experience, the unexpected often meant a complication. It was with this in mind that he and Francine exited their car and approached the couple. Before they had gotten close enough for introductions, Sue, with a raised voice aimed in their direction, was giving substance to Mickey's fear of a monkey wrench at work.

"This is Dr. Bartholomew Lewis. He is a psychologist and a colleague of Dr. Simpson's. Dr. Simpson had arranged for Dr. Lewis to become the legal custodian of all our client records in the event of his death. As a result, Dr. Lewis is ethically obliged to protect the confidentiality of all of our clients."

Lewis, a lean man who looked to be in his early thirties, was three or four inches shorter than Mickey. He had neatly trimmed jet-black hair which matched the colour of his equally neatly groomed moustache and goatee. Mickey shook the man's extended hand and felt the soft and supple skin of his palm and fingers which hadn't seen hard labour in a long time, if ever. He didn't like Lewis already even though not a word had passed between them yet. That didn't change when Mickey asked the question to which he was afraid he already knew the answer.

"Good afternoon to you, too, Ms. Reynolds. Pleased to meet you, Dr. Lewis. I'm Detective Sergeant MacKinnon and this is Detective Constable Deveaux. May I assume you are here to assist us with our enquiries?"

Lewis spoke in a decidedly prissy manner.

"You might well assume such a thing, Detective Sergeant, but you would be mistaken. I am here to protect the confidentiality rights for which Dr. Simpson's clients have a reasonable expectation. In other words that you might understand, it is like doctor-patient privilege. I am here to see that you don't violate the rights of the many simply because of some notion of yours, with no evidence of which I am aware I might add, that there might be a suspect among them. Bottom line, there will be no review of Dr. Simpson's client files today, or ever, if I have my way. Go seek your warrants if you wish, but if I am not mistaken, you would be wasting your time. I believe the law supports my position on this matter."

Mickey experienced dual emotional reactions to Lewis' words and tone. One was the intensification of his dislike for the arrogant SOB, and the second, a profound sense of disappointment that a fertile line of enquiry might be made unavailable to them. Straightening to his full six foot, two-inch height and stepping into the Psychologist's personal space, Mickey angled his head down so that his face was just inches from that of Lewis.

"A colleague of yours has been murdered, brutally murdered in fact, and you honour his memory by smugly trotting out some vague arrangement in an attempt to impede the investigation. You have no authority here, so move your ass, now!"

Lewis had leaned back slightly to avoid further specks of Mickey's saliva hitting him in the face, but otherwise stood his ground while producing a document and a business card he handed to MacKinnon.

"Huff and puff all you want, Officer. I believe you will find the documentation naming me as custodian in order. If you have any questions, here is the card of my attorney who will be happy to further your education on the law in this matter."

Quickly reviewing the paper, Mickey handed it to Francine while glaring at Lewis and then Sue Reynolds. Mickey had noticed that the prick of a shrink had referred to him as "officer" rather than Detective Sergeant.

"This will not go unchallenged, Lewis, you can bet your sweet ass on that! You work fast, Ms. Reynolds. The boss you say you adore is not two days dead, and one of the first actions you take is to call in this guy to obstruct a potentially fruitful line of enquiry. What a loyal employee!"

Jumping to Sue's defence, Lewis continued in his haughty manner.

"Look MacKinnon, by contacting me, Ms. Reynolds simply did what she was instructed to do by Dr. Simpson. Besides I was aware of Peter's passing and was prepared to act as custodian immediately. Both of us want Peter's killer brought to justice but not at the expense of the violation of the fundamental rights of a whole group of citizens. Surely you can understand that. You will have to conduct your enquiry within the law this time, Officer."

With this, Francine figuratively eased herself between Mickey and Lewis.

"Thank you, Dr. Lewis. We will seek legal advice on the matter. In the meantime, a review of Dr. Simpson's client files will not take place. Ms. Reynolds, I would appreciate it if you would have a chat with us, perhaps over a coffee at the restaurant across the street. It won't take long and it would be helpful."

Sue, hesitant in responding, gave an opening for Lewis.

"Ms. Reynolds, you don't have to speak to these people without an attorney present. And given the bullying tactics I've witnessed just now, I would suggest you contact yours immediately."

This comment seemed to aid her decision.

"Thank you, Dr. Lewis, but I do not need a lawyer. I'd be happy to talk with you, Detective Constable, but just you."

CHAPTER 24: JUST WANTED TO HELP

It was nearing 2:00 pm when they were seated by the waitress at a small table isolated from the few diners who remained from the lunch hour rush. The interior of the restaurant was rather nondescript, the kind of establishment one might patronize, and later, have little memory of it. The dining area had several small wooden tables covered with red and white checkered vinyl tablecloths with knives, forks and spoons wrapped in rather coarse paper napkins for each diner. Faded plastic flowers, perhaps roses, it was hard to tell, acting as decorative touches, extended from the necks of slim vases at the center of each table. They seemed the only concession, as meagre as it was, to gentility. In a sense of style which might escape many, the restaurant's designer had the kitchen constructed with only a waist-high counter separating it from the dining area, thus, diners got an up-close and personal view of the hairy short order cook manning the greasy grill on which their orders sat and spat. The waitress quickly delivered their drinks, decaf coffee for Francine and green tea for Sue. Francine had requested seating where some privacy could be assured.

Mickey had grudgingly agreed to wait in the car where he contented himself listening to the *Bachman-Cummings Songbook* playlist. He was smarting from the loss of control he demonstrated in dealing with Lewis and the consequent fallout of being excluded from the Reynolds interview. Pretentious, haughty men, like Lewis, who seemed to be looking down their noses at an unworthy world, had always rubbed him the wrong way. He had sometimes scared himself with thoughts of perpetrating violence on people like Lewis. He knew his intense reaction to the perceived contempt he saw in the attitudes and tones of Lewis' type probably found its genesis in his humble childhood environment and upbringing, a sort of inferiority complex he had somehow taken on. It was a hot button for him and he knew he needed to exercise caution when dealing with little men like Lewis.

Back in the restaurant, beverages having been served, Sue apologized for the approach Dr. Lewis had taken and explained that she was just following Dr. Simpson's direction about the disposition of client records. She emphasized that she certainly was not trying to hinder the investigation. In fact, she said she was anxious for the police to find the guilty party.

"Anything that I can do to help you with your pursuit of this despicable human being, I am most glad to do."

Pausing for a moment, Francine seemed to be considering Sue's offer, then asked a question that clearly shook Sue.

"Why have you been lying to us, Ms. Reynolds?"

Shocked by the sudden accusation, Sue blustered indignantly.

"Lying? What on earth are you talking about? Why would I lie? I can't believe you are accusing me of lying! I'm leaving!"

Sue had started to stand up when she heard a command that left no doubt it was to be obeyed.

"Sit down now or we'll move our little chat to an interview room at Police Headquarters where you may well be charged with obstruction. Do you understand?"

Though she hadn't raised her voice, Francine's tone and ferocity were so unexpected that Sue froze, looked at the young Detective's intense glare, and then quickly slid back into her seat.

"That's better. I would rather drink restaurant coffee in pleasant surroundings - well, more pleasant than an interview room at Police Headquarters that smells of sweat and urine - wouldn't you?"

Sue nodded in agreement and Francine honed in.

"Ms. Reynolds, you are a terrible liar. You lied when you were asked what time you left the office on the day Dr. Simpson was murdered. You lied again when asked if you had witnessed anything unusual at the office, anything out of the ordinary."

Recovering from the alarm that Francine's tone and intensity had first created, Sue made a last attempt to maintain her façade of innocence.

"How would you know that for goodness sake? Are you saying someone told you something different? That's impossible! Who could it possibly be? There was no one else there ..."

Too late, Sue stopped talking, unable to mask a facial expression which screamed "I'm guilty". Francine continued to look her directly in the eye and waited. Sue finally dropped her eyes and the next words she spoke signalled that, at least, a closer approximation of the truth would be forthcoming.

"Please forgive me for not giving you all the information I could have when you and Detective Sergeant MacKinnon first spoke to me. What I am going to say next will explain why I didn't tell you everything when you asked me those questions. You are right. I didn't leave the office at 5:00 pm; it was closer to 5:30 pm when I left. You are probably wondering why I would lie about such a thing. Well, I lied because I did something of which I am very ashamed. You see, Peter... Dr. Simpson was acting strangely concerning a last-minute appointment with someone named Samantha Henning. Apparently, Dr. Simpson had previously spoken with this person but not in the office when I was there. He agreed to see her on a priority basis, but she wasn't referred through the usual channels that someone being seen as a priority would be. This, in itself, was unusual. It also concerned me that he did something that went against his practice policy. You see, he agreed to see Ms. Henning at 5:00 pm, the time I usually leave for the day. If I left as usual, there would be no one else in the office when therapy was being conducted and he is ... was adamant about there being someone else present. I even offered to remain beyond 5:00 pm in order to accommodate the appointment, but Dr. Simpson actually insisted I leave at 5 o'clock. It didn't make sense. Also, after I mentioned that Samantha Henning had called seeking an appointment, his demeanour changed, he seemed more distracted, anxious. I was worried, and because of this, I did something I shouldn't have done. I pretended that I was leaving as usual at 5 o'clock and then hid in the outer office so I could see this Henning woman for myself. Within five minutes, a female entered the office, one who looked very young, maybe late teens, or early twenties. It crossed my mind that she might be one of the students Dr. Simpson sees at the Teen Health Clinic at Lillian Metcalfe High School. Anyway, I remained in the outer office until the young woman was gone, after which I left as quickly and quietly as possible."

Scribbling notes in shorthand unique to her, Francine was nodding her head and mentally preparing follow-up questions.

"You were there for the entire therapy session. During that time did you hear or witness anything?"

With a big sigh, Sue now seemed resigned to providing information that she wished she could avoid revealing.

"I didn't see anything other than the girl coming and leaving. Dr. Simpson's office door was closed which made it difficult to hear what was being said, but I did hear raised voices from time to time. And when the girl was leaving and walking through the outer office, she called Peter a creep and a criminal and that he would answer to God and to her."

Francine had discontinued taking notes and seemed deep in thought. Finally, she looked from her notebook back to Sue.

"You neither saw nor heard anything else?"

"No, I didn't."

"And as far as you know, neither Dr. Simpson nor this Samantha Henning was aware that you were in the outer office during this time?"

"Yes, that's correct."

Francine pondered what she was hearing before probing Sue Reynolds' motivations once again using a tone of voice a friend might use.

"You had feelings for Peter, didn't you, Sue? You suspected that something was wrong about his relationship with Samantha Henning, didn't you?"

"I loved him, Detective Constable. Not in the way of husband and wife, more in the way of brother and sister or mother and child, maybe. I just wanted to see him succeed and to be part of his life. So, yes, his attitude and treatment of Samantha Henning worried me. I just knew something was amiss but I didn't know what. I thought if I could find out, I might be able to help."

"You loved him in the same way you did Manning Mahoney?"

An expression of profound sadness replaced that of the calm resignation which had been present on Sue's face when talking about her relationship with Peter Simpson.

"My, you do your homework, don't you, Detective Constable? Yes, I loved Manning as I would the child I will never have. He was a bright light, a man with a fascinating life and an enviable future. I wanted to help and be part of it. However, when my job ended there, so did my contact with Manning. It seemed like I had also been made redundant in Manning's life as well. So, Detective, I have now lost two people I loved, admired and respected and just wanted to help."

If I'm being had, thought Francine, *this woman deserves an Oscar.* Francine couldn't help feeling a flash of compassion for Sue Reynolds. She decided to end the interview, believing Sue was more a victim than a suspect.

"Sue, thank you for telling me the truth, and I am truly sorry for your loss."

CHAPTER 25: THE BRAIN TRUST

On the way to Police Headquarters, Mickey had decided to eject the musical comforts that Randy Bachmann and Burton Cummings had been providing, so he could listen intently to Francine give the highlights of her interview with Sue Reynolds. Occasionally, he posed a clarifying question or requested an interpretation from his young partner. In the end, he nodded and gave the smile of the self-satisfied. He had been right about Sue Reynolds as an unlikely suspect. In response, Francine feigned sticking a finger down her throat.

After arriving at HQ, they both used the time before the start of the Team meeting at 4:30 pm to write their reports and to read previously unread reports submitted by other Team members. By the time they had made their way to SIR-2, all Team members were present and accounted for. Wasting no time, Mickey brought the meeting to order, thus suppressing the hum of voices which had predominated to that point.

"Listen up, boys and girls, I want to hear the progress we've made to date. I see that Terry and Henry are with us, so I am guessing that they have something to report. However, I'm going to start with Francine who will provide information regarding the review of the Simpson client files and a second interview with Sue Reynolds, Peter Simpson's secretary. With that, he nodded toward Francine, who remained seated, occasionally referring to her notes while presenting her report.

"The review of the Simpson files was a non-event. Simpson had appointed a custodian or caretaker, a Dr. Bartholomew Lewis, for his client files in the event of his death. Lewis effectively put the kibosh to any review of client files in the near future. As custodian, Lewis' responsibility is to protect the confidentiality rights of the innocent while giving short shrift to any suggestion that a murder suspect might well lurk among the former clientele of the departed Dr. Simpson. Mickey has asked the legal beagles for advice with regard to Lewis' authority, but we've yet to hear a peep or a woof if you prefer.

"It seems Sue Reynolds has not taken to our Detective Sergeant MacKinnon here and would only agree to be interviewed without the Detective Sergeant present. Hence, yours truly conducted the interview solo."

Following the provision of the highlights of her interview with Sue Reynolds, Francine offered her interpretation and hypotheses.

"Whereas I did not believe everything Sue Reynolds told us during the first interview, I believe what she told me during the second. I think she's lonely, and has no one in her private life, only those she associates with at work. She wants to feel needed, to feel close to somebody, so she selects someone at work, in both cases males, with whom she attempts to build a special relationship. She maintains they are not sexual ones, but ones built on the idea of becoming a significant other in the life of that person. I'm not sure I buy the non-sexual motivation, but I believe they serve her need to bond with another human being and her need to feel valued and appreciated. She remains a suspect, but not a prime one in my view."

George Garcia's voice was the first to be heard following Francine's report.

"I don't know, Francine, she sounds psycho, seeing relationships with men where there are none. I thought behaviour like that was considered delusional. She sees Simpson entertaining a young woman after hours, alone in his office, and she goes a little off her tree and takes him out in a jealous rage. How do you figure she's a low-priority suspect?"

Francine stood abruptly, and leaning across the table in the direction of George Garcia spat a caustic response.

"Weren't you listening? I clearly explained why we think Reynolds is not considered a prime suspect! For Christ's sake, tune in!"

With this, she sat down as suddenly as she had stood just seconds before. The room was still, the only noise heard being the gurgle of the coffee machine as it brewed the next pot of coffee. As moments ticked by, the silence was finally broken by Francine herself as she, in a muted voice, addressed the room and then George Garcia without looking at him directly.

"I apologize to all of you, and particularly to George, for that unwarranted outburst. It was unprofessional and I'm … well … I'm sorry, George. To answer your question, first of all, she has no history of violence. Two, she's a small woman and the fatal blow was delivered with considerable force according to the ME. Three, Reynolds is a very private, retiring person whose pattern is to withdraw rather than strike out when faced with adversity. Four, if you believe her, and I do, nothing happened between Simpson and Henning to warrant Reynolds attacking her boss. And five, my 'copper's nose' tells me she's not the one. You know as well as I do, George, we weigh everything we see and hear during suspect interviews. What I saw and heard was a woman telling the truth, one who was extremely embarrassed by this whole situation with Simpson and Henning. She is also one of the worst liars I have ever met. There were no tells during the second interview. Now, please excuse me for a few minutes."

Without further comment, Francine Deveaux quickly exited SIR-2.

No one spoke until the Detective Constable had left the room and closed the door behind her. Garcia's question asked and answered, Mickey took the opportunity to move on to the next item on the agenda.

"Terry, glad you could make it this afternoon. What do you have for us?"

Terry Tremblatt, as stunned as anyone present, knew better than to reference the exchange they had just witnessed.

"A couple of things, Mickey. First, the analysis of stomach contents indicates that Simpson had not eaten anything since lunch. Second, the preliminary tox screen is positive for ethanol or alcohol but negative for the usual suspect drugs and poisons. The lab is reluctant to do further analyses unless you can give them some idea of what to look for. Otherwise, it is like looking for the proverbial needle in a haystack and will put increased pressure on an already overwhelmed system."

Pausing, looking around the table inviting comment or questions and hearing none, Mickey addressed Tremblatt.

"I think we perhaps have gotten what we can from the tox screen, Terry. Besides, we don't have any indication that Simpson had consumed a particular drug or other toxin, so, no, further tox analyses at this point are unwarranted. I'm sure that's something the beaker-and-test-tube-gang will be happy to hear. The finding of alcohol present in Simpson's blood further supports our theory that a bottle was present in the office, and it was this bottle that was used to strike and kill Simpson. It also suggests that the murder may not have been pre-meditated, but rather spontaneous or impulsive."

Mickey thanked Terry and called again on George Garcia.

"George, give an update on the progress of the expanded canvass in the area of the Simpson offices."

George Garcia cleared his throat and put on his reading glasses before addressing his colleagues. He held a document to which he occasionally referred while speaking.

"As you may be aware, we expanded the canvass to a two-block radius of the building where Simpson had his offices. Marlene and I, with Henry's help, identified sites that we considered the most viable. That is, sites more likely to be frequented by the girl or young woman mentioned by witnesses as being present in the small park directly across from the Simpson office. In this regard, we got a break. The only public transit in the canvass area is by bus, and there are only three bus pickup and drop-off spots. We started with the bus stop closest to the scene of the crime and began visiting businesses where there was a view of the bus stop. And bingo, we hit pay-dirt first try. Marlene, you give this part of the report, it was your interview."

Standing up, Marlene Stott looked slightly dishevelled, her pants showing wrinkles and creases, the neck tag of her cardigan sweater peeking above its collar, and wisps of hair escaping what looked like a hastily bound ponytail. Upon seeing her like this, someone who didn't know her better might assume that she had been under some type of extreme time crunch which had forced her to wear the clothes she'd worn the day before and to take grooming shortcuts. However, those who had come to understand her more fully had learned that how she looked today was a fair representation of how she presented herself to the world daily. That said, the Detective Constable's outer appearance belied her strengths as an investigator – a dogged determination to thoroughly and efficiently complete the assignments and actions she'd been given and a focused vigilance on ways to contribute to the objectives of the investigation. She was well on her way to developing into the kind of detective Mickey had envisioned when he first met her and subsequently encouraged her to pursue a career path to Homicide. Absentmindedly, Stott tucked a strand or two of fly-away hair behind an ear and began.

"The business that George is referring to was the very first on my list for this area, a beauty salon. The bus pickup and drop-off point is directly in front of its large street-side window.

It turns out that two of the hairdressers who work there noticed an older teenager, meeting the general description of the female seen in the park, sometimes disembarking from or catching the bus at this stop. They estimate that, between the two of them, they have seen her five or six times over the past month. The reason the girl caught their attention was because she was often carrying what looked like a backpack, the kind used by school students, and they wondered why she was there so regularly since there are no residential buildings nearby. Only one of the hairdressers was working the day Simpson was murdered and she does not remember seeing the girl that day. I realized that this might be the 'park girl'. I mapped the shortest route from that bus stop to the little park and George and I walked it. We looked for signs of CCTV cameras which might capture people walking along the sidewalks on both sides of the route. We found four possibilities and were able to get some footage from three of these cameras. We have submitted those recordings to Henry for review. Unfortunately, the footage is far from complete for the days leading up to the murder and the day of the murder. One camera was not working for part of that time and another was not always turned on."

Garcia quickly picked up his reporting after Stott finished.

"You will remember that an ATM camera was identified directly across from the park which pointed in the general direction of the building in which Simpson had his office. We secured the recordings for six days including the day of Simpson's murder. Marlene and I spent some time with Henry in his high-tech kingdom just before we convened and we have something to show you. Henry?"

While George was speaking, Henry DeLong had finished making the connections necessary to project images from his laptop through an LCD projector on a pull-down white projection screen. He was ready before George called upon him.

"Before I begin with the recordings, I want to report that I have had no luck determining the provenance of the threatening call Karen Simpson received on Saturday morning. I'm guessing the caller used a pay-as-you-go. Now, for the good stuff. I have looked at the recordings from the ATM. Unfortunately, the ATM camera is distant enough from both the park and the Simpson office building to significantly impair image quality. Plus, the view only covers a small portion of the park and only part of the Simpson office building parking lot, and not the building at all. Despite this, I believe there are things of interest to this enquiry on more than one day of recordings. The resolution of the images I am about to show you has been enhanced using digital filters so image quality is improved but hardly pristine. The first images are from Tuesday, the day Simpson was murdered. Someone snap the lights off, please."

On the projection screen appeared a static view showing a portion of the park on the far right, the office building parking lot in the background, and a dark blur at the far left edge of the screen which DeLong described as a passing car in the foreground. In that portion of the screen which shows the park stood a human figure, apparently female with long dark hair dressed in a dark coat, back to the camera. Henry demonstrated that zooming in on the figure provided little improvement in visual detail. He now spoke from in front of his laptop set up at one end of the conference table.

"This may be our girl. She enters the screen momentarily at 4:46 pm, the time that this image is caught by the ATM camera, and is gone within seconds, only to be caught again in approximately the same position for 22 seconds at 5:59 pm the same day. Here's that image captured at 5:59."

A second image is flashed on the screen and once again shows what appears to be the same person, wearing the same coat, standing back to the camera looking in the direction of the Simpson building. Once again, zoom provided no additional detail. Henry's fingers flew over the keys on the laptop and as they did, he began speaking about another image which came up on the screen.

"This image is from the same day, time 5:34 pm. Note the figure in the parking lot. It is a woman who walked from the direction of the office building to a car, cleaned the snow and ice off it, and drove off. You see the static image is of her facing in the general direction of the camera and zoom suggests she is wearing a lighter-coloured coat and a scarf over her hair. However, her car was parked back to the camera and we improved the resolution enough to get its licence plate number. We checked and the car is registered to none other than Sue Reynolds.

"It should be noted that the figure who could be Sue Reynolds is shown walking from the direction of the office building to the same car shortly after 5:00 pm on recordings from previous days. And one last image, again of the parking lot which you will see is snow-covered as soon as the video comes up. There it is. Watch now. There, see the female figure, dark hair and coat. She walks to the car on the far left of the screen. I know it is hard to see because the parking lot is not well-lit there. But she seems to circle the car, pauses to lean over the car's hood for a few seconds and then walks away in the direction from which she came. That also may be our girl. Impossible to get the plate number, but it looks like a 'beemer'. We are confident the car is Simpson's for two reasons. First, Marlene checked with the Registry of Motor Vehicles and confirmed that Simpson did, indeed, drive a BMW. Second, the next image coming on the screen now was taken from the same recording for the same day only a bit later at 5:36 pm. You can see an adult male, who we believe is Simpson, getting into the BMW. By the way, this recording dates to five days prior to the murder. Tomorrow morning, Marlene and I will be going through the additional recordings that she and George submitted, the ones from cameras at points along the route they mapped from the bus stop to the park. And now, let there be light, please. How do you like me now, Boss?"

As the light illuminated the conference room once again and the last image faded from the projection screen, squinting Team members chatted excitedly for the few moments before Mickey spoke, effectively quieting the hubbub.

"OK, folks. First of all, Henry, you know I love you. Second, let's review what the information reported here today tells us. Anybody?"

Marlene Stott's voice was the first to be heard.

"The video recordings place the unknown young female, possibly a high school student, near the murder scene at a time which falls within the estimated window in which Dr. Simpson was thought to have been killed. She appears to travel to the area by bus and may have shown interest in Dr. Simpson's car a few days before his murder. This information, considered with the description provided by Sue Reynolds of the young female she saw leaving Simpson's office on the day he was killed and Karen Simpson's characterization of the voice uttering threats during the anonymous phone call she received, would suggest a person of interest."

Mickey nodded and added his confirmation of her assessment.

"Exactly, Marlene. The recordings also support the information provided by Sue Reynolds during the second interview regarding the time she left the office - at approximately 5:30 pm. This piece of evidence further suggests she may not be our killer. Also, the tox results tend to further support our theory of a bottle being the murder weapon, that it was likely present in the office rather than the killer bringing it, and that the murder was an impulsive act rather than a pre-meditated one."

George Garcia, clearly needing to further affirm an earlier point he'd made, particularly in light of the fact that Francine had not returned to SIR-2, addressed the group.

"I hate to belabour the matter, people, but Reynolds leaving the office when she said she did doesn't mean she didn't come back, park elsewhere and top Simpson."

"Point taken, George. I would add that although the tox screen suggests that Simpson was not incapacitated by drugs or poison at the time of death, it is highly likely he was drinking. Is it possible that the effects of alcohol dulled his perception of the threat his killer posed?"

Mickey, feeling all that could be gained from the Team meeting had been achieved, quickly scribbled a note and then moved to wrap up.

"OK, folks, as I see it, potential suspects are thin on the ground. Sue Reynolds, though less likely to be our perp, nevertheless remains a suspect. The young female is someone we need to identify and interview. Please excuse the pun, but video evidence and other information appear to put her squarely in the frame. Adding to that, Sue Reynolds mentioned that Simpson saw high school clients at the Teen Health Centre at a local high school. That needs to be explored. Could the girl in the park be a client of Simpson's either through his office or through the Health Centre? We may have more luck getting access to client information through the Centre and the high school than we have through Simpson's office. I also want to re-interview Karen Simpson. I want to tighten the screws a little more now. Both Francine and I left the first interview feeling there was more to be had. So, here's how I see us moving forward. George, you and Marlene continue the canvass, but before doing so, take some time to visit Lillian Metcalfe High School and its Teen Health Centre ASAP to see what you can find out about kids being seen by Simpson at the Centre and his office. Identify who they are, if possible.

Also, take the best image of the 'park girl' Henry can provide and show it around, see if it jogs any memories. Speaking of pictures, I have another field assignment for you, Marlene. I want you to take a copy of the picture Henry provides to you and George with you to show to Sue Reynolds. She saw a girl at Simpson's office who could be our mystery girl. It's a long shot but see if she recognizes anything about the girl in the picture. The girl Reynolds saw gave her name as Samantha Henning. Henry, check out that name, look for adolescents and young women up to the age of 25. Francine and I will be visiting Karen Simpson this evening to conduct the second interview. That's it for today, everyone, we meet same time tomorrow."

CHAPTER 26: A GOOD NEIGHBOUR

After the Team meeting, Mickey made it a priority to seek out his partner. Her sudden outburst and hasty departure from the Team meeting was so unlike her that an unsettled feeling was now beginning to make a home in the pit of his stomach. He found her sitting alone on an overturned blue recycling box outside a rear entrance of the building housing the HRPD HQ. She was smoking a cigarette, something he'd never seen her do before.

"Francine, what the hell is going on? That thing with George Garcia earlier … getting pissed off with me about how Sue Reynolds rates as a suspect … it's like you're wound so tight that the mere hint of criticism sets you off. This stuff is not you. It's not how you normally handle things. And what's with the smoking?"

In response, she gave him a perfunctory half-smile and a prolonged silence. Then, after taking a last long pull on the cigarette she was holding, she flicked it to the ground and proceeded to stare at the smoldering tobacco as it expelled lazy curling wisps of smoke.

Mickey waited for her. Finally, she addressed him while continuing to study the expiring cigarette.

"I have apologized to George, to you and to everyone who was there, for my behaviour. I will do better in the future. I appreciate your concern, really I do, but there is nothing wrong with me that a good night's sleep can't cure. I'm sleep deprived. I am irritable and more emotionally … I don't know … emotionally vulnerable. And no, I am not a smoker. I just like to have a puff once in a while."

He knew well before the words had escaped his mouth that this was not a wise thing to say, but he had never been very good at aborting a social faux pas before he found himself knee-deep in shit.

"You're not pregnant, are you?"

A withering look accompanied a response that made clear that their conversation was over.

"Don't we have an interview with Karen Simpson to get to?"

***

Fine china saucers, holding matching cups of steaming tea were on the coffee table in front of the expensive-looking fabric sofa on which they were sitting. Mickey and Francine thanked Karen Simpson for her hospitality and for agreeing to see them.   It was 6:30 pm, a scant two hours after the adjournment of the second meeting of the Investigative Team. They had had just enough time to return to their offices to check messages, grab something to eat from the canteen, and for Francine to check on her friend before leaving for the Simpson residence. In the car, Francine had told Mickey that when she had contacted her, Karen had seemed very open to their meeting again. Now, they sat across from a woman whose face communicated the insidious consequences of the tragedy she was experiencing.   Yet, despite the pale complexion marked by tiny worry lines that had become noticeable, the by-product of nagging, intrusive stress, and the red, sore-looking eyes, Karen Simpson's striking beauty remained transcendent.

Before the heavy lifting, Francine, as she and Mickey had discussed during their drive to the Simpson house, tried to rehabilitate herself in Karen Simpson's eyes.

"I understand how difficult this has been for you so I appreciate you're willingness to see us again to answer a few questions relative to our investigation. How are you and Solynn doing?"

Karen Simpson's answer seemed rather unguarded, almost as though the strained interaction with Francine just hours before had never happened.

"Oh, as well as can be expected I suppose. It still doesn't seem real to me. I keep expecting Peter to call or walk in the door. I haven't said anything to Solynn yet. I think she is too young to understand, but she has missed him already. If she hears someone at the door, she calls 'Daddy'."

Karen's eyes started to moisten and she reached for a tissue.

"Damn, I wish I could stop crying. Anyway, I arranged for Solynn to be with Ida, my neighbour across the street, while we talk. My parents are due to arrive from Toronto this evening. What can I do for you?"

As they had previously decided, Francine began the interview with a plan to initially revisit some of the information Karen had given during their first meeting the morning after her husband's death.

"Mrs. Simpson, when we first talked, you told us about a threatening phone call you received. You said you took the call later on Saturday morning, that the caller's voice sounded like that of a young female, that the caller suggested that she knew your husband and said that he was evil, was keeping a secret and needed to be stopped. She also used your daughter's name and seemed to know that your husband would be home late that evening. She even advised you and your daughter to get away from him. Is that essentially correct?"

"Yes, yes it is. She also said that I should ask him why he was late."

Nodding, Francine proceeded.

"Is there anything else I didn't mention just now, or that comes to mind that you didn't tell us about that call?"

Lifting her left hand to her face and pinching the bridge of her nose between her thumb and index finger, Karen paused, seeming to make a great effort to marshal her concentration, to consider the question.

"Well, there are a couple of things, one I can't believe I didn't remember when I first told you about the call. Did I mention that I had gotten a call a couple of days earlier? The caller didn't say anything, and I said 'hello' a couple of times, then hung up?"

Noting Francine shaking her head, Karen added detail.

"That was on Thursday previous to the Saturday call, but it was later in the day, mid-to-late afternoon."

Looking at Karen as though waiting for her to continue, Francine prompted.

"You said there were a couple of things you forgot to mention."

"Oh, yes, forgive me. My mind … my thinking is ponderous, I'm afraid. When I told Peter about the second call, he started asking me questions about it, you know, 'What else did the caller say?', 'Did you notice anything else?' - stuff like that. It triggered a memory of noise in the background. I recognized it. It was the noise chainsaws make. A tree-trimming crew was felling a dead tree just across the street from our house that morning. You can see the stump and sawdust if you look. At the time, I was so certain the call had been made from just outside our house that I ran to a front window to look. Of course, there was no one. The girl would have been long gone if she was ever there. I realize now it may have just been a coincidence."

Mickey, a self-taught student of brain function, had always envisioned his mind as a myriad of pathways, representing neural strings, along which chemical sparks flew at the different connective points as energy coursed through them, much like the electric trams of old. He was sure his mind was a mass of chemical sparks now as he made connections

- the park, Simpson's office and his residence, the anonymous phone calls, the multiple sightings of the girl - 'park girl' was becoming the common factor. The excitement of that possibility was mitigated by a suspicion as to why Karen Simpson had not mentioned this potentially significant piece of information during the initial interview. To him, it seemed reasonable to connect the apparent knowledge the caller had of the Simpson family with the idea that someone was in a position to observe the family. Maybe Karen had been too distraught to think clearly when they first talked to her. Still ....

Francine's voice abruptly brought him up short and back to the task at hand.

"Had you noticed someone hanging around the house or loitering in the vicinity at other times?"

The immediate reply surprised both officers, but they outwardly remained calm, matter-of-fact.

"Yes, actually, I have. On two occasions, I have seen what I believe was an older teenage girl or young adult standing outside the Williamson's house on the opposite side of the street from our house. She was just there, by herself. The first time I saw her was when I looked outside from one of the front windows. On that occasion, she seemed to be watching our house. The second time, I was coming back from getting groceries with Solynn and she was in the same spot but was not looking at Solynn and me or the house when I saw her. I really didn't think much about it at the time. Do you think that girl could have had something to do with this?"

Francine, hitting on all cylinders now, was voicing Mickey's questions, almost as they formed in his mind.

"We have to look at all possibilities, follow all leads. This is a lead we will follow along with the others we have. Did you recognize the person? Have you ever seen her before? Please describe her as best you can."

Karen Simpson sat upright and crossed her legs, intertwined the fingers of her hands and slipped them over one knee.

"No. I have never seen her before. Let me see, her description … she was tall, maybe five foot, six inches or more. It was hard to tell. She was wearing a full-length dark coat, maroon colour, I think, but I believe she was of average weight, not heavy anyway. She had long dark hair, brown most likely, maybe black. Although I didn't get a good look at her face, I had the impression she was pretty. I'm not sure why. That's about it."

Starting to glance toward Mickey, wondering if it was nearing the time to begin their preplanned strategy, Francine made a mid-glance decision and turned back to Karen.

"Did you notice anything else about her, her clothing beyond the coat, for example? Did she act or move in any way that caught your attention? Was she carrying anything?"

Karen, eyes slipping into that unfocused state that signals an absorption in thought, appeared to be casting her mind back in time before she spoke.

"No, I can't remember anything else. She probably had gloves and boots on, but I can't say I remember them. I didn't see her move, like walk, so if she had a limp or anything like that I wouldn't have noticed. I don't remember her carrying anything. Now I remember, she had her hands in the pockets of her coat."

Dans des sou, dans un livre, thought Francine and put forward her follow-up question.

"She didn't have a school bag, a backpack?"

"No, I told you she wasn't carrying anything. Do you think she's a schoolgirl? Is that what you think? Anyway, the days I saw her were Saturdays, not school days."

Shifting topics, Francine made a show of consulting her notes as though getting her bearings for the next series of questions. She wanted to review the period before Karen Simpson contacted the police to report her husband missing. In response to Francine's recitation of what she had previously told them, that is, what she did and when she did it, from the time she had expected her husband to when she contacted the police, Karen simply confirmed the information. On cue, Francine started the heavy-lifting.

"I still find it hard to believe that you waited some five to six hours after your husband was due home to contact the police. He had given no indication to you that he would be late. You couldn't reach him by phone, office or mobile at 9:30, yet you waited another 90 minutes before contacting the police. And you say you didn't even think to check your voicemail till then. It sounds like you weren't overly concerned."

Karen bristled. Glaring at Francine, her anger spilled over into her posture which had become tense and rigid, and into the pitch of her voice which had become shrill. She angrily jabbed a finger at Francine, her voice cracking with emotion as she spoke.

“You… you know nothing about Peter and I! Yet you presume to make this kind of ridiculous judgement. We loved each other, we cared for each other. Think what you like, but I was concerned about him being so late. It was just that I felt he would appear at any moment and I hung on to that until I couldn't hang on to it anymore. His being that late, without contacting me had never happened before, so excuse me if I didn't follow your goddamned protocol governing behaviour in this kind of situation."

Unrelenting, Francine gave her no breathing room.

“Mrs. Simpson, just how solid was your marriage? Could your husband have been seeing someone else? Maybe the anonymous caller heightened an already fomenting suspicion on your part? Or created one? Were you happy in your marriage?”

Karen Simpson's face looked stricken, and she looked from Francine to Mickey, who immediately stood facing his partner, a stern look on his face.

"That's enough, Detective Constable! Mrs. Simpson doesn't deserve this sort of treatment. I will finish this interview and we would like some privacy, if you don't mind."

Francine looked shocked, but stood and while slowly exiting the living room stopped to offer an apology.

"My apologies, Mrs. Simpson, sometimes I get carried away."

Mickey remained standing until he heard the front door close. Only then did he resume his place on the sofa.

"I'd like to apologize for my partner, Mrs. Simpson. I hope you're OK. If you are, and as distasteful as it is, it is important that I ask you some difficult questions."

Karen nodded that she was alright and for Mickey to go on.

"Mrs. Simpson, I'm sorry to be asking these questions but did you have any reason to question Peter's faithfulness? Any reason to suspect he might be seeing another woman?"

Having used the time during which Francine had been ousted from her house Karen composed herself and then gave a little wave to indicate an acceptance of Mickey's apology.

"None at all. We adored each other. I know he loved me and he wouldn't do anything to hurt Solynn and me. If you think he might have been killed by a jealous lover, I think you're bark .... My God, you think it was me! You think I did it! That's why you're asking these questions! Talk about being twice victimized!"

Keeping his voice calm and his manner supportive, Mickey sought to reassure Karen.

"We don't think anything at this point. These are simply the questions we must ask as part of our enquiry. By the way, we are aware of the charges made against Peter by a co-ed at Memorial University when he was there. Are you aware of that?"

"Yes, I am. If you did your homework, you will also know that the charges were fabricated because Peter would not agree to alter the student's grade in exchange for sex. Peter was totally vindicated."

Nodding slightly and watching Karen's face intently, Mickey spoke quietly.

"Not vindicated actually, charges were dropped because the complainant had engaged in similar behaviour previously and that weakened her credibility. You weren't the least bit suspicious?"

Glaring at Mickey, Karen's voice became strident and accusatory.

"It's true, isn`t it? Once that kind of accusation is made, it follows you. No matter the lack of evidence, the lack of credibility of the accuser, or the findings of innocence ... the accused is never thought to be guiltless. He's held to be somehow at fault even by those responsible for upholding the law. What a society we live in!"

Pressing his lips together after a period of silence, Mickey altered course and asked Karen about Peter's involvement in the Teen Health Centre.

"Karen, we understand that your husband was seeing some students at the Teen Health Centre at the high school. Did he tell you much about his work there?"

Still fuming, Karen Simpson took a deep breath.

"I hope we are just about finished. I have to pick up Solynn from Ida's. Peter didn't say much of anything about his Teen Centre clients other than he enjoyed the work and said he felt more effective as a therapist with clients in that age group. His only negative comment was about the lack of teacher coverage at the Center when he was engaged in therapy sessions. He was a stickler about having another person nearby during therapy for the protection of both the client and the therapist."

"He said nothing else about his work there, about any of the students? Nothing came up that was concerning to him or you?"

Standing while checking her wristwatch, Karen sought to end the interview.

"Look, Detective Sergeant, I've told you everything I can. Now I have to get Solynn."

Feeling that the interview was nearing the end of its usefulness, Mickey left his seat and accompanied Karen to the front vestibule where they retrieved his coat from a closet and made for the front door. When Karen opened it to see Mickey out, they found Francine standing on the step holding Solynn.

"I've just had a nice chat with your neighbour, Mrs. Williamson, who was about to bring Solynn over. Since Solynn and I hit it off right away, I offered to bring her back. Hope that's OK?"

Karen, at a momentary loss for words, finally managed to say "thank you" while gathering the little girl in her arms and closing the door.

As the Impala sped away from the Simpson residence, Francine asked Mickey about the part of the interview with Karen Simpson she missed.

"MacKinnon, you are one mean SOB. You had me quaking in my boots. Did it help?"

Shaking his head, Mickey broke out into a huge smile.

"I must admit kicking your ass like that was fun. I should have been an actor. Yeah, I'm not sure it helped though. She denies having any suspicion of philandering on her husband's part. She maintains they had a rock-solid marriage. She is also adamant that the MUN business was a matter of Peter being caught in a game that was none of his doing. She gave me nothing about the Teen Health Centre, although I thought she got very anxious toward end of the interview when that topic came up. In short, I got zilch. So what did you do with your downtime?"

Francine, acting coy, took a quick look at her partner.

"What downtime? Let's see - I had a call from Stott. Apparently, she got right on to Sue Reynolds with the picture of this park female. As expected, the best Reynolds could say was that it might have been her, the dark hair and the dark-coloured coat being the same as far as she could tell. And as I said, I had a nice chat with Ida Williamson. I went over to the house to say 'hi' and ask a couple of questions. I learned they don't have CCTV as part of their security system as I had hoped, so no picture of the young female. However, Ida said she had noticed the girl in front of her house a couple of times on weekends too. She gave the same general description as Karen Simpson. Then we got to talking about the tragedy which has beset the Simpson family and about the support that Mrs. Simpson, now a single parent, will need, I commented on what a good neighbour Ida was looking after Solynn the way she has been. Well, Ida told me that this was nothing new, that she enjoyed looking after Solynn and that she'd frequently done so for Karen and Peter. In fact, she shared that she had done so for a couple of hours on the day Simpson was murdered ..... between 6:00 and 8:00 pm she said.

CHAPTER 27: A KILLER AT LILLIAN METCALFE?

Thursday, January 25

The bedside digital alarm clock read 2:32 pm. For almost two days now, her room had been cloaked in a darkness that hadn't seen sunlight beyond the little that seeped around the drawn curtains during the day; while at night, the only light was that cast from the hallway through the cracks around the bedroom door. The sole reason she was aware that it was Thursday was because her mother had told her on the last trip to check on how she was doing. Cloistered here, she knew she was hiding from a reality that did not seem a reality at all, more a fantasy, something made up. The gloom was somehow a shroud of protection keeping at bay the light which brought truth with it.

While Sheila had been able to use her involuntary retching in response to hearing of Peter Simpson's death to feign a physical illness, resulting in her being ordered to bed, she knew this could not go on much longer. Despite her awareness that the shelf life of her closeted existence was fast being depleted, she had been glad to have had the time she'd had. Her mood had spiralled down and down toward something bottomless, something beyond her imagination, something which had embraced her and pulled her even further into its depths. At its worst, she could barely get out of bed to go to the bathroom, each movement requiring an energy that seemed to dwarf her capability. Eating had been a physical impossibility. Only recently, in the last hour or two, between gagging fits, had she managed to force down small quantities of food. She recognized that her mother was concerned and fearful, confused by the fact that she did not have a fever. Unless some sign of recovery was imminent, she knew her mother was poised to take her to the Emergency Department at the hospital. She could not let that happen. She understood that she must extract herself from the emotional quicksand which was sucking her under and confront the truth. But she also knew from experience that reason did not necessarily lead to emotional control.

As Sheila tried to marshal the resolve and energy required to escape her dark sanctuary, she thought about one positive consequence that resulted from the systemic illness she was assumed to have. That singular bright spot was the fact that both her mother and her sister had not quizzed her about her whereabouts last Tuesday evening. As more time passed, she felt it less and less likely that they would.

With the intent of demonstrating recovery, Sheila, using every fibre of her being and fighting her body's demands that she do nothing, got out of bed and made for the bathroom. The image she saw in the mirror, the first in two days, startled her. Her skin was pale, tinged with grey in places. She had dark patches under her eyes and her lids appeared to be swollen. Her long hair was tangled and in disarray. Her lips were dry and cracked, skin flaking from them, and her teeth, far from sparkling white, had grown a fuzz like that of peaches. The jolt she experienced seeing her face in that condition lent a further impetus to her emerging belief that she had to do something. She couldn't just lie down and die. That poor choice of words brought an immediate spike in her anxiety level which she recognized was going to repeat itself time and again given her heightened state of sensitivity. She would need to get a handle on it or go insane.

***

Showered, legs shaved, teeth brushed, hair shampooed, blow dried and combed and dressed in jeans and a cropped, black long-sleeved top, Sheila descended the stairs to the sound of her mother bustling around in the kitchen. Her mother must have heard her coming because she was looking straight at her expectantly when she rounded the doorway.

"It's so good to see you up and around, sweetie. You had us worried. How are you feeling?"

It pleased her to see the smile and happiness registered on her Mom's face.

"Still not 100 percent, but much better. I think I will make myself a cup of hot chocolate and watch a little TV."

The words had barely escaped Sheila's mouth when the front door opened and was closed with a loud bang that caused percussive aftershocks in its wake. Maggie's excited voice could be heard on the heels of her dramatic entry

"Mom, you're not going to believe this! Wait 'til I tell you!"

Maggie virtually exploded into the kitchen bursting to share her news. Noticing Sheila, her eyes widened.

"Hey, Sheila, you feeling better?"

Sheila had hardly had time to nod, let alone say anything before Maggie was into the story she just had to tell.

"You guys are just not going to believe this! The cops were, like, everywhere at school today. Well, not everywhere, but there were two cop cars there. Well, not the kind with flashing lights on top, but they were cop cars. Jimmy Adler, a guy in my class, told me the teachers and some kids were being called to the office one by one to talk to the cops. One of the kids who had to go told Jimmy that the cops showed him a picture of a girl and asked him if he recognized the girl or suspected who she might be. But Jimmy said the kid couldn't tell them because the picture didn't even show the girl's face and it could have been anybody."

Betty Munroe listened intently to her daughter and attempted to ask a question but was cut short, mouth open.

"Wait! Wait! That's not all! Some parents had to come to school to be with their kids when they talked to the police. Just like on that TV show we saw. What was it called?"

Betty used Maggie's need to take in oxygen as an opportunity to comment on her revelations.

"Jimmy Adler is quite a source of information, isn't he? Did he say why the police were interested in identifying the girl?"

Maggie, clearly enjoying the spotlight, quickly answered her mother's question.

"It wasn't Jimmy who told me about the parents coming to school, it was Frances Abbott. She was one of the kids the cops talked to. She said she thinks it has something to do with Dr. Simpson's murder because the cops knew she was seeing him at the Teen Health Center and they asked questions about that. Frances also said that she thinks most of the kids they talked to were seeing Dr. Simpson."

Betty Munroe's face had become a study in consternation as she replied.

"Obviously the police think there is a possible connection between Dr. Simpson's death and his work at the Teen Health Center. I do hope none of the students at the school are involved."

Looking very pleased, Maggie outlined what she and Frances thought.

"We, like me and Frances, figure that the girl in the picture they were showing is tied up in it. She might even be the murderer! Just think about it, we might have a killer walking around Lillian Metcalfe!"

Walking rapidly away from the kitchen and her hot chocolate, Sheila made it to the downstairs bathroom in time to heave the soup and crackers she had eaten an hour ago into the toilet bowl.

***

Later that evening, again in seclusion in her bedroom but with the lights on, Sheila sat on her bed mentally berating herself. Once again, she came to the conclusion that she was never going to maintain her sanity unless she could control her emotions and the strong visceral responses that had been accompanying them. She was sure she had been on her way to a mental breakdown in the short time since Simpson's death, and that would continue unless she could turn things around. *OK, Sheila girl, it's time to let reason take over from emotion. Consider what you know or think you know. If Maggie, or rather Jimmy Adler, is right, the cops have no idea who the girl is and the picture they have doesn't even show her face. I don't even know that the picture is of me, but what are the chances it isn't? And if it is, where did they get it? Obviously, with the face not shown, it isn't a posed shot. It must have been part of the background of another picture taken by someone else. How else would they have gotten it? Of course! CCTV! I didn't even think of that. Wait. Not to worry, if they had a better picture, they would be showing that around, not the shitty one.*

Sheila's attention was then drawn to the bedroom door which was opened partway after a light knock. Maggie poked her head through the opening, her face a mask of apprehension.

"Hey, big sis, are you really feeling better? I hate to be selfish but I don't want to come in if you are still sick and risk catching it."

Smiling at the brutal honesty of her little sister, Sheila waved her into the room while reassuring her.

"I'm feeling a whole lot better, Maggie. Come on in. I'm sure I'm not contagious anymore."

Entering and closing the door behind her, Maggie took a seat on the bed.

"You know this is like the first time in days we've had a chance to talk. What, with you being sick and my germ phobia. What do you think about the cops and all that at school today? I thought it was cool at first, but now it's kinda sinking in. That thing I said to you and Mom earlier, 'bout a killer roaming around school; that could be true, you know. What do you think?"

Maintaining a calm and neutral facial expression and tone of voice, Sheila sought to temper her Maggie's concerns.

"To tell the truth, I'm not worried. It's not likely the murderer is a student at school. It's more likely they are looking for this girl because she is a witness and may not realize it, or maybe she's not and the cops just want to make sure. Now we're on the topic, Maggs, how are you doing? I mean about Simpson being dead. How are you feeling?"

It was almost as if Maggie had been taken by surprise by the question. Sheila saw astonishment flicker on her face before it moulded itself into one expressing resignation. The split second over which this transition occurred was disconcerting to Sheila.

"What? Me? Oh, yeah. You know what? Like I told you, I made my peace with what happened between me and Dr. Simpson. I'm certainly not freaked because he's dead, but I didn't want him to die either. Know what I mean?"

What the hell? thought Sheila. *She talks as if it happened to a complete stranger, not someone she knew and trusted and who assaulted her.*

"For God's sake, Maggie, you refer to him as Dr. Simpson after all that has happened. You seem totally unconcerned, untouched by it all. I don't understand."

Standing and turning to look down at her sister still seated on the bed, Maggie gestured with both hands, palms facing up with arms extended and to the sides while using a voice tinged with mild exasperation.

"Bottom line, Sheila, I want this behind me. Dr. Simpson is gone. There is nothing to be gained by continuing to discuss what happened. You may think I should feel this way or that way, that I should somehow be an emotional wreck, but guess what, I'm not. End of story."

Finding it hard to fathom what she had just heard from Maggie, Sheila got to her feet and looked Maggie right in the eye.

"Whoa! Whoa! As I remember it, when we first talked about this, you were so upset. What the hell has happened since then to cause such a turnabout?"

On her way to exit the bedroom, Maggie spoke over her shoulder in answer to her sister's question.

"I'm not sure your memory is that good, Sheila. I think you were more upset than me. Anyway, things change. People change. Things are put into perspective. I don't know. All you need to know is that I am OK. This is the last time I want to talk about this."

CHAPTER 28: IDA SAID

K aren Simpson sat cross-legged on the family room floor of her house playing with Solynn, inserting shapes into same-shaped holes on a board - a Christmas present she and Peter had given her. She marvelled at the adaptability of her daughter, her rapid adjustment to the absence of her father in the short time since his death. The little toddler had already reduced the frequency with which she asked about Peter. When the door chimes sounded or the phone rang, she wasn't automatically calling out "Daddy" now. This development brought mixed feelings for Karen. On the one hand, she was heartened by the fact that Solynn seemed to be adjusting so quickly to life without her father, but on the other, it saddened her to think that someone as important to Solynn as Peter could be so easily erased from her thoughts.

Karen couldn't abide thinking in terms of murder, and certainly not using the word *murder* to categorize Peter's passing. It wasn't denial she told herself because she knew full well that her husband was dead, and that his death was not a natural one. It was simply that the term conjured up such unpleasant thoughts that its avoidance seemed sensible given her need for emotional self-preservation. She was sure that this need also influenced her decision to tell Solynn that her "Daddy" had gone on a trip and would not be back for a long, long time. Really, what else could she tell a four-year-old?

Unexpectedly, tears began to escape, finding their way down her cheeks. She immediately dabbed them with the handkerchief that had become an essential accessory for the past two days, and likely, for days to come. When she noticed her daughter looking at her with a questioning look on her face, she flashed a comforting smile and hastily distracted the toddler by asking her to find the star's home on the board.

God, I miss him! It wasn't supposed to be like this. Never in her wildest dreams could she have anticipated this happening. The emptiness and deep sadness she felt were staggering and debilitating. However, she knew she could not give in to it. Solynn needed her. She could not book off from being a mother to meet her own selfish needs.

Karen recognized that she was feeling grief, but felt she had bypassed the earliest of the five stages, denial, anger and bargaining, and catapulted to depression and acceptance. She suspected, no, not suspected, knew that this modified progression of emotions was the by-product of the intense feeling of guilt that had settled in and showed no sign of abating anytime soon. When she allowed her mind to go there, she could not fathom how she had come to do what she had. What was it in her that allowed her to become so primal, so base? Jealousy, suspicion and anger had gone wild. During that short period, she had become someone she didn't know, someone capable of acting so contrary to the human being she thought she was. Once again taking stock, as she had done countless times over the last couple of days, she told herself that no matter her culpability and accompanying feelings of guilt, as the surviving parent, she had a commitment to her daughter. That commitment trumped everything else, *so suck it up and continue to do what needs to be done*!

Karen checked her watch in response to the front door chimes. It was 10:30 am, that is, 10:30 am Thursday, two days post-Peter. It seemed that everything that happened since Peter's death was referenced by the time marker *post-Peter*. This had become a persistent point of orientation which had asserted itself in her awareness. She heard her mother's footsteps in the front vestibule, the front door opening and voices raised in greeting. Moments later, a stylishly dressed, handsome older woman with uniformly white hair, Karen's mother, entered the family room to let her know that Ida Williamson was here to visit.

"Do you feel up to it, Karen? I can make excuses for you, if not."

Getting to her feet, after kissing Solynn on top of her head, Karen raised and waved a hand dismissing her mother's concern.

"It's fine, Grammy. Would you mind filling in for me? Solynn is doing a great job finding the right shapes. I know she would like to show you how she does it. OK?"

***

Sinking into the green leather chair in the living room after Ida had taken a seat on the sofa with tea and biscuits within arm's reach, Karen waited for her friend and neighbour to initiate the conversation because it looked like she had something on her mind.   The short period of silence before Ida began was punctuated by a crackling noise from the wood fire Karen's father had built in the fireplace before leaving to pick up groceries and wine.

"I know your Mom and Dad are with you now, Karen, but I wanted to let you know that Ned and I are available to help in any way we can. We're just across the street, you know. How are you getting along, anyway?"

Watching Ida's face closely, Karen thought to herself, *no, that's not what you came for*, then answered her long-time friend.

"I'm doing OK, Ida. I think it's going to take a long time for me to be anything like normal, but I can function. I have to, Solynn needs me."

Nodding her head, but her face communicating her thoughts were elsewhere, Ida appeared to continue the holding pattern she seemed to be in. Karen had experienced this before with Ida, who appeared to frequently see herself as a source of social slights and miscues for which she felt compelled to apologize, but not necessarily with haste.

"You know I'd be happy, and so would Ned, to care for Solynn any time you need a break or need to attend to things. Maybe you want your Mom and Dad to go with you? I love that little girl, you know that. I was telling that policewoman, the pretty French one, how I have been happy to do that since little one was born. Particularly, since I have no kids myself. I'm just like an aunt, Auntie Ida, wouldn't you say?"

Karen, aware that Ida was circling the real reason for her visit and not having the patience to let her friend get to it in her own time, cut to the chase.

"You have been a godsend, Ida. We are so lucky to have you and Ned as neighbours and friends. Ida, you seem to have something on your mind. What is it?"

Ida gave Karen a quick smile, drew herself up on the edge of the sofa and took a deep breath.

"Christ, am I that obvious? No career as secret agent, then. Listen, I need to tell you about something I did. Something I said actually, without thinking. OK, here goes. You know when those two police officers who came to see you yesterday? Well, that policewoman was asking if we had CCTV as part of our security system and if I'd seen anyone hanging around your house in the last few weeks. So, I told him about the girl I saw and she said you had seen her too. We gave similar descriptions apparently. Anyway, she and I were chatting away about this and that and we got onto the topic of neighbours helping neighbours. Well, she told me what a good friend I was by caring for Solynn at a time of crisis. I told her that I loved looking after Solynn and did it regularly, crisis or not. I don't know how it came up but I ended up mentioning that I had looked after her for a while Tuesday evening last and she got all interested and asked for specific times. Have I said something I shouldn't have, Karen?"

Inwardly, Karen felt an immediate panic, shortness of breath and rapid heartbeat, similar to the emotional and physical reactions she had experienced when finding herself in enclosed spaces. Outwardly, she managed to maintain a neutral facial expression which evolved into a smile while waving away Ida's concern with a raised hand while making a 'psss' sound with her lips.

"You worry too much, Ida. You didn't say anything out of line at all. Has this been worrying you? If it has, you can stop now."

Fifteen minutes later, Karen was watching from the vestibule window as Ida crossed the street on the way back to her own house. As she watched, she chastised herself for being so stupid. Telling the police a lie which could be so easily laid bare, what was she thinking? It wasn't even a lie which gave her an alibi so she really could have told them anything that explained her leaving the house that night. She could have simply said she went for a drive to get a break after a long day of child care and didn't stop or talk to anyone. Although it didn't provide an alibi either, it was at least partially true and unlikely to be refuted. Self-flagellation completed, she turned her thoughts to damage control.

CHAPTERS 29: SINNERS, REPENT

Sue Reynolds was dusting and polishing the countless figurines, picture frames, and decorations in her apartment, plus any surfaces on which they sat. She gave particular attention to the large number of religious items, many of which had belonged to her father. As she did so, memories of her father flourished in her mind. She smiled as she remembered "Daddy". He was so proud of his little girl, so proud that she could quote scripture from such an early age and participate in the services and rallies he conducted. She was Daddy's little prodigy. Daddy should have been a full-fledged Reverend Minister, not just a lay preacher. She remembered what he had said when she had told him this following one of his rallies which always left her intensely excited. *Sue, God speaks to those who can hear, rich or poor, famous or not, book smart or not, college degrees or not. I can hear Him. He tells me what I need to know. That's all I pray for, I need nothing else. Do you understand? I am His special son as I know you are His special daughter.*

Another memory, this time of her mother, Myrtle, Daddy's wife, a housewife and cook, *but she was not Daddy's true partner like me. God bless her soul, mother knew that was true and the will of God. She accepted and rejoiced in the glow with which our Saviour surrounded us, Daddy and me. Dear Lord, I know you had a purpose in taking Daddy, but I do miss him so.*

The momentary joy generated from such memories, and the outer calm she demonstrated in her careful handling and attention to the cleaning of her memorabilia, was a contradiction of the overwhelming inner tumult she was presently suffering. As was always the case, the source of this pain was the conflict between the expectations of virtue for "Daddy's little girl" and the disturbing thoughts that gained unwanted access to her mind. One of the most devastating of those imaginings which she could not seem to expel from her consciousness was of a teenage Sue in bed with Daddy. Although this had never happened, the mental impression was nonetheless persistent and was a source of consuming shame. Compulsively, she once again cycled through the ruminations most recently sparked by her interview with the young Detective Constable. Her thoughts took the form of confessions to herself and her God and always involved the same self-condemnations.

I am a disgusting, immoral woman who is tempted by sins of the flesh, a fornicator at the ready. My unwelcome dreams are those of a fallen woman. I have neither the conviction to cast such thoughts from my mind nor the strength to do other than hide them. My weakness has made me a stalker and a liar. God, please forgive me. I am so weak. Please help me become your special daughter once again.

As the cycle progressed, self-condemnations transitioned into the comforting judgements of the behaviour of others, most prominently that of Peter Simpson.

Peter, my darling, you were weak as well, a sinner, a fornicator like me. You were a man, like many, unable to resist young whores, cheating on your wife, on me. Why, Peter, why did you do this to us? We were happy, we had each other and you threw it away. You surely didn't expect to go unpunished?

CHAPTER 30: BANISHED

Arthur Munroe sat in the neutral-coloured armchair which complemented the neutral-coloured bedspread in his single room with neutral-coloured walls at The Queen Royal Hotel on the outskirts of Halifax. It was 5:45 pm and he was finishing his second pre-supper rum and coke, dark rum with a splash of Coca-Cola, no ice. Lately, he'd noticed that it took a third drink before he was able to detect the welcome effect of the alcohol. He was two-thirds of the way there. He couldn't remember the last time a single drink had done it for him. *I am sick, twisted*, he thought, *a drunk, a pervert and a criminal, a man with an addictive personality.* How did he get to be this way? If, indeed, he had an addictive personality, where did he get it? Was it inherited? How could it be his fault, for pity's sake? He hadn't asked to be this way. He remembered posing these questions and more to his former therapist, a specialist in one addiction or another, he couldn't recall exactly which one. The therapist had told him that no one knew the answers for sure, but studies had shown that people with addictive personalities were impulsive, experienced difficulty delaying gratification, were anti-social in their orientation and felt socially alienated. At the time, he hadn't thought that these things described him, although he hadn't argued the point. What had severely pissed him off though was the therapist's comment that the studies also pointed to another characteristic, a high tolerance for deviance. All he had heard was the "quack" calling him a deviant, a pervert. That had short-circuited any chance that he would continue with therapy.

With his continuing denial and with the length of time it had taken for his life to finally implode, he hadn't seen it coming until it was too late. As he sat there by himself in this monochrome room drinking the third rum and coke which had mysteriously appeared in his hand, no wife, no family, and no friends and suspended from his job, he finally understood.

Arthur didn't blame Betty for ousting him from the home and taking steps to protect herself and the girls from his influence, and his perversions. He had reluctantly agreed, although being cut out of his daughters' lives completely was something he hoped might be reversed sometime in the future. Deep down, however, he understood that such a hope was likely to be a bridge too far. If he was in his wife's shoes, he would have done the same thing.

No wonder he didn't have a wife, a family, friends, and soon maybe a job. Given the horrendous things he'd done that he could remember, he shuddered to imagine the things of which he had no memory. That realization made him grimace as a crippling anxiety gripped him, a mimic of cardiac failure.

With a full-body shudder, Arthur tried to shake off these poor-me thoughts and consider his life going forward. Despite the ugliness that had frequently been visited upon him, he thought of himself as a survivor. Goodness knows he had had a lot of experience at picking up the pieces when things had blown up on him. What was happening now was simply the progression of a well-established pattern, one with which he was very familiar. It was there to be overcome and he had his passions to help him cope. Those passions seemed to go hand in hand, one being the catalyst for the other. Yes, passion in a glass led to the passion he could not pursue without it. Checking his watch, he noted it was 6:14. Good, time for one more drink before supper.

CHAPTER 31: ANOTHER CASSEROLE

"Yes, may I help you?

Rose Pendleton was standing at the front door of the Simpson residence addressing a woman standing on the step clutching a Pyrex dish covered with aluminum foil. Rose eyed the object in the woman's hands and wondered where they were going to store another offering of food. They were overrun with lasagnes; casseroles of every variety, cookies, cakes, dessert loaves, sandwiches - the list went on and on. She feared they were going to have to throw out a lot of it.

Sue shifted uneasily while she assessed the elderly, trim and alert-looking lady in front of her. She wondered if this was a friend or neighbour or, perhaps, the Simpsons had employed a maid or an assistant of some kind. She thought the latter unlikely if she was not aware of it.

"Yes, I'm Susan Reynolds, here to visit Mrs. Simpson if she is up to seeing me."

Adopting the demeanour of a gatekeeper, a task which she seemed to take on with relish, Mrs. Pendleton asked Sue if she was a neighbour or a friend. Only when she had established Sue's relationship with Karen did she invite her to step inside the vestibule to wait while she checked to see "if her daughter was up to a visit".

Less than a minute later, Karen walked into the vestibule and, without a word, walked directly up to Sue and gave her an extended hug, the Pyrex dish trapped between their bodies. As Karen stepped back, Sue, eyes brimming with tears, was quick to express her condolences.

"Mrs. Simpson, I am so sorry about Dr. Simpson. I wanted to tell you that in person. He was such a good person and a wonderful therapist. He helped so many people. I will miss him greatly. I know you may not need it but I brought you a chicken casserole. And listen, I don't have to stay. I understand that you may not feel up to visits yet. You know, since it's only been two days ……"

As Sue started to turn toward the front door to exit, Karen placed a hand on her shoulder.

"Nonsense, Sue. I can't think of anyone I would rather see than you. Thank you for the casserole. You're very thoughtful. Please come into the living room and sit for a while. I will ask Mother to get tea and cake, or coffee if you prefer."

Sue was pleased to be invited in and quickly handed off the casserole she'd been carrying to Rose Pendleton. This was the first time she had visited the Simpson house since beginning work for Peter. Sitting in the spacious living room, which could have made the pages of a magazine on interior design, gave her a glimpse of a previously unknown reality. The luxury of the room represented a part of Peter's life in which she had not been involved, and therefore, in which she had been unable to exert her influence. The room, somehow, was a physical reminder that she had shared him, that he had not been hers alone. Sue was taken by surprise by the fact that this realization seemed to cause her as much distress as the death of the man himself.

After a few minutes during which the two women exchanged the obligatory comments about how each was managing under the circumstances, the conversation gravitated toward the police investigation. It was a comment made by Sue which set it on this course.

"I can't imagine anyone wanting to harm Dr. Simpson, but I'm sure the police will discover who is responsible. In fact, I met two of the investigating officers and they scared me half to death just asking questions. I wouldn't want to be a criminal in their path. They even asked me to account for my whereabouts during the time ... well, you know, as though I was a suspect in their minds. Even when I told them I was home watching TV all evening, they seemed suspicious. What a horrible job they must have if it makes them doubt everyone's veracity."

Nodding her head in agreement and sympathy, Karen smiled briefly.

"You mean the big guy with the young female partner, MacKinnon and Deveaux? They are just doing their jobs, I suppose, but I know what you mean. I found him intimidating just because of his size. As for Deveaux, she seemed to take an instant dislike for me for some reason. She practically accused me of negligence in reporting Peter missing on the night he .... died. They haven't told me much about the investigation, but I think they're looking for a girl, more an older teenager, or young woman, they've yet to identify. I've actually seen her just outside the house on a couple of occasions. It is hard to believe someone so young could have anything to do with Peter's death. By the way, believe it or not, early on they wanted me to produce an alibi as well, as though I was capable of murdering my child's father! Like you, all I could say was that I was home where I am most evenings caring for Solynn."

Looking at Karen over the rim of her teacup as she was about to take a sip, Sue's face projected, in quick succession, expressions of mild surprise, and then recognition followed by anxiety.

"My goodness, Mrs. Simpson, I saw a tall, dark-haired girl leaving Dr. Simpson's office on the day he was killed. I told the police of course. But you saw her outside your house? Please be careful! Are you receiving police protection? I didn't see anyone on guard. Are they hidden?"

Karen gave a little laugh and sought to assure her visitor.

"Don't worry, Sue. We're fine. No, we don't have police officers protecting us, but we have an excellent security system and my parents are here. Anyway, it may not be the same girl. Even if it is, she may have nothing to do with Peter's death. And even if she does, there is no indication that she intends to harm me or anyone else in the family."

Sue shifted her sitting position to the front edge of the sofa, then stood while responding to Karen's reassurances as though less than convinced.

"Well, if you think so, Mrs. Simpson. Anyway, I should be going now, I've stayed too long as it is. Please call me if there is anything I can do, anything at all."

After a final hug and exchange of goodbyes by the front door, Karen watched Sue make her way along the sidewalk to the street and, within seconds, out of sight. She was unaware, as was Sue, that they both had learned something during their conversation that had aroused their respective interests. Karen wondered why someone who was home all Tuesday evening did not answer a telephone call made to her home at 9:30 pm. Sue, walking with her head down to protect her face from the freezing wind cutting into her flesh, pondered how someone could be home looking after her daughter Tuesday evening while at the same time be driving down Fletcher Avenue, three blocks from Peter's office. Although not known to Sue, Karen had already told the police that she couldn't raise Sue by phone at 9:30.

CHAPTER 32: AND THEN
THERE WERE THREE

Friday, January 26

It seemed absurd to Sheila. *How can the woman stand up there blatting about the French Revolution when my life is disintegrating right in front of her? Why can't she see what's happening? Why can't she see me?* Sitting near the back of the classroom, head down reading proclamations of love on her graffiti-laden desk, Miss Patton doing her best to make French history captivating, Sheila was grinding her way to the end of the first day of her return to classes at Lillian Metcalfe. Although she found it hard to generate any interest in her classes, her re-introduction to her school had been easier than she thought it would be. Predictably, life went on around her, the organized and prescribed routine. The social interaction of the typical school day forced activity upon her, drew her in, and distracted her. An added factor which facilitated the ease of re-entry was the absence of police officers and police cars. Sheila was relieved that the focus of the investigation seemed to have taken them elsewhere. Consequently, she had less time and fewer reminders to dwell on her situation. This brought with it a reprieve from the depressive feelings which had been gnawing at her very soul.

Change of class buzzer sounding, Sheila looked to gather and pack her History materials only to find that she had not taken them out of her backpack in the first place. Leaving the classroom and making for her locker, she saw Noah Baldwin approaching her. Even the prospect of attention from a guy like Noah, someone she had been admiring from afar for a while, did not give her the little inner shiver it had done in the past. The fact that his approach left her shiver-less was certainly not Noah's fault.   Over six feet tall, lean but muscular, with longish curly blonde hair and chiselled facial features, Noah was considered "fit". If the fantasized activities of Sheila's dream world were an indication, then she and Noah would be considered among that world's most amorous denizens.

"Hey, Sheila, I like the new hair. You look like a different person. How come you decided to go for the Miley Cyrus look?"

Stopping in the hallway next to her locker, surrounded by the noise of the moving human mass that was class change time, Sheila turned toward Noah.

"Oh, I wanted a change, Noah. I was getting tired of the old me, so here's what I ended up with. So you think it makes me look like a different person?"

In that moment, raging hormones started to battle her depressive mood with hormones establishing the upper hand. She looked at him leaning against the adjacent locker as though he was settling in for a bit. Noah took an up-close and personal look at Sheila's new hairstyle as he answered.

"Oh, yeah. I had to look a second time before realizing it was you.   I gotta say I think it looks really great. Listen, I was wondering if you'd like to take in a movie with me some time? Maybe we could get something to eat first?"

Taken completely off guard, Sheila's face couldn't hide her surprise. Inexplicably, her mind nimbly raced to find excuses for turning the man of her recent dreams down. Maybe the power of hormones was overstated. She was about to trot out one of a number which came to mind when her common sense prevailed. Resurgent hormones pounded out the not-so-subtle message "don't be so fucking foolish" while Sheila articulated something else.

"I'd like that Noah. That would be fun."

Noah gave every indication that he was a guy quite pleased with himself as he hustled off to his next class with the promise of calling Sheila soon to arrange "something". Closing her locker, she began to slowly walk to the school library for a scheduled study period, a blank in her schedule during which no instruction took place but was to be used to work on academic activities of the student's choice. Meandering down the hallway, she considered the number of comments about her change in appearance she'd received from fellow students since her return to school. She was beginning to fear that the steps she had taken were having an opposite effect to that which she intended. They were serving to call more attention to her than she wanted. Although Noah and others had focused on the short hair, she had made other adjustments. Among them, she had effectively followed a make-up plan suggested in one of her glamour magazines which had accentuated her eyes, making them look bigger and appear to be set wider, enhanced her cheekbones and changed the shape of her mouth. When she had inspected herself, she, like Noah, thought she looked like a different person. But her efforts to transform herself did not stop there. She judiciously selected a wardrobe and shoes which detracted from her height, rather than highlighting it. She had also abandoned the wearing of her full-length maroon Hudson's Bay coat and gone back to the old coat, still serviceable. None of this had set well with her mother, but unexpectedly she had not put up the stink Sheila was anticipating, particularly about her hair. Rather, her mother had given her what seemed like a token admonishment and then slipped into the distracted, disengaged person she had been before her rebirth as the nurturing, attentive mother during Sheila's illness.

***

Using the after-effects of her recent 'illness' as an excuse to beg off basketball practice once again, Sheila bumped into Maggie after school dismissal and they walked home together. This opportunity seldom presented itself because the respective extra-curricular activities of the sisters had them leaving school at very different times for the most part. They used it to talk about many things as they travelled the familiar route but no mention was made of the topic Maggie had put off limits, her involvement with Peter Simpson. This was annoying Sheila to no end because she had questions she wanted to ask Maggie, questions coming out of the disquietingly cavalier attitude and apparent emotional suppression her sister was exhibiting. However, she had made up her mind she was not going to make an issue of it so soon after Maggie had asked her to drop it, plus she had her own problems to deal with right now.

Entering their home, both girls quickly dispatched their school paraphernalia and, as was their practice, made for the kitchen to prepare a snack and get themselves a drink. They found their mother sitting at the kitchen table, looking at them as they entered. Her face was etched with tension. Sheila had the distinct impression that she had been waiting for one or both of them, an intuition which was confirmed by her mother's first words.

"Girls, please sit down, I need to talk with you."

Sheila's anxiety momentarily leapt. She was sure that the police had been in touch with her mother. *No, no, that couldn't be it. She wouldn't be talking to both of us together if that was the case. But it's something bad.* She knew that from the pain her mother's face could not hide. She seated herself alongside Maggie and waited anxiously for her mother to continue. In the moments of silence that followed, Sheila became aware of previously unheard individual sounds, the ticking of the wall clock, the hum of the fridge and the whirr of its ice-maker, a creak in the ceiling, all of which seemed to create a virtual cacophony.

"Girls, I love you both very much, you know that. I hope you also know that I would never do anything that would hurt you if I could avoid it. In fact, as a parent, and as a mother, I have always tried to make decisions that are in your best interests. Recently, I had to make a decision that I'm going to tell you about, a decision which I feel is in your best interests as well as mine, but will likely hurt you as it has me."

Quickly glancing at Maggie, Sheila saw her sister's rapt attention riveted on their mother, eyes wide, face wearing an expression of anticipation mixed with apprehension. She knew her mother's preamble to what was coming next had given a home to a sick feeling in the stomachs of both of them.

"I am not so unaware that I think what I am about to tell you will come as a complete surprise. You know that your father and I have been having problems. The difficulties have been going on for some time now, at least two years. Among the things at the root of the friction between us are your father's drinking, which has gotten much worse over the past six to eight months, his unwillingness to get help, and the fact that his behaviour is negatively impacting the family. For example, he is missing work and has been threatened with dismissal. He has been siphoning off money from the family account to buy alcohol, and he is abusive to me when drunk. Most importantly, he is a very negative influence in the home and I've had enough. Earlier today, I told him I wanted him out of the house, that I wanted a separation and, eventually, a divorce. He has agreed. He packed his things and left this morning. And before you ask, there is no chance this decision will change."

Both girls sat, stunned and in silence. Even though Sheila had made no secret of her animosity towards her father, the rocky relationship between her parents had been so much a part of her life that she had become inured to it. To have her mother take such decisive action after literally years of marriage free-fall was a shock. Yet, despite the suddenness of the announcement and the initial fear it might be expected to generate, a kernel of optimism germinated. Within seconds, it blossomed.

"You did the right thing, Mom. He was dragging you down. As far as I am concerned, every day with him was another day in our lives lost. This will probably sound strange, but I am happy for you, I am happy for us."

Having said this, Sheila spontaneously stood up and hugged her mother. Then, both of them looked to Maggie who had said nothing yet, but gave the impression of being conflicted. Finally, she smiled a smile which said this is my brave face, not the way I really feel. She addressed her mother and asked questions her mother had anticipated and already answered.

"If this will make you happy, I'm with you. Are you sure you won't change your mind? Even if he agrees to get help and stops drinking?"

Betty Munroe looked at her younger daughter with compassion and answered calmly.

"Sometimes, honey, things get beyond the point of no return. What I am trying to say is that, over the past two years, the relationship between your father and me has been so damaged that it cannot be repaired. I don't love him anymore, and he certainly shows no sign of loving me."

Maggie stared at her mother for a protracted period, then started to cry silently, tears streaming down her face. Betty Munroe, tears in her own eyes, moved to hug her daughter and comfort her.

"It's going to be OK, darling. I know it's a shock, but we're all going to be OK. There, there, please don't worry."

As Sheila watched the two people she loved most in this world embrace, she was struck by the notion that although there were just the three of them now, it was as it was meant to be.

She couldn't help feeling that things were unfolding as they should and that the Munroe family had just put itself back on course after having lost its way for a time. For the first time in days, she experienced a feeling of peace, or, at least, a temporary absence of stress.

After a few minutes, Maggie seemed to get her emotions under control and stopped crying. Betty had returned to her chair and it was clear to Sheila from her mother's body language and facial expression that she was wrestling with some inner thoughts. Then, Sheila realized that there was more to come, her mother hadn't finished.

"What is it, Mom? You look like you have more to say."

As Betty looked at her, Sheila had the feeling that her mother's face, in that moment, captured the agony of mothers through the ages required to make heart-breaking decisions. That insight made her fearful as Betty spoke.

"There is something else. Your father agreed not to contest custody and will not seek visiting privileges. I will have 100% custody. We both agreed that this would be best under the circumstances. I do not see this changing in the future."

Her mother's words unleashed a fury in Sheila which was so sudden and so intense she started to physically tremble.

"What a miserable excuse for a father, for a human being! He can't get his fucking head out of his ass long enough to see what's important! God, I hate him! You know what? Any time spent thinking about him is wasted -"

Sheila stopped mid-rant. She had noticed that far-away gaze in her mother's eyes, the pain imprinted on her face. She suddenly realized that her mother had left something else as yet unsaid. That recognition instantaneously de-escalated the angry, hostile tirade and she addressed her mother almost in a whisper.

"There's something else, isn't there, Mom? Something you haven't told us."

After a stifled sob and a sigh of resignation, Betty Munroe looked intently at first one daughter then the other.

"Your father's addiction was not limited to alcohol. Pornography has been added to his list. I didn't know about this until recently, but when I confronted him, he admitted it. I don't want him near either of you. I'm sorry to have to put all this on you. I debated and debated whether or not to tell you, but I felt you deserved to know in order to understand the decisions I have made."

Sheila's heart broke for her mother. While she was initially blown away by her mother's revelation, she had long since ceased to have any expectations for her father. Nevertheless, she knew this must be devastating for her. And Maggie, she must be rocked by this. As she turned her attention to her sister, Sheila was surprised by the impassive expression on Maggie's face, as if what their mother had said hadn't registered yet, or as if she was not surprised. Had she known or guessed?

CHAPTER 33: THE LADY DOTH PROTEST

Sheila was lying on her bed staring at the ceiling while Taylor Swift's "Paper Rings" filled the room via her wireless speaker. The fact that she was actually in her bedroom in street clothes listening to her favourite pop artists, rather than huddled under the sheets in pyjamas with the room cast in darkness, was a good sign she thought. Perhaps it had to do with the feeling she had that the last few weeks, particularly the last three days, were starting to seem like a distant memory, somehow more remote to her than they actually were. She marvelled at the mind's ability to protect itself although she knew from recent experience it also had the potential to do you in. She considered the fact that some good things had happened, were happening, and understood that these developments were, without doubt, contributing to her positive change in mood. She had taken action, arisen from her catatonic state and forced herself to face the world as the new Sheila Munroe. *Positive.* She was flying under the police radar to date. *Positive.* Her mother was finally divesting herself of 81 kilograms of human waste. *Positive.* Despite the many negatives associated with it, the removal of further threats to Maggie was also a positive. Maybe the destiny of the Munroe females is to be shiny and bright and happy after all.

Having repeated several times, Sheila decided to give "Paper Rings" a rest and engage in another of her interests, reading crime mysteries. She had acquired a substantial collection of novels including titles by authors such as Martha Grimes, Ruth Rendell and Ian Rankin, her favourite. Recently, she was enjoying the works of some of the Scandinavian authors whose novels had been translated into English, writers such as the late Stieg Larsson and Jo Nesbo. She had propped her head up with a pillow preparing to continue reading about another investigation by Grimes' Richard Jury when Maggie knocked and then opened her bedroom door.

Sheila had been expecting her. She could read Maggie like a cheap crime mystery. Therefore, she had anticipated that Maggie, once she had heard their mother's startling pronouncement, wouldn't be content until she had asked a million questions, including those of the 'what now' variety. When Sheila left the two of them, Maggie was in the early stages of unleashing her barrage of queries on their mother. Knowing Maggie to be an equal opportunity inquisitor, she had guessed that it was only a matter of time before she would be engaging Sheila in a similar question-and-answer session.

After closing the door and sitting at the foot of Sheila's bed, the anticipated Maggie dam burst.

"My God, did you see that coming? I was asking Mom, what now? I mean where do we go from here? I mean like for money and stuff. Like, I was thinking about the house. Will we have to move? Change schools? Where is the money going to come from? What about - ?"

Sheila held up an outstretched arm with the palm of her hand facing Maggie, a stop-right-there-and-take-a-breath gesture. If she was being honest with herself, she had always known that Maggie was a bit selfish, a little too consumed with her own needs, and in times of stress, this egocentricity became more evident. So, it was not surprising to Sheila that her sister's reaction to their mother's announcement would be motivated by thoughts of what it would mean for her.

"Whoa! Slow down! To answer one of your questions, I knew they were having problems but would never have guessed porno. Absolutely disgusting! And no, I didn't see Mom kicking the fucker out coming. I guess it had been going on for so long, that I had gotten used to it. It was like the new normal if you know what I mean."

Although Maggie was looking her in the face, Sheila had the distinct impression from the unfocused eyes that she was looking right through her, invested in some inner thoughts to which Sheila was not privy, at least, not yet. As her sister's gaze gradually became more focused, it was apparent she was back and going to speak.

"Yeah, me too. Dad's drinking wasn't always such a big problem, was it? I mean Mom and Dad were happy once, earlier on. I just hope she hasn't given up too soon. What if he gives up booze? What if he changes? People can change, you know. What about us? Mom doesn't have a job and without Dad, we won't be able to pay our bills. We'll be poor!"

It struck Sheila as interesting that Maggie had not expressed any shock about their mother's disclosure of the pornography. She then remembered Maggie's impassive, unruffled reaction when their mother was telling them about it.

"We'll be alright. Mom will get a job and I'll get one, if necessary. Hey, I think I should get one, necessary or not. I gotta say, Maggs, you seem to be taking the pornography stuff really calmly. I was shocked and nauseated, but you don't seem to be. Did you know about it before she told us?"

Maggie immediately looked away from Sheila and down at her feet when answering.

"God, nooo! Don't be so foolish! I was shocked like you. Just because I don't show it like you, doesn't mean I wasn't surprised. Where'd that come from? Man, you can be weird sometimes. You're too suspicious all the time. You overthink things. You need to chill."

Listening to Maggie's rapid-fire reply, part emphatic denial, part bluster and part personal attack, a quote from Shakespeare's Hamlet, part of her course in English Literature, came to mind, "The lady doth protest too much, me thinks."

CHAPTER 34: THE TRUTH WILL
SET YOU FREE OR NOT

Saturday, January 27

"**S**heila! Sheila Munroe!"

It was Saturday morning and she had just left Lillian Metcalfe High after attending final auditions for a major part in the school's planned rendition of the play, *High School Musical*. She had missed the previous two audition sessions due to her "illness". The try-out had been fun, refreshing and distracting, giving some relief from the events which had been eroding life as she knew it. It was during her solitary walk home along a snow-lined sidewalk, engrossed in mental run-throughs of the role in which she hoped she would be cast, that she heard the woman's voice. She had only been vaguely aware that someone had been there, but now she stopped and turned around to face the person who had spoken.

Recognition set off a massive adrenaline expulsion. She felt weak at the knees as though she needed to steady herself on something for fear of collapsing otherwise. She did not, rather could not, respond to the woman in front of her, the person who called her name. Her mind was thrown into neutral, paralyzed, and the silence grew.

Karen had seen recognition register on Sheila's face as she, herself, had confirmed Sheila's identity when she turned around. Despite the short hair and the make-up, she knew she had the right person. She also knew that what she said next was critical if she was to gain this girl's trust and learn what she desperately needed to know.

"Sheila, I am very aware that you know who I am. I would like to talk to you, just you and I, anywhere you suggest."

Hearing the woman's voice again seemed to have the effect of kick-starting Sheila's brain. As a tangle of thoughts was slowly being sorted, she responded in a voice an octave or two above normal.

"You're Karen Simpson. I've seen your picture in the newspaper. How do you know my name? What do you want to talk about?"

Karen had been prepared for the possibility of Sheila stonewalling. She had her response ready. She did not want to frighten the girl off. Quite the contrary, she needed to establish a relationship with her, a rapport. She proceeded using a calm and friendly tone.

"Sheila, I am aware that you know where I live. I have seen you outside my house a couple of times. I know you have visited my husband's office, someone has seen you there and told me, and I believe you and I have talked on the phone, although you did not introduce yourself at the time. I found out who you were with the aid of a Lillian Metcalfe yearbook I borrowed from a friend of mine. Sheila, I need your help. I need to find out what you meant by what you said during the phone call. I need to know what you know. Please, this is very important to me. You should know that I have not told the police about this nor will I, but you have to realize that if I can find you the way I did, they will too. Will you talk to me?"

Labouring to make sense of the presence of one of the last people she could have anticipated confronting her in the street, Sheila concluded that she had no option other than to agree to the woman's request. Besides, she needed to know what the woman wanted. There was only one way to find that out. However, she was unable to suggest any place they might go to talk in private, a place where she could be relatively certain they wouldn't be seen together. She certainly didn't want to remain in the open like this, so she consented to Karen's idea of using her car parked not five minutes away in a public parking area. An awkward silence hung between them as they made their way to the parking lot, a silence broken only by the phone call Sheila made to her mother to let her know she would be a bit later getting home from the audition than expected.

Upon entering the automobile, Karen turned on the engine and dialled up the heater. Sheila's mind continued to race, invoking all manner of possibilities that might explain Karen Simpson's sudden appearance, including a hidden microphone on Karen or in the car with the police at the other end listening, or a kidnapping by Karen intent on exacting revenge, a psychotic Karen. She told herself to calm down, the die was cast now and she would soon learn exactly what was going on. She turned her head to look at Karen and waited.

Every reason for not doing what she was doing at this very minute had been ignored, allowing the present moment to become a reality. Turning to Sheila, Karen began to articulate the reasons for the conversation that she felt compelled to pursue, but first, she sought to reassure the young girl sitting in the passenger seat.

"Sheila, please know that I am not working with the police, making a citizen's arrest or acting like a vigilante in any way. I am simply seeking information and, at this point, you are the only one I know who can provide it. When you spoke to me on the phone last Saturday, I could tell that you were genuinely upset. You made some allegations regarding my husband, Peter, which I didn't understand. But I had no doubt that you believed what you were saying. I could hear the emotion in your voice. I have come to recognize that either you know something about Peter I don't, or you think you know something about him you believe to be true but may not be. I'm not sure why I feel such an overwhelming need to find out which, but I do. Maybe I need to know that the man I loved and shared my life with was the man I thought he was, but if he wasn't, as hard as it will be to hear, I need to know that too. So Sheila, please explain what you meant, why you called him evil, said he had secrets and fooled people, why you felt he needed to be stopped and from what?"

With Karen looking intently at her, Sheila panicked. *This is it! It's over! Oh, God almighty, I'm screwed!* She glanced briefly at the door handle and considered wresting open the car door and fleeing. As though reading her mind, Karen spoke again.

"I can tell from your expression that this is hard for you. Maybe talking to me will make you feel better. Please, Sheila, I just want to know what you know. I'm not here to harm you."

During the few seconds it took Karen to speak her words of encouragement, Sheila started to feel less unnerved, her mind less scattered. She quickly reviewed her options. *One possibility would be to play dumb and deny, deny, deny. Deny everything. Tell this woman that she is mistaken, that I am not the person she saw outside her house, not the person she heard on the phone. Another possibility would be to admit part, but not all. Pretend I made the call but as a joke, a lark. Say it was stupid, foolish, but just a prank. But then how do I explain being outside their house, in Simpson's office? No, if I'm to make any admission, I have to be all in. Jesus, what am I going to do?* After a protracted period of silence, she glanced again at the woman seated beside her. She then made her decision.

***

There it was again, a noise. Maggie was in her bedroom organizing materials for a research assignment for her Economics course scheduled to be presented to her class next week - *The Economics of Buying Locally*. Photocopied articles and papers, with notes, jotted in the margins, covered her desk's top and part of the bed. She had been in the process of sorting the articles she had decided to use in the order they would appear in her paper, when she heard the first noise - a soft, but distinct thud which she strained to identify and interpret, but couldn't. After listening intently for a minute or two, she had decided it was nothing and had gone back to sorting. Then she heard the second sound. This time the sound was identifiable, a creak on the stairs. Maggie momentarily froze. She was home alone. She knew Sheila was at an audition and had called to say she would be later getting home and her mother had left shortly after receiving Sheila's call to post some job applications she had completed. Instinctively, she scanned the bedroom for a weapon, something she might use to fend off an intruder. *Nah, it couldn't be, the doors are locked.* She'd seen to that herself. The sound of footsteps in the hallway just outside her bedroom door and the knob on the door turning sent her to the bedroom window with the thought of flinging it open and screaming her lungs out if necessary. Tugging at the handles of the window, back to the bedroom door, she heard a familiar voice.

"Maggie girl, cumin gif your Daddy a hug. Aren't sha glad to schee me?"

Turning in the direction of the voice, she saw her father teetering on his feet, clearly intoxicated. In addition to his unsteadiness and slurred speech, Maggie noted his dishevelled appearance. His overcoat and trousers were dirty and she assumed that he had fallen at least once. Her face conveyed both displeasure and disgust, but her voice was level, subdued.

"It's you. What are you doing here? You're not supposed to come here. Leave now and I won't tell anybody."

Arthur Munroe put his hand on one side of the doorway to aid his balance and a smile joined the drooping lids, two-day stubble and spittle dribbling down his chin.

"Can't a Dad visit hish fav'ite girl in hish own housch? Cumin, Maggie, gif me a li'ul hug."

Arthur had taken one tottering step into the room and toward her and she had shrunk from him pressing herself against the bedroom wall. He continued to advance smiling and was so close to her now she could smell the stench of alcohol on his breath. Almost in a whisper, his next words triggered an overwhelming feeling of defeat, a resignation in Maggie.

"Dun be schared, darlin', I jus' misch ya' scho mush."

Her body reacting to her mind's capitulation, she relaxed and she stopped pressing against the bedroom wall. She closed her eyes as he reached out, his fingertips gently tracing a path down one cheek. Behind closed eyelids, she prepared to embrace the darkness, her breathing audible in the silence which had settled in the room. Then, unexpectedly from the foot of the stairs, Betty Munroe called to her.

"Hey, Maggie. I picked up some groceries. Give me a hand carrying them in from the car, will you?"

Arthur withdrew the hand immediately and Maggie, as though returning from another dimension was infused with a new energy. She quickly took the initiative and whispered to her father.

"Listen, I'll go help her at the back door. While I'm doing that, go out the front door and don't make any noise. Got it?"

Minutes later, she was entering the kitchen through the back door with arms full of grocery bags while her mother gathered more bags from the trunk of the car. As she set the bags on the kitchen counter, Maggie heard the front door close with a gentle thump.

***

Once Sheila had arrived at her decision, her words came in a torrent. She told Karen everything or almost everything. In Sheila's slightly sanitized confessional, Maggie was an unnamed close friend, and she hadn't returned to Simpson's office after making her demands of him. For her part, Karen listened throughout the rush of words, from time to time nodding her understanding. Sheila's monologue had gone on uninterrupted for so long that when it ended abruptly, a period of silence ensued after which she took a good look at Karen's face. She was surprised to note the absence of any apparent emotion, no anger, no astonishment, no shock, no pain, no stress or anxiety, nothing. She suddenly realized that she had been so intent on telling her story, of unburdening herself, that she had not considered its impact on Karen.

"Mrs. Simpson, I am so sorry about this. I didn't want to tell you any of this, but I felt you left me little choice."

Karen Simpson inhaled a huge volume of air and slowly let it out while turning to face Sheila.

"I don't believe any of this! My husband was not a pedophile, a child molester. You can't live with someone for years and not know or, at least suspect, that sort of thing. It would have gone against everything he believed and valued. Besides, you have nothing but someone else's word about that, and why hasn't that person told her parents or the police?"

Karen paused as if gathering her thoughts and asked another of the many questions which had formed in her mind during Sheila's chronicle.

"Something else which makes no sense at all is why you should take it upon yourself to seek revenge for a friend, no matter how close. You describe taking inordinate risks, going to such elaborate lengths to compromise a professional Psychologist, for God's sake, someone who makes his living observing and analyzing the behaviour of others. You would have me believe that you not only convinced him you were an older woman but enticed him to make sexual advances. Are you really expecting me to believe this?"

For some reason unknown to Sheila, she suddenly felt it extremely important that Karen Simpson believe her. Maybe, after having kept Operation Samantha to herself for so long, finally discharging herself of the responsibility of secrecy brought with it an intense need to be validated rather than be dismissed. This need drove her next comments.

"Mrs. Simpson, I understand that what I have told you is a shock, but I am telling you the truth. You sought me out and took me by surprise. Do you think I could have made up a story like that, one that accounts for all the facts you know, on the spur of the moment? You said yourself that I sounded genuinely upset on the phone and that I sounded like I believed what I'd told you. If that doesn't convince you, I have a tape of my meeting with your husb – "

Stopping abruptly, Sheila suddenly remembered the copy of the recording she had forgotten she'd given Simpson. *Oh shit, the police would probably have it now.* Having read so many crime mysteries, she knew she had served up evidence for voice analysis on a platter.

Reading Sheila's face after her aborted comment, Karen quickly zeroed in.

"What were you saying about a recording? Are you suggesting you recorded your meeting with Peter? I want to hear it if it exists. Why did you stop mid-sentence? You remembered something, didn't you? What was it?"

While rummaging in her book bag which was on the floor of the car by her feet, Sheila told Karen about the memory stick she had given Peter. Within seconds of exploring her book bag, she produced a small digital recorder.

Karen listened to the recording in its entirety, her husband's voice, and the girl's, using words which made clear the temptation and the suggested betrayal. He had stopped, it seemed true, but he had gone farther than Karen could have ever imagined. She had wanted to scream at the girl to turn it off, to make it go away, but she hadn't. She had been transfixed, hearing a man she trusted, thought she knew, speak from the grave. Now, she was reeling, feeling overwhelmed. She had lost a partner whom she'd loved dearly and wanted to spend the rest of her life loving, only to learn he was not who he appeared to be, but rather a weak man who was easily seduced, betraying and humiliating her. She was suddenly overcome with the need to be alone, to be rid of this messenger of destruction. Without reference to the recording, she put the car in gear, mumbling to Sheila that she would drop her off at her house if she would please provide directions.

Driving to the Munroe house, Karen's mind was flooded with thoughts, but as the minutes passed, these thoughts began to coalesce centred around her humiliation and the need to protect Solynn. She did not want Solynn to know about her father, to be subjected to the derision and teasing of peers when she got older. She thought about the position she, herself, enjoyed in the community, the social status, the reputation, and the advantages, most of which would be threatened if what she had just learned got out. As these notions passed in and out of consciousness, she realized how resilient she was, already into damage control. Then and there, Karen decided that she would not be the facilitator of her public humiliation, the catalyst for her daughter's disgrace. She would not be the one to further disseminate the information that she was now sorry that she had pursued.

Pulling up to the curb in front of the Munroe residence, the silence was broken by Sheila's thank you and a final apology.

"I'm so sorry."

Karen nodded acknowledgement. Grabbing her book bag, and reaching for the door handle, Sheila turned to push the door open when Karen spoke for the first time during the trip to the house. Her voice was calm, almost subdued.

"Sheila, I never want to see you again."

CHAPTER 35: EXORCISING DEMONS

Arthur woke with a start. A high-pitched loud mechanical sound was coming from the mouth of the small alley, a garbage truck hoisting a dumpster. He was lying on his back in a little recess in the alley wall with cardboard covering his body. He became aware that he was involuntarily shivering and feeling extremely cold. Attempting to move, and change his position, additional sensations were apparent. First, he was finding it extremely difficult to get his muscles to do what he wanted them to do. And second, he felt a powerful diffuse pain explode in his brain. The head pain he recognized, the punishing muscle stiffness was a new experience. There was sunlight, but he didn't have any idea of the time of day, or what day it was for that matter. He did, however, recognize the alley, he had been here before. With excruciating effort, he slowly sat up and removed the remaining cardboard covering the lower half of his body. It was then that he noticed that the fly of his pants was open and his genitalia exposed. Spontaneously, a memory came to him, that of a familiar black-haired woman. He assumed the usual exchange had taken place, a few tugs on his bottle in return for services rendered. As he feared, the slow migration of his right hand to the back pocket of his trousers confirmed that his wallet was missing. With difficulty, he zipped up his fly. Exerting concentrated effort, it took him a full five minutes to get himself into a standing position and walk from the alley. Did he have his car? If he did, where did he park it? No keys in his pocket, he wondered if they had been stolen along with his wallet. His mind was Swiss cheese, full of holes. He couldn't remember much of anything. Indistinct images or impressions, like that of the black-haired woman, cycled through his mind, providing little in the way of connections to what might have filled the past 24 hours of his life. At the point of giving up on his fruitless attempts to bring to mind anything which might give insight into where he'd been and what he had been doing for the past day, an image of Maggie pushing him, whispering to him, then running downstairs flashed in his mind. Stairs? Where? Then another image materialized, one which caused an intense throbbing in a brain floating in toxin.

***

Having completed the finishing touches on the church bulletin for the coming week, Sue set about printing the document in preparation for photocopying. In addition to preparing the bulletin, she had accompanied Jack on visits to two members of the congregation who were hospital-bound, and acted as a sounding board for Jack as he rehearsed his sermon for the up-coming service tomorrow. All done in one morning.

Remembering she had agreed to help clean out a long-neglected storage room in the manse today, she quickly slipped into her coat and made her way to the large two-story stone residence adjacent to the church. As she walked the pathway which connected the two buildings, she momentarily lost herself in a reverie about the men in her life, Daddy, Manning, Peter, and now, Jack Moore. She'd mourned the loss of her father, of course, and remained saddened by Manning distancing himself from her; however, Peter's sudden passing, while tragic, had provided her with an opportunity. She would fill the void in her life that he had so abruptly left by funnelling more of her energies into helping Jack, the new minister at her church only two months into his new assignment. Despite her feeling of well-being, and no matter how great the effort made to suppress it, she couldn't prevent the fear she felt that somehow Jack would also leave her. Associated with those thoughts was a feeling of panic and a desperate need to somehow prevent it from happening.

Finding the front door of the manse open as Jack had said she would, she entered and immediately ascended the dark oak stairway to the second floor where the storeroom was located. At the head of the stairs on the second floor, she found the Minister waiting there carrying a tea service on a tray along with a plate full of various dessert sweets.

"Hello, Sue. Right on time, I see. I thought we'd have a little tea and some goodies. It's such a nice winter day, I think we will be relatively comfortable in the sunroom at the front of the house."

Giving her no time to respond, he proceeded to walk, tray in hand, to the doorway leading to the small sunroom. Hesitating for a moment or two, Sue followed with a somewhat puzzled look on her face. She was, indeed, intrigued by the Minister's behaviour. In the time she had been volunteering, he had never done anything like this before. She hadn't expected it.

The sunroom was bright and, as good as its name, sunny. Furthermore, despite it being a January day, the temperature was reasonably pleasant. Two comfortable cushioned chairs with a small table between, on which the Minister set the tray, had been arranged in a manner which would allow their occupants to face one another. He motioned Sue to take one of the chairs to which she responded with a question.

"Reverend, I thought we were to go through the old storeroom today?"

With a smile, he took her coat with one hand and guided her to a chair with the other.

"I think we have known each other long enough now for you to call me Jack. Don't you think? As for the storeroom, it can wait. I would very much like for us to talk, to get to know each other better. Is that alright with you?"

Effectively giving her answer by taking a seat, she waited

while he poured the tea and offered her a square from the plate. Thanking him, she waited again and an uncomfortable silence gripped the sunny room. Finally, Jack, face flushed, apologetically explained.

"I'm sorry, Sue. I'm forty-two years old and I'm acting like a silly schoolboy, actually worse than a schoolboy. I'm not good at this, so I'll just be out with it. I like you, Sue, I'm attracted to you. I think you are a very kind person, a righteous person, someone I truly respect and admire. If you are willing, I'd like us to get to know one another better, to spend time together."

Sue couldn't believe what she was hearing. No man had ever spoken like this to her, had ever suggested the type of interest in her that the Rever...Jack had just done. Her heart was racing and she felt slightly faint, but she managed to respond in a way that could never be confused with playing hard-to-get.

"Oh, Jack, you are a sweet man! You've made me so very happy. I want to know all about you."

Forty-five minutes later, tea gone and only a few sweets left, Sue and Jack emerged from the sunroom having addressed numerous topics during their get-to-know-you conversation ...family, religion, politics, health, preferences, dreams, hopes and more. Sue had invited Jack to have dinner at her apartment the following night. He had accepted. Walking along the second floor landing to the head of the stairs on the way to the front door, they paused in front of an open doorway, the doorway to Jack's bedroom. They looked inside the room and then at one another and blushed in unison. Smiling, he took her hand in his and they walked on to the top of the stairway.

***

Later in the day, Sue sat in her apartment surrounded by religious figurines the eyes of which she was sure were gazing disapprovingly at her. She knew that was impossible, of course, but they served as reminders that she had betrayed her beliefs, her faith. She had wanted Jack to take her to his bed. She had wanted to fornicate out of wedlock. And to make things worse, she had wanted this with a man of the cloth. She would be the willing Jezebel in his fall from grace. Exacerbating her emotional turmoil was her inability to prevent feelings of lust from creeping into her awareness. It caused her no end of misery that she could not suppress such thoughts and emotions. She had eventually become so mentally fatigued in the effort that she had finally given herself over to her base desires … entertaining mental images of their nakedness, the anticipated feeling of Jack's body moulding to hers and the touch of his hands caressing her skin.

Sue sought sleep as a reprieve from her warring feelings and thoughts which were tearing her apart, causing her grasp on what was real to slip. However, even this escape eluded her, for she tossed and turned, and finally, she abruptly sat up in bed. Suddenly, she realized what she had known since leaving Jack's. *Yes, she is a sinner, lusting after a man, thinking unclean thoughts, but Jack, was the tempter, the Devil's helper. He needs to be punished!*

***

Sitting alone at the kitchen table in her home, Sheila continued to replay her encounter with Karen Simpson in her mind. Her mother, Betty, had run out to post additional job applications and Maggie was at a friend's studying. *More likely listening to music and gossiping* thought Sheila. The sudden appearance of the Simpson woman had been a shock but also a wake-up call. It had generated a realization of just how vulnerable she was. However cathartic spilling her guts to Karen Simpson might have been at the time, the euphoria had soon evaporated as second thoughts took a stranglehold in her mind, fuelled in particular by the last words Karen had uttered to her. "I never want to see you again." *What the hell? Does the woman blame me for her husband's behaviour? I'm not the one going around screwing young girls! More likely, she thinks I killed her husband. If that's the case, why not just ask me? Why say she never wants to see me again?* Sheila replayed the seconds after she disembarked from Karen's vehicle. They had looked at one another for a moment or two through the open passenger door before Karen had given a small nod of her head and turned to look through the windshield. Suddenly, it dawned on her. *That's it! She believes me! She doesn't want it to get out. She's saying that she is going to let it go.*

In another very important way, Sheila's experience with Karen Simpson was impacting her, but in a delayed fashion. Karen had brought into the full glare of reality the tragic fallout of her husband's death. Sheila's intense hatred of Peter Simpson, her obsessive drive to exact revenge, and, yes, her ego involvement in the challenge of pulling off Operation Samantha - she could hardly tolerate the name now - had effectively blinded her to the fact that innocent people would be hurt, traumatized. The full force of that realization was hitting her now.

On the other hand and from a purely selfish point of view, an unintended yet instructive consequence of Karen Simpson's unexpected appearance, thought Sheila, was her full appreciation of the fact that the police would eventually find her. With that advanced warning, she had some time to prepare.

At that moment, the kitchen door opened and Betty Munroe entered the room with a smile on her face and carrying the day's mail and newspaper. Shedding her coat and with excitement her face couldn't hide, she took a seat at the table across from her eldest daughter.

"Sheila, I have some wonderful news! I have a job interview. The job is for a Human Resources Officer position with the

Nova Scotia Power Corporation. You know my friend, Judy Morrison. Well, we met for coffee yesterday and I was telling her about the separation and the fact that I would need to get a job. She asked what I wanted to do and I told her that my degree and work experience was in the area of Human Resources. One thing led to another and she offered to ask her husband, who just happens to be the Director of Human Resources at NS Power, about any possibilities. Well, he called this afternoon and asked me to apply, and then he went on to set a time and date for an interview. I don't want to get my hopes too high, but this is so encouraging. As perhaps you can tell, I'm a bit excited."

Sheila expressed her happiness for her mother and they talked about the job prospect for a couple more minutes before the phone rang and Betty left the room to answer it. It was so good to see her mother happy. She deserved some joy given the little she'd had with Arthur for the past couple of years. Still smiling about her mother's animated announcement, her gaze fell on the newspaper her mother had left with the mail on the kitchen table. Her eyes were drawn to an article heading on the front page, 'Police Search School for Person-of-Interest'. Scanning the short article, words and phrases jumped out at her, 'unnamed source', 'Lillian Metcalfe High', 'possible connection to the murder of Dr. Peter Simpson', 'Simpson counselled students at the Teen Health Center housed in the school'. It dawned on Sheila just how short the time to prepare for the coming of the police would be. She also wondered if her mother would have any chance of being Nova Scotia Power's new Human Resources Officer once the police arrived on their doorstep.

***

"I'm glad you came to see me, Maggie. The last time we saw each other we seemed to have a misunderstanding. I thought you loved me as much as I love you. I thought you wanted our love to go to the next level. Maybe I misinterpreted the situation and upset you. I'm so sorry if I was the cause of any unhappiness you might have experienced. You are my special girl, you know, now and forever."

Maggie sat beside him on the sofa, her head buried in his chest and tucked under his chin. He held her gently with one arm around her shoulders, stroking her hair with the other hand.

After helping her mother with the groceries and confirming that her father had left, Maggie fled the house as quickly as she could and started walking aimlessly, thinking about the shit heap that was her life. *What a lovely world I live in. My parents separated and getting a divorce. I have a mother I am now dependent on who is unemployed. I have a father who is an alcoholic and a porn addict and I can't bear to think about his showing up in my bedroom. And to top it off, I have a gorgeous sister who is both prettier and smarter than me, and never makes a mistake. How can I compete with that? God, I need someone to talk to, but there's no one - well, maybe there is.*

She'd needed someone in whom to confide, someone who she knew would tell her things would be OK, someone who would make her feel valued and powerful. He'd picked her up as he had in the past, and they drove to a small, older home in the north end of the city. He'd only taken her here once before. At that time, he'd said it was the house of a friend he was checking on while the friend was on vacation. It had been here that it had happened, and now, she was back, voluntarily, and more than that, she wanted to be here …. with him.

She'd broken down in the car on the way to the house; deep, throbbing sobs racking her body. She'd fought to get her crying under control while he'd murmured sympathetically, asking what was wrong. By the time they'd arrived at their destination, the heaving sobs had abated, but her tear-stained face and red and puffy eyes remained as a testament to the emotional desperation she'd been feeling.

The sofa creaked as he stopped stroking her hair and tenderly cupped her chin with the fingers of his freed hand while slightly maneuvering his upper body so her face was tilted upward to his.

"You do know I love you, don't you, my beauty? Everything will be alright. I will always look after you. You know that."

Maggie gave a little smile. She wanted so much to have the reassurance he gave her, the approval, the admiration. She needed it … she needed him and his caring, desperately.

"That's right, my star. I love that dazzling smile."

Tilting his head forward, he kissed her on the forehead, and then on the mouth. She kissed him back. *He loves me and I need him and he wants me. I am his special girl. Everything will be alright.*

***

Sheila was glad Noah Baldwin had called. She needed a distraction, a bit of sanity in her life. Noah had been sweet about what movie to see. She'd known that he would have liked to have seen *Arcadian* or *Damaged*, but she just couldn't do fantasy or dark right now. Given her emotional state, she'd even have agreed to *Kung Fu Panda 4* if he'd suggested it. As it was, Noah had made the sacrifice and agreed to *Wicked Little Letters*. Over their pre-movie meal, a club sandwich for him and a Thai grilled beef salad for her, they chatted about school, their teachers, their classmates, their likes and dislikes and, eventually, the hot topic of the police invasion of Lillian Metcalfe came up. Noah had introduced the subject innocuously enough.

"The cops sure created a buzz when they came to the school, didn't they? All kinds of rumours are going around about why they were trying to find that girl. You know … the one whose picture they were showing everybody to see if anyone knew who she was. Some people think she was the one who killed that Psychologist, Simpson. Some think she didn't kill him herself but was an accomplice or a witness."

This was a conversation Sheila did not want to have, so she attempted to redirect the course of the exchange.

"Yeah, I heard the picture was really poor, didn't even show the girl's face. Listen, are you sure you're really OK with seeing *Wicked Little Letters?* I can't imagine it would be your first choice."

Noah smiled, putting his perfectly straight, very white teeth on display.

"Listen, I would watch *Kung Fu Panda 4* as long as it was with you. I know who the girl is."

Sheila had started to smile at the compliment Noah had just given her when the last thing he said hit the mark. Smile frozen, she took in his expression, his unflinching gaze as her eyes locked on his. *He knows!*

CHAPTER 36: HOW DO YOU LIKE ME NOW?

Saturday, January 27

Day 4 of the investigation was ushered in by a grey winter's day which, in turn, cast a kind of pall over the City which seemed shrouded in a persistent haze hanging in the still frigid air. It was cold but not snowing, leaving the streets and sidewalks clear except in front of those businesses and residential properties whose owners, good citizens all, never removed snow from the sidewalk. *Another City by-law never enforced. What was the point? Human beings are what they are,* thought Mickey. On the one hand, you have your citizens who complied because it was a rule and on the other, you have your citizens who didn't comply for the same reason.

Mickey was commencing a working weekend following a full Friday lost to the Simpson investigation due to commitments to other cases, primarily in the form of several hours of testimony on behalf of the prosecution. His irritability because of this was assuaged somewhat by Francine's request that he pick her up outside a Tim Horton's near the building in which she had her apartment. He hoped this would mean an extra large double, double and maybe something very unhealthy to eat. And there she was, waiting for him at the curb, holding two waxed paper cups in her hands as well as a small brown paper bag. Entering the car after he had reached over to open the passenger side door, she handed him his caffeine fix and the bag which contained a single banana chocolate chip muffin. *Ah, life had its moments.* Greetings were quickly exchanged, a brisk "good morning" on Francine's part and a small nod in return on Mickey's, muffin crumbs already escaping freely from his open-mouthed mastication.

Despite her greeting and remembering to provide caffeine

and sugar, he couldn't help observing once again how tired the young Detective Constable looked. Obviously, that "good night's sleep" she had claimed would see her right had not happened yet. He decided not to comment beyond judging the muffin which had just ended its short-lived existence. "Not bad."

Given the results of their interview with Karen Simpson and a call from an excited Henry DeLong, Mickey had decided to move the Investigative Team meeting, previously scheduled for 4:30 pm, up to 9 o'clock this morning.

"Frannie, after I regale our colleagues with highlights of our follow-up interview with Karen Simpson, I want you to tell them about Ida Williamson's little bombshell. We'll see what new information we have this morning to determine where we go from here; but there's one thing for sure, we need Karen Simpson to explain her apparent lie."

All members of the Team, save Terry Tremblatt, had assembled by the time Mickey and Francine arrived at SIR - 2. Walking to the head of the conference table, depositing his reports and notes on the surface in front of him, he unleashed his first salvo designed to light a fire under the Team.

"I hope you've got something for me this morning. We're into the fourth day and we have no one we can tie to what little evidence we have. I selected you because you're supposed to be the best. For Christ's sake, start producing to the level of your reputation. OK, what have you got for me regarding the canvass, George?"

George Garcia's face took on the tell-tale signs of a man who is royally pissed. Brow furrowed, eyes slightly squinting and mouth firmly set, he turned to his Investigative Team leader.

"Son of bitch, Mickey. You call us out like that and then you ask me to report first. Jesus Christ! We got fuck-all! Nothing shows on the CCTV footage taken from businesses along the route between the bus stop and the park. Marlene and I think we've probably gotten everything we can from the canvass, but we'll continue to expand the radius if you want. The administrator at Lillian Metcalfe High gave us full cooperation. We had access to all teachers, identified the students being seen by Simpson at the Teen Health Center, and interviewed all those students in the presence of their parents. Despite all that, we got nada. You know the picture of the 'park girl' we have is shit. Nobody could give us anything based on that. All due respect, given the legwork Stott and I have put in, I'm not impressed with the suggestion that we are not working hard or aren't smart enough."

At least one cage rattled thought Mickey.

"Thanks, George. I'll decide on the canvass perimeter after we've heard from everybody. Henry, you look like the cat that swallowed the canary. What have you got?"

Henry DeLong rose from his chair at the table and walked over to the small portable sound system he had brought into SIR-2 before the meeting convened. He offered a smug smile to his colleagues while reporting that he had unearthed only one person by the last name of Henning in the whole of Halifax Regional Municipality, but it belonged to a 63-year-old widower with the first name of Gunther. An expanded search had not yielded any better results leading him to conclude there was no one registered under the name Samantha Henning in or around Halifax.

Mickey stared at the young computer phenom.

"That can't be all! Jesus, what's with the smile? I thought you had something, for God's sake."

The words had barely escaped Mickey's mouth when Henry, without any preliminary introduction, pushed a key on his laptop and the room came alive with a dialogue between a woman, who introduces herself as Samantha, and a man, who the woman refers to as Dr. Simpson. No one in the room said a word as the dialogue went on for more than twenty minutes. When it stopped playing, all eyes fell on Henry from whom some explanation was anticipated. Now his smug grin was a broad smile.

"That, my colleagues, is what we call a result. Chalk one up for the DeLonginator. What you just heard is contained on a jump drive collected from the middle drawer of the desk in Simpson's office during the search by Forensics. How do you like me now, Boss?"

Mickey, captivated by what he had heard on the recording, broke out in a broad grin of his own.

"That, indeed, is a result. Assuming it is a genuine recording of a meeting between Samantha Henning and Simpson, what does it suggest? Anyone?"

A pregnant silence gripped the room before Marlene Stott, seated to Mickey's right, made an offering.

"I estimate the length of the recording to be twenty to twenty-five minutes long so it could not have been made at their meeting on Tuesday because witness information indicates that meeting was much shorter in length. Therefore, it might well be a recording of the first meeting to which Samantha Henning refers in her exchange with Sue Reynolds when arranging the follow-up appointment."

George Garcia followed on the heels of his partner.

"I was thinking about motive. Why make such a recording? We found no recording equipment in Simpson's offices so it doesn't appear that he records his sessions as part of his case histories. And why record that particular meeting? I think the content of the recording may give us a clue. Who does the content of the recording make most vulnerable? Rhetorical question, folks, the answer is Simpson. He appears to have stepped over the line ethically. I can't see that he would want this getting out. I'm thinking blackmail, Mickey."

Francine got into the act addressing Garcia's thoughts and building on them.

"OK, say the motive is blackmail, who is the blackmailer – Samantha Henning or a third party who recorded them? I think the answer may go back to what George asked – 'Why this particular session?' Since this is the only recording of its type found, it suggests this session was the focus. How many people outside the two involved in the session are likely to have known what the session would be about? I should think none, and I agree with George, it is highly unlikely Simpson would record it. That leaves little Miss Samantha as our blackmailer."

During the brain-storming session he had set in motion, Mickey had left his chair at the table and started making notes on the SIR-2's large whiteboard. He now paused.

"I like what I'm hearing. I agree that it seems unlikely that Simpson would record the session. However, it is still a possibility that he did. Knowing he would control the product, he could've thought he had time to decide what he wanted to do with it. Time to erase or destroy it, if that was his wish."

Henry DeLong had been sitting back and enjoying the positive energy his contribution to the investigation had generated. He now felt the need to join the discussion.

"True, Mickey. However, consider the fact that the recording is the product of a two-step process. What I mean is the session would first have to be recorded. Then, the recording would have to be copied on the jump drive. It would be one thing to simply record it for later reference before deciding what to do with it. However, taking the step to duplicate it suggests a decision had been made regarding the use of the recording. I think this argues against Simpson as the recorder unless we are missing some key information."

What was happening in the room right now is what drew

Mickey to major crime investigations. The pursuit and sharing of information, of facts, and the sorting and sifting of those facts using the combined analytic capabilities of a team are what did it for him. It was his drug. He loved the process, embraced the team methodology, and truly respected the members of the Team. Pausing to finish his whiteboard entry, Mickey walked back to the table to return to his chair.

"Good stuff. I'd like to leave that for a bit and move on with a report on our follow-up interview with Karen Simpson. And while I think of it, Henry, will you see if you can run down a separate recording of Simpson's voice so you can do a voice identification match with the male voice on the drive? I want to be sure it's his voice."

After Henry nodded his assent and committed to seeing what he could do, Mickey summarized the second Karen Simpson interview.

"Here are the highlights of the interview yesterday evening. Mrs. Simpson added some important details to her earlier statements. First, she informed us of another anonymous call, lasting only seconds, during which the caller said nothing. This was on the Thursday previous to the Saturday morning anonymous call. Second, with regard to the Saturday call she received, she remembers hearing the sound of a chainsaw in the background on the caller's end and associated it with the felling of a dead tree on the property of a neighbour across the street which was happening at about the same time. Third, she said that on two previous Saturdays, she had seen a tall girl or woman, five-six or taller, with long dark hair and wearing a long maroon-coloured coat, standing on the sidewalk across the street from the Simpsons' house. She said the girl may have been watching the house. Finally, Mrs. Simpson maintains that she and her husband had a strong marriage, that she had no reason to be concerned about her husband's fidelity, denied any possibility of an affair, and defended him vigorously concerning the MUN incident involving the co-ed."

Some chatter broke out among those gathered around the large conference table but no one asked a question. Consequently, Francine, fielding a nod from Mickey, took center stage.

"I would like to add a bit more to what Mickey just told you. We did a little good cop-bad cop during the interview with Karen Simpson and I quickly became persona non grata and was banished from the interview which Mickey continued on his own. I used the time to visit and talk with the neighbour across the street, Ida Williamson. I was checking for possible CCTV as part of the Williamson's security system. No luck there. However, it turns out she had also seen a young female of the same general description as given by Karen Simpson, on the sidewalk in front of her house. As fate would have it, while I was waiting for Mickey, Mrs. Williamson and I got to talking about this and that including a chat about Mrs. Williamson's role as a babysitter for the Simpson's daughter, Solynn. Mrs. Williamson enjoys doing this and has done it frequently in the past, including for a period between 6 and 8 o'clock on the night Peter Simpson was murdered. It seems Karen Simpson lied to us about her whereabouts that night during the first interview and did not correct that falsehood during the second."

Spontaneous conversation created a hum which filled SIR-2 while Francine paused to let the information she had just imparted find the mark. She felt a sudden flash of irritation when she saw Marlene Stott immediately raise her hand. She'd hoped to allow the Team a bit more time to consider the implication of Karen Simpson's lie before engaging in a give-and-take discussion. When she acknowledged Stott's hand, her tone clearly betrayed her annoyance.

"Yes, yes, what is it, Marlene?"

Marlene Stott must have heard it too because she slowly

lowered her hand while apologizing, although she wasn't sure for what.

"I'm sorry to interrupt, Francine, but I thought I should mention that the 'park girl's' name is Sheila Patricia Munroe."

The room became quiet immediately and remained silent. Anyone who had been engaged in activity, note-taking, texting, checking e-mail messages, or day-dreaming, stopped. Francine sat down. All eyes initially targeted Marlene Stott with some pairs shifting in Mickey's direction shortly thereafter. To say the least, Mickey was taken aback. At first, he thought she was joking, highly inappropriately, but quickly remembered that this was Marlene Stott, the straight-laced, nose-to-the-grindstone Detective Constable who was talking. Taking greater notice of the earnest expression, Mickey responded.

"Explain, Stott."

Marlene cleared her throat. She had taken some initiative that had paid off. She had considered the information they had gathered, and based on that had deduced and pursued a reasonable path of enquiry. She had nothing to be sorry for.

"Yes sir. I have been reading the interview reports from the Team members, listening to the reports given at our Team meetings and, like everyone else here, noted the frequency with which 'park girl' popped up. Given that Sue Reynolds, our only witness who saw her close up, said she thought the girl looked like an older adolescent, I got to thinking about that. I also considered that Dr. Simpson worked at Lillian Metcalfe's Teen Health Center and wondered if 'park girl' might be a student at the high school. I figured if she is, there would be a good chance that she would be pictured in their yearbook. I have a family member whose son is a senior at the school and obtained the most current edition from her. I arranged to meet Ms. Reynolds before the meeting this morning. I had her start with senior classes, grade 12 classes, with the instruction to consider the pictures of female students. She selected Sheila Patricia Munro within five minutes and claimed she was as certain as she could be that the picture she chose was of the girl she saw in Simpson's office on the day of his murder. I got back from Ms. Reynolds' residence just before the meeting so hadn't had a chance to tell anyone."

Unbelievable, thought Mickey. All this experience and training sitting around the table and the rookie fashions what could be a breakthrough in the case. *Why didn't I think of it? Why hadn't anyone else on the Team?* He took a glance around the table before addressing Marlene Stott.

"Well done, Detective. Have you the yearbook with you? I'd like to see the picture. We need to get the personal details of the girl."

Marlene fetched the yearbook from her briefcase and pushed it, open to the appropriate page which had a post-it marking it, along with a piece of paper, across the table toward Mickey.

"Yes sir. I have the yearbook right here. Me and Henry got the personal information you need before the meeting and it's written on this paper. Sheila is 18 years old and a grade 12 student at Lillian Metcalfe. She lives at 435 Dunromin Street with her parents, Arthur and Elizabeth Munroe, and a younger sister, Maggie, fifteen. Sheila is a strong student. She is a superior athlete, playing on a number of varsity teams. She's also heavy into drama. Not exactly a profile one would associate with a murderer, sir."

Mickey accepted the yearbook and paper and while looking closely at the picture, replied to Stott.

"Ah, Stott, murderers come in all forms, all ages, from all types of backgrounds. You can't dismiss anyone as a suspect because they don't fit your perception of how a murderer should present himself, or in this case, herself. By the way, it's 'Henry and I' not 'me and Henry'."

As he referenced the short list of assignment responsibilities he was about to distribute, Mickey could not help but smile to himself. He was unsure what he had seen in Marlene Stott which had caused him to ask for her assignment to the Investigative Team. Maybe it was simply that he saw something of himself in her when he first started as a cop. Perhaps he did see star potential in her but he couldn't, for the life of him, identify any of the signs that might have tipped him off. Or, maybe he had just been playing to his ego, the big man allowing a peon an opportunity to bask in the glow of his success as an investigator.

"OK, listen up everyone. Thanks to Detective Constable Stott, here, we have advanced this investigation considerably. We'll certainly follow the path she opened up. Henry, in addition to the sample for the voice analysis match for Peter Simpson, I want you to check the Simpson landline records for the first anonymous phone call Karen Simpson received on the Thursday, in the late afternoon. Also, see that some high-quality glossies from the yearbook picture of Sheila Munroe are made and give them to George and Marlene. George, you and Marlene show the picture to Karen Simpson, her neighbour, Ida Williamson, and all the witnesses you identified on the canvass who said they had seen 'park girl'. You know, the hairdressers and the employees of the businesses near the park. Make sure the picture is one in a line-up of six."

At this point, Mickey took a break to acknowledge Henry DeLong's hand which had been raised since he'd given him his assignment. By doing so, he learned that Henry had already checked the Simpson phone records for Thursday and had identified the call in question. Like the threatening call, it could not be linked to a registered user.

"OK, Henry. Moving on then, Francine and I will be interviewing both Karen Simpson and Sheila Munroe as soon as possible. Francine, please arrange a time with Karen

Simpson for later on today. I think we can leave the Munroe interview until Monday."

Hearing her name mentioned, Francine looked up as she closed the door to SIR-2 after taking a message from one of the secretaries attached to Special Investigations.

"That was a message from the front desk, Mickey. It would seem that I don't need to arrange a meeting with Karen Simpson. She's at the front desk now asking to talk to you."

Immediately gathering the materials he'd brought to the meeting from the tabletop in front of him, Mickey precipitously adjourned the meeting after setting the time for the next one at 9:00 am on Monday.

"Francine, please escort Mrs. Simpson to our office and bring your notebook."

CHAPTER 37: SETTING THE RECORD STRAIGHT

By the time an extra chair, Karen Simpson, Mickey and Francine were all squeezed into the office that the two detectives shared, there was little room to move. Unknown to the two detectives, the confining nature of the enclosure was already causing Karen Simpson to question the wisdom of coming to HRPD HQ for this meeting. So closely were they seated to one another that any one of them could have reached out and touched any of the others without leaving his or her chair. Mickey noticed Karen Simpson looking around the cramped space with a pained expression on her face - a look he took for mild disdain or contempt.

As he prepared to take his seat, he further noted that Karen looked tired and drawn, but beautiful. It had always amazed him how vulnerability somehow enhanced the attractiveness of some women while detracting from the appeal of others. She had her hair scooped up on her head in some kind of swirl and fastened there with a decorative clip. When she shed her full-length black leather coat, elasticized black leggings and a snug pink knit sweater showed off her figure to advantage. She had accessorized with silver hoop earrings and a matching thin silver chain around her neck. Mickey could smell her perfume, something expensive no doubt. He recognized that any advantage the confined quarters afforded him might be lost by the intimidating effect that this beautiful woman had on him at this moment. He cursed the limitations of the male gender.

"I'm glad to see you, Mrs. Simpson. There are more follow-up questions I need to ask so it is very convenient for us that you visited today. But you wanted to talk to me, didn't you? What's on your mind?"

Taking a sip from the bottle of Perrier mineral water she had brought with her, the reason she gave for declining Francine's offer of a beverage, Karen looked directly at Mickey and during the next few minutes her gaze didn't waver.

"Detective Sergeant, I'm afraid I wasn't completely forthright with you and Detective Constable Deveaux about my whereabouts on the night Peter died. I'm ashamed of myself for misleading you and I want to correct my misinformation and explain why I didn't tell you the truth in the first place."

Mickey nodded his head to let her know that he was listening, and Karen continued after taking another small sip from her bottle.

"I told you I was home all night on Tuesday, but the fact is that I asked Ida to come in to stay with Solynn and I left the house for a while, roughly between 6 and 8 o'clock. I didn't tell you this before because I was embarrassed and ashamed to admit the reason I left the house. I'm afraid that reason had to do with the doubts that anonymous phone call had created in my mind. My imagination had gone wild and I was thinking all kinds of thoughts of my husband with another woman. It was an intrusive obsession, an unrealistic fear I realize now, but one I acted on. After Ida came to look after Solynn at about 6:00, I drove to Peter's office to see if he was there. Seeing his car parked in the lot and no other car, I recognized that I was being silly, a fool, and drove away after deciding not to go into the office to see him. I hadn't had any supper because I had been waiting to eat with Peter when he got home, so I decided to go to a restaurant - Faubert's on Carlisle Avenue. After that, I picked up a couple of items from the Shoppers Drug Mart in the Kingston Heights Mall and drove home, arriving just before 8:00. I am sorry about not telling you this earlier. I hope I haven't caused you any problems."

Leaning forward in his chair slightly, putting his face that much closer to Karen Simpson's, some thoughts tumbled in Mickey's mind. As he'd listened to Karen's explanation, he appreciated that she was, at the same time, providing a motive for murdering her husband while serving up an alibi of sorts to suggest she didn't kill him.

"Mrs. Simpson, your failure to be upfront with us from the beginning has resulted in a delay in dealing with certain matters that could have been cleared up well before now. Fortunately, I don't believe this has compromised the investigation in any significant manner, but I'm sure you can appreciate that withholding information, and in your case, lying to investigators, is a very serious matter. Although I in no way condone your procrastination, shall we call it, I'm glad you decided to come to us with the truth. You understand you have suggested a motive for murder, and you put yourself at the scene near the time of the murder. We will need to check with Faubert's and the drugstore. Are you able to tell us the names of anyone who may have seen you at either establishment?"

Rummaging in her purse, Karen retrieved two slips of paper and handed them to Mickey.

"These are the receipts, one for the meal and the second for the items at Shoppers Drug Mart. They are dated and time-stamped. They know me at Faubert's, so I would imagine you will have no problem confirming I was there. You will note that the waiter's first name is printed on the receipt. I'm sure he will remember me. I am less certain about the clerk at the drugstore. It was a young man with dark hair. But I did use my Visa card for payment."

Taking the receipts, Mickey thanked her and emphasized that everything she had told them would have to be checked out and confirmed. He paused, thinking to himself how slick this woman was - beauty and brains. He strongly suspected she had found out that he had learned of her lie, and what he had just witnessed was Karen Simpson engaged in very effective damage control. Now, he leaned back in his chair, a signal of a relaxation in the interview he hoped would cause a commensurate lowering of Karen's guard.

"What else haven't you told us, Mrs. Simpson?"

There it was, that little hesitation and flicker of the eyes. Mickey saw it. *She is going to lie again.*

"I've told you everything, Detective, everything I can think of. If I think of anything else, I'll get in touch."

Giving her no time for recovery, Mickey immediately posed the next question.

"Did you kill your husband, Mrs. Simpson?"

No hesitation or flicker this time, but surprisingly less expression of indignation than he thought appropriate.

"No, I did not."

CHAPTER 38: FAUBERT'S

T he temperature had taken a further downturn over the past couple of hours, producing the kind of frigid air which hurts your lungs with each breath in and produces huge plumes of vapour with every breath out. Another climatic condition had asserted itself as well. Adding to the discomfort such days bring to those who venture outside was a steady wind from the northeast which had been absent earlier in the morning, and which now seemed intent on tearing at any exposed flesh while penetrating the most robust of overcoats. Mickey and Francine had just run this icy gauntlet after leaving Police Headquarters following the interview with Karen Simpson. Coats drawn tightly around their necks, they swiftly entered the unmarked police sedan. The car's engine, subject to the elements all night, turned over, but not without complaint. Car idling, Mickey's suggestion that they flip a coin to see who scraped the frost from the vehicle's windows was met with a you-must-be-kidding stare from Francine. In response to his complaint that the feminists' demand for equality between the sexes was rather selective, came an unfeminine retort about stopping his whining and getting busy with the scraper.

Both heater and fan dials in the car's dashboard turned to the maximum, Francine was driving toward their first destination, Faubert's on Carlisle. Since it was not much out of their way, Mickey thought it an expeditious use of time to first stop off at the restaurant to check with the employees about Karen Simpson's claims of having been there on Tuesday evening. Francine had called ahead to make arrangements and found out that both the waiter, whose name was on the receipt Karen had given them, and the maître d' were both in-house this morning. Absentmindedly, she'd also put in a call to

Lillian Metcalfe High to organize the Sheila Munroe interview. A recorded message had informed her that the school was closed until Monday. *Of course, it's Saturday! Only suckers like her were working weekends.* Deciding she would keep this little lapse in concentration to herself, she made a note to call the school early Monday morning to set up the interview.

Mickey had never been a patron of Faubert's. However, he knew it to be an up-scale establishment, a restaurant where the chef's name was publicized along with an accompanying biography; where the size of entrées were served as artistic offerings meant for dwarfs; and, where astronomical prices were charged for the pleasure of being able to say that one had dined at Faubert's. Having parked nearby, they were now climbing the three carpeted concrete steps leading to the full-glass front doors of the bistro. Not open to the public for breakfast, the doors were locked, but before Mickey could knock, a thin man of medium height with greying black hair and dressed in jeans and a black crew neck sweater unlocked the doors to admit them.

"Good morning. You must be Detective Constable Deveaux. I'm Rene d'Entremont, Faubert's maître d', we spoke on the telephone. Please come into the main dining area. Mason, the waiter who served Mrs. Simpson, is waiting for us there."

After Mickey's introduction to the maître d', both detectives produced identification for d'Entremont's perusal and then followed as he led. Surveying the dining room as they entered, Mickey took in the subdued lighting with a unique frosted glass fixture specific to each table, the solid wood dining tables and chairs, the fine linen table cloths, the silver serviette holders, the heavy silverware settings, and the fresh flowers everywhere. What he saw told him that, as a paying customer, it would cost him a day's salary just to breathe the air in this room. He noted a young man, dressed in formal black waiter's attire, seated at one of the tables drinking coffee.

Introductions were made once again as everyone was seated and Francine took the lead.

"Thank you both for speaking with us. When I called you earlier this morning, Mr. d'Entremont, you were able to confirm that Mrs. Karen Simpson did dine at Faubert's on Tuesday evening past and that Mason was the waiter who served her. The receipt from Faubert's that Mrs. Simpson provided us is time-stamped for 7:28 pm. So we know when she left. At what time did she arrive?"

The maître d' looked at his young waiter before speaking and then proceeded to answer.

"Mason and I talked about this before you arrived. Our best estimate and that's all it can be, of course, because we had no reason to check for the exact time she arrived, is around 6:20 pm, maybe a bit later. That's the best we can do."

Mickey had been sitting there thinking about the approach he was going to take with the upcoming interview with Sheila Munroe when the part of his brain that was still monitoring d'Entremont's voice started sounding an alert. Abandoning his thoughts of the interview to come, he fully focused on the one at hand. Before he could ask the question, he heard Francine ask it for him.

"I assume Mrs. Simpson had a reservation. It's my understanding that dining at Faubert's is by reservation only."

Looking at Francine with an expression that suggested a hint of arrogance, d'Entremont proceeded to educate one who wasn't of Faubert's world.

"Yes, of course, that's true. Faubert's does not accept walk-in custom. However, as you can appreciate, there are certain exceptions, clients whose patronage Faubert's holds very dear. These clients are welcomed without reservation. Mrs. Simpson and her husband are among that very small group. So, in answer to your question, Mrs. Simpson did not have a reservation."

Connard, thought Francine, before asking her next question.

"How did Mrs. Simpson seem? Was there anything about her behaviour that caught your attention, anything out of the ordinary or unusual?"

For the first time, Mason made as if to speak, only to be cut off by d'Entremont.

"Sorry, Mason, I just wanted to say that I did notice one small thing. Her attire was not the usual for Mrs. Simpson. She was wearing cord slacks, a checked shirt with a V-neck sweater and ballerina-style flats for shoes. Although Mrs. Simpson is a woman who can wear anything and look absolutely stunning, she is usually dressed immaculately in a style in keeping with the clientele of Faubert's when she dines with us. I'm sure you know what I mean. Mason, did you notice anything?"

Now permitted to respond, the young waiter reported also noticing that Karen Simpson was dressed down and added another observation.

"She seemed a bit preoccupied. I had to approach her table a couple of times to ask if she was ready to order. She hadn't even opened the menu on both occasions. She finally asked my opinion on a selection but didn't seem to hear me when I made one. She seemed a bit into herself, you know what I'm saying?"

***

The weather had not improved during the time Mickey and Francine had been in Faubert's. It remained extremely cold with wind chill temperatures now approaching minus 27 degrees Celsius. It was the kind of cold which caused a crunching sound when boots came into contact with snow. Luckily, the car engine had not had time to cool significantly while they were in the restaurant, and within minutes much-welcomed heat was flowing from the car's interior vents.

Francine had been pensive for the first minutes of the drive back to HRPD headquarters, but now she vocalized her thoughts.

"I think everything we learned from d'Entremont and Mason supports what Karen Simpson told us. I think it helps to exclude her as a viable suspect in her husband's murder."

In response, Mickey posited another possibility.

"I hear you, but consider the fact that despite the timing of her appearances at Faubert's and the drugstore, Karen Simpson still had time to kill her husband, clean up the glass, dispose of it and then drive home. Granted, the timeline would be extremely tight, but I think she could have done it."

Shaking her head, Francine poured cold water on the scenario Mickey had just articulated.

"I don't know, Mickey. Do you think she could have impulsively caved in her husband's skull with a bottle, come to the realization he was dead, and then calmly cleaned up the glass and disposed of it on the way to Faubert's? Once there, she appears mildly distracted if anything, with no signs of the kind of distress and upset one might expect if she had just murdered her husband. That's extremely hard for me to accept."

Mickey remembered that he had made a similar argument regarding the probability of Sue Reynolds being the killer and Francine's consequent caution about downgrading or excluding suspects based on preconceived ideas. He felt that this was, perhaps, not the best time to bring that to his partner's attention.

CHAPTER 39: MOTHER WARRIOR

Monday morning, January 29

Francine navigated the unmarked Impala into the visitors' parking area of Lillian Metcalfe High School. The school was a two-story, flat-roofed brick building housing almost 1,200 students enrolled in grades 10 through 12, the second largest school in the City. Despite the cold and the fact that classes were in session, Mickey noticed a couple of dozen or more adolescents, apparently students, hanging around the school premises, hovering in crooks and crannies smoking, making out and, no doubt, conducting business in some instances. He couldn't imagine the reasoning behind forcing the enclosure of 1,200 hormone-hyped teenagers, whose approach to life and learning is encapsulated in the motto "I'll try anything once", in confined spaces for five to six hours a day. *Brilliant!* Making their way past even more students congregated just inside the front entranceway to the building, he heard a loud male voice refer to smelling pork as they passed. *Another anonymous rebel entertains the herd.*

The administration offices of the school were a short walk from the front entrance just off a large atrium featuring natural light from a prominent glass dome in the ceiling and a central botanical display. Mickey wondered why the kids hanging around the front entrance, never mind those doing God knows what outside, hadn't been dispersed since they were in plain sight of anyone coming and going from the administrative area. He was able to answer his own question when he and Francine entered the door marked Administration off the entrance lobby. It was over-run with students waiting for two harried receptionists to answer questions, provide materials and literature or shunt youngsters to a Principal and two Vice-Principals who were churning out one interview after another. These people couldn't come up for air in here, let alone check the front entranceway for malingerers. He could see that the visit he and Francine were paying was going to cause a bottleneck with a dominos-like effect. He chuckled to himself when he realized he didn't give a damn.

Seated in Principal Richard Foreman's office, introductions made and identifications exhibited, Mickey addressed the Principal and a Guidance Counsellor who had been asked to be present by Foreman. Apparently, the Counsellor was on hand in his capacity as a student support professional and someone who might be better equipped to answer certain questions. Neither Mickey nor Francine objected to his presence although Mickey could not see its purpose.

"Mr. Foreman, we appreciate your cooperation in this matter. As you know, we have been seeking to identify an older female adolescent or young woman who we feel may be able to help us with our enquiries into the murder of Dr. Peter Simpson. Detectives Garcia and Stott, whom you met a day or two ago, were here for that purpose. Since that time, however, we have obtained further information allowing us to identify the female in question as Sheila Patricia Munroe, a grade 12 student here at Lillian Metcalfe. Based on this identification, Detective Constable Deveaux made the call to you earlier this morning to confirm that Sheila Munroe was in attendance and to arrange for the use of an office or room in the school which afforded some privacy to interview Miss Munroe with her mother present. In addition, Detective Constable Deveaux called Sheila's mother asking her to meet us here."

Despite the nod of understanding, the professional bearing, and the solemn expression on Foreman's face, Mickey knew the man was itching to know all the details. That was not going to happen, and Richard Foreman's ensuing remarks suggested he knew as much.

"Sheila's mother has arrived already and we made her comfortable in a small board room behind the admin area here. You can use that room for your meeting and you will not be disturbed there. There is coffee and tea, water and some doughnuts laid out for you. Help yourselves as you wish. No message should be read into the fact that we are offering doughnuts as part of the refreshments."

Foremen paused momentarily waiting for the detectives to acknowledge his little joke at their expense. Quickly reading their faces and realizing he would not get it, he moved on.

"Once you are ready in the board room, we can send for Sheila to leave class and come to join you there. As Constable Deveaux instructed us by phone, we have not said anything to Sheila about your visit and will contact her teacher using the PA system asking only that Sheila be sent to the admin offices. Is there anything else you need?"

Mickey shook his head. He was about to thank Foreman once again for his assistance when the Guidance Counsellor, who had introduced himself as William Freeman, offered information he felt compelled to add.

"I'm not sure why you need to speak to Sheila and I don't expect to be told, but I do want to say that she is one of our top academic students, an elite student-athlete, and very active in extra-curricular activities, particularly drama. She is truly a student of whom we are proud."

Mickey thanked Freeman without a follow-up comment. He then asked Mr. Foremen to give him and Francine five minutes to chat with Mrs. Munroe before sending for Sheila.

***

Betty Munroe had been seated in Lillian Metcalfe's small board room for approximately fifteen minutes now. She was edgy, and nervous, and had been since receiving the phone call from a Detective Constable Deveaux an hour ago. The detective had said that she and her partner wanted to interview Sheila concerning a case they were investigating, that Sheila may have been a witness without realizing it and might have information which would be helpful to the investigation. She went on to invite Betty to be present during the interview, if it was convenient; and said that she was sorry about the short notice, but time was of the essence in the matter.

Looking around the room painted in light beige and decorated with posters containing pictures and quotes meant to inspire students and teachers alike, Betty tried to think positively, to avoid a feeling of impending doom from consuming her. She studied the poster images and read the slogans and quotes again. Her exploration of the room also included the small counter in one corner on which there was a coffee percolator with freshly made coffee, hot water and tea bags, bottled water, and a plate of assorted doughnuts. As her stomach had done when she first arrived and had been offered a beverage by a smiling receptionist, it started to flip again just thinking of food and drink. Quickly looking away, searching for other sources of distraction, Betty's attention was directed to the unusual table at which she was sitting. Unusual, that is, for a public school, for it had a large polished granite top supported on a wrought iron frame and legs. It looked very expensive, and a thought about tax dollars frivolously spent had just passed through her mind when she saw the commemorative plate indicating that the table had been donated by Toffer Granite Works to mark the opening of the school. Betty had started fantasizing about the people who might sit in the eight black office chairs arranged around the table when the door to the room opened and a young woman and a huge man walked through the doorway. Seating themselves directly across the table from her, the woman introduced herself as Detective Constable Deveaux, while referencing their earlier phone call, and her partner, Detective Sergeant MacKinnon. They each proffered their identification for inspection. Betty's gaze lingered on the male detective's face, a face that seemed menacing even when one would expect it to hold a neutral expression.

"Mrs. Munroe, as I mentioned on the phone, we are investigating a matter with which we believe Sheila might be able to help us. She may not know that she possesses information that might be of use to us. We will be asking her some questions that will enable us to determine if she can contribute to our investigation. She will be joining us in a few minutes at which time we can begin. Do you have any questions?"

The fact that the two people sitting in front of her were detectives was not lost on Betty. She was also cognizant of the fact that Deveaux had used a lot of words but told her virtually nothing about the "matter" being investigated.

"Yes, I have some questions. What is this all about? I mean what is this investigation about? I don't understand why you think my daughter might be able to help you?"

Betty thought she noted a hint of pity, or was it compassion, in the face of the young detective as she responded to her questions. That, plus the answers sent Betty's mind into a tumultuous tangle of thoughts of which she could make no sense and caused an intense wave of nausea. Betty knew she was panicking.

"It is a murder investigation, Mrs. Munroe. Witness reports place a young female, who we now believe to be Sheila, near the scene of the crime close to the estimated time of death. She may be a potential witness, someone who may have seen something or heard something that could help us. It is important that we speak with her for this reason."

Phrases penetrated the cognitive blizzard rendering Betty's reasoning temporarily paralytic – "murder investigation", "near the crime scene", "close to the estimated time of death".

Her heart started thumping and she felt her chest tighten. She recognized fear. From somewhere deep inside came a single thought, one which had been shared with her by her father on more than one occasion during her childhood: *When we feel threatened, we are all afraid. What separates success from failure in dealing with the threat is how one manages the fear.* That memory summoned the same strength and the same motivation she had felt as a child when old enough to understand her father's message. Her mind cleared, and her mental paralysis lifted. Returning the Detective's gaze, Betty cleared her throat and spoke in a voice that she only hoped sounded as determined as she meant it to be.

"Detective, is Sheila considered a suspect? Surely, you don't think she had anything to do with the murder?"

Using the same words she had witnessed Mickey use in past cases, words she had used herself a few times, Francine sought to calm Betty Munroe's fears.

"Our job is to follow up on all possible avenues of enquiry and this is just one of many. At this point, we don't know who committed the murder and we have no evidence suggesting Sheila was involved. We are seeking her assistance as a potential witness, someone who may have seen or heard something important."

A mother warrior now, Betty recognized a non-answer and pressed Francine with her next question.

"Detective Constable Deveaux, I ask again, is my daughter considered a suspect?"

Francine was aware that Betty Munroe was fully engaged and firing on all cylinders. She was intelligent, a mom responding with a sense of purpose and not amenable to the latitude that might be taken with someone who was less focused due to the unsettling impact of shock or upset. So, the Detective tried again.

"No, Sheila is not considered a suspect at this ti -."

Francine was interrupted by a light knock on the board room door, which was then opened by Richard Foreman who ushered Sheila Munroe into the room while introducing her. Upon seeing this, Betty Munroe stood up and walked toward her daughter while addressing first, the detectives, and then, her daughter.

"Detectives, this interview is over. You will not be questioning my daughter without a lawyer present. Sheila, you are coming home with me."

Before Betty Munroe uttered those words, Mickey had been about to suggest that Foreman had made a mistake and had summoned the wrong student. At first glance, he would not have recognized the girl who had walked into the room with the Principal as the subject of the yearbook photo he had seen, her appearance being so physically changed. Yet, something on closer examination, the height, build, eye colour or some combination perhaps, triggered recognition. As Betty Munroe started guiding her daughter toward the door, Mickey spoke to her for the first time.

"With all due respect, Mrs. Munroe, I think Sheila should make those decisions. Have no doubt, we will be interviewing her. We can do it here, in your home or down at police headquarters, with or without an attorney present. It is her choice. However, if you leave today without talking to us, we will have no option but to bring her into HQ for questioning. It's Sheila's call. I suggest we leave you and Sheila here to talk in private before making any decisions. Detective Constable Deveaux and I will wait outside until you have finished. Take your time."

Betty Munroe did not look in Mickey's direction, did not respond to his words, but simply steered Sheila past a stunned Richard Forman out of the room and out of the building. She felt sick to her stomach, a visceral reaction to her realization that her life continued to disintegrate.

***

Richard Foreman's mouth stood agape as he looked from the departing backs of one of his star pupils and her mother to the two police detectives sitting at the boardroom table. A period of silence stretched over several seconds with no one speaking. Then the Principal turned and exited the room closing the door quietly behind him.

The door closed, Mickey turned to Francine and asked for her impressions. She had worked with Mickey long enough to have anticipated the request. She was ready.

"The girl is trying to hide in plain sight. She's changed her appearance and done a pretty good job of it, I have to say. I'd guess she got wind of the visit George and Marlene and company made to the school, heard that they had a picture of a girl they were looking for. As for the Mom, she was taken totally off guard. Her reactions suggest to me that she had no idea what her daughter had been up to. She was initially stunned but recovered quickly, her concerns immediately centred on protecting Sheila. Betty Munroe is intelligent and articulate and has some knowledge of individual rights before the law. I am concerned that we lost the advantage of surprise here, Mickey. We let her mother waltz Sheila right out of here. We could have taken her in for questioning. We have enough evidence to have done that. What are you thinking?"

Listening to his young partner, his alter ego and devil's advocate, Mickey gave thought to her words before responding. He recognized that he had had a mild spike of anxiety in reaction to her comment about an advantage lost. Of course, he realized she was right, an advantage had been lost. They could have played hardball and marched Sheila out of the school, mother in tow, right into an interview room at Police Headquarters for questioning. That would have scared the shit out of both of them, but would also have cemented an adversarial relationship between parent and police, something he wanted to avoid if possible. From what he had seen of Betty Munroe, in those few minutes of interaction after being introduced, told him that scared shitless or not, she would function, stand her ground, and call upon every resource at her disposal to limit any perceived or actual harm which might befall her daughter. Mickey felt he needed Betty Munroe's help to get at Sheila's story because he knew she had a story to tell whether that be of a witness or a suspect. Corralling the anxiety, he replied making a concentrated effort not to sound defensive.

"Frannie, I'm thinking you're right about the advantage lost. But I'm also thinking that the mother might well be the key to any useful information we get from Sheila so I don't want her totally pissed off with us if it can be helped. Let's give them a few hours of breathing room, time for them to talk and see what happens after that. We'll follow up if we don't hear from them."

CHAPTER 40: ADVOCATE

Monday afternoon, January 29

Neither mother nor daughter spoke a word until they were safely in the family car and headed for home. They had exited the school swiftly, not stopping for school books and materials or to provide explanations. Betty was still in shock. She had been blindsided by what the police had told her. She knew enough to understand that her daughter's situation could be very serious. She also recognized that she was at a disadvantage. She needed an explanation from her daughter and she needed it right away. What worried her most was that, if there was an innocent, simple explanation for the police interest in Sheila, why had she made no mention of it? Betty knew something was being hidden from her. It had been on their way out of the Lillian Metcalfe parking lot that she finally spoke, seeking to get to the truth.

"What on earth is going on, Sheila? I need to know and I need to know now!"

Sheila had been using the silence before her mother spoke to deal with her thoughts. Despite not being dressed in uniforms, and before her mother referred to them as detectives, she had assumed the man and woman sitting in the boardroom were cops. She had told herself this day would come; it hadn't been a matter of 'if' but 'when'. She had fantasized about many possible scenarios comprising how the police would get to her. A school visit had been one of those scenarios so she felt she was as prepared as she could be when she had heard the PA request for her to come to the administration offices. What did not fit with the imagined circumstances of this particular scenario was the presence of her mother. That had truly surprised her, as did the fact that she was not led out of the school in handcuffs. The unimagined reality was that, despite having her in their sights, the cops had allowed her to be escorted out of the school by her mother. What did that mean? Turning to look at her mother driving, she could see she was very upset and frightened, so she knew that they had told her something bad, but what?

"Oh my God, Mom, I was going to ask you the same thing! I get called down to the office and taken to that room with you, and that man and woman are sitting there and then you jump up and take me right out of the school. You called them detectives. I can see you're freaked. What did they say? What did the guy mean about decisions I should make?"

In the expression on her mother's face, when she took her eyes off the road momentarily to turn toward her, Sheila saw both fury and desperation.

"Don't you dare play games with me, Sheila! Don't you dare lie to me! Those detectives as much as said you were a suspect in a murder case …. Jesus, Sheila, a suspect in a murder case! They said you were seen near the scene of the crime close to the estimated time of death! Oh God, I'm going to be sick! What is going on, for God's sake?"

As she listened to her mother, she was struck by how similar the actual information provided by the cops was to what she had imagined in one of her invented scenarios. She had not taken her eyes off her mother's face, the face of the woman she loved and admired, and she felt heartsick that the next words out of her mouth would be both cruel and painful.

"I won't lie to you, Mom. But to avoid that, I will not be able to answer your questions. I will need a lawyer and I will answer his questions. I will tell him everything. Please don't worry, Mom, it will all work out. I love you very much."

Battling the effects of what seemed like an electric shock which traversed the length of her body, Betty immediately, with arm and hand movements made difficult by the muscle weakness that had come over her, pulled the car to the curb and put it in park. Mother and daughter faced one another and after a few moments of silence, tears flowing down the cheeks of both, mother sought her daughter's hand and held on as if their very lives depended on it.

***

Betty Munroe scanned the room yet again. The walls were some sort of earth colour, perhaps a shade of very light brown, with several framed pictures of landscape scenes placed here and there. The receptionist had told her that one of the firm's partners was an amateur photographer and the pictures were a product of her work. They were rather good and, under different circumstances, Betty would have taken some time to examine them with greater care. As it was, she had been sitting in a soft black office chair, one of six in the waiting area adjacent to the receptionist's desk, for more than an hour now. Apart from the receptionist, she was the only person in the room. Sheila was just behind a closed office door some twenty feet from where Betty sat, telling Ms. Rosalind Lund, LL.B. something she couldn't bring herself to relate to her mother. Oh, she had tried to get her daughter to open up, telling her that she would always love and support her no matter what and that she would always be there for her. No manner of reasoning, cajoling or pressuring had moved Sheila to confide in her. Sheila had simply parried all Betty's efforts with responses which emphasized that she loved her mother and that she needed her mother to trust her, and to have confidence that she was doing the right thing. If only she could, but that would mean she would have to let go and trust in the unknown. That kind of trust had not rewarded Betty recently. She quickly reprimanded herself for thinking this way for this was Sheila, not sick and twisted Arthur. Looking at the closed office door, wishing she could be with her daughter, she took some solace in the fact that she had been able to arrange a consult with Rosalind Lund so quickly. The appointment had been scheduled less than five hours after the meeting at the high school with MacKinnon and Deveaux. About to begin another panoramic sweep of the room, Betty made an involuntary short gasping sound as the office door which had been the subject of her intense concentration opened.

****

Sheila had told the lawyer almost everything. In fact, after the preliminaries, including introductions and a short discussion of Ms. Lund's specialty area of practise, that being criminal law, and attorney-client privilege, the floodgates had opened. Sheila had engaged in a continuous monologue broken only occasionally by Rosalind Lund's clarifying questions. When she finally ended her story, she had covered Maggie's revelations, her revenge, planned and executed alone and in secrecy, and Peter Simpson's death and the subsequent police investigation that led them to her. Lund was a relatively short woman in her mid-forties with bottle-blonde hair cropped close to her head. This short hairstyle gave her an elfin appearance which somehow complemented her petite figure and sparkling blue eyes. She wore reading glasses which had alternated between being perched on the end of her nose and hanging from a silver chain around her neck. She had listened intently to Sheila's account, occasionally shaking her head and once she whispered the word "amazing". When it was apparent that Sheila had finished, and Rosalind had asked all the questions she was going to pose for the time being, the lawyer had instructed her client.

"Yes, you do need a lawyer, and yes, I will represent you. As your lawyer, I am directing you not to say anything to anybody. I do not care who it is, family member, friend, Guidance Counsellor, nobody. Understand? You and I are the only ones who know all the details of your account, your situation. I want it to stay that way. Are you clear on that? In particular, do not talk to the police. If they should contact you, direct them to me. I will let the police know that I will be representing you and tell them that they are to go through me to talk to you. However, they don't always play by the rules so if they should pick you up and take you to Police Headquarters to be interviewed, tell them you want your lawyer, but say nothing else. Here's my card with contact numbers. I will give one to your mother as well. You are my client so my obligation is to you in this matter, nobody else. I will follow your instructions not to divulge any of the information you have given me to your family, not even to your mother. I will arrange a meeting with the investigating officers as soon as possible to see what they have to say, and to try to determine what facts they have. At some point, it may be advantageous for you and me to meet with these officers; however, we'll cross that bridge, if and when necessary. Try not to worry Sheila, I've already started working on your behalf. OK, that's enough for today. I'll be in touch."

CHAPTER 41: WARRANT

Late afternoon, Monday, January 29

"I t's about time. I thought you had succumbed to the charms of Judge 'Don Juan' Davidson and the two of you were to be found in a cozy wine bar somewhere."

This was Mickey's greeting to Francine as she entered their office at Halifax Regional Police Department Headquarters at 4:30 pm waving a piece of paper. She gave him a crooked smile and rolled her eyes while responding to his taunt.

"Honest to God, Mickey, I'm going to have to write you up for blatant sexism. You think Davidson wants to get in my pants so you never fail to send me to make the case for a search warrant. Well, you're wrong. He's a nice old man who can't help drooling all over himself when near anything in a skirt. After all, he is male."

Francine handed the paper to her partner who quickly reviewed it. No sooner had he finished reading than he got up from his desk chair and moved to retrieve his coat from the coat rack.

"Excellent. The good Judge agreed that our argument for the need to search for the maroon coat, glass from the bottle, a copy of the recording and recording equipment was reasonable. Don't take your coat off, Frannie, we're going to execute this warrant right now. I have alerted George and Marlene and they are going to look after Lillian Metcalfe. The teaching staff may have gone home, but I called the Principal to ask that he be on stand-by subject to the approval of the warrant. Better to do it when school is not in session anyway. You and I are taking the Munroe home."

***

They both knew Maggie suspected something was amiss, she was not stupid and they were not so robotic that their acute anxiety and distress could be hidden from her successfully. However, Sheila and her mother had agreed that it was best not to divulge anything despite Maggie's questions and puzzled expressions when claims of everything being fine were made. Besides, Rosalind Lund had instructed them to tell no one, including family. Whereas she initially had thought that direction from her lawyer would be impossible to follow in her sister's case, Sheila was finding that her ability to stonewall Maggie was something she could do, and would do. That resolve was made moot with the sounding of the front door chimes of the Munroe dwelling. From her bedroom where she had spent most of the time since returning from the lawyer's office with her mother, she heard Maggie's muffled voice as she answered the door. Then another voice, male she thought, also muffled. She got up from her bed and walked to her bedroom door and opened it to hear the voices more clearly. Intelligible now, Maggie's raised voice, mid-sentence, sounded mildly alarmed.

"- bunch of cops here and they want to talk to you. Mom, can you hear me?"

A few seconds later, she heard her mother's voice sounding cautious, wary.

"Yes, what can I do for you?"

Next came a male voice in response, matter-of-fact, unemotional, sterile, one she thought she recognized.

"Mrs. Munroe, we are here to execute a search of the premises, the house, any outbuildings and the grounds. Here is the warrant for your information. We are a team of five officers. We will leave things as we found them to the degree that it's possible. For convenience, you might want to have any family members present congregate in one area of the house while the search is being conducted, or, if you'd prefer, you could leave the house until the search is finished. That's up to you, of course."

Given the sound of footsteps moving in multiple directions in the house, Sheila realized the search had begun even as her mother responded to the male voice.

"Have you cleared this with our lawyer, Rosalind Lund? Does she know what you're doing? Good Lord, what are you looking for anyway?"

Sheila did not hear clearly what the male voice said in response, something about not needing their lawyer's permission and that was about all. With a jolt it hit her, the second storage drive with her copy of the recording on it and the Hilroy scribbler with her surveillance notes, they were in her bedroom. She thanked God that she had returned the mini-digital recorder and wire microphone to Noah Baldwin. Using every ounce of willpower she had at her disposal, she blocked a numbing wave of panic from taking possession of her. With a presence of mind she did not know she possessed, she immediately located both items. She moved quickly knowing that a cop could enter her room at any minute. She slipped the drive into a small tear in the lining of her bra. Next, she placed the Hilroy notebook on her small desk along with her *Introduction to English Literature* text hurriedly writing 'English Literature – Poetry' on the notebook's front cover, and then opening it to the first blank page whereupon she started to compose a poem. She had the first couplet composed when a light knock and the announcement of "Police" preceded the opening of her bedroom door. A female officer entered first, stationing herself just inside the door, followed by the big detective she had seen at Lillian Metcalfe earlier in the day.

Mickey entered the bedroom, typically adolescent with a small wireless speaker with connectivity to her mobile phone, no doubt, and several posters featuring the Jonas Brothers and Taylor Swift. He prided himself on knowing who they were.

He invited Sheila Munroe to join her family in the kitchen if she wished while he searched her room. She declined, stating the need to complete a poetry assignment which was due tomorrow. Mickey would have much preferred the girl to be elsewhere while he searched but he felt he couldn't force her to vacate the bedroom. Despite his years of experience and training, he was embarrassed to have his hands, gloved though they were, sorting through panties, brassieres and other very personal items in full view of the female to whom they belonged. Despite his discomfort, he conducted a thorough search of wall hangings, shelves and books, closets and clothing, dresser draws, bags and purses, the bed and the area under it, vents, electrical fixtures, and the area under a small rug. While combing through the room, he asked, tongue in cheek, who her favourite artists were as if he couldn't tell by the posters surrounding him. In response, she simply gestured to the walls of her room. He then commented on her collection of crime mystery novels enquiring when she first acquired an interest in the genre. He went on to say that he had noticed that she had some titles by Scandinavian authors, and wasn't it great that translation of their works had allowed a broader exposure to their writing? Forty-five minutes later he was finished and, just before departing and taking the female officer with him, asked how the poem was coming along. In response, Sheila invited him to look at the scribbler page on which she was doing her composing and asked what he thought. She now had three stanzas completed. He read the poem-in-progress and complimented Sheila on her creative abilities which he suspected went well beyond poetry. Without further comment, he left as did the female constable and Sheila began to involuntarily shiver. She wondered if she might be having a seizure.

Unbeknownst to Sheila, Rosalind Lund had arrived at the house as the police were leaving with Sheila's maroon Hudson's Bay coat carefully placed in a plastic evidence bag.

The lawyer demanded to see the warrant authorizing the search, and after having read it, nodded her confirmation. She asked Betty if the police had given her a receipt for the coat to which Betty answered that they had. Rosalind had taken the opportunity to speak with the detectives on the front walkway outside the front door before they drove away. While conferring with the detectives, she noted the movement of the partially opened curtains of the house across the street and the overt gawking of the people outside on either side. It was obvious that the Munroes' neighbours had just been provided with some entertainment and fodder for gossip. She knew life would never be the same for the family, and if she had allowed herself time to acknowledge emotion, she probably would have felt sorry for them.

Back inside the Munroe residence, she was besieged by questions from Betty with Sheila and Maggie all ears looking on. *Was the search legal? Can they do that? Why did they take the coat? Why were they looking for an audio recorder and broken glass? What's that about?* Holding her hand up to stop the flow of interrogatives, Rosalind patiently addressed Betty's concerns to the degree her professional ethics would allow.

"The search was legal as was the removal of the coat. As they explained to you, they will return it to you in due course, meaning when they are finished with it. As for your other questions, I will not answer those because to do so would contravene my advice to my client who, I must remind you again, is Sheila, nobody else. I have instructed her not to say anything to anybody about what she told me about this case, and not to talk about anything related to the case at all. And that includes family members, friends, counsellors, ministers or priests, and certainly not the police. I can't emphasize this enough. If you are inclined to pressure Sheila to provide information, you will, in effect, be trying to get her to ignore the direction of her lawyer which will put her at risk. Am I clear about this?"

Pausing to receive a grudging acknowledgement from Betty and Maggie, the lawyer quickly moved on to the next item on her agenda.

"OK, I'm glad you both understand the need to support Sheila in this way. Now, since I'm here, I would like the opportunity to meet with Sheila privately. Is there a place in the house where we could be alone?"

Ten minutes later Sheila and Rosalind were ensconced in Sheila's bedroom with a tray containing a steaming teapot, cups and saucers, spoons, milk and sugar, and a small plate of sliced supermarket jam roll for which Betty apologized, but insisted they take with them anyway. Referring to papers she had taken from her leather attaché case, Rosalind opened their conversation.

"Sheila, I need to review the information you provided during our interview earlier today. First, I want to make sure the details are correct. Second, I want you to add anything I might have missed or anything you may have forgotten to tell me. Third, I will ask some clarifying questions and your answers will help with my understanding. OK?"

Taking Sheila's slight nod as an indication of her acknowledgement of the process and what it would entail, Rosalind proceeded.

"You told me that a chain of events was generated in response to a confidence shared by a person close to you, someone you will not name and who reported that she was sexually assaulted and raped by Peter Simpson. In response to what you were told by this person, you created and carried out a plan to lure Simpson into a compromising situation, one that involved sexual intimacy between the two of you. You did this to punish Simpson because the person who confided in you did not want the information shared with anybody including the authorities. To carry out your plan, you conducted preparatory surveillance on Simpson's office and his home. You then established a persona by the name of Samantha Henning, disguised and presented yourself to Simpson as Samantha Henning, an individual seeking therapy. You met with Simpson at his office twice. The first time, as Samantha Henning, you were successful at getting him to make sexual advances involving embracing and kissing you. No sexual intercourse took place. You were also successful at generating an audio recording of that meeting using a hidden mini-recorder and a wire microphone. That meeting was on Monday, January 22, shortly after 5:00 pm. You subsequently copied the recording on two storage drives, one of which you gave to Simpson during a second meeting the next day, Tuesday, January 23, again shortly after 5:00 pm. This time you came as yourself, not Samantha Henning, and you made several demands in return for your silence about Simpson's unethical, if not illegal, behaviour during your first encounter. None of those demands involved money for you. You estimated that this second meeting took thirty minutes or less. You left with the understanding that you would meet with Simpson again in two weeks to receive proof that he had acted on your demands. When you left, Simpson was alive. Is that essentially correct?"

Sheila had been listening intently and decided to add something she had neglected to mention in her initial meeting with the lawyer, that being the fact that Simpson had followed her home in his car on that Monday evening. Rosalind made a note of this before looking up from her notebook and into Sheila's eyes.

"This, my dear, is an incredible story. Don't get me wrong, I am not saying you're not being truthful with me but it just seems so unlikely that you, an 18-year-old high school student, would have the know-how and the moxie to pull this off. It would be a great help if there was any way you could confirm your story or at least some part of it."

After a pause during which Sheila appeared to be struggling with a decision she might make, she replied and included a question.

"It may be hard for you to believe but not for me. I'll admit I almost gave it up several times, thinking I was totally in over my head, but I got past it. I have a question. As my lawyer, if you come into possession of something, like evidence, that might make me seem guilty, do you have to give it to the cops?"

Rosalind made it clear that defence attorneys were under no such obligation. Even if evidence came into their possession that left no doubt of their client's guilt, it did not have to be turned over to the police or the prosecution voluntarily. The only circumstance under which an attorney is required to turn over such evidence is when the police seek specifically identified evidence from the attorney directly. Hearing that, Sheila fished her fingers down the neck of her sweatshirt, and after a few seconds of tugging and pulling, retrieved the storage drive she had hidden there. She handed this and the Hilroy notebook from her bedroom to Rosalind explaining what they were and how she had kept them from being discovered during the police search. Rosalind Lund silently accepted both items.

CHAPTER 42: A FOUL-SMELLING CREEK

Tuesday, January 30

It was 8:35 am and, much to his chagrin, Mickey was driving his own car, a dark blue 2022 Volkswagon Passat sedan to work. Mickey knew the Passat was the nicest car he would ever own and he treated it like the prized possession it was. The exterior was washed and waxed frequently in the summer, less so in winter. He used a special wax-based product designed to assist in retaining the richness of the colour of the interior surfaces of the vehicle. Vacuuming was a once-a-week ritual. The time and effort he devoted to keeping the Passat well-maintained and in pristine condition contrasted starkly with that he invested in housekeeping. Images most likely to be remembered by visitors to his apartment were those involving a kitchen sink full of dirty dishes crusted with the remnants of left-over food, layers of crumbs covering the floor and carpet, particularly around the sofa in front of the television, and the mountain of dirty laundry which never seemed to get smaller despite his best intentions. Seldom did he drive the Passat to work because he had convinced himself that, if he did, circumstances would conspire to require its use on the Job, and as a consequence, it would be damaged. Therefore, the fact that he was now driving his beloved car to work was not the best of omens in Mickey's mind.

Having arrived at HRPD Headquarters without incident, and then, parking as far away from other cars as possible, he took some heart from the fact that so far his Passat remained whole. Turning his attention to the task at hand, he called the Team meeting to order.

"Good morning, mes amis. This is the fourth Investigative Team meeting regarding the murder of Dr. Peter Simpson.

First of all, thanks to Henry, George and Marlene for their reports which were on my desk when I arrived this morning - my apologies for not having had time to read them yet. Your oral reporting to the Team will be virgin material to everyone including me. Let's start with you, Henry. Any luck with the identification of the voice on the jump drive being that of Simpson's?"

Slouched in a wheeled office chair, Henry used his feet to propel the chair closer to the table while assuming a more upright sitting posture. His attitude communicated that of an expert charged with a task that was mere child's play.

"Piece of cake, Boss. The internet coughed up a wealth of voice samples for Simpson - speaking engagements, educational seminars, and the like. Knowing how much you enjoy a discussion of the technical and the technological, let's just say there is better than a 95% probability that the voice on the drive is Simpson's."

Mickey smiled at the young tech-wizard.

"Excellent work, Henry. And I much appreciate your consideration of my sensibilities. It would be great to have the same match done with the female voice as well. I'm sure we will be talking with Miss Sheila Munroe again and we will attempt to get a recording to use for comparison. Alright, let's move on to George and Marlene. Give us an update on witness identification of Sheila Munroe's yearbook picture and the search at Lillian Metcalfe."

Garcia and Stott looked at one another and then George nodded to the Detective Constable.

"You take this, partner."

"About the picture identification of Sheila Munroe, we lifted a yearbook picture of Munroe and five other females of similar age, ethnicity and hair colour from that same yearbook. Thus, we presented a picture lineup of six head and shoulder shots as alternatives for each witness to consider in making their selection. We showed the lineup to the six witnesses - Karen Simpson, Ida Williamson, the two hairdressers and the two employees of businesses which have a sight line which takes in the park near the Simpson offices. We got a 50% hit rate. Ida Williamson and both of the hairdressers from the salon by the bus stop selected the picture of Munroe without hesitation. Karen Simpson said she was unsure, but when pressed, selected Munroe. One of the employees chose a picture other than Munroe's and the second employee told us she did not see the individual well enough to make any selection. As for the execution of the search warrant at Lillian Metcalfe, the warrant only included areas specific to the use of Sheila Munroe, for example, her locker and her desk. We found nothing specific to the warrant; however, we did find a small black carrying or overnight case in her locker - you know the kind of small case you might use for taking clothes and stuff for a short stay somewhere. It contained a short skirt, a V-neck sweater, push-up bra, pantyhose, high-heel shoes, a brush and comb, make-up and other hygiene supplies. I did wander down to the school's Audio-Visual Department and learned that the school does not have mini-digital recorders. That's it."

After thanking both Jack and Marlene for their efforts, he called upon Francine to share the results of the search of the Munroe residence including the confiscation of the full-length maroon-coloured coat. Upon the completion of her report, Mickey sought to summarize the Team's progress and set assignments going forward.

"Here's where I think we are. We now have a primary suspect, Sheila Munroe, to whom some specific circumstantial evidence points. She can be placed near the crime scene on the day of the murder possibly just an hour before the estimated time of death. There is evidence in the form of the recording on the jump drive found in Simpson's office that she had a relationship with the deceased, and we have speculated that the relationship may have been that of blackmailer and victim. Of course, this poses the question of why the blackmailer would murder her victim. We also have witness evidence that she may have been stalking Simpson, both at his office and his residence, in the days leading up to his death. She has made a credible attempt to change her appearance by altering her hairstyle and cosmetically making over her face. We suspect that this was in response to George and Marlene showing up at her school and flashing a picture of her around. The residence search has yielded a coat which closely resembles the one that witnesses remember the girl they saw wearing. In addition, she has lawyered up without even attempting to explain any of the things I have just mentioned. By the way, her lawyer is Rosalind Lund, the Scottish bulldog, so make sure you dot all your 'i's' and cross all your 't's' on this one.

"We also have Sue Reynolds and Karen Simpson, both of whom can't be eliminated as suspects. Reynolds' relationship with Simpson, as it was with a former boss of hers, Manning Mahoney, was odd. And I have the feeling Karen Simpson hasn't told us everything she knows about this case. We have no evidence from witnesses or forensics that places any of these suspects, or anyone else for that matter, at the scene of the crime at or around the time of death. We have found no weapon, or in this case, pieces of the weapon. We have no clear and compelling motive for any of the suspects, although you could speculate that Reynolds somehow felt rejected by Simpson, but we have no suggestion that was the case. And, if indeed that was her reason to kill, why had she not murdered Manning Mahoney when she was unceremoniously dismissed from her previous position? With Karen Simpson, the motive might have been related to suspicions that her husband was having an affair. However, we have no incontrovertible evidence he was having an affair, or that his wife would have had anything more than suspicions, if that. This brings us to Sheila Munroe who may have been attempting to blackmail

Simpson, but as I said previously, that's pure speculation at this point. So, where does this leave us?"

"Up a foul-smelling creek with no means of ambulation?" Henry DeLong, a smile on his face, impulsively quipped from his seat at the table.

A few pained smiles broke out on the faces of those assembled, but everyone appeared to understand that a critical point in the investigation had been reached and any sign of blatant frivolity was not appropriate. If the sheepish expression that had settled on Henry's face was any indication, even he got it, albeit belatedly. Mickey, his face a statement of the gravity of the situation, continued to address the Team.

"The question was rhetorical, Henry. I am going to tell you where it leaves us, and that is with much more slogging to be done. I suspect there is a very good chance that we will never find the murder weapon, or in this case, pieces of it. They have likely been discarded and by this time carted away by City Waste Disposal. That leaves us with obtaining a confession or providing the crown prosecutor with very convincing circumstantial evidence. I want us to renew our investigative efforts. I want a heavy push to see what we can add to what we have at present. To that end, here are your assignments. Marlene, I want you to arrange to have Sue Reynolds and Karen Simpson come in to look at the coat we found at the Simpson residence to see if they recognize it. Call me with the results when you have them. Henry, I want you to find out everything you can about Sheila Munroe. George, you identify Sheila Munroe's friends, and neighbours, as well as those of Karen Simpson and Sue Reynolds. Go see them, and see if you can flush out anything that might be helpful. As for Francine and I, we will be re-interviewing Karen Simpson and Sue Reynolds, as well as meeting with Sheila Munroe and her attorney later this morning. You may not be aware of this, but Peter Simpson's body was released yesterday morning and I understand the funeral is scheduled for tomorrow afternoon. Francine and I will be attending. Our next Team meeting will be the day after tomorrow at 9:00 am. I want you to have completed your assignments by then or have the most compelling reasons I've ever heard for why you haven't. George, you may be pressed to complete yours in time, so overtime is authorized and you can pull Francine and Stott in to help if you feel the need. Let's get going then. Good hunting."

CHAPTER 43: PUSH COMES TO SHOVE

Sheila and Rosalind Lund had been waiting in a small barren-looking interview room in HRPD Headquarters for almost thirty minutes now. Containing a grey metal table bolted to the floor as were the four metal chairs of the same colour arranged around it, the room had a light shade of pea green on the walls, but no wall hangings of any type. There was one window with security bars and the only other source of light was a single overhead fixture which was protected by a mesh screen made of metal. Sheila had noticed that the door to the room was very heavy, the side facing into the room covered with a sheet of metal, When it closed, it did so with a pronounced thud. She had seen enough cop shows on TV to know that the sizeable rectangular mirror covering a large part of one inside wall was a two-way mirror. She assumed eyes would be on her.

Sheila's mind drifted back to the prep session she'd had with Rosalind Lund prior to coming into this terrifying place. They had sat in Rosalind's office going over the details of Sheila's story again and again. She answered the lawyer's questions patiently even though she knew that many times the questions were about the same thing, just asked differently. She knew that Rosalind harboured suspicions that she was not telling her everything. More than once, the lawyer had emphasized the need for Sheila to be totally up front with her to avoid being blindsided by something important that Sheila had not told her. Concerning the interview about to take place, Rosalind had been adamant regarding her rules of client interview conduct.

Do not speak unless I give you permission. We will talk about what went on in the meeting afterwards. For us, the goal of the meeting is to find out as much as we can about the evidence they have which has led to their interest in you. For them, it is to intimidate you, us, to make you feel you have to explain, to convince you that it is in your best interest to tell them everything, to break you down. Sounds scary and it is. However, you'll be with me, someone who has been through it many, many times, so you don't have to worry. Simply say nothing, let me do the talking for you.

Rosalind's voice brought her back from the well-lit, expensively furnished and appointed interior of the lawyer's office to the depressive surroundings of the vomit-green room. In doing so, she caught just the last portion of what Rosalind was saying.

"…..delay in the start of the meeting is a calculated tactic. It's designed to heighten your anxiety, make you more edgy, and more likely to blurt out something you shouldn't. Try to relax, and let them play their little games. We will simply stick to our game plan. OK?"

Sheila was about to tell the lawyer that the "little games" were, indeed, increasing her stress and that she felt like she was ready to jump out of her skin when the door opened and the same detectives who she'd seen at her school walked in. The big guy spoke first.

"Sorry to keep you waiting Rosalind, Miss Munroe. We've met before but not been formally introduced. That's my fault. I'm Detective Sergeant MacKinnon and this is Detective Constable Deveaux. I want to thank you for meeting with us this morning. There are just a few things which we believe you can help us with. We'd like to exclude you from further consideration as a person of interest, and I think your answers to our questions will facilitate that."

Rosalind met Mickey's smile with a winning one of her own, and as Mickey and Francine took their seats at the table opposite the lawyer and her client, she took charge.

"Good morning, Mickey, Detective Constable Deveaux. Mickey, your hospitality has decidedly taken a turn for the worse. No refreshment has been offered, and making us wait half an hour, tut, tut. Just so you know, Mickey, I have instructed my client to say nothing. All questions are to be addressed to me. I assume you will be recording the session, which is fine, I like to perform. I would like to have a copy of the recording, of course."

Sheila's initial surprise and dismay at the fact that first names were being used by those who were supposed to be combatants was quickly erased by the way her lawyer took control and set the parameters for the meeting. With a pleasant smile, the man called Mickey continued his exchange with Rosalind.

"Setting the tone as usual I see, Rosalind. Look, we simply want to eliminate you from consideration in our enquiries, Miss Munroe. We can't do that without some explanations from you on a couple of issues. Those explanations may well assist us in the pursuit of Dr. Simpson's murderer. Had you ever met Dr. Simpson before his death?"

Her voice controlled but now more emphatic, more authoritative, Rosalind chided the Detective Sergeant.

"What part of 'all questions will be directed to me' did you not understand, Mickey? If this interview is to continue, you will honour that request from now on. Of course, my client knew Dr. Simpson, who didn't? The local media were all over him, quite a celebrity. Show me someone in Halifax who hadn't heard of him. Why do you ask that question, anyway?"

Realizing his error, but too late, Mickey replied too quickly.

"We have a witness statement indicating that Miss Munroe met with Dr. Simpson at his office. We'd simply like confirmation from her."

With a dismissive wave, Rosalind put an end to further consideration of the question.

"Come on, Detective Sergeant. My client is not going to confirm or deny what amounts to hearsay evidence from an anonymous source. Next question?"

And so it went for another fifteen minutes, with Mickey asking questions about the jump drive and why Sheila had recorded it, the stalking of Simpson at his office and home, and her presence at Simpson's office on the day of his murder. Answers to such questions included what amounted to the following evasive non-answers:

"My, my, now stalking is defined as my client walking past the Simpson residence and reading in the park across from his office, a very creative interpretation I must say."

"You have a recording, you say. If one exists and I'll take your word for it for now, what makes you believe my client recorded it? We are dismayed to hear that you have possession of such a thing. What is the world coming to?"

"My client is simply not going to comment on information provided by some unnamed source regarding her whereabouts at any time."

Anger born of frustration, something he commonly experienced when dealing with defence lawyers, and particularly with Rosalind Lund, Mickey abruptly ended the interview.

"Thank you for wasting our time, Counselor. I had hoped Miss Munroe could help nail a murderer; however, it appears that both of you are intent on protecting one. If you had no hand in this death, Miss Munroe, you need to talk to us. Right now it looks like you and your lawyer are focused on protecting you which, of course, gives rise to suspicions about you. Are you our murderer, Miss Munroe?"

With that Rosalind shot up from her chair and began donning her coat while addressing Mickey.

"That's enough. Are you charging my client? If not, we're outta here. No? I thought not. Come on, Sheila."

***

Light snow was falling as Rosalind drove Sheila back to her school to resume classes. Sheila felt her life had become surreal, one in which someone treated as a murder suspect was expected to function as a high school student as though everything was unchanged, normal. She couldn't see how it could be done. During the drive to Lillian Metcalfe, Rosalind had shared her take on the meeting with the detectives. She explained that they obviously did not have enough evidence to charge Sheila or they would have done so already. She had gone on to say that if they had nothing more incriminating than that suggested by their questions then she wasn't surprised that charges hadn't been brought. The lawyer's parting comment when Sheila was getting out of the car at the student drop-off area in front of Lillian Metcalfe was an instruction that Sheila conduct her life as normally as possible and continue to say nothing to anybody about the case. With that, she had driven off in her gold-coloured Lexus sedan with Sheila looking at the departing car and experiencing an overpowering feeling of being deserted. She had an urge to yell after Rosalind not to leave her. Momentarily, the car with its exhaust plume wafting in the air passed from her view. She turned and squinted through the falling snow at the large red brick facade of the high school. She wanted to walk away, run away, anywhere, but she didn't. Rather, she took in a deep breath of cold air, held her head erect and walked toward the front doors. She understood that she had made the decisions she had for the best of reasons, that she had created the challenge she faced, and that she was not going to run from that challenge.

***

She could see Maggie bearing down on her with a determined

look on her face. Sheila was eating her lunch, or rather poking at her food as it congealed on her plate, in the cafeteria. She hadn't been hungry, nor felt sociable when lunch break had been shepherded in by the customary buzzer. She'd paid little attention to what she chose to eat as she floated through the buffet queue. Carrying her tray, she'd shunned the company of her peers, preferring to sit at a table some distance from the animated throng of students trying desperately to impress each other. She looked at them for a minute and saw performing monkeys, engaging in silly, predictable behaviours with the expectation of eliciting equally silly, predictable responses. *God, how juvenile.* After she'd sat down, she had caught a glimpse of Noah Baldwin, sitting with some guys from his class, watching her. He'd started to stand up with tray in hand, preparing to carry it over to her table to join her she'd guessed but had thought better of it when Maggie stormed over to Sheila. He resumed his place with his peers.

Throwing herself into a chair opposite Sheila, Maggie went on the attack.

"OK, Sheila, what the fuck is going on? You and Mom have gone deaf and dumb on me since the cops searched our house. I have asked you both nicely what this is about and you act like it's some big secret that I can't be trusted with. I'm a member of this family, the three musketeers, you do remember that? Except, it seems that one of the musketeers is not a musketeer after all. You both seem to think I'm too stupid, too weak, too …. I don't know what … to be a real part of the family. And I don't care what that woman lawyer says, we're sisters, I would never do anything to hurt you or Mom. You have to know that, don't you?"

Maggie paused in her onslaught long enough to take a breath, but not long enough to allow Sheila to reply. Although the din of the cafeteria at lunchtime had absorbed her raised voice as a sponge would a drop of water, she lowered her voice, not much louder than a whisper now, as she continued.

"Look, Sheila, I'm getting worried. I'm not as big a moron as you and Mom seem to think I am."

Anticipating a protest from her sister, Maggie cut her off.

"No, no, let me finish! I have been putting together some of the things that have been going on and what they add up to is scaring the shit out of me. First, you start skipping school, no explanation that makes sense when I ask you about it, but you swear me to secrecy. Second, you're seen in the little park by Noah's friend, a park that just happens to be opposite Dr. Simpson's office. Third, the police turn up at school looking for a girl they want to question. They have a shitty picture of this girl that doesn't even show her face, but you know what it does show? The park! Noah told me it shows the park, for Christ's sake! That picture is of you, isn't it? The police were looking for you, and now they've found you, hence the search. What did you do, Sheila?"

Visually scanning the immediate area around the table for eavesdroppers, and feeling confident none were present, Sheila hissed at her little sister.

"Not here! Let's go to the storage room across from the janitor's office on the second floor so we won't be heard."

With that, they both stood, Sheila, heading for the garbage and recycling bins to dispose of her untouched meal, Maggie waiting for her. They, then, exited the cafeteria and ascended the stairs to the second floor on their way to an inner sanctum they had used for privacy before. Fortunately, the storage room conveniently housed surplus chairs in which they sat to continue their exchange. Sheila immediately addressed the comments of her sister.

"I didn't do anything wrong, Maggie. It is just a misunderstanding. The police have me confused with someone else. This will all go away once they realize they've made a mistake. Don't worry, everything will be OK"

It crossed Maggie's mind that her big sister was the second person to assure her that everything was going to be OK recently, but she wasn't accepting that answer from Sheila.

"I think that's bullshit, Sheila! Don't patronize me! I think I know what this is about and the guilt is driving me around the bend. All this, the skipping, the secrecy … the overnight bag on the day Dr. Simpson died …. What was that about? No, no, don't answer. I want to get this out. This all started after I told you what happened to me. Didn't it? Don't lie to me, Sheila. You became a vigilante for me, didn't you? Please, God, you didn't kill him, did you? Please say you didn't because he wasn't the one who hurt me! He was trying to help me!"

Maggie was crying, looking beseechingly at Sheila, seeking relief, while Sheila stared back at her sister in shock. She was having trouble making sense of what she had just heard. Everything she'd done, all that had consumed her for the past few weeks, and the risks she'd taken leading to the legal threat she now faced, were based on what Maggie had told her. She had presumed her sister, her Maggie, would not lie to her about something like that. *Why would she lie to me? Oh my God! What a god-damned awful fucking mess?*

Maggie, tearful and trembling slightly, could see by her sister's reaction that she had hit the mark, she had guessed what Sheila had been doing.

"I am so sorry, Sheila! I was so upset when I confided in you. The stuff I told you did happen, except it wasn't Dr. Simpson. It was someone else. You saw how upset I was. I couldn't hold it in. It just poured out of me. I shouldn't have said anything. I'm really, really sorry! But listen, I'm OK now. Honestly!"

Sheila could not believe what she was hearing.

"Maggie, I'm absolutely stunned. You're now saying you were not raped by Simpson – that you said it was Simpson just to get me off your back rather than tell me who it really was?"

Maggie, dabbing at her eyes with the cuffs of the sleeves of her top, started to nod her head in the affirmative, before answering.

"Yes …. well …. no! I wasn't raped, but I had sex but not with Dr. Simpson. That's what I'm saying. I know I am responsible for what is happening to you, and I want to help you as much as I can. I want to be on the inside with you and Mom, not on the outside. We'll make everything OK! You'll see!"

Emotionally, Sheila felt as if she had been run over by a truck. She had virtually put her life on hold for weeks, had mortgaged her future, at the very least, and forfeited it, at the worst. Yet, her response to her sister was unexpectedly subdued.

"Things will not be OK, ever again, Maggie."

***

Mickey was sitting at his desk in his office staring into space. He was so absorbed in his thoughts that he had not noticed Marlene Stott and Henry DeLong appear in the open doorway of the office. DeLong, in his cheeky, bordering-on-insubordination manner, broke through MacKinnon's trance-like state.

"There you have it, folks, our Team leader in full deductive splendour. And you wonder why he gets paid the big bucks."

Mickey quite enjoyed Henry's impertinence. He thought the young detective colourful and entertaining, even when Mickey was the target of his jibes. He responded to DeLong in kind.

"Henry, you do understand that many cops pounding a beat have backgrounds in computer science? Why, a good-looking lad like you, all decked out in uniform, would be a credit to the force, a source of feelings of security riding his bike through the downtown. You can ride a bike, can't you, DeLong? What do you two want anyway?"

Marlene took a step away from Henry for fear of contamination by association, while DeLong responded.

"Jesus, Mickey, do you always kill flies with an elephant gun? I'm not going to ask you to come out and play anymore. I wanted to tell you about a couple of interesting things I unearthed regarding Sheila Munroe. Her school attendance has been a bit spotty in the past few weeks - seems our Sheila has been bunking off classes from time to time. It is particularly noticeable because it is a change in pattern from her almost perfect attendance before this period. She had to carve out some time for stalking Simpson somewhere. Also, hot off the grapevine, Daddy Munroe, Arthur, is a heavy drinker which has cost him his job and his marriage it would appear. Arthur and Elizabeth have recently separated and he has moved out of the house. I'm still digging, but I thought you might like to know what I have found to date."

Nodding, Mickey thanked Henry and then raised his eyebrows in question as he looked toward Stott.

"I wanted to let you know that Karen Simpson was here to look at the coat taken from the Munroe residence, the one belonging to Sheila Munroe. She said that if it wasn't the same one, it was highly similar."

Waving a hand in acknowledgement of the information his Team members had provided him, Mickey slipped back to the inner thoughts that had occupied his attention before the interruption. Those thoughts caused him an uneasiness born of his experiences of the many murder cases he had investigated since moving to Homicide. Cumulatively, the understanding generated by such experiences told him they needed more to make a case that a Crown Attorney would be satisfied to take to trial. The cast of potential suspects was small, with one in particular shining like a beacon on a starless night, but how to make her shine brighter was the question. Possibly he was too close to the case, too committed to assumptions made, too set in the investigative paths presently being followed. He felt a need to step back and look again with new eyes. Decision made, he would devote the rest of the day to other case responsibilities, knock off early and have a drink or two before heading home for order-in pizza and a Toronto Raptors game on TV.

CHAPTER 44: FAREWELL, PETER

Wednesday, January 31

There was not enough seating available in the nave of Saint Matthew's. Every pew, including those in the balcony, was full and the overflow left people standing on both sides and at the back on the main floor. Some people had given up and left when they saw such overcrowded conditions, and now people were being turned away due to fire regulations. His first time in Saint Matthew's, Mickey marvelled at the architectural grandeur of the building. The nave was an enormous, airy, but cold room with a high vaulted ceiling supported by stone pillars strategically placed throughout. On both sides were expansive areas of stained glass windows, in red, yellow, green and blue, depicting various biblical scenes. The exterior sunlight made the glass come alive. Huge candelabra chandeliers hung from chains from the ceiling to offer interior lighting and lend the gold-framed portraits of significant religious personages hanging from the stone pillars an ethereal appearance. The large room boasted a wide central aisle and a concentration of pews on the stone-look floor tile which he calculated could accommodate four to five hundred people

Mickey once again thought how fortunate he was to have Francine as his partner. She had had the foresight to hustle him along to the funeral service well in advance of its commencement. One of her reasons for prodding Mickey into early arrival was evident in the mass of humanity now congregated inside the church. A second reason given was to allow them access to a prime location to better observe those attending the funeral to see if any unexpected "players" put in an appearance. They had chosen a position in the church foyer in order to have an unobstructed view of every person entering the church. Though both officers had noted Sue Reynolds' arrival, the knots of people entering together made it extremely difficult to track all faces. On several occasions, Mickey thought he recognized a face but couldn't identify a name or even where he had seen the person before. He was finding the whole undertaking frustrating. He was just about to suggest to Francine they give it up as a bad idea when he locked on another familiar face to which he could put no name or context. Francine's elbow gently jabbing him in the side announced that she wasn't having the same problem putting a name to the girl whose face he had just registered as somehow noteworthy. In response to Mickey's questioning expression, she whispered, "That's Maggie Munroe, Sheila's younger sister."

The service was longer than most funeral services Mickey had attended. This was due to the number of people who had been asked to speak during the observance, including the eulogist, a colleague and friend of Simpson's, the City's Mayor, and Karen Simpson, herself. The speakers used terms that put one in mind of the kind of tribute that might be offered for a famous statesman, a fabled physician or a well-known philanthropist. "A loss to the world community", "a clinician with a worldwide reputation", "a highly regarded expert in the field of abused children", "a respected academic with many peer-reviewed articles published", "a pillar of the community", and, of course, "dedicated husband and father" were just a few of the descriptions sprinkled through the speeches. Indeed, Simpson had seemed to have been a solid citizen, a credit to his family and his community. *Why then, did someone murder you?* Mickey wondered to himself. Standing at the back of the church during the ceremony allowed Francine and Mickey to exit the building just before the close of the service. Establishing a vantage point just beyond the front doors, they observed Karen Simpson accompanied by her parents and people Mickey assumed to be other family members follow the casket and walk out of the church and directly to Levinson Funeral Home limousines parked at the curb adjacent to the front doors. Media photographers, kept at a respectable distance by uniformed police, started taking pictures of the casket and the family with zoom-lensed cameras. Mickey gave a slight nod to Karen Simpson as her eyes briefly locked on his as she passed. She made no visible response.

People were pouring out of the church now and the detectives scanned the faces of the departing carefully, looking for one in particular. Mickey saw her first and tapped Francine on the shoulder while discreetly pointing toward the young teenager who had just come into view. As they had pre-arranged, Mickey watched as Francine walked through the milling crowd to catch up to the girl who was making her way down the sidewalk away from the church. She appeared to be unaccompanied. Head down, walking slowly, she seemed to be startled when Francine spoke after falling into step with her.

"Hi, Maggie, do you remember me? Detective Constable Deveaux? I was a bit surprised to see you at Dr. Simpson's funeral service. I didn't realize you knew him."

Maggie stopped walking, so abruptly that Francine had taken a step or two before she, too, halted her forward momentum.

"Yes, I know who you are. I saw you at the funeral with that big cop. Where is he anyway?"

Francine smiled and stepped back toward Maggie, who was still rooted to the spot where she had suddenly stopped and seemed to be looking around for Mickey.

"Oh, I decided to ditch him so I could say 'hi' to you. Did you know Dr. Simpson, Maggie? Is that why you came to his service?"

Maggie certainly seemed uncomfortable. Francine also noticed the young girl's hesitation before responding, as though considering what she should say. Then, as tears formed in the corner of her eyes and in a voice which cracked with emotion, Maggie answered in a whisper.

"I knew him … not well … I talked to him about, you know, being a Psychologist 'cause I was thinking about studying to be one, you know, at university… when I go. He was at the Health Center at the school. He was nice … once he gave me a ride downtown after school. I liked him."

Francine didn't have to be a psychologist or social worker to see that Peter Simpson's death was emotionally significant to Maggie. Maybe the loss of her father to a family break-up, as well as an apparent mentor whom she liked and trusted, had created the conditions for the sadness which appeared to be gripping the young teenager. She wanted to let Maggie know that she understood.

"I think I know how you feel, Maggie. It must be very hard to lose someone you look up to, like Dr. Simpson, and cope with your parents' separation at the same time. It would be confusing and painful for anybody."

At that point, two things happened so close in time that it would have been difficult to pinpoint which preceded the other. One was Francine's recognition of the momentary expression of weariness on Maggie's face, as if to say, *You don't know how I feel at all!* The other was an auditory experience, also Francine's, wherein she heard a voice, one she recognized, Rosalind Lund's.

"That will be all, Detective Constable. Maggie, please get in the car and I will take you home. Detective Constable, you know better than to question a minor without a parent or an assigned guardian present. You may expect a complaint to be filed."

Obediently, Maggie quickly moved to get into the back seat of the Lexus that had parked at the curb, the driver's side window rolled down. Without further word, that window closed as

Rosalind Lund immediately guided her car back into traffic and was gone.

CHAPTER 45: PROSECUTION SCORNED

By Wednesday afternoon, all recent actions Mickey had assigned to Team members had either been completed or were in the final stages of completion. More specifically, Marlene Stott had arranged for Sue Reynolds to look at Sheila Munroe's coat which Reynolds thought was very much like the one she saw Samantha Henning wearing as she left the office on the day Dr. Simpson was murdered. Henry DeLong's research, along with the interviews conducted with friends, neighbours and associates of Karen Simpson by George Garcia and Marlene Stott, produced background information that could only be described as untarnished, not even a ripple on the smooth surface of Karen's exemplary life. Some interesting details were unearthed about Sheila Munroe and Sue Reynolds, however. While the overwhelming feedback from their digging pronounced Sheila a bright student, well thought of by all those she had come in contact with, she had been "a bit wild" when she was younger said a couple of her friends, "dating older guys", "partying", and "drinking too much". These same friends had assured the detectives interviewing them that such behaviour was a thing of the past. Henry had added that Sheila had not come to the attention of law enforcement during her "period of rebellion". More significantly, however, George Garcia interviewed a male student and friend of Sheila's by the name of Noah Baldwin. Among other things, Baldwin, "whose interest in Sheila seemed more than that of a friend" said Garcia, had told him that he not only owned a mini-digital recorder but had loaned it to Sheila at her request during a period which made it the likely recorder she'd used with Simpson. That recorder was now in police possession and deemed an item of evidence.

Two neighbours living on the same floor in Sue Reynolds'

apartment complex described Sue as a quiet, almost reclusive, individual. They said they seldom saw her and that she had tended to shun any invitation extended to join them in recreational activities or social get-togethers. One of these neighbours, an older widow, said she had once asked Sue to go to a weekly bingo sponsored by her grandson's hockey team and Sue had gone "religious fundamentalist" on her, all but suggesting that the neighbour was a sinner, as was her grandson, for having anything to do with gambling. Another source of information was Sue's Minister whom George characterized as a "frustrated evangelist". Garcia stated that the clergyman's sermons were of the fire and brimstone variety with "a lot of 'hallelujahs' and 'praise the Lords' from a congregation of swaying bodies and uplifted arms". When asked, the Minister said that Sue was a "devout Christian, a righteous servant of the Lord". As a testament to his portrayal of Sue in this light, he had gone on to tell George that there wasn't a day that went by that Sue wasn't at the church doing something to "assist the Church's mission on this earth". Further questioning clarified what "assist the Church's mission" meant, and that was helping out with the administration of Church affairs, dealing with correspondence, organizing events, assuming volunteer roles in those events, accompanying the Minister on home and hospital visits, and participating in the Church's services as an assistant to the Minister. The Minister, unmarried, had high praise for "Sister Reynolds" for the way she had assisted him personally, aiding with the cleaning of the rectory, even attending to the cleaning, pressing and setting out of ecclesiastical garments for his use. When asked about Sue's remarkably high level of involvement in the affairs of the Church, he had reflected for a moment before saying it was somewhat unusual, but that over time he had come to see Ms. Reynolds as indispensable to his ministry. In response to the pressure of George's questioning, the Reverend admitted that Sue's "fervency" could sometimes "set her apart, make her appear a little extreme, a little unbending in the application of her faith". When asked how this translated into specific behaviour, he offered only that Sue expressed the strong conviction that sinners who would not mend their ways forfeit their right to walk among the righteous and made no concessions in expressing that view.

Further, the results of the third interviews which Mickey and Francine conducted with Karen Simpson and Sue Reynolds produced nothing that was not already known. And a silent Sheila Munroe remained every defence lawyer's ideal of the model client. Thus, Team members were left considering what they had gathered in the way of evidence to date and where that left them going forward. Following a painstaking period of information regurgitation, members concluded the obvious, that a host of circumstantial evidence pointed to Sheila Munroe but without clear motive and established opportunity. A further fly in the ointment was the lack of the murder weapon, unlikely to be found. Hence, it was decided that while the investigation continued, Mickey would take what they had to the Crown Attorney for consideration. For the first time since the Team was formed, Mickey gave no new assignments. Rather, he challenged each Team member to review everything they had done and had in the way of product - every interview, every search, both in the field and on the Web, the results of every telephone tip, and the reports that had been generated - to look for anything that might have been missed. It had happened before and Mickey hung on to the slim hope that it might prove to have occurred in this case as well.

***

Bernard Borgman, no one called him Bernie to his face, was a rotund Senior Crown Attorney. Some described him as obese, again not to his face. An arrogant, officious man who walked with a swagger, his pomposity had alienated many an investigating officer as well as countless victims of crime and their families. Married, many imagined his wife to be a long-suffering, submissive woman who must not only be blind, but in absolute denial regarding the man she married. Those who engaged in these speculations had not met Mrs. Borgman, a professor in Women's Studies at nearby Mount Saint Vincent University, and a feminist in every sense of the word. Bernard, despite his aura of self-importance in the Halls of Justice, was Bernie at home. Mrs. Borgman didn't suffer fools, especially male fools, lightly, and Bernie was no fool.

The fact that Mickey had drawn the Borgman straw didn't bother him in the least. With Borgman he knew he was getting the most experienced CA available, one with the best conviction record among his peers, and one on whose opinion, though sometimes delivered derisively, a lead investigator could rely. After passing muster at reception, he stood in front of Bernard's office door now, pausing to fortify himself for the Borgman experience before knocking. A deep cultivated voice bade him enter immediately upon his rapping on the door. The office was nothing special, not large, not especially well-appointed, the furniture was solid wood but ancient, the padding on the chairs worn and in need of replacing. Despite the old and faded appearance, the office was considered the best of the pickings at the downtown Halifax home of the Nova Scotia Public Prosecution Service. The fact that Bernard Borgman was its long-time occupant was a measure of both his longevity as a Crown Attorney and the respect he had among his colleagues at the NSCPS.

Borgman waved Mickey to a chair at a small wooden office table adjacent to the large antique which was his desk. There was a thick file folder already sitting on the table. As was his practice, the Crown Attorney had already thoroughly read and dissected the information contained in every document connected to the Simpson case. When he met with lead investigators, he was almost as familiar with their cases as they were. After seating himself in a chair that groaned with recognition, Borgman's first words formed a question.

"Detective Sergeant, tell me why you want me to waste the taxpayers' money prosecuting this case, that is, if you ever decide to charge anybody?"

Familiarity with the CA's manner and style told Mickey that no answer was required, so he let the silence that followed stretch. Borgman continued.

"For want of anyone who is a better fit, it seems you have an 18-year-old schoolgirl to whom you want to provide prime seating at a first-rate demonstration of criminal prosecution. A young lady who is not only highly intelligent, academically proficient and an accomplished athlete and school citizen, but one who, incidentally, you cannot place, either forensically or through witness report, at the scene of the crime when the reprehensible deed was done. Heaven forbid we should have a murder weapon. And, pray tell, where is the motive? Surely, it's not the cock-and-bull about blackmailing the victim? A wet-behind-the-ears Legal Aid rookie would shred such a proposition in less time than it would take to make the argument. I'm surprised, Detective Sergeant. I thought you better than this. There must be villains aplenty out there. Why don't you investigate one and provide me with a case which won't result in me being laughed out of court? Scoot now."

To himself, Mickey chuckled while thinking what a perfect prick Bernard was, a fat patronizing prick. However, that characterization of the offensive barrister never saw the light of day, while other of Mickey's words did.

"Your analysis of the case is essentially that of the Investigative Team's, Bernard. But here's the rub. Of course, we will continue to investigate, re-visiting what we have done to date, but I believe that there is every chance that at the end of the day, we may have no more than we do now. If that should be the case, if we can squeeze no more to the surface, would you consider trying the case as it is?"

A hint of annoyance crept into Borgman's facial expression, yet his voice retained a resonance and cadence which spoke of privilege and social standing.

"My, my, we have trouble taking 'no' for an answer, don't we? Let me put it in words that I'm sure you will understand. Your investigation is incomplete. It's 'shit' if you will. I have no intention of taking on a case that is DOA from the start. You can fuss and fume with the Chief if you choose but I think it highly unlikely she's going to make a contrary decision once she knows where I stand. Good day, Detective Sergeant, I'm a busy man with well-investigated cases to pursue."

It wasn't that Mickey couldn't "fuss and fume" with the best of them, rather it was that he knew the fat shit was right. The case was shaky, very shaky, and he was aware that the Chief Crown Attorney would never override a decision made by Bernard Borgman. Like a dog, he retreated with his tail between his legs, sufficiently chastened, but reasonably intact given a close encounter of the Borgman kind.

CHAPTER 46: IF I COULD TURN BACK TIME

Wednesday, January 31

Sheila had been unable to concentrate on anything other than her sister's astonishing disclosure. During her school classes, all she'd heard was background noise created by her teachers' efforts to provide insights into chemical formulae, French literature and differential equations. Their labours came up short in competition with the preoccupation generated by her inner turmoil. Her Chemistry teacher, Mrs. Broderick, had even asked her if she was feeling well.

What her sister had told her had laid bare the unimaginable - that the vengeance she had taken on her sister's behalf, the sister she had thought had been raped, had targeted an innocent man. Not only had she done it all for nothing, she had caused so much heartache for others – Karen Simpson and her little daughter, Solynn, and her own mother. *If only I could wish this away, or turn back the calendar! Oh God, if I could, I'd do it in a heartbeat!*

The last thing she remembered was the buzzer announcing an end to the school day before she found herself outside Lillian Metcalfe. She'd been so distracted that she couldn't recall how she got there. A familiar voice calling her name had brought her out of her stupor. Looking in the direction from which the voice had come, she saw Noah Baldwin standing at the end of the school walkway where it joined the street-side sidewalk. He was waiting for her to catch up to him. Upon seeing him, she felt her mood lift a little, and then a little more when he flashed that smile of his as she came up to him.

"Hey, Sheila, you looked lost in thought there. You OK?"

"Yeah, I'm fine, Noah. You know me, just daydreaming."

"Do you mind if I walk with you for a bit?"

Despite her feelings of acute anxiety and guilt, she couldn't help smiling at him. In his company, she felt the support she so desperately needed right now. She experienced a sudden desire for physical contact so she reached out and took his hand in hers. Hand in hand, they began to walk in the direction of the Munroe home. For a few minutes, they moved together in silence, seeming to be content to just be together. Finally, Noah broke the spell.

"Sheila, listen, I don't know if you've heard, but some rumours are starting to circulate, you know, about the cops being at your house yesterday. Some of them are wild. I'm not fishing for information or anything. I just wanted to let you know that I'm here if you need someone to talk to."

Sheila was a bit shocked to hear that word had gotten out already, but she had been reconciled to the fact that it was going to get out sometime. *Did it matter whether it was today or tomorrow or next week?* She'd just hoped to be able to float under the radar for a little longer. Now that that possibility had evaporated, she would have to ready herself to face all the questions, the finger-pointing and suspicions, and the gossip. With eyes cast downward, she tried to find a calm, take-it-all-in-stride tone as she lied to Noah.

"Thanks, Noah, I appreciate that. Yeah, the police were at the house. They were acting on some misinformation, but I think it is straightened out now."

"Good, I'm glad. But I'd still love to talk to you, anytime really."

They'd fallen back into another period of comfortable silence as they continued to stroll along the sidewalk. This time, Sheila ended the quietude.

"Noah, you knew that picture the cops showed you was of me. Did you tell them that? Did you tell them I borrowed your mini-recorder?"

Noah stopped in his tracks, and turning toward her, gave an anguished look.

"I'm sorry, Sheila. I did tell them you borrowed my recorder. They asked directly and I didn't want to lie to them. I didn't tell them that I thought it was you in the picture. To be honest, I wasn't sure it was you. You couldn't see a face. They asked me if I recognized the person in the picture, and I really couldn't recognize anybody from that picture. So, I wasn't lying. Are you in serious trouble, Sheila? I hope I didn't make it worse for you?"

Her eyes resumed their study of the ground as she lied to him once again.

"Of course not, Noah. Don't worry about it."

***

Despite the affection communicated by a kiss she and Noah had shared at the head of the driveway to her house before he departed, Sheila's mood quickly turned sour as she approached the back door. Her anger had been simmering under the cover of a diligent high school student during afternoon classes and an attentive girlfriend on her walk home with Noah. So when she entered her home and saw Maggie stuffing her face with grapes and flavoured yogurt at the kitchen table, it bubbled over. Remembering that her mother was at a job interview for the Human Resources position she'd applied for, she took the opportunity to reproach her sister.

"Maggie, you out and out lied to me. You have no idea what trouble you've caused. For God's sake, we're sisters! Why would you feel the need to lie?"

Maggie looked a bit like a deer caught in the headlights. After an extended pause, however, she reiterated her lunchtime explanation.

"I told you, Sheila. I was really, really upset when I confided in you. I wasn't thinking clearly. I shouldn't have said anything. I'm sorry. What can I say?"

Sheila determined not to be deflected, persisted.

"OK, Maggie, you were upset and not thinking clearly when you told me about being raped. Let's say I buy that, but what I don't understand is why you didn't, at least, tell me the truth later - that it wasn't Simpson. Why did you continue to let me think it was?"

Maggie was getting agitated by Sheila's persistence.

"There you go again saying it was rape. It wasn't rape! I wasn't forced or anything. I agreed. Look, Sheila, it just seemed easier to have you think it was Dr. Simpson rather than telling you it wasn't and having you pester me about who it was. Besides I didn't know you were going to go all Rambeau on me. I didn't ask you to do any of that. So don't go pointing your finger at me as though it's all my fault. Take a good look at yourself."

Sheila thought it ironic that the girl who had just thrown her sister into a lifetime of shit should be making accusations. She was not finished with her little sister yet.

"Another thing I don't get is why you won't tell anybody, even me, who raped … had sex with you, particularly since Mom and Arthur have split. It doesn't make sense to me unless you are afraid of him. Is that it? Did he threaten you?"

Sheila responded to Maggie's silence in the face of these questions by applying greater persuasive pressure.

"You told me today that Mom and I were freezing you out of the family, that we didn't trust you and were keeping secrets from you. Well, aren't you doing the same to us? Don't you trust us? What about the three musketeers? Aren't you being the lone musketeer here? You seem to want to be one of the three musketeers, but only on your terms. Why on earth would you want to protect this guy?"

If a crimson face and the wide, unblinking eyes were any indication, Maggie had become very annoyed that her argument of a few hours ago was being used against her.

"For sure I'm not telling you and have him wind up dead!"

It was an arrow to the heart and they both knew it. Sheila, face frozen in shock, stared briefly at her sister and then turned and headed up the stairs on the way to her bedroom in full retreat. Maggie, in apparent disbelief that the words had passed her lips, ran after her.

"I'm sorry! I didn't mean it! I was just pissed off!"

While tears found their way to a pillow in a bedroom upstairs, Maggie stood at the bottom of the stairwell wishing she had not had to hurt her sister, but the comment had achieved its intended job of short-circuiting an irritating and dangerous exchange. *I may be younger, and I may not be as pretty or as smart, but I know how to win.*

CHAPTER 47: PURSUIT

S heila felt particularly alone and isolated. Her best friend - and Maggie was her best friend - had sucker punched her. How could someone she loved, someone she'd risked her future for, turn on her like that? *If my sister doesn't have my back, who's going to?* Working furiously to control the hurt Maggie had inflicted, her rational brain took control and she knew who would have her back – her mother, for sure, and, maybe, just maybe, Noah. He seemed to like her and she liked him. Even though everybody knew the police had been swarming all over her house yesterday, he still wanted to see her, to talk to her, and to be seen with her. *He doesn't think I'm a murderer, but my sister does. How fucked up is that?*

The sting of Maggie's assault was lessening the more she thought about it, and the more she thought about it, the more she analyzed it. *Maggie's accusation had come when I was pressing her about the identity of the son-of-a-bitch she had sex with. She'd been irritated, that was easy to tell. She didn't like being questioned, being called out as a hypocrite. She wanted to end the discussion. Well, she certainly achieved that.*

While she was ruminating about her altercation with Maggie, Sheila heard what she assumed was her mother coming in, followed by a murmured conversation. The back door then opened and closed. A sudden burst of thoughts paraded through Sheila's mind, rapidly coalescing into conjecture as she quickly moved to her bedroom window and watched Maggie walk to the sidewalk at the front of their house, stop and pull out her mobile phone. As Maggie punched in numbers to make a call, Sheila was running down the stairs to put on her boots, coat and gloves, conjecture quickly becoming conclusion. *She's up to something.*

Running past her mother who was working at the sink in the kitchen, Sheila told her that she was going to meet Noah for a milkshake at MacDonald's.

"I'll be back in time for supper. Where's Maggie going?"

Her mother's answer was barely audible as Sheila bolted out the back door she'd just opened.

"Leave room for your supper. Maggie's off to Kate's."

By the time she got to the sidewalk, Maggie had a fifty-yard lead on her. *Perfect.*

***

Another cold northeast wind had piped up since Sheila had walked home from school with Noah, and there was a snow flurry in the air. As she followed Maggie at a distance and using what cover she could find in case her sister turned around unexpectedly, Sheila was wishing she still had her long maroon coat the police had seized. From what she'd observed, her sister seemed to be walking with a purpose and certainly not toward her friend Kate's house. Sheila was almost certain Maggie wasn't meeting Kate, although the two friends might be meeting somewhere other than Kate's house. Refocusing on her surveillance, she'd walked on a few steps before she reacted to the fact that Maggie had stopped at a bus stop about three hundred feet ahead of her and about three blocks from the Munroe residence. Taking cover behind a parked car, Sheila maintained visual contact with the figure of her sister now seated behind the clear Plexiglas of a bus shelter. Sheila's fear that Maggie was there to catch a bus was mitigated somewhat when two buses came and went without her sister making a move. Ten minutes became fifteen minutes, then, fifteen became twenty. Having been stationary, crouched behind the parked vehicle, for that period of time, Sheila was starting to cramp, unable to ease tense muscles, and to benefit from the body heat physical movement would have generated. She was becoming chilled to the bone. She considered giving up her vigil, but making that decision was pre-empted by Maggie standing and walking toward the curb. She detected the car in her peripheral vision a split second later. It was travelling in her direction but was slowing, finally coming to a stop at the curb in front of the bus shelter. The car was too far away for her to identify the driver, but there was no one in the passenger seat because Maggie opened the passenger side door and hopped in. Once her sister was inside, the car pulled back into traffic and began accelerating toward Sheila. She ducked down further between parked cars to avoid being seen by anyone in the vehicle as it passed her position. This maneuver, while assuring no one in the car saw her, had prevented her from again getting a look at the driver. However, she'd had time to study the car for the second or two it took to pass by. While she was a self-acknowledged dunce when it came to cars, unable to tell one make and model from another, she had noticed some details about the car. She tried to cement in memory the things she'd observed. It was big and looked new and expensive - lots of chrome, large shiny wheels, silver in colour, and big fancy headlights and taillights. *Shit! I didn't get the licence plate number.* And something else was interesting as well. It looked familiar.

***

She'd called him because she needed his support and reassurance. She needed him to tell her everything would be OK. She needed to hear she was beautiful, special. She needed to feel loved. And most importantly, she needed him to share her burden. However, it had started within minutes of her getting into his car. He'd placed his right hand on her inner thigh and moved it slowly up toward her crotch. She had pushed his hand away, telling him to stop. "Not here!" He'd complied and excused his behaviour by expressing how much he missed her, how much he wanted her, and that he was beside himself with desire for her. His words had provided the drug she craved. She'd wanted more. Consequently, after arriving at his friend's house, their hidey-hole, they had barely crossed the threshold before they had begun kissing frantically while tugging themselves out of their clothes. All the while, he'd spoken the words that fuelled her need. He'd administered the drug.

Lying on the bed in their perspiration, after making love for a second time, he rolled over on his side facing her.

"You are an amazing woman, Maggie. I can't get enough of you, I really can't. I love you so much. I want us to be together forever."

Maggie never got tired of hearing how much he wanted her, how much he loved her. When he said things like that, she felt powerful and in control, and she had learned how to gain and maintain that power. She maneuvered her body so she was facing him, then leaned in to kiss him while reaching down under the covers with one hand to stroke him. She could feel him respond to her touch, to her kiss. She smiled to herself, then broke off the kiss and the caress and jumped out of bed.

"It's getting late. I have to get home."

With that, she started dressing.

***

On their way back from the house, he was quiet, pensive. She'd seen him like this before and it usually was a forerunner to his questioning of her about some issue or problem he perceived in their relationship. On more than one occasion, it had been about his feeling that Maggie wasn't "as committed to him as he was to her". He had even accused her of seeing another man once. At other times, it had been about his concern that she was careless about keeping their relationship a secret. It would often start with him accusing her of something she'd done wrong or he thought she would do wrong which she would vigorously deny. Even though these accusations almost always had no basis in fact, she would start feeling guilty and end up apologizing for something she hadn't done.

To break the extended period of silence, she finally asked him if something was bothering him. He began by saying that while it was great that she had called, he wondered if there might have been another reason she wanted to see him that she hadn't shared. It often started as innocently as this but she knew it could get tense in a hurry if she didn't see where it was going and try to head it off. She sought to reassure him.

"Other than I love you and want to be with you – and you already know that – I think I have shared everything, and I do mean everything, with you."

She gave a little giggle at her attempt to lighten the mood but he demonstrated no outward reaction, keeping his face expressionless. After a minute or two during which Maggie was kept in suspense, he replied.

"Maggie, I am very unhappy about your sister bringing the police so close to us. Do you think she killed Dr. Simpson?"

Maggie was shocked that he would even ask such a question but also because he knew she was a suspect. She tried to cover her surprise but, in doing so, as much as admitted that she knew that her sister was a person of interest to the police.

"No! No, certainly not! Not Sheila! The cops have got it wrong."

Turning to glance at Maggie briefly before again casting his gaze back to the street ahead, he followed up.

"What puzzles me, my sweet, is why the police might consider your sister a suspect in the murder of Dr. Simpson. I mean why would they think she might have killed him? Did she have a relationship with him? If she did, you never mentioned it? Do you know why she might be considered a suspect?"

Maggie understood that he would not accept "I don't know" or any type of hedging in response to his questions. Feigning ignorance had not worked well with him in the past, and not wanting a return to having to deal with his anger and hostility, she answered his questions as fully as she could. She told him about misleading Sheila by naming Dr. Simpson as her lover, about her suspicions that her sister had been engaged in seeking payback from Simpson, and about telling Sheila that Simpson hadn't had sex with her after all.

"I told her it was someone else, but I didn't tell her it was you. I will never tell anyone that!"

After listening attentively to her explanations, he smiled at her reassuringly.

"I'm not angry, Maggie, but I do wish you had told me about this matter with Sheila before now. Something like that could lead to the end of us. I have some questions though. OK? Why made you think of Simpson as the culprit? Why did you choose his name above any others? It suggests that his name was front and center in your mind, very familiar to you. Now, why would that be?"

Maggie could feel the oppressiveness of his questioning. It made her anxious, like she had done something improper but she hadn't, had she? Her skin experienced the sensation of a trickle of sweat running down her side. She tried to think why he was asking these questions and what he wanted her to say, but such considerations did not make her explanations any easier.

"It….er….just popped into my head. I mean I didn't… um …think much about it. I knew he was…you know….a Psychologist. He visited our school to counsel kids who needed it."

Without taking his eyes off the road, he asked more questions.

"Did you need counselling from Dr. Simpson, Maggie? Did you talk to him?"

A glimmer of insight dawned as Maggie considered his last questions. *He thinks I had a thing going with Dr. Simpson! Not again!*

"He and I were not getting it on if that's what you think! I just went to see him about getting advice on how to become a Psychologist, that's all. He was helping me with that."

He gave her that comforting smile once again.

"There, that wasn't so hard was it? That's all I want, my star – to be kept informed about everything that happens in your life. You are the most important thing in the world to me. Please promise me you'll tell me everything in the future. Don't hold anything back. OK? Promise?"

She was relieved that her admission hadn't incurred his wrath and that she was escaping with just having to reaffirm a promise to tell him everything about her life. She put her hand lightly on his leg while offering the pledge he required.

"I promise."

He dropped her off within three blocks of her house but at a location different than the one where he'd picked her up. They'd never used the same pick-up and drop-off spot twice. Before she exited the car, they set a date and time for their next rendezvous, much sooner than she expected and was their practice. *He's totally into me.*

***

Sheila, back in her bedroom after she'd parried her mother's teasing about how little time her milkshake date with Noah had taken, was deep in thought. She had tried, but she hadn't been able to identify why the car she'd seen Maggie get into was familiar to her. Consequently, she'd decided to adopt a strategy often recommended by her mother when the brain stubbornly refuses to give up its information. She would not purposely seek to bring the knowledge to mind, but think about other things and see if it would pop into consciousness unbidden. She'd given over her attention to thoughts of Noah when she heard her mother call her for supper.

Maggie hadn't returned. However, Sheila had noticed that her mother hadn't laid out a place setting for her, suggesting that she knew Maggie would not be joining them for supper. Sheila was just about to ask her mother where Maggie was when the back door opened and her sister appeared uttering an apology and an explanation.

"I'm sorry, Mom, but Kate's folks had a meeting they'd forgotten about, and they had to leave in a hurry so we had to postpone supper for another time. Anything left for me?"

Assuring Maggie that there was more than enough left for her, her mother set about getting it ready while Maggie quickly ran up the stairs to "freshen up". *Wash the sex off her more likely,* thought Sheila. It also crossed her mind how easily her little sister again lied to her family.

After Maggie had come back downstairs and joined them at the table, Sheila watched her closely as she skillfully handled her mother's questions about Kate and her parents and the meeting they'd "forgotten". She was again both shocked and impressed with the ease and guile with which Maggie deceived others. In many ways, she did not like what she was seeing and hearing. Somehow, her vulnerable, naïve little sister had evolved into a devious, manipulative woman-child who, at fifteen years of age, was likely engaged in a sexual relationship with an unknown lover she was hiding from everybody. *Who could she be seeing?* Sheila had a very bad feeling about what was going on. She couldn't see anything positive coming from this, rather she thought the whole situation signalled disaster. Thoughts of teenage pregnancy, venereal disease, drug use, and Maggie impulsively dropping out of school were just a few of the consequences that crossed her mind. She had to find out who her sister was seeing. She hoped she'd discover it was just a boy from school who was old enough to drive his father's car, and that Maggie keeping it secret was just her being a drama queen. However, her better judgment told her that she was involved in wishful thinking; that all the signs pointed to something more sinister. Sheila realized now that to unmask Maggie's guy, she needed help, and she knew just who she could ask.

***

Noah Baldwin had a varsity basketball practice scheduled for that evening. As was his habit, he arrived at the Lillian Metcalfe gymnasium boys' locker room at 6:30 pm to tend to a minor but nagging injury, in this instance a healing sprained ankle, get his gear on, and carry out his own limbering up routine before the start of practice at 7:30. None of his fellow team members approached preparation, training and practice with the same dedication and vigour that Noah did. He loved playing basketball more than he did any of the other sports he pursued. As the starting point guard for the Warriors, he was a team leader, and as such, played a significant part in the team's success. He enjoyed the rush that he felt when the Warriors won, for if the team won, it was usually because he'd played well.

This evening, the 90-minute practice now history and Noah showered and dressed, he left the locker room and headed for the exit door of the gym. He hadn't seen her during the few seconds it had taken his eyes to adjust to shifting from the bright helium lighting of the gym to the low intensity illumination provided by the fixture above the exit door. He'd felt someone grab his arm, and squeeze it while calling his name.

***

They sat across from one another drinking coffee lattes in a nearly deserted café located near Lillian Metcalfe High - her treat since she was the one who waylaid him after his basketball practice in order to ask him "something important". She waited until he had a chance to take a few sips of his latte before deciding to plunge in, but then, delayed further after witnessing the frothy moustache those sips produced. *Oh my God, he's cute!*

While he was wiping away the residue from his upper lip she zeroed in, leaning toward him across the table and lowering her voice.

"You want to be a spy?"

His quizzical look sparked a comprehensive explanation from Sheila; one that covered Maggie's claim that Simpson introduced her to sex, her later recanting of that allegation, and Sheila's suspicion of a mystery boyfriend whom Maggie was keeping secret. She told him of her theory that her sister had randomly named Simpson to avoid naming her secret boyfriend, then disavowed the claim when she thought Sheila had acted as a vigilante in pursuing Simpson on her behalf. She also confessed to Noah some of what had transpired in her efforts to shame and punish Peter Simpson. He sat there, his face suggesting that Sheila would proclaim she was just joking with him at any minute, but no such claim was forthcoming. Slowly, he understood that she was serious.

"Now, I totally get why the cops are interested in you. But, you're not in jail. You're drinking lattes and going to school - being normal. They can't think what you did was that bad."

She knew she was at a critical point in her attempt to get Noah on side. She needed his help and she knew she wasn't going to get it if he thought she was losing it.

"I know, I know, I can hardly believe it myself. I did it for Maggie, for all young girls really. I didn't know Maggie had lied. It was a shock when she admitted it. But I still think she could be in danger, Noah, and I need your help to find out whether or not she actually is."

Noah was no fool, she knew, and following his initial astonishment he asked a very reasonable question.

"Why don't you just tell your mother? Let her look into what Maggie is up to."

She'd anticipated this response.

"She won't tell Mom any more than she told me, which is nothing. I need to find out who she's seeing to determine if I do have anything to worry about. If I don't, all's good. If I do, then I'll decide what to do next."

Nodding his understanding and after a short pause, Noah's response had reconfirmed Sheila's faith in him and in her feelings for him.

"How do I fit in?"

Smiling, Sheila articulated a plan that she had conceived while lying awake in her bedroom in the early hours of the previous morning. An unsmiling Noah had listened intently. They left the café twenty minutes later.

CHAPTER 48: DOLDRUMS

Thursday, February 1

It was Thursday and more than a week since Peter Simpson's body had been found. Mickey had been in his office at HRPD headquarters since 8:00 am as had two other members of his Team, Henry DeLong and Marlene Stott. Francine had called to say she would be late "due to unforeseen circumstances" and would be there by 11:00 am. They had previously spent several hours re-examining much of the information the investigation had unearthed and were determined to continue to plough through the remainder today.

The call from Mark Harvey had startled Mickey and shattered his concentration on an interview report he'd gotten invested in. Harvey wanted to see him for a chat. *Apparently, the Inspector had come in early as well, how unusual*, thought Mickey. He felt a little frisson of unease as he got up from behind his desk, and started the short walk to Harvey's office. He was pretty sure he knew what was coming and he had been wracking his brain trying to formulate an argument which might forestall the Inspector's anticipated orders. The problem was that he realized that the investigation of Peter Simpson's murder had bogged down with no further leads to follow up on right now. If he were being totally honest with himself, there was nothing on the horizon which might have the potential to advance the investigation. In the end, Mickey had not been able to come up with any compelling argument to offer his superior officer. Thus, fifteen minutes, one coffee and a "we can't win them all" comment later, Mickey, a man unused to failing, left the Inspector's office feeling like a failure. Speaking of the steps that were to take place in light of the status of the Simpson case, Harvey had informed Mickey that he had until the beginning of the next week to turn up something that would warrant continuing with a full Investigative Team. If his Team hadn't found something promising by then, measures would be taken to scale back the investigation. Special Investigations Room-2 would be reassigned to another Team, and Mickey and Francine would be assigned a new case or cases to go along with the ones they'd already been given. Harvey had assured Mickey that the "Simpson matter" would remain active but the case would become just one of a number being handled by George Garcia and Marlene Stott. Mickey's argument that the Inspector consider assigning the ongoing Simpson investigation to him and Francine was politely denied with reasons given which, unfortunately, made administrative sense. So it was produce in the next few days or the Investigative Team would effectively be no more.

Cases did stall, Mickey knew this. It happened with a regularity that would shock the general public if the statistics were generally known. Most often, it had nothing to do with the thoroughness and tenacity of the investigators. In the past, Mickey had heard many of his colleagues blame limited resources for unsolved cases, but that had not been the problem in the Simpson case. He and his Team had just not been able to uncover anything to take them over the top. That knowledge, however, did not help mollify the intense sense of frustration he felt. A man had been murdered and Mickey was on the verge of failing to lead his Team to a positive result - the apprehension and charging of the responsible party.

After returning to his office, he made it a point to contact every member of his Team by email informing them of Harvey's ultimatum, although he didn't call it that in his message, and challenge them to an even greater effort to run Simpson's killer to ground. Within five minutes of sending his message, he began getting responses from those he'd contacted informing him that he could count on them, some voluntarily giving up previously approved time off to come in to work. The responses touched him, forcing him to suppress a welling of emotion. He was in the process of tamping down this sudden surge of feeling when the ringing of his desk telephone finished the task for him. It was Rosalind Lund.

"Good morning, Mickey. A little birdie, who shall remain nameless, has informed me that the Simpson investigation is going to be scaled down because you are not in a position to bring charges. Can I tell my client that she can return to being what she should be, a high school student, instead of the innocent target of the police?"

God, the woman has informants everywhere, thought Mickey. He could see the day when defence attorneys like Rosalind Lund were telling him about internal police decrees before he knew about them himself. His thoughts momentarily shifted to Sheila Munroe, and briefly considered what she must be feeling if, indeed, she was innocent. Maybe it was the disappointment he was feeling, maybe it was some compassion he felt for Sheila, or maybe it was the sense of resignation that had come over him. Whatever it was, he decided to be frank with the attorney.

"Good to hear from you, Rosalind. What a surprise. In answer to your question, we have a limited basis on which to charge your client at present. The fact that the case might be scaled back at some point - and I emphasize the word 'might' - should not be a reason for your client to celebrate. When and if the investigation should be scaled back, it does not mean it will be abandoned."

Rosalind thanked Mickey for being less than helpful as usual and told him he hadn't said anything that she hadn't already surmised. Mickey, tongue in cheek, had responded that he was glad to have been of service. Before she could hang up, Mickey blurted out something he'd thought about asking Rosalind for a while but hadn't formed the intention to do so until this very moment.

"Rosalind, I was wondering if you would like to have a drink with me sometime. That is if it wouldn't make you feel uncomfortable, us being on opposite sides, so to speak."

A long pause followed during which Mickey mentally cringed at the impulsive stupidity he had just demonstrated. Rosalind's answer, however, when it did come, was a testament to the capacity of humans to heal one another as Mickey's melancholy measurably lifted.

CHAPTER 49: UP CLOSE AND ...

Thursday, February 1

Sheila felt it Thursday morning at school. Life, for her, was changing. Within an hour or two of arriving at Lillian Metcalfe, she began feeling like an outsider. If there had been anybody who had not been privy to her crossing paths with the law previously, it seemed they were now, students and teachers alike. From so-called friends, she learned that school scuttlebutt ranged from Sheila, a witness to something important to the Simpson case, to Sheila, a mistress scorned who had sought revenge on her lover, Peter Simpson. She felt she was being scrutinized, being watched, eyes turned away at the last second when she looked in that direction. Many students, some with whom she was unacquainted, were bold enough to question her directly about what was going on, about the rumours. Even her friends made clumsy attempts to reap any salacious details to be had while hiding this curiosity behind a transparent screen of concern for her. The teachers were too sophisticated and socially astute to stoop to the depth of the gracelessness some of her peers did, but she could tell by the way they interacted with her that they, too, had their questions. The one shining light in the morass which school had become was Noah Baldwin. Rather than distancing himself from her, as some of her so-called friends had done, he made efforts to talk to her, to hang with her. He chatted about anything and everything short of her relationship with the police and the Simpson murder.

During lunch hour, they sat together in the cafeteria. It was there that she had almost broken down for the first time when she told him how much she appreciated his company and support. Despite his being there for her, and how much she loved him for it, she couldn't help asking why he was being "so nice" when so many others had started treating her like she had leprosy. In response, he looked her in the eye while his words buoyed her morale and fortified her resolve.

"Because I like you…a lot. I think you're kinda dope, you know…really brave."

She'd lost it then, trying to stifle sobs which seemed to explode from her body unchecked. In response, he simply stood, walked around the table, and sat down beside her, holding her in his arms without regard to the curious stares of classmates-turned-strangers around them.

She had told Noah a lot, but not everything. She desperately wanted to unburden herself but she knew it wouldn't be fair to put him in such a compromising situation. And if truth be told, she was still uncertain to the degree she could trust anybody. So, she remained Rosalind's obedient client.

***

It hadn't taken long. And it turned out to be relatively simple. After school on Thursday, Sheila suggested to Maggie that they get a couple of friends over to play a game of Monopoly, a game both sisters enjoyed. Discussing her sister's availability to play had enabled Sheila to determine dates and times her sister said weren't good for her. Only one of those dates and times involved Maggie going to her friend Kate's for the supper she'd unavoidably missed. *I'll be heading to Kate's right after school.* That date was tomorrow. As soon as she was alone, Sheila immediately called to advise Noah. He had called her back twenty-five minutes later to confirm things were a go from his end.

***

Friday, February 2

Friday at Lillian Metcalfe was a repeat of Thursday. The same stares and hushed whispers as she passed students in the

300

hall. The same dumb questions. The isolation. What was new, however, were the verbal challenges and taunts by a couple of students she'd had run-ins with in the past. *I can't believe you're not in jail yet. Did you kill him because his dick wasn't big enough? Guess we shouldn't be surprised that the daughter of a drunk would be fucking bananas.* She knew the barbs were meant to hurt so she resolved to avoid giving any hint that they had hit the mark. She consistently ignored them and walked on by the offending students without acknowledgement. When she was able, she took refuge during any out-of-class time by spending it with Noah or alone in the storage room. During the lunch hour, while sitting with Noah she suddenly realized he was getting his fair share of abuse as well when a boy stopped at their table and brayed at Noah. *I bet she's a great fuck, Noah. I'm sure that shrink did too, but look what happened to him.* Noah sprang to his feet, sending his chair flying into an adjacent table and pushed the other student so hard that he went sprawling to the floor. As Noah stood over him, waiting for him to get up to receive more punishment, chants of "fight, fight, fight" erupted from other students in the cafeteria as they quickly circled the pair. As the boy Noah had pushed struggled to get to his feet, Sheila broke through the throng of students and took a position between the combatants, facing Noah.

"Stop, Noah, please! Let's get out of here! Please!"

Noah, breaking off his glare at the other boy, looked at Sheila, and when she took his hand, allowed her to lead him out of the cafeteria, to taunts of "whim" and "coward". She took him to the storage room to recover and to talk.

"Noah, I don't want you fighting because of me. You don't have to stick with me. It's alright if you back away. You shouldn't have to take this kind of abuse because of me. I don't want you to get in trouble or to get hurt."

His heart and respiration rates were beginning to slow, but

his emotions were still high, although starting to ebb as he addressed her appeals.

"What, and abandon my best friend? No way, no way in hell! You got me whether you like it or not. So let's not have any more talk like that."

Sheila, tears streaming down her face, wrapped her arms around his neck and kissed him with the tenderness of someone who might have just come to understand what love is. They spent the rest of the lunch period in each other's arms, reaffirming their bond and talking about the plan.

CHAPTER 50: … VERY PERSONAL

Friday, February 2

Noah was in his father's car with the engine running, his mobile phone connected by Bluetooth to the vehicle's speaker system. Sheila's voice was audible as she informed him of her location as she followed Maggie.

Her sister had immediately left the Lillian Metcalfe property at the end of the school day. Sheila had been waiting for her and had taken up surveillance following at a discreet distance. In the meantime, Noah had quickly gotten into the Ford Fusion his father had allowed him to use to visit a friend in the hospital following a non-existent basketball practice after school. The plan was for Sheila and him to be in constant contact by maintaining an open line via their mobile phones, and for Noah to keep re-positioning the car based on Sheila's reports of where Maggie was going.

"Noah, she's just gone into that little café on Desmond Lane. I'm just in front of Jasmine's, you know that women's clothing boutique a couple of doors down from the café. See if you can find a parking spot on the street. I'll look for you and come to the car when you get a spot."

He found a parking slot almost immediately. As luck would have it, the spot was located to give an excellent view of the café's front entrance. Within seconds, Sheila opened the passenger-side front door and got in. Noah was the first to speak.

"What do you think? Do you think he's in there and she's gone in to join him?"

Sheila was shaking her head in the negative before he'd finished his question.

"Nope. They don't want to be seen together, or at least, he doesn't want to be seen with her. If they are hooking up today, she's waiting for him to pick her up."

Noah considered her response, then posed another possibility.

"Maybe she went in the front and out a back door on the way to meet him somewhere else."

Sheila's response carried the confidence of someone who had done a lot of thinking about their strategy and the possible obstacles it might face.

"When I followed her last time, she took no evasive action. She has no reason to believe she's being followed, so I don't think it likely that she's gone out the back. If she has, our plan is in the toilet. We'll just have to hang around to see."

What seemed like a long time had passed since they had first started watching the café, but a glance at the digital read-out of the dashboard clock told Noah it had only been twenty-five minutes. He was beginning to wonder if they might be on a fool's errand.

"Maybe I should go over and take a peek in the front window to see if she's still in there."

Without taking her eyes off the front entrance, Sheila sought to reassure him.

"Patience, patience, partner. I have a feeling we are right where we should be. I think it will happen soon. Hang in there."

Noah had barely let out a big sigh at the prospect of sitting in a cold car indefinitely when Sheila spoke animatedly.

"There it is!"

The same car that Sheila had seen pick up Maggie at the bus stop, appeared from behind them, slowing, and then stopping in front of the café. Sheila could now see through the car's back window that the driver was a male, but he was facing front so she could only see the back of his head. She examined the head intently trying to discern any clue which might suggest an identity. *Nothing.* She turned to Noah.

"Ready? Don't follow too closely, OK?"

Maggie had darted from the café entrance to the waiting car as Noah started the engine and was preparing to pull out. He was delayed in edging his car into the street by three vehicles he waited to let pass allowing the car Maggie had just gotten into to accelerate into a stream of traffic and pull well ahead of the Fusion. However, the car was still in view when Noah finally got his father's car up to speed.

Sheila had waited until Noah had them in an advantageous position behind the car they were following.

"Did you see him? Did you recognize him? Anything about him seem familiar?"

Noah's response reinforced the chill she'd felt when she first saw the head of the driver.

"No, I didn't recognize him from the back of his head, but I got the impression that he is a man. I mean a mature man, not a teenager. You know what I'm saying?"

Unfortunately, Sheila knew exactly what he was talking about because she had had the very same impression.

Noah turned on the windshield wipers in response to the sudden start of a snow shower. The wap-wap sound of the wipers filled the silent void between instructions from Sheila about the path the car ahead of them was taking.

"He's taking a right at the next street, Noah. You're doing great, not too close or too far away that we might lose them."

She smiled at him and reached out a hand to squeeze his knee. He smiled back at her.

They'd tracked the car Maggie and the mystery man were in

for about fifteen minutes before it pulled off a residential street into the driveway of a rather small, somewhat weather-beaten house in the City's north end. Noah and Sheila drove past the house, turned around in the driveway of another home further down the same street, and returned to find a parking place which allowed them a view of the tatty residence. By that time, the car in the driveway of the house was empty. Maggie and the guy had obviously gone inside. Turning off the engine, Noah glanced at Sheila.

"What now?"

Her blank expression didn't inspire confidence in Noah, but her words were thoughtful just the same.

"I'm not sure, Noah. I didn't think beyond following them to where they were going. I thought we might get a good look at the guy, but we didn't. When they come out, we might have better luck."

Noah considered what she'd said, then floated an idea.

"We could just go and knock on the door and see who's there."

As anxious as she was to learn the identity of Maggie's secret boyfriend, she was wary of doing anything that might blow up in their faces or further alienate her sister. *What if the guy is a teenager entertaining Maggie at home with his parents present? What if the guy is not even the boyfriend she seems to have? Then, why the secrecy, the cloak and dagger stuff?* She didn't have the answers, and after a mental tug-of-war, she opted for the status quo. They would wait and watch to see if anything transpired to help them decide what to do next.

"Let's not be too hasty, Noah. Let's take a wait-and-see approach. You OK with that?"

Although he would have preferred to take some immediate action, he recognized this was Sheila's show, so she was entitled to call the shots, within reason, that is.

They had been hunkered down for about fifteen minutes, Sheila examining the house for any detail that might present a clue as to what might be unfolding before them. Nothing suggested itself. As she yawned deeply, she let her mind drift. In doing so, images of the little park near Simpson's office played in her mind. She recognized the memories from that Tuesday evening after earlier delivering her ultimatum to Simpson. They were flooding her consciousness after being suppressed for days, as though her brain had made them off limits until now. She was experiencing them in a fragmented form as one might view a trailer for a film. She saw herself walking back to the small park across from Simpson's offices with a vague determination that she would exact a greater price from this sexual predator. She remembered getting to the little park and stopping there, sitting on the bench, at a loss for what she might require of Simpson as a further measure of justice. She had lingered there for better than twenty minutes during which time she made aborted promises to give up further vigilantism and go home. But something had kept her there. She was unable to simply walk away from the responsibility she felt to all females, herself included, because statistics said Simpson, and men like him, would do their worst again and again. She had decided she would turn him in to the police. She would give them the memory stick as evidence of his assault on her. If that didn't work, she would break her promise to her sister and tell the cops what he had done to Maggie, and then beg for her sister's forgiveness. She'd felt the overwhelming need to deliver the news to the man face-to-face, to witness his recognition of the implications of what she was going to do. She saw herself striding purposefully to the office building after observing that Simpson's car was still there. Like someone having an out-of-body experience, she could now see the closed inner office door and her hand reaching out and grasping the knob, twisting. She remembered things in an almost kaleidoscopic fashion after that, a mental blur through which occasional pristine sensory impressions had emerged … Simpson slumped on the floor, unmoving, the smell of booze wafting around her, and the blood. Fear of being discovered and the horror of the scene propelled her out of his office and the building into the night.

In the Fusion, Sheila suddenly sat up ramrod straight and stared through the windshield at the car that was parked at the house they were watching. She then shouted at Noah.

"I remember! I remember that car parked on the street in front of the building where Simpson has his office! It was there the night he was killed!"

Her sudden movement and shout startled him.

"Jesus, Sheila! You just about gave me a heart attack! What are you going on about?"

Sheila was animated and alert and starting to get worried. She pointed toward the driveway.

"See! I saw that car in front of Simpson's office building on the night he was murdered!"

Noah's expression suggested he needed more information to understand what she was saying. So, she decided she would no longer be Rosalind Lund's obedient client and she told him what she had witnessed on the evening Peter Simpson was killed. After hearing her out, he sat there stunned. Gradually regaining his wits, and slotting what she'd just told him into place, he looked at Sheila wide-eyed.

"Are you saying that car over there might belong to the murderer? I mean, holy shit, Sheila! Couldn't there be another explanation?"

Sheila was beginning to feel a greater urgency to act now, but she needed Noah on board so she explained her thoughts further.

"Sure, maybe there could be. But think about it. I see the car at the scene of Simpson's death on the evening he was killed. That car would appear to belong to Maggie's mystery boyfriend. Maggie was seeing Simpson for counselling. She says it was to check out a career possibility, but what if it was about the boyfriend and her relationship with him? The boyfriend insists on secrecy, and does not want to be identified; he doesn't want to be seen with her. If Maggie told Simpson about the boyfriend, and the boyfriend found out, maybe the guy decided to eliminate Simpson to keep the secret."

Noah nodded his understanding but countered.

"If Simpson was told about the sex, then, as a Psychologist, he would have to report it to the police, wouldn't he? I mean if the guy was older."

Almost hyper with nervous energy now, Sheila responded.

"He couldn't if she didn't tell him who it is. He may have been trying to persuade her to tell him."

Noah could see Sheila's reasoning but started to blurt out something he realized too late he shouldn't have.

"Yeah, I get it, but why kill Simpson, why not just kill Mag……? Oh, sweet Jesus, Sheila, we've got to call the cops!"

Sheila was already pulling a business card out of her jeans pocket.

***

The woman on the switchboard had informed Mickey that he had an emergency call from a Sheila Munroe, did he want it transferred to his desk phone? Emphatically stating that he, indeed, wanted to take the call, he'd called out to Francine and Stott, the only two Team members within earshot, to alert them to the call. He wanted them on hand when the call came through. That happened just as Stott hurried into his office, following Francine. He'd mouthed the name Sheila Munroe to his colleagues as he picked up the receiver and greeted the girl.

"Hi, Sheila, what can I do for you?"

He listened for a minute or two before asking if it was OK with Sheila if he put her on speakerphone so two members of his Team who were with him in the office could hear what she was saying. Apparently, she'd agreed, because he subsequently punched the speakerphone button.

"OK, Sheila, everybody can hear you now. You said you have an emergency involving your sister, Maggie. That you think she could be in imminent danger. Could you tell us what the emergency is and why she might be in danger?"

For the next few minutes, the three detectives listened to Sheila Munroe's voice fill the small office with a rapid accounting of what she witnessed at Peter Simpson's office on the night he was killed, her sister's claim about Peter Simpson and her subsequent recanting of the assertion, the vehicle which potentially connected the Simpson murder to her sister's present situation, and the reason why she and Noah were sitting in a car outside a house with her sister inside with a possible murderer.

By the time Sheila had finished, Mickey had grabbed pen and paper off his desk.

"Where are you, Sheila? Give me the address."

He wrote down the information on a post-it and tried to hand it to Francine, who made no attempt to take it, as he continued speaking to the girl on the phone who was starting to sound more and more frantic as the phone call went on.

"Listen, stay right where you are! Stay in the car! We are on our way and should be there within minutes. Do not try to intervene in any way. The situation is potentially very dangerous! Understood?"

A strained voice sounded from the speaker.

"I understand. Please hurry!"

Stott had quickly left the office to don a Kevlar vest while

Mickey was pulling on his own vest after having called for backup. Francine remained seated in the same chair she had taken when first entering Mickey's after the Sheila's call had come in.

****

"OK. Let's just sit tight until the cops arrive. If they leave the house before the cops get here, we'll follow them and let the cops know where they go."

Sheila, so deep in thought that Noah figured she hadn't heard him, replied in a subdued manner that made it clear how grave she thought the situation was.

"She's not leaving that house alive, Noah. You said it yourself, he kills Maggie and he thinks his problem is gone. She may even be dead now. If she isn't, every second of delay increases the chance she will be! I have to do something!"

With that, Sheila opened the passenger door and got out and, amid Noah's protests, started walking toward the house. Shouting an expletive to no one in particular, Noah also exited the car and jogged to catch up to Sheila.

"OK, Sherlock, what's your plan? If you don't have one, I do!"

He stopped her forward march by grasping her upper arm near the shoulder and turning her body to face him. He asked again.

"Do you have a plan?"

Sheila shook her head to indicate that she didn't, at which point he huddled with her to explain his plan before he returned to the car to get a large screwdriver from the trunk.

Two minutes later, Noah had crept noiselessly to the back of the house. He'd hugged the side of the building as he went, ducking under the windows he encountered, then stopping at each trying to get a glimpse inside. His efforts proved fruitless because every window had drawn blinds, impenetrable. Although the sun was nearing the horizon and darkness was near at hand, he knew that had anyone looked out of one of those windows while he was doing his surreptitious peeking, he'd have been on full display. No one had or, at least, he didn't think they had. His heart continued to pound in his chest as he pulled his mobile phone from his parka and whispered his report to Sheila via the open line they had again established between their phones.

"I'm at the back door now. Tried to get a look in the windows but couldn't see anything through the blinds. I'm ready when you are. Just tell me a second before you start, OK?"

Sheila had made her way to the front door and was standing within a foot of it when she received Noah's hushed message. Although Noah's voice came as a faint whisper as she pressed her phone to her ear, in her present state of heightened anxiety, she was sure it sounded like he was using a megaphone. She almost asked him to keep his voice down, but instead, she whispered, "OK. I'm starting now."

***

He was startled, then alarmed by the sudden loud hammering on the front door. The sound seemed to resonate and echo throughout the small house which was largely empty of furniture except for the bed he was presently on, a couple chairs and some kitchen items. Whoever it was certainly didn't seem to appreciate that a lighter, intermittent knock was all that was required. He began to worry that the constant hammering would draw attention from outside the house. Therefore, he knew he couldn't ignore it and hope whoever it was would go away. He rolled off Maggie who just lay there staring at the ceiling as though she was asleep with her eyes open. He quickly covered her body with a blanket, donned a dressing gown, and went to deal with the racket after closing the bedroom door. Making his way to the front of the house, he began to speculate about the intrusion he was about to investigate. He was almost certain it had nothing to do with the girl being here. He'd been too careful, too well prepared. However, he was concerned about what she'd told him about her confessions to her sister. *The little bitch just couldn't keep her mouth shut! Well, that's not going to be a problem much longer.*

***

Noah could hear the pounding from his position by the back door. As soon as he did, he turned the knob to see if it was unlocked. *No luck.* He then extracted the screwdriver from inside his parka where he'd stuffed it in the waistband of his sweat pants. Quickly, he jammed its sharp end with considerable force into the spot between the door and the door frame where the lock was located. With both hands, he wrenched the shaft of the screwdriver violently. He saw the frame splinter and felt the door give just a bit. In quick succession, he repeated the maneuver two more times, the door springing open on the second of the attempts.

***

Sheila's arms were starting to get tired from hammering her fists on the door. A mixture of exertion and adrenaline was working against her, but she knew she needed to keep up the barrage. She'd begun the assault on the door with renewed vigour when it was violently opened and a man with a terrifying look on his face stood before her in a dressing gown. She was so stunned she didn't move or say anything as the moments ticked by. She knew this angry man ..... *Jesus, it's Foreskin*! Seeing an expression of confusion register on Sheila's face, Richard Foreman took the initiative. His angry man demeanour changed instantaneously. He smiled at her.

"Why, this is a pleasant surprise, Sheila. Maggie didn't tell me you'd be dropping by. We are just finishing up her tutorial now."

He then turned his head to call into the house.

"Maggie, look who's here."

Turning back to Sheila, he stepped aside inviting her to enter.

"Come in, Sheila. I'll rustle you up a drink while you wait for Maggie."

Sheila did not move but gave him a quick head-to-toe study before responding.

"Always give tutorials in a dressing gown, do you?"

Then, looking past Foreman, she yelled Maggie's name into the house announcing her presence.

"Maggie! It's Sheila. Come on out!"

Richard Foreman moved so rapidly that she had no time to react. He'd taken one quick stride toward her, plunged a hand into her hair, and clutching it tightly in his closed fist, yanked her into the house. In one continuous motion, he frog-marched her by her hair across a small foyer slamming her head into a wall opposite the front door with as much force as he could muster. The brunt of the impact was taken largely on Sheila's forehead and was so violent she must have lost consciousness briefly because when she regained her senses she was on the floor and he was on top of her. Noticing her coming around, Foreman taunted her as he set about violently ripping at her top and bra.

"Hey, Sheila, you're back with us, I see. I'm just going to give you a sample of what Maggie's been getting. You're going to love it. You know what they say, 'Once you've had Dick, you can't go back'."

She tried to fight him off, but the blow to her head seemed to have robbed her of all her strength. Her scalp burned and she felt dizzy. Her efforts to dislodge him were futile and she started to panic. *Oh God, I'm going to be raped! Then he's going kill me!* She made one final effort to throw him off, but he put a stop to her struggling with a punch to the face. She physically folded. She was helpless. She closed her eyes. She didn't want to be looking into that merciless face as he humiliated her.

Waiting for the inevitable, she stopped writhing, but even now, her survival instincts were active. She'd save her energy by abandoning her useless efforts to stop him from raping her while waiting for greater physical recovery and an opportunity to get out of this. She'd expected to feel him inside her, grunting and thrusting like a pig, but instead, she felt something very unexpected. His body weight which had been pressing down on her suddenly fell away. His hungry, grasping hands were no longer holding her down while pawing at her. She opened her eyes. If she ever wondered what an angel looked like, she was now staring at it in the face of Noah Baldwin. He stood over her with an expression of intense concern holding the screwdriver. On the floor, lying face-up next to her was a prone Richard Foreman. She noticed that he was breathing which resulted in a fleeting feeling of disappointment until she thought of the impact his death would have on Noah.

As Noah stooped to help her up, he dropped the screwdriver on the floor. That was when she first noticed the blood on its shaft. Her head throbbed when she moved but she was alert enough to assess the damage to her body. The breast that Foreman had managed to wrest free of her bra was bloody from scratches. She saw that her jeans were wrapped around one foot and she couldn't find her panties. *The SOB is an absolute animal!*

She felt a blanket being wrapped around her and was aware of Noah leading her to a chair to sit down. She tried to smile at him, but couldn't quite manage it. From her position on the chair, she could see Foremen on the floor, coughing occasionally, his breathing rapid and shallow. *Die, you bastard, die!* That thought was quickly chased from her mind by the wail of a siren in the distance. Then she remembered. She looked up at Noah beseechingly.

"Maggie?"

Noah pointed toward the back of the house.

"She's in there! She's alive, but out of it. He must have given her something. She acts like she's stoned."

***

Mickey was the first to note the Ford Fusion, with no one in it, parked on the street a hundred feet from the driveway at the address to which they were heading. Scanning the area for Sheila or her friend, Noah, he'd been unable to spot them on the street or in front of the house. He was starting to get a sinking feeling in his stomach. The unmarked police car glided to a halt in the driveway behind the expensive-looking large sedan parked there. Stott had killed the siren a couple of minutes before they arrived to try and avoid alerting the suspect. Both detectives disembarked and hurried to pre-determined strategic positions while assessing the scene. Stott, assigned to cover the back of the house, was the first to report, informing Mickey by mobile that the back door was ajar and looked like it had been forced open. Mickey told Stott to hold her position in case anyone went out the back door, while he moved to one side of the front door. He then knocked on the door while announcing their presence in a booming voice.

"Police! Open the door and place your hands where we can see them."

Within seconds the door opened to reveal a teenage boy going down on his knees and placing his hands on his head while shouting.

"Don't shoot! Don't shoot! My name's Noah Baldwin, Sheila Munroe's friend! Sheila's the one who called you! The murderer has been neutralized. His name is Richard Foreman. He's our Principal."

CHAPTER 51: CROSSING T'S
AND DOTTING I'S

Both Sheila and Maggie had been examined by paramedics before being whisked off to hospital by ambulance. Likewise, Richard Foreman, deemed to have by far the more severe injuries, had been earlier treated at the scene before being taken to the same hospital. Mickey had sent Stott to accompany Foreman in the Emergency Health Services ambulance. The paramedics had told Mickey that the shaft of the screwdriver had not appeared to have punctured or otherwise damaged any vital organ. Foreman had been very lucky. Noah Baldwin was assessed by paramedics after which he was interviewed briefly by Mickey before he was allowed to leave with his father who had been called by police. Noah insisted on being driven to the hospital to check on Sheila.

Arriving at the Victoria General Hospital, Noah found Betty Munroe in the waiting room of the Emergency Department. When she saw him, Betty stood and gave him a big hug. After they sat down together, she told him that Sheila was still being assessed for a concussion and was having skin lacerations treated. It was expected that, if she passed concussion protocol, she would be discharged within a couple of hours. Maggie, on the other hand, was being monitored due to the effects of the drug, suspected to be GHB, Foreman had likely put in her drink. Otherwise, she was injury-free. Maggie, too, was expected to be discharged soon. Betty broke down when she told him that her youngest daughter, her baby, had agreed to have a rape kit administered.

"I can't believe it, Noah. Where was I? Why didn't I know? My God, why didn't they tell me?"

These were questions Noah couldn't answer, and shouldn't,

even if he thought he knew what to say. He was young, but he understood that questions like the ones Betty Munroe was posing were best answered by her daughters. He had to content himself with professing ignorance and encouraging Betty to take heart in the fact that neither daughter was seriously hurt physically. He wasn't as sure about the mental damage their ordeal might have caused.

After being filled in by Noah about what had happened, his father seemed dumbfounded. He then vacillated between scolding his son for lying about why he needed the car and taking the risks he had taken and praising him for the heroic behaviour he had demonstrated.

Mickey arrived at the VG Hospital just minutes before both girls were deemed fit to go home. He asked each of the girls if they felt up to a short interview before leaving the hospital. If not, he would be fine with arranging interviews with them at a later time. Both girls agreed to have the interview right away, Sheila with her mother present, but Maggie was reluctant to have her mother hear what she had to say. However, she finally relented.

Over approximately thirty minutes, Sheila told Mickey everything she knew, or thought she knew, about what had transpired from the time of her little sister's disclosure of being raped to the time the police had arrived at the house Foreman used for his trysts. Betty Munroe wept quietly from time to time as her eldest daughter, still just a teenager, related her account.

Mickey suspected the interview with Maggie would be extremely difficult for both mother and daughter. When the interview got underway, Maggie, at first, related information which largely paralleled that which had already been provided by Sheila when it came to her involvement with Peter Simpson and what she had told her sister. About Richard Foreman, she provided new details. She said she and Foreman had been in a relationship dating back to October, almost six months ago. She stated that she was in love with him and wanted to marry him. When asked how she and Foreman had first gotten together, she said that he had called her to his office and told her that he had observed that she was a particularly bright student, and he wanted to help her develop her exceptional skills and talents. From there, he'd set up tutorials after school in his office to work on things like public speaking, creative writing, and even how to walk the catwalk when modelling.

"He told me I had the beauty and body of a model."

She said they had sex the first time he'd taken her to his friend's house. He had been in the habit of taking pictures of her in a number of outfits, dresses, pantsuits, and bikinis, he'd brought with him.

"Then he asked if I'd be OK with some nude pictures because modelling agencies often want to see what a potential model's body looks like without being covered with clothes. I kinda knew what he might be up to, but I did it anyway. I wanted him to like me."

When asked, Maggie said she couldn't remember having sex with Foreman at the house earlier today. She appeared devastated to learn that Foreman was suspected of murdering Peter Simpson and shocked to hear that Foreman had probably intended to kill her and Sheila when she showed up unexpectedly.

The Munroe family left the hospital with instructions for Betty to monitor Sheila for any belated symptoms resulting from the blows she'd received to her head. A shell-shocked Betty could not stop hugging her daughters. It was as if she feared not being in physical contact with them somehow made them less safe. For the time being, neither Sheila nor Maggie was complaining.

***

Friday, February 9

Over the week since Richard Forman's arrest, Mickey and his Team had worked tirelessly to cement the case against him. All 't's' were being crossed, all 'i's' dotted. So far, despite Foreman's lack of cooperation, Mickey felt they were in a position to formally charge him with two counts of aggravated sexual assault, one of which involved a minor, one count of the rape of a minor, one count of attempted rape, one count of forcible confinement, and one count of administering a noxious substance for the purpose of sexual assault involving a minor. Although he thought it unlikely the Crown Prosecution Service would agree, he would consult them about a charge of attempted murder stemming from Foreman's attack on Sheila Munroe.

Despite Sheila's revelation that she had seen a car identical to Foreman's in front of the building in which Peter Simpson had his office, the crown prosecutor, Bernard Borgman, was reluctant to prosecute a charge of murder. Borgman's reasons were three-fold. First, there was no evidence to establish that the car seen in the parking lot was Foreman's even though a witness said she thought it looked highly similar. Second, there was no evidence, witness or forensic, that put Foreman in Simpson's building, let alone in his office. Third, Foreman's attorney would surely call into question the motive the prosecution would put forward, that is, that Foreman killed Simpson to shut him up about the relationship between himself and Maggie Munroe.

"The problem, Detective Sergeant, is that Miss Munroe has stated that she didn't tell Simpson about the relationship, and what's more, that she informed Foreman she didn't tell Simpson. So, we are left with asking a jury to assume Miss Munroe lied in this instance and did tell Foreman she'd confided in Simpson. Alternatively, we could ask the jury to assume that Foreman killed Simpson because he didn't want to take the risk that Miss Munroe had confided in Dr. Simpson but lied about doing so. Both assumptions are a bridge too far when it comes to reasonable doubt. No, it's a non-starter as it stands, I'm afraid."

As for Foreman, he remained in an isolated hospital room, with posted guard, until he was deemed medically fit to be transferred to the Central Nova Scotia Correctional Facility. The stab wound he received, though deep, had not caused life-threatening damage and he was recovering "quite nicely" according to the attending physician.

CHAPTER 52: REVERBERATION

Friday, February 16

Two weeks after she and Noah had rescued Maggie, Sheila and her sister found themselves walking home from school together. Despite living in the same house, this occasion marked the first time in days they enjoyed time spent with just the two of them present. Since Maggie's rescue, there had always seemed to be someone else around competing for their time – the police, the media, friends, and other family members. For Sheila, things at Lillian Metcalfe had settled back into the normal pre-Simpson routine. Her detractors had returned to the dark recesses of the psychological swamps from which they had emerged. Her fair-weather friends had taken to hanging around with her again, attempting to bask in the glow of a heroine, someone who risked her life to save her sister. Noah had been getting much the same treatment. He'd told her the kid he'd shoved to the floor in the cafeteria for making crude comments about her had even come up to him to apologize. Maggie, unfortunately, was not experiencing the same response from her peers. While many of her classmates had been hot to hear the sensational details of Maggie's affair with Dick Foreskin, she'd noted some of the female students were not so enamoured with being seen with such a "slut", while a few of the boys treated her like something exotic, not of their world.

Sheila and Noah saw one another at every opportunity. Their ordeal seemed to have had the effect of drawing them closer together. She understood that she had the good fortune of loving a guy who had stuck with her, had taken grave risks to help her rescue her sister, and who saved her from being raped and likely, murdered. He, on the other hand, had fallen in love with a girl whose efforts to protect and find justice for her sister were awe-inspiring, who had shown the persistence and dedication that he thought made her a very unique person. Her loyalty to her family and her beliefs endeared her to him.

Sheila and Maggie stopped walking while Sheila checked her phone's screen in response to hearing its ringtone. She saw that the call was from Rosalind Lund. Even though she was no longer under suspicion, her heart spontaneously started beating rapidly and she felt slightly short of breath. She'd come to associate Rosalind with the most stressful and terrifying period of her young life. She finally summoned the courage to answer and after greeting Rosalind, listened for about thirty seconds after which she said "thank you" and "good-bye" before ending the call. During the phone exchange, Sheila's facial expression had not changed, although since ending the call, a smile had started pulling up the corners of her mouth. Noticing this, Maggie pressed her sister about the call.

"That was Rosalind Lund. She told me that the police had formally advised her that they no longer consider me a person of interest in the Simpson murder case. More than that, she said Noah and I are going to be nominated for the Nova Scotia Medal of Bravery. She also told me Foreman is not cooperating, thus, I may be needed as a witness when his case goes to trial. They'll probably want you to testify too, Maggie."

They continued their slow walk home, enjoying each other's company, much as they had done on many days prior to the mess in which they had been caught up. Sheila was beginning to feel more and more like her old self, but she continued to worry about the scars her victimization by Foreman would leave on Maggie's psyche. Even now, as she glanced at her sister walking beside her, Maggie seemed very distant. Sheila was suddenly overwhelmed by the sickening feeling that the sister she knew and loved was being lost to her forever.

CHAPTER 53: ONE SATURDAY IN APRIL

Saturday, April 20

It was one of those Spring days that gives a glimpse of the Summer to come. Although it was mid-April, the sun was a brilliant globe of gold, high in the sky and concentrating its intense warming rays on the cobblestones of the Castle Gate patio. The management had been quick to take advantage of the unusually temperate day and had set up tables and chairs outside. It turned out to be an inspired idea as virtually every table had been occupied since shortly after the pub opened for business.

At one of these tables, enjoying a pint on a Saturday, sat Mickey MacKinnon and Marlene Stott whom he'd cajoled into joining him. Since becoming partners, Mickey had sought to continue the practise of engaging in informal reviews of the cases they were presently pursuing much as he had done with Francine until she'd been lost to him and the Job. It had been so sudden and so complete that he hadn't seen or talked to her since early February. Her last words to him had been spoken on the very day Richard Foreman had been taken into custody and as he rushed out of his office at HRPD HQ tugging on his Kevlar vest after trying to get her to do the same. Those words still haunted him.

"I'm so sorry, Mickey. I just can't do it anymore."

Since then, she had steadfastly ignored his repeated attempts to make contact. He'd even tried to reach her through her therapist who'd told him that she thought Francine would change her mind about seeing him at some point, but that it might be best in the interim if he gave her some space. Although he had not learned much about Francine's condition, he had been able to garner a few facts which both saddened and shamed him. Saddened him because it seemed she had felt the need to create an alternate reality to explain the symptoms she was experiencing rather than feeling she could confide in him, her partner, her protector. He had been devastated to learn that there had been no single mom friend or birth by C-section or late night feedings or diaper changing or baby vomit on a sweater. The elaborate fantasy had been easier for Francine to create than admitting she was human. Shamed him because he taken her for granted - she had been his rock, always there, forever dependable, untouchable. But the debilitating symptoms of PTSD had reached out and ensnared her, reduced her and he hadn't seen it coming. He'd failed her and it caused him great pain.

Thinking of Francine, he watched and half listened to Marlene Stott now as she engaged him in re-hashing one of their cases. He closed his eyes and inhaled deeply in an attempt to control a wave of anxiety which flowed through him at the thought of being responsible for yet another young detective, so keen, so open, so vulnerable.

As far as the Simpson matter was concerned, Mark Harvey had made clear that the future responsibilities of the two detectives would be limited to providing testimony for the prosecution when the Foreman case came to trial. Nevertheless, Mickey and Marlene were keen to keep up with what was happening in the investigation because, to date, Richard Foreman had not been charged with the murder of Peter Simpson.

Foreman had now been an inmate of the Central Nova Scotia Correctional Facility since his transfer from the VG Hospital almost two months ago. Another investigative team from Sex Crimes was currently pursuing an enquiry into how extensive his predatory sexual behaviour had been. They were looking into how many other young girls he may have cultivated in order to sexually exploit them. So far, two others had come forward, one fifteen years old, the other only fourteen, both students at Lillian Metcalfe, both professing Foreman had been their boyfriend. Although that investigation was ongoing, Foreman, upon the advice of his attorney, had confessed to two counts of aggravated sexual assault, one count of the rape of a minor, one count of attempted rape, and one count of administering a noxious substance for the purpose of sexual assault. The charge of forcible confinement was dropped. He maintained he had not sexually interfered with any other young girls beyond the three identified. The detectives in charge of the case thought this claim unlikely and had extended their investigation to include communities in both the Northwest Territories and Ontario where Foreman had previously been a teacher. Be that as it may, it was thought it would be some time yet before he went to trial on any charges which new evidence might support. Despite his cooperation on the exploitation charges, he had steadfastly maintained his innocence concerning the murder of Peter Simpson. He'd suggested to detectives that either the car that Sheila saw parked on the street in front of Peter Simpson's office building was one that was similar to his, a coincidence, or that Sheila was simply mistaken in her identification. He was adamant that he had never set foot in Simpson's office, ever.

Although Foreman had yet to face justice in the courts, he'd faced some rough justice while incarcerated. He had been beaten senseless by a fellow inmate who held the view that pedophiles were the lowest of the low and took it upon himself to communicate his view to Richard Foreman in the best way he knew how. Another stay at the VG Hospital saw the former Principal back at the correctional facility looking forward to a future of constantly looking over his shoulder.

Taking a swallow of his second pint of ale, Mickey commented on the status of the Simpson murder case.

"You know something, Stott. I'm beginning to think Foreman

is going to skate on the murder charge. Unless something else falls into our laps, the Crown Prosecutor is resolute in his belief that there is no reasonable expectation of a conviction based on the evidence we have now."

Marlene, who had moved from lager to white wine, was thoughtful for a few seconds before responding.

"I know we discussed this before, but I wonder if Simpson might have been killed by someone else. I mean the CP is right, there is no evidence placing Foreman in the Simpson offices. The only thing that suggests he could have been there is the Munroe girl's sighting of the car. And consider this, how many times does a perp leave a crime scene trace-free? Terry Tremblatt would say 'never'. So how does Foreman accomplish it? We either missed something or he wasn't there."

Giving a sigh of resignation, Mickey acknowledged his partner's reasoning.

"I know. I know. It just galls me. Listen, what happened when you did your 'social worker' bit with Karen Simpson and that fruitcake of a secretary, Sue Reynolds?"

Mickey knew Marlene had visited both women in the last day or two but hadn't had a chance to talk to her about it. Stott wanted to see how they were and to follow-up on a commitment she'd made to Francine to keep both women updated on where things stood with the investigation, scaled back as it was. Since it was not one of her cases now, she had checked with George Garcia, whose responsibility it had become, about making the contacts before she did so. Getting a thumbs up from George, she had arranged to see Karen first.

The day she'd arrived at the Simpson home on Sanford Avenue had been overcast, dreary and damp, with more rain threatening. Karen had greeted her dressed for work it seemed, wearing a luxurious, form-fitting pantsuit with the jacket pinched at the waist, two-inch heels, make-up and a rather elegant hairstyle, hair gathered in an intricate braid at the back of her head. Marlene's first impression had been that she'd caught the woman on her way to a formal meeting or gathering of some sort, but that thought had been short-lived as Karen had stepped back to let her in the house. Despite Karen's apparent effort to dress up for the occasion and her initial artificial cheeriness, Marlene had seen that she'd lost weight and that the make-up hadn't fully disguised the purplish patches and bags under her eyes. The gloom of the day had seemed to match the darkness that had pervaded the interior of the house, with no curtains fully open, and no lights on. As they'd seated themselves in the living room, Marlene had noted that Karen had set out a carafe of coffee with cups and saucers and some dessert squares. Again, another effort to portray a return to normalcy, routine, which had seemed at odds with the fragility the Detective Constable thought she'd detected in the woman. Thirty minutes after she'd entered the house, conversation at a natural end, Marlene was at the front door bidding Karen Simpson goodbye and promising to stay in touch. What Karen had shared, over the half hour the two women had talked, Marlene had heard before from grieving family members who'd lost loved ones. Yet, it made it nonetheless tragic. Karen had told Marlene she continued to struggle with the loss of her husband, that there were times when she forgot momentarily that he was gone and expected to see him or hear his voice. In those moments, those split seconds, she was whole again, only to be emotionally numb once more, when memory took hold. She had assured the young detective that she was getting "wonderful" support from her parents and Ida Williamson. *And, of course, Solynn gives me the energy and the will to heal.* Apparently the smile Karen had flashed at the mention of the little girl's name had seemed to Marlene like the first genuine expression of happiness of the visit. That smile, however, had been quickly followed by tears as Karen confided that it broke her heart to see how Solynn had seemed to have forgotten her father.

"She rarely refers to him now. Yet, sometimes, on infrequent occasions, like when the door between the garage and the main house opens and closes as it did when he used to come home from work, Solynn will still spontaneously call out, 'Daddy' and look for her father."

As Stott had backed out of the Simpson driveway, she'd observed another vehicle waiting to pull in off the street. Once her car had reversed into the street, she had a better view of the driver of the other vehicle as the two cars passed each other travelling in opposite directions, hers headed to Sue Reynolds' apartment, his to the Simpson driveway. His gaze directed straight ahead, no glance in her direction, she'd recognized Dr. Bartholomew Lewis behind the wheel. It had crossed Marlene's mind that maybe the expensive pantsuit, the make-up and the fancy hair hadn't been for her after all.

Gaining access to Sue Reynolds's apartment had turned out to require running the same security gauntlet Francine and Mickey had been forced to negotiate when they had visited in the past. Like then, Sue Reynolds' curt voice, imbued with undisguised wariness, had greeted Marlene's push of the intercom buzzer button. She'd had to assure Reynolds that she was who she said she was by displaying her police ID through the glass of the front door before she was permitted entry. However, once Sue Reynolds was satisfied the Detective Constable was legit and they were seated in the same cluttered apartment Francine and Mickey had been forced to navigate, she treated her visitor like a long-lost friend. *Oh, yes, I'm fine. Bartholomew, I mean Dr. Lewis, has been ever so helpful to my recovery from the shock of Peter's death. I'm working in his practice now, you know. He's such a smart man, so upright. I am so lucky to have the opportunity to work for a man like that. I truly believe he is a righteous man put on this earth to serve God's will. I have prayed for him and for the opportunity to do my small part to oblige his mission. I have learned it is not always men of the cloth who have been legitimately called to serve. I recently had an experience with a so-called minister who turned out to be Satan's helper. He was a fraud, an imposter. I told him so myself. I contacted members of his congregation to warn them of the heathen masquerading as a man of God. But, you know, some people just can't see the light. When I spoke to many of them, you could tell he'd already taken possession of their souls. He even got a cease and desist order to prevent my contact with his misguided followers. Imagine trying to stop someone from telling the truth, from doing God's will! There is a place in Hell awaiting Jack Moore!*

Mickey was making circles in the air with his index finger while pointing to his temple as Marlene related the details of her visit with Sue Reynolds.

"Like I said, Stott, she's a bona fide fruitcake. Someone needs to take a good look inside that brain."

Taking another sip of her wine and watching her partner over the rim of her glass, Marlene observed Mickey starting to retreat into inner thoughts. They had been together long enough now that she recognized the look and knew he was probably mentally reliving the case …. or thinking about food. In the past, she had gained some important insights into investigative thinking when Mickey shared his thoughts after withdrawing into this type of reverie.

"A penny for your thoughts."

"You know, Stott, the whole case was based on a bunch of presumptions that turned out to be untrue. If you think about it, these presumptions created the context in which Simpson's murder took place. They went unquestioned, and because they weren't, they were given a power greater than they should have had. Do you know what I mean?"

He could see the puzzled look on Stott's face even with her wine glass obscuring the lower half of it.

"What I'm saying is that key players presumed or believed things that were not true. For example, Sheila believed

Maggie when she said she was raped by Peter Simpson. She didn't question it, presuming her sister had spoken the truth. Maggie, in turn, presumed Sheila would simply keep her secret, certainly never dreamed she'd so directly seek justice on her behalf. Both girls presumed sharing Maggie's confidence with their parents would damage the marriage, a marriage they would eventually learn was beyond repair. Richard Foreman presumed Maggie had or would confide in Simpson and identify him as her boyfriend, exposing him as a sexual predator, so he killed him. See what I mean? Things could have been very different with less presuming and more questioning."

Quite out of character, Marlene had drifted off during Mickey's ramblings about the role erroneous presumptions had played in influencing the course of events that led to murder. She was more concerned about some nagging loose ends, ones she was thinking about now. Although the HRPD and the Crown Attorney's Office seemed content with the probability that Richard Foreman murdered Peter Simpson, she was not. No evidence tied him to the assumed weapon or placed him at the scene, and evidence supporting motive was unsubstantiated. On the other hand, Simpson's wife, Karen, by her admission, was near her husband's office about the time of his death. Her alibi, including the timing of her dining at Faubert's and the time stamp on the drugstore receipt, did not completely exclude the possibility that she could have carried out the attack. She also thought that not enough had been done to exclude Sue Reynolds as a suspect. Sue was certainly odd, eccentric, and a bit of a religious zealot, which in and of itself did not make her a murderer. However, her disturbing relationships with male work colleagues give rise to questions about how stable she is and how she might react to perceived transgressions given her propensity to interpret events in narrow hell and brimstone terms. George Garcia was right about the video evidence. The fact that she was shown leaving the office shortly before Simpson's estimated time of death doesn't mean she could not have come back and attacked her employer. And finally, Sheila Munroe whose statements to police put her in Simpson's office around the time of his death and who had a motive to kill the Psychologist since she believed he had raped her little sister, needed a closer look. It was Sheila who said that she had seen a car like Foreman's parked outside the Simpson offices on the evening he was murdered. However, no other witness was found to corroborate her report.

She tuned back just as Mickey was finishing his spiel. Nodding her head in agreement with whatever he had just said, she wondered if those erroneous presumptions he was going on about shouldn't include some made by the police.

EPILOGUE

One Year Later

A call from the Crown Prosecutor's office had informed them that Richard Foreman would not be facing a jury of his peers. He'd confessed and pleaded guilty to three counts of sexual exploitation of a minor, two counts of aggravated sexual assault - one involving a minor - and one count of administering a noxious substance for the purposes of sexual assault involving a minor. These were the charges laid in Nova Scotia. The murder of Peter Simpson was not among them. They'd heard the rumours that Foreman faced several similar charges in both the Northwest Territories and Ontario. Although Mickey had spoken little about the Simpson case for a number of months now, the flurry of activity surrounding the Crown Prosecutor's announcement had brought him briefly in contact with Karen Simpson and Sheila and Betty Munroe.

He had seen Karen at the Nova Scotia House Assembly where he'd unexpectedly been requested to accompany a small contingent of HRPD brass to update a legislative committee on the Simpson case. Mickey had never been ordered to do anything like this in the past; however, when he'd seen Karen Simpson in the foyer conversing with some of the politicians who were members of the committee, the glimmer of an explanation presented itself.

She'd made time to chat, telling him that she was doing much better now, that her "zest" for life had returned with the help of Bartholomew, her new significant other, and the irrepressible force that was Solynn. When he'd asked her whether or not she'd heard anything from Sue Reynolds, Karen's bright and beautiful face turned sour. She'd said that she was surprised that they hadn't heard, but "Bart had had to fire the Reynolds woman. She became obsessed with him, trying to insert herself into all aspects of his life. He was convinced that she was mentally ill and needed help. When he tried to discuss the situation, she became enraged, refused to seek help, and started accusing him of being in league with the Devil. She withdrew herself from his personal life which was a good thing in one way, but she carried it over into her everyday work in the practice. She became obstinate, often refused to follow his directions, and did things in her own time. It became intolerable. After he let her go, she started calling his clients and ranting about Bart being an imposter, a fraud. We had to get a cease and desist order in place to stop her."

On the brighter side, volunteered Karen, she was pleased to tell Mickey that the memory of her late husband would exist beyond the memories of those who knew and loved him. "Of course, those memories will sooner or later extinguish or fade into oblivion. Very soon now", she'd teased with a smile, "you may find yourself on a particular route in Halifax which takes you along a street identified with a large white-on-green overhead sign which reads 'Dr. Peter Simpson Way'".

As Mickey was about bid her good-bye, he was caught by surprise by Karen asking about Francine. His response was perfunctory and a lie.

"She's doing fine. Looking at changing careers. I'll tell her you asked after her."

What else could he say after all? Certainly not that he hadn't seen or talked to her for more than a year or that he, in her mind, represented the toxicity of the circumstances in which homicides bloom and had to be avoided at all costs, or that she had attempted suicide. No, he couldn't say any of those things.

Mickey's short conversation with Betty Munroe, on a bench in the hallway outside the Crown Prosecutor's office, had been depressing, to say the least.   She told him that Maggie, just a couple of weeks into it, had discontinued therapy designed to assist her in dealing with the emotional scarring caused by her exploitation at the hands of Richard Foreman. Betty said she'd been told by Maggie's therapist that he felt Maggie was dealing with guilt that she somehow encouraged the exploitation. Betty, dabbing her eyes with a tissue, disclosed to Mickey that soon after Maggie quit counselling, her school attendance started to suffer until she dropped out of school completely. She lamented her daughter's decision to leave the family home and the prospect that she was living rough on the street or with "God knows who". Betty, a shadow of the woman Mickey remembered her to be, expressed her fears about how Maggie might be supporting herself.

Following his conversation with Betty Munroe, Mickey reflected on how differently the tragedy that had sucked in both families had affected Betty versus Karen Simpson. Betty still grieved while Karen was almost born again. He thought he understood the contrast. Karen lost a husband through no fault of her own. On the other hand, Betty was engulfed in the guilt of a disastrous choice of husband, a menace she allowed to stay in the family far too long, and of somehow failing to see the peril her younger daughter was in before it was too late. A mother who may well have lost that daughter because of what she feels she did, and because of other things she should have done, but didn't. While Karen's pain was no doubt intense, the event that caused it was over, and had been for over for a year. The source of Betty's agony was a living and breathing part of her, her child was out there on the streets, at risk every second of her life. Betty's was a living nightmare that gave no hope of waking up. When Mickey had tried to be helpful in suggesting things Betty could do to distract herself, to look after her health, it became clear from her responses, that the woman seldom left her two-bedroom apartment where she lived alone. Although she continued to work as a Human Resources specialist, hers appeared to be a to-work-to-home-to-work kind of existence. She said she had not accepted any of the number of invitations for coffee, a drink, a movie or dinner she'd received since her separation. She simply couldn't bring herself to trust her judgement when it came to men. Mickey had found the only light that seemed to shine in her otherwise bleak mental outlook was the apparent pride she felt in her oldest daughter, her lifeline to the fact that she was not a complete failure as a mother.

Betty told him that Sheila had graduated from Lillian Metcalfe High School first in her class in aggregate academic standing. At her graduation ceremony, she won the Governor General's medal, the Female Athlete-of-the-Year award, and was offered three scholarships, one being a $ 5,000-a-year renewable scholarship to Saint Mary's University. In the months leading up to graduation, she was heavily recruited by the coaches of three university basketball teams with offers of tuition relief and other considerations if she decided to attend their university. Ultimately, said Betty, she'd chosen Saint Mary's, not because of the scholarship or other inducements "but because she felt I needed her close a little longer".

Mickey's chance meeting with Sheila Munroe had occurred when he bumped into her in the lobby of the Maritime Centre where the Crown Attorney's Office is located on Barrington Street. Sheila was there to pick up her mother. As they made small talk about how each of them was doing and what was going on in their lives, Mickey could see the same inner strengths and resources, the resiliency, in the young woman now facing him that he'd seen in the teenager who'd risked her life to save her sister. After a few minutes, Sheila broke off the conversation, excusing herself, so as to not to cause her mother worry by being late.

As she walked away from Mickey, Sheila had a sudden frisson of sorrow, one tinged with regret. A memory of Noah Baldwin flitted into her mind - a mental image of his handsome, earnest face; his sparkling, deep brown eyes; his curly blonde hair, his warm and endearing smile. A tear threatened as she remembered them dancing at their graduation prom. It was their last date. Afterward, they'd gone their separate ways. It had happened so suddenly. Noah had changed his choice of university, opting to attend an upper Canadian university rather than St. Mary's as they had planned. His purposeful distancing himself from her had hurt her deeply at the time, and truth be told, it still did, but she understood his decision. She'd asked far too much of him and had required him to carry too big a load. She had looked to him to help share the burden of her deeds, to be her confidante in all things. So, she had told him everything - about the confrontation with an inebriated Simpson to tell him face-to-face that she was going to expose him; about his pleading for her to reconsider; about her refusal and verbal assault on his character; about his anger-fuelled charge at her and his hands around her throat; about breaking free of his grasp and finding the liquor bottle in her hand; about swinging the bottle at his head with an adrenaline-infused strength; about cleaning up the pieces of glass. She had told him all this on a clear, warm and sunny day in June. As a light breeze rippled his curls, he'd listened to her confession as they sat alone in the bleachers behind Lillian Metcalfe. There, she'd seen the light fade from his eyes as his face first registered disbelief, then shock followed by despair. No manner of assurances that she'd checked that Simpson was still breathing and had a pulse before she abandoned him and fled into the night eased his despair. No pleas to consider the most logical perpetrator of the Psychologist's death ("Remember, I saw his car parked there!") brought him back from a place where she couldn't reach him. Helpless, she watched him as he, with his head down, shuffled slowly away from the bleachers, away from her. She knew then as

she did now that they would never be together again but that
she would always love him as she suspected he would always
love her. He communicated that love each and every day she
remained free.

ACKNOWLEDGEMENT

Could I have written Fatal Presumptions without the helpful insights of some very perceptive individuals whose opinions and suggestions I trust? I don't know but I am so thankful that I didn't have to try. One thing I do know, however, is that there is no question in my mind that Fatal Presumptions spins a better tale, providing the reader with a higher quality reading experience, because of them. Linda, Heather, Al, Jennifer, Chris and Emma, I owe you my sincere gratitude.

Merville Thomas

Merville Thomas is a man of mystery. Little is known about him. It has been suggested that Thomas is a shy, reclusive person living in Nova Scotia, Canada. Someone whose acute understanding of aberrant human behavior and law enforcement serves to make his gripping storytelling both believable and compelling. On the other hand, there are those who think he is an arrogant, mentally unbalanced and criminal personality, who couldn't give a fig about his readers - a person in hiding risking exposure only to satisfy his desperate need for literary acclaim, albeit a step removed. Whether a shy, timid and reclusive person or an arrogant, unempathetic fugitive, Thomas' novels will keep readers compulsively turning pages to learn what happens next.

Shadows Over Spectral Waters

A barbaric crime ushers a demented evil out of the shadows!

On a dreary rain-soaked late September morning, Detective Sergeant Mickey MacKinnon, following up on a tip, finds a decomposing mutilated body on a rural property. The finding sets in motion one of the most bizarre and tragic murder investigations of MacKinnon's career as a homicide detective. As he pursues his inquiry, he not only learns that the perpetrator of this barbaric crime is clever, methodical and seemingly a step ahead of the police, but suspects that he has killed before.
Creating portraits in death and playing cat and mouse with the police are perverted ways the murderer deals with the demons which haunt him relentlessly. However, this self-styled ghastly therapy brings him face-to-face with a challenge which ultimately forces him into a life-or-death situation.

FATAL PRESUMPTIONS

345